Jack opened the l— ity or awkward gr————— —just a simple "Hi" followed by an exclamation point. Jack couldn't resist that simple familiarity, as if he and the writer had been friends for years. The script was even smaller in the letter, as if the writer might be a little shy on self-confidence. He squinted, trying to decipher every word, suddenly needing any illusion of warmth and companionship he could find:

I can't help but wonder what fascinating part of the world you are in now and what Christmas traditions you are observing and, I hope, taking part in. Do they celebrate Christmas where you are? Are the colors and tastes and smells and sounds different from those we are used to? Will you share your experiences with me through a letter?

LETTERS FROM A STRANGER

Paper crackled under Angela's hand where she'd laid the mysterious letter from a major stationed in Germany. The strokes of the major's pen were angry slashes, in some places almost tearing through the paper, as if he had fought against writing the letter as his hand moved the pen:

I've wondered why my men haunt the mail room and spend so much time answering letters written by complete strangers. Now I know. Those letters make them feel less forgotten and alone, more significant. I've been sitting in my office, thinking about having someone to share the loneliness with, but your letter made me realize that it's a contradiction in terms. If you're sharing, how can you be lonely?

PRAISE FOR CONNIE RINEHOLD AND HER WONDERFUL NOVELS:

Letters from a Stranger

"Connie Rinehold wields her pen like a master swordsman in *Letters from a Stranger.* Her words flow and stab at the reader's heartstrings as she draws you into the realm of imagination that is very close to the reality of our everyday lives. So full of life are her characters and their conflicts, they leap off the page to wrap themselves around your heart. A poignant story of today, one that shouldn't be missed."   —*Rendezvous*

"Fast-paced, sensitive, poignantly humorous, *Letters from a Stranger* is the best book you'll read all year."
          —Beth Anne Steckiel, owner of
          Beth Anne's Books, Colorado Springs, CO

"*Letters from a Stranger,* Connie Rinehold's new release, touches your heart with her emotionally compelling tale . . . a warm, thoughtful and tender story of love triumphing over the painful, emotional scars of the past."
          —Jill Smith for *Romantic Times*

"Connie Rinehold has a unique voice, a gift for tapping into a woman's most private feelings. The characters are so real and honest that they climb off the page and into your heart. This is power—powerful, unforgettable characters, and the emotional power of Connie Rinehold's writing style. She not only touches the reader, but moves her, leaving her with a soft, private smile, a feeling of being lit up from the inside. I LOVED THIS BOOK!"
          —Jennifer Greene, author of *It Had to Be You*

MORE THAN JUST A NIGHT

"Connie Rinehold has a way of telling a story that makes it linger in the mind long after the last page has been turned."
—Mary Kirk, author of *Miracles* and *Embers*

"This is my kind of book . . . one you'll read again, and again, and again."
—Bertrice Small, author of *A Moment in Time*

"High romance with just a twist of fantasy . . . love and adventure in this haunting story of a man lost and in search of home . . . and himself."
—Laura Kinsale, author of *The Shadow and the Star*

"With vivid characterizations and Connie Rinehold's flair for picturesque phrasing, *More Than Just a Night* is a compelling tale of romance and suspense."
—Catherine Hart, author of *Tempest*

"I was captivated from the first page to the last by the powerful and compelling love story, and held spellbound by Ms. Rinehold's rich, expressive prose and depth of emotion. *More Than Just a Night* is alive with all the raw passion and emotion of the West."
—Kathe Robin for *Romantic Times*

"Superb reading. The longing, tenderness, and ache of unfulfilled love . . . so vividly expressed will keep you turning the pages. Outstanding!"
—*Rendezvous*

"[A] feast for the reader. Ms. Rinehold has the imagination, skill and delightful character development which makes this truly a romance for the discriminating romantic."
—*Heartland Critiques*

Also by Connie Rinehold
MORE THAN JUST A NIGHT

CONNIE RINEHOLD

LETTERS FROM A STRANGER

A DELL BOOK

Published by
Dell Publishing
a division of
Bantam Doubleday Dell Publishing Group, Inc.
1540 Broadway
New York, New York 10036

The trademark Dell® is registered in the U.S. Patent and Trademark Office.

ISBN: 0-440-21402-5

Printed in the United States of America

Published simultaneously in Canada

May 1993

10 9 8 7 6 5 4 3 2 1

OPM

To new friends who enrich my life with your presence and who have shared so freely your experience and time. I wish there were room here to name all of you, but I have a long memory and there will be other books. But for now . . .

Beverly and Chris Allen for being with me from the first and for six weeks in Germany that led to an off-the-wall idea for a book.

Erica Winkler, Francie Stark, Bertrice Small, Mary Kirk, Christine Monson, Catherine Hart, and Katherine Kingsley for aid, comfort, and support above and beyond the call of friendship.

Lydia Lee and Ozzie Green for proving that the nicest people find love in unexpected ways.

Judy and Rex Covault for more than I can say.

Katerina . . . because you are so special.

Especially to my husband Sam, for the letters that made our long-distance romance the stuff of dreams.

With special thanks to Bruce Kendall and Manuela Payne for allowing me to introduce Angie and Jack to the magic of Cordillera.
And to Jennie Cissell Thompson for sharing your special gift of speaking the language of the heart.

To all of you with love.

A NEW BEGINNING

She wakes up every morning to the sound of emptiness.
  One more lonely day to face, she calls it selfishness.

It never seems to end, this desolate road she walks.
  She thinks more than her share, and it does no good to
  talk.

She's standing confused and sore; her world is crashing in.
  She needs someone to wipe her tears and point her
  straight again.

If you'll take her hand and guide her and speak softly to
  her heart,
I'm sure she'll be okay, Lord. She just needs a place to
  start.

—Jennie Cissell Thompson

PROLOGUE

*1*973

Angie had been taught that nightmares and fairy tales weren't real. She knew better.

This was real—nightmare and fairy tale combined as colored lights surrounded her and danced through the air and a soft mist curled around her feet on the stage. Behind her, twin stairways curved in from the wings, ending in a magical ballroom where she had danced just a short while ago. Between the stairways a queen sat on a golden throne that rose from a red-carpeted dais. A queen who would be replaced and forgotten within a few short minutes.

It had happened before.

Angie stood on the stage where dreams would be granted and crushed within a single moment. She felt a thousand stares from the crowd below, saw the blur of faces as they waited for the final decision, heard the hushed voices and the collective rhythm of people breathing as she waited for it to be over.

The fairy tale, where she strutted and smiled and performed and tried to convince herself that it wasn't a nightmare, that it wasn't real.

Someday it would end.

She *had* to believe that.

"The second runner-up is . . ." The announcer's voice seemed to boom in her ear as he read the name.

The girl on her right gasped, then took her place in the background. Angie closed her eyes for a moment, wishing it had been her, stepping back, fading away.

Only two were left.

She and Sara clasped hands, holding tightly in anxiety, in anticipation. No other signs of their tension showed. No one else knew that Angie was being smothered by fear, that Sara was paralyzed by hope.

They stood in a fairy-tale setting, bathed by colored lights, their long gowns glittering with pearls and crystal beads, the hems stiffened with strips of crinoline to exaggerate the sweep and flow of the finest fabrics.

"And the first runner-up . . ."

Another gasp, a sob, and Angie felt Sara's hand go limp and turn cold before Sara smiled and took her place among the props opposite the other girl.

Instinctively, Angie held her breath and huddled in the smallest space she could find within herself, blanking out the one she was in.

It had happened before—the roar of the crowd that never failed to frighten her, the voice of the announcer that always followed her into sleep for nights afterward, the hands of that other queen and nameless others grasping and pushing at her, adjusting and straightening her, jerking her away from herself. In the wings, she saw her mother, a beautiful smile on her face, a smile of happiness and fulfillment and pride.

Angie knew that only she had the power to bring out that smile and make her mother feel as beautiful as she wished to be. Moments like this were her mother's raison d'être.

On nights such as this her mother found her own private dream.

Charlotte Winters's daughter was once again judged the best, the most beautiful and talented, the brightest jewel in Charlotte's own imaginary crown. Charlotte saw only the fairy tale. Angie lived in the nightmare.

It had happened before, and it would happen again.

But Angie couldn't think about the next time. She had to believe that each time was the last. She couldn't let it touch her—the fear that burned in her stomach and strangled the breath in her throat. She had to think of her mother's pride, her mother's dreams, her mother's need.

She was only now beginning to understand about Charlotte's need, and her own. She was only now beginning to wonder why they weren't the same, why one was more important than the other.

Her eyes widened, and her mouth curved into the sweet smile that had become famous on the circuit—just the right blend of innocence and confidence. She felt the heat then as her face flamed and a velvet robe trimmed in fur was fastened around her shoulders. Only a few knew that the fur smelled old and sour and that it was as fake as the happiness she displayed.

She was so very good at faking it.

The lights became brighter, warmer, and tears combined with makeup to drip down her face like hot candle wax, melting everything that she was supposed to be. The familiar weight of a crown settled over her brow, tangled in a strand of hair stiff and gummy from perspiration mixed with hair spray.

As she walked down the runway, her stomach rolled with the odors of cosmetics and perfume, mold, and the two dozen pink roses she'd been given. She could taste the bile in her throat—a lingering threat of the illness that emptied her stomach before every appearance.

She smiled and glided above spectators she could no longer see or hear. She'd found her secret place where tears were invisible and anger was silent.

At the end of the runway she focused on the man standing below her with an eight-millimeter movie camera, following every step of her progress. Her father, recording her victory for her mother to study and criticize for the next time. Shuddering at the thought, she paused for him and slipped one aching foot, then the other, in and out of her high heels—just for a moment, too quickly for anyone to notice what she was doing. How she missed the patent-leather Mary Janes that she'd worn until now.

How she hated growing up feeling as if she'd never been a child.

Her father lowered his camera, and watched her as she posed for the official contest photographer and curtsied to the judges. As she turned for the walk back to take her seat on the throne, she imagined that she could hear the whir of his camera begin again.

She wondered why he didn't smile.

She posed for more pictures, holding the roses, then holding the trophy and a check that would disappear into a trust fund with her name on it. Until she was ready for college, the money would simply be a series of numbers in a bank book. She thought of the other award she had won tonight: Miss Congeniality, the friendliest and sweetest, the easiest to get along with. That prize had disappeared into her mother's safekeeping, and Angie wondered why it was less important than the robe and crown and the trophy that she now held.

The lights dimmed suddenly, and the stage was empty. A woman removed the robe, handed the trophy down to Angie's father, and led Angie to her mother, who waited in the wings, still glowing and beautiful.

She noticed the silence as they walked into the long dressing room backstage, not absolute but punctuated by soft whispers and sobs, and the cacophony on the other side of the wall. The fairy-tale setting was being torn down —just plywood and paper and rented flowers. The orchestra members called to one another, joking about the pageant and the stumbles and missed notes of some of the contestants. Men on the stage crew cursed the props and shoved them into the bowels of the auditorium.

It was all like a secret that was told, then tucked away until it could be told again.

People stood all around her, watching her, sidling out of her way, mothers pulling their daughters from her path, all of them watching her, then dropping their gazes.

It had happened before, more times than she wanted to remember. But this time she understood the looks being cast her way. She understood the resentment, the hostility. And she felt the bitter disappointments being experienced around her.

She felt her own disappointment even more keenly.

Angie walked on through the subdued crowd, her back

straight, her eyes wide, unblinking, her expression blank. She was a winner. She had to act like one.

Sara, her friend, stood just ahead, her head raised, tears streaming down her face. She wore a dress similar to Angie's, blue chiffon to Angie's ivory lace. Both dresses were demure yet fitted perfectly over budding curves. They were wearing earrings and high heels for the first time, going from children to young women in the time it had taken to change their shoes.

Angie stopped in front of her friend and smiled. The other girl said nothing, did nothing as Angie held out the bouquet of roses she clutched in her hand. She would give Sara everything she had to take the look of bitter hurt from her eyes.

Sara ignored her offering, let it drop to the floor as Angie's hand opened. Then she turned and trampled Angie's flowers, crushing the petals into the floor as she ran away— crushing Angie with her rejection.

A few of the other girls snickered. Some whispered behind their hands as they cast sidelong glances Angie's way. Others averted their gazes or left. None spoke to Angie.

It had happened before.

And as before, she wondered why nightmares and fairy tales were the same.

Why she always lost more than she won.

1

Colorado Springs—December 1990

What have I done? Angie wondered as she watched her
students file into the studio, their tights and leotards pris-
tine, their hair caught neatly in ponytails, braids, and little
buns at the back of their heads.

Today would be their last class before Christmas vacation. Today would be her last class, period, the last time she
could claim to be one of the owners of the Winters-Haley
Academy of Dance. After the school closed for the day, her
partner, Margot Haley, would become the sole proprietor
of a successful enterprise, and Angie would be retired at
the age of twenty-seven.

A has-been.

Catching their collective reflections in the mirrors lining
the large studio, Angie's dark brown eyes sparkled as she
tucked a stray hank of her auburn hair behind her ear. She
stuck out like a sore thumb in the crowd of pint-size prima
ballerinas, with her neon-red leotard and iridescent yellow
tights. She looked the same as she always had, with the
beauty that she'd cursed more than once before she'd
learned to accept it for the shallow perception it was. Inside, she was the same, too. It was her perceptions of herself that were changing, and in the confusion she'd found
her life changing, too.

It hadn't happened. She couldn't possibly have made
such an impulsive decision. Not Angela Winters, who more
often than not killed an impulse by thinking it to death.
Not when she'd found a nice, safe little niche for herself
where her success protected her from expectations and demands. She couldn't possibly have put herself in the position of having to meet her own expectations, demand more
from herself.

Angie knew her actions had been totally out of character. Poor Margot. No wonder she'd been watching Angie as if she expected a change of mind at any moment.

All on impulse. An irresponsible whim, her mother had said. But then, her mother had considered Angie's determination to open the academy an equally foolhardy whim.

Her mother had thought she was too young to start a business, too naive and sheltered to make it in the outside world, too well trained and talented to lower herself to teaching. So what should she do, she'd asked her mother in a rare fit of pique, become a dancing nun?

Charlotte didn't understand the difference between real talent and acquired technique. She didn't see that her daughter was short on the first and long on the second. Angie could certainly dance and loved it, but that didn't make her a *dancer*. Angie was simply an overachiever, driven by the need to succeed, to prove to everyone that she would not be a disappointment ever again.

She'd proven that and more and had found no satisfaction in it. With the success of the school, Charlotte had changed her tune to sing her daughter's praises to anyone who would listen. With the passing of years, Angie had become more bored, more disillusioned.

She'd been, she realized, disappointed in herself.

Until she'd sold her old life at a respectable profit—a completely irresponsible act, considering she didn't know what to do next.

Take the money and run.

She'd proposed that Margot give her a down payment and monthly installments, so she could fool herself into believing she was still earning a living.

Give it a rest, Angie, she told herself firmly. It wasn't as if she'd have to stand in line at the unemployment office or apply for welfare.

When her father bowed out of his marriage, he defied his wife by setting up a trust for Angie, giving her material control over her own life on her twenty-first birthday. When Charlotte Winters remarried four months ago, Angie's father had deeded her the family home. Materially, she had control over her life. She would be doing what she wanted—as soon as she figured out what it was. There was absolutely no reason to panic.

She hoped.

Illusion and irresponsibility, Angie had learned, went very well together. One made it possible to indulge in the other.

The floor shook as a dozen eight-year-olds performed the tumbling exercises that preceded every dance class. Already the air in the studio carried the unique scent of active children, not perspiration exactly, but a combination of various fabric softeners used on just-washed leotards, the heavier odors of their mothers' perfumes, and the dust that children seemed to collect just by walking from point A to point B.

The mothers were banned from the lessons, but that didn't stop some of them from jockeying for position in front of the small window set into the door. The girls in this class were the serious students, either because they loved dance or because their mothers loved the prestige of being able to brag about their daughters' accomplishments, to live out their own frustrated fantasies through their offspring.

In the beginning, she'd thought she could make a difference to mothers and daughters alike. She should have remembered that nothing could make a difference but the daughters themselves, and she knew better than anyone how difficult that was. She focused on Laurie Gilbert, the only success story in the bunch, not because Laurie was good—she wasn't—but because Laurie was working her buns off for the sheer love of it. Because she wanted to.

"Okay, ladies, everybody face the mirrors and take first position," she said on a sigh. It was all routine, all repetition. Only Laurie's eyes reflected excitement, enthusiasm. Only Laurie saw each lesson as new and unique.

Two of the students took opposite ends of the line—the two girls whose mothers were staring through the window. Away from the studio, Mary Beth and Jennifer were friends. At three o'clock on Mondays, Wednesdays, and

Fridays they became rivals. From bitter experience, Angie knew well which would prevail.

Mary Beth Johnson's mother opened the door to stand in the threshold, openly directing her daughter's "performance." Everything Mary Beth did was a performance as far as her mother was concerned. The more she directed, the more stiff and clumsy Mary Beth's movements became. The petite eight-year-old was working up a righteous anger as she deliberately botched the positions.

Good for you, Mary Beth.

Angie made a decision. One final act before she left these girls to stumble in their mothers' wakes.

"Laurie," she called out to the child who always kept a little apart from the others. The girl who concentrated and practiced and dreamed of a future on the stage. The girl whose mother dropped her off for class and picked her up after but rarely came in to wait. A mother who fretted over her child's dedication and worked overtime to pay for her daughter's dream. It didn't matter that Laurie's coordination was hampered by dyslexia, or that she was quiet and shy. What she wanted mattered. Her courage mattered.

Laurie glanced up at Angie, eager for instruction and fearful that she might be corrected for that last awkward turn. "Yes, ma'am?"

Angie kept her voice even, casual, businesslike, as if what she was about to say should be no surprise to anyone. "Practice starts for the recital next month. Be sure to get plenty of rest. I don't want the lead dancer to have circles under her eyes." Silence fell as the other girls stilled, one by one. That hated silence. But Laurie didn't notice. Her skin flushed as she lowered her gaze to the floor.

"Me?" she asked in a small voice.

"You're the only Laurie in the class," Angie said gently, knowing that the girl had more ambition than confidence, more desire than skill. As far as Angie was concerned, it was the ambition and tenacity that would earn Laurie her dreams. Besides, this was only Laurie's second year in dance. Maybe a little confidence would help her catch up that much faster. "You'll have to practice extra at home."

Laurie's head snapped up as if she'd just realized that Angie was serious. "I will. I'll push my bed against the wall and move the rest of the furniture out of my room. The floors in there are wood."

Again, Jennifer snickered.

Mary Beth's breath whooshed out of her, and she smiled in triumph. Angie knew Mary Beth had no interest in doing more than putting in her time, and her smugness could have been anything from being let off the hook to knowing that Jennifer hadn't won the coveted lead position.

Angie raised her eyebrows at Jennifer, pinning her with a look she'd perfected over the years, and stifled the urge to give Mary Beth a thumbs-up.

Angie sauntered toward the door and firmly shut it in Helen Johnson's face. She didn't even bother to smile. What was the use? She was invisible—no longer one of the powers-that-be at the academy. Invisible was good. Out of sight, out of mind. She'd developed a real talent for dropping out, period.

Except that this time, she knew, deep down, that she wasn't failing.

It had been a bad idea to think she could make a difference, and an error in judgment to believe she was capable of trying. Her friend Gena was right. Sometimes she *did* think too much.

Except when life was handed to her on a silver platter. Then she simply talked herself into believing it was what she wanted. She was so good at adjusting and conforming, and she always managed to find an ideal or two on that silver platter that appealed to her.

"Some ideals are great in theory, but suck ducks in practice," Gena had said. "Look at the Crusades. Hundreds of years of armed missionaries fighting for Christianity, and the Moslems still outnumber the Christians."

Angie hadn't bothered to point out that Gena's life was built on a crusade. For Gena it worked.

Angie went through the motions and checked her watch every four minutes. Hair straggled from her students' ponytails and buns, and their tights began to wrinkle and bag on coltish legs. Somehow—Angie had never quite figured it out—their white leotards became dingy, though the studio was kept spotlessly clean. Next month the class would graduate to black.

Brilliant, Angie, putting the younger ones in white. Shows just how tuned in you are to the ones you wanted to help.

It had taken years to realize that it was herself she'd wanted to help. Now she'd helped herself right out of a career.

"Shouldn't you be generating a little anxiety?" her mother had asked during a frantic call from Paris. Angie hadn't had the courage to tell her mother of her decision in person, so she'd waited until Charlotte was too far away and would have to pay over a dollar a minute to argue. "It would be redundant, Mother," Angie had answered. "You're doing fine without me."

"You need to have a goal, Angie."

"I do, Mother—"

"You love to dance," Charlotte interrupted. Charlotte always interrupted.

"Yes, for myself."

"Those children need you."

"No." The children knew more about life than she did. They were independent and assertive, even in the third grade. They didn't need a wuss for a champion. She didn't need a crusade to give her life meaning. She'd already spent too much time pretending to enjoy ideals that didn't agree with her.

She sighed with relief as the hands on the clock finally completed their hourly sweep. All that was left was to wait for Margot to finish her own class so she could tell her of the decision she'd made about Laurie. Margot would be surprised at Angie's choice, but what the heck. The condemned were usually granted a last request.

Condemned to what? she wondered.

Wiping her face with a towel, Angie waved at the girls as they left the building and tried to ignore the sick panic twisting in her stomach. She strolled into the office and carefully shut the door, then sagged in the chair behind the desk.

For months, she'd been high on freedom and the concept of choices. She'd forgotten that when you overdose on anything, you inevitably had to crash.

She'd been pretending for months. Pretending to know herself and what she wanted. Pretending to know exactly where she was going. She'd fooled herself into thinking that she was ready for this, welcomed it. She'd thought only of tomorrow, forgetting that tomorrow was easy. It was the day after tomorrow that worried her.

In a few days she'd meet Margot and their lawyers, sign the closing papers, and walk away—no more going through the motions, no more frustration.

No more pretense.

It scared her to death.

Irritated with her self-centered absorption, Angie picked up a pen and rooted around the messy desk for paper and envelope. It would be another half-hour before Margot finished with her class. No way was she going to wallow in her own insecurities for thirty more minutes.

As she always did when she couldn't find enough of herself to hold on to, she reached out to another who might be lonely and confused.

She wrote a letter to a stranger.

STRANGERS

I'm nobody! Who are you?
Are you—Nobody—Too?
Then there's a pair of us?
Don't tell! They'd advertise—you know!

How dreary—to be—Somebody!
How public—like a Frog—
To tell one's name—the livelong June—
To an admiring bog!
                              —Emily Dickinson

2

Germany—Christmas Eve, 1990

You didn't have to stop breathing to be dead.

Jack Caldwell had learned that basic truth at age ten. Months had stretched into years as he'd witnessed life and death trying to crowd each other out, a struggle that seemed separate from the heart and soul, a battle that had no winners. It had been a concept then, too frightening and complicated to be verbalized. Until eight months ago, he'd believed that he'd succeeded in wiping the memory out of his mind. It wasn't a part of *his* life. It would never be a part of his life.

Until the words had been said to him, *about* him.

Truth delivered down and dirty by his wife, calculated to damage, maybe even destroy. He hated her for saying it, for reminding him of what he'd already known and worked so hard to forget. Kay had to be wrong. He saw and heard and felt. Oh, God, how he had felt that night.

For a few minutes past and present had closed over him, dragged him down. He'd been out of control as he fell into a hole with nothing to hold on to, nothing to get a fix on.

The first time he'd felt himself pitching over the edge, it hadn't been like that. At ten, he'd seen everything with innocence and clarity. At ten, he'd reacted with honest emotion and had immediately been forgiven by his family.

Hell, they hadn't even noticed what he'd done.

It hadn't taken him long to calm down, grow up, and learn patience the hard way. He'd learned then what it took to push him in directions he didn't want to go.

It took betrayal. And loss.

Damn her for making him remember!

He heard the hesitant knock on the door, then the quiet swish as it was opened.

"Why don't you go home, Major? It's Christmas E—"
The young lieutenant's voice trailed off as his superior officer turned to look at him. Major Caldwell had that cold,
blank expression that warned against trespassing on his
personal space. Lieutenant Baker flushed and stared at the
wall as he realized what he'd done. The major's personal
space was probably as cold as winter on the moon.

Lieutenant Baker saluted and backed out of the office.

Jack swiveled his chair around and returned his gaze to
the view outside his window as he sipped from a mug of
lukewarm coffee. *Home,* he thought grimly. Didn't Baker
know? The office was his home. He'd had to move out of
their quarters after Kay had left, and the Bachelor Officers'
Quarters held no appeal with their institutional decor and
mainly young and single inmates.

Single.

Divorce papers had come in this morning's mail.

Merry Christmas, Jack.

He listened to the party sounds in the background, the
singing and laughter and good will, and he wondered if he
had fallen again, if he was going under for the third time.

"No," he said under his breath. Not him. He wasn't a kid
anymore. He was a major in the Air Force, known for his
patience, his ability to concentrate on scattered bits of intelligence and fit them all together. He was quick and con-
cise and all business. He knew what the people in his unit
thought of him: a man who spoke only when he had something to say, did what had to be done, without temper,
without anything more than professional interest. No one
knew what he took personally and what he didn't. If one of
his subordinates had a problem, he listened. When he offered criticism or advice, it was just to make sure the unit
kept working properly. It was part of the job. It was part of
the image.

It meant control.

No, he wasn't going under at all, he decided. It was just a
memory, something that was over and done with. Another
ending that he didn't want to think about.

Denial. Wasn't that one of the stages, like anger and

grief and acceptance? It had been explained to him a long time ago. It was okay to be angry. He'd believed it until his anger had deprived him of something precious. Then he'd learned that denial could be a form of acceptance. Don't think about it, and it won't be real.

The only reality was the job, the plans he'd made when guilt had evolved from anger. Once, Kay had liked that about him—the way he wanted life to be laid out all nice and neat, like soldiers standing formation, row after row of plans, ambitions. He hated it when those plans got screwed up. She wanted the same thing, she'd said. She wanted to know where she was going.

He would be the model officer, the perfect husband, and she would be the ideal officer's wife and woman of the eighties, juggling her duty to him and her duties to herself.

He should have seen it coming when she'd used the plural for one and not the other.

The situation wasn't all that unusual. It happened all the time—wives just packing up and leaving without notice. Overseas assignments weren't all glamour and great shopping. Prices in Europe had soared so high that most servicemen couldn't afford to do anything. They lived in large apartment buildings, families stacked on top of each other like crackers in a box. They couldn't even argue without everyone on base knowing the details.

And on a base that had more chiefs than Indians, the jockeying for position was a little more desperate, a little more vicious. The wives' social life revolved around the Officers' Club and their own organization within an organization. Kay had hated the political maneuvering, the obsessive ambition some of the women indulged in, not for themselves but for their husbands.

Peace on earth. Good will toward men.

No, the situation wasn't unusual. Maybe he wouldn't have felt anything at all if she'd gone about it in the usual way . . . if he had reacted in the usual way.

Jack closed his eyes against the sight of falling snow, Christmas lights, the frosted trees of the Black Forest just beyond the perimeter of the base. A white Christmas.

Just like the ones we used to know.

Before Germany, he and Kay had always enjoyed the holidays. Last year, she'd wanted to go stateside for Christmas. He couldn't get leave. Then she'd wanted to send plane tickets to her widowed father and her grandmother, but his paycheck wouldn't stretch that far.

Not that it had started when they'd come to Germany two years ago. Their marriage had been a time bomb from day one. Kay had her own ideas on what she wanted and expected him to deliver. He'd been willing to give all he could, had even compromised his career plans. A marriage was worth saving, and he'd loved Kay once. He wanted to love her again.

He'd expected her to feel the same way.

Not in this life.

Laughter floated down the hall as the last of the men left the mail room. It had been chaotic when the last shipment came in: packages from home, letters from sweethearts, and bags of mail in response to servicemen's pleas for pen pals. Having pen pals was back in style, and there were even people in the states who wrote letters as a hobby. Many of them were female and single, and the men gave them nicknames such as Angel or Baby or Our Girl. He often heard the men reading their letters aloud, sharing a link to the States with their buddies, speculating on the attributes or lack thereof of their pen pals. It passed the time, and a couple of marriages had resulted from the correspondence. Jack held up his mug of coffee in a silent toast to his reflection in the window.

Romance lived . . . somewhere.

"Sir?"

Jack ignored Baker, the happiness and anticipation charging the atmosphere—hell, he wanted to ignore the whole damn world. But the world wasn't about to return the favor. Baker was a sincere do-gooder, and Jack was afraid that the lieutenant was dangerously close to inviting him to share the holiday with him and the girl he'd met on base—a Filipino nanny who worked for one of the families.

Baker's romance worried him. The girl was hiding something. Not even Baker's closest friends knew anything about her, and Baker had taken to constantly looking over his shoulder. Do-gooders like the lieutenant were ripe pickings for opportunists no matter what language they spoke.

He wiped his hand over his face. God, had he ever been that young and naive?

His concern aside, Jack knew that in his present state of mind, he'd probably wind up playing the Grinch by advising Baker to forget his mysterious girlfriend and find a pen pal instead.

He heard Baker tiptoe into the office. In the window, he watched the lieutenant's reflection as he placed a decorated tin on the desk and pulled an envelope from his pocket to lay on top of the tin. "Merry Christmas, sir," Baker whispered, then shut the door on his way out.

He didn't want to see what Baker had brought, didn't want to be reminded of Christmas and good will. His reflection wavered as the headlights of a car swept over the window and disappeared.

Jack spun around to face the desk. The tin could hold only one thing: Mrs. Baker's homemade fruitcake. She sent her son one every year. Jack hated fruitcake, but that wasn't the point. Baker loved it and he'd just handed it over to him.

Damn, but he hated being pitied.

His gaze caught on the envelope addressed in a handwriting so small, he could barely make it out. LINK INTERNATIONAL was stamped in the lower left-hand corner. It was from Colorado Springs—home, though his parents spent most of the year living out of a motor home and put down temporary stakes whenever and wherever the mood struck them. How long had it taken Baker to dig through the mailbags to find it? If Jack had any sense, he'd file it in the wastebasket.

He had enough strangers in his life—himself in particular.

The envelope glared brightly on the drab government-issue desk, inviting him to satisfy his curiosity, promising him relief from the memories.

Why not?

Reaching for the letter, he opened it and stared at the salutation. No formality or awkward greetings here—just a simple "Hi" followed by an exclamation point. Jack couldn't resist that simple familiarity, as if he and the writer had been friends for years. The script was even smaller in the letter, less legible, as if the writer might be a little shy on self-confidence and worked hard at fading into the paper. He squinted, trying to decipher every word, suddenly needing any illusion of warmth and companionship he could find.

December 2—

Hi!

My typewriter is broken—dead, actually—so you'll have to suffer through my handwriting. I really must think seriously about getting a computer to save your eyes and to save me from myself, but frankly, I'm terrified of anything that is smarter than I am.

I can't help but wonder what fascinating part of the world you are in now and what Christmas traditions you are observing and, I hope, taking part in. Do they celebrate Christmas where you are? Are the colors and tastes and smells and sounds different from those we are used to? Will you share your experiences with me through a letter?

I am celebrating the holidays much as I did when Mother was here. She remarried a few months ago, and she and her husband are on an extended around-the-world cruise. After that, she and my stepfather will settle in his house in Gennessee. It's been difficult adjusting to an empty house—empty nest syndrome in reverse, I suppose. On the other hand, the freedom is nice.

Anyway, I made a resolution to buy a small tree this year, but found myself dragging a twelve-footer through the front door. The attic has enough decorations and lights for ten trees, so rather than let them go to waste, I strung lights all over the trees in the front yard and around the windows. I broke another resolution by painting holiday scenes on every window. What fun. Washing the paint off, however, is a nightmare. Next year, I must be strong. And practical.

At least sanity prevailed, and I bought a small roasting hen instead of the twenty-pound turkey I had my eye on. I hate turkey soup and turkey hash and turkey casserole. Will you be having turkey and dressing and mince pie? My mouth waters at the thought.

In honor of the freedom I mentioned earlier, I made a decision that has turned my life completely inside out. Acting on impulse is an interesting concept. I may have to try it again sometime. In the meantime, I am committed to doing my own thing. Now that everything is about to become final, I'm starting to panic. I still don't know what my own thing is.

Time has escaped me again. It is five-thirty and I must melt a friend for dinner at seven. Please take care and enjoy the holidays in your host country enough for both of us.

> *Best wishes,*
> *Angela Winters*

Melt a friend for dinner? Jack held the page closer in an effort to read the last paragraph. No, it was just an oversize E, not an L. He put the letter down and reached for the tin. The fruitcake was already sliced, and one piece was missing. Poor Baker. The aroma of Grand Marnier wafted up from the cake. He wondered if Angela hated fruitcake as much as he did.

The letter drew his gaze over and over again. Between the cheerful lines there was a poignancy, a loneliness he understood all too well. Angela was celebrating Christmas alone—no mention of festivities or parties or gifts to exchange. Even he'd received gifts: a book from a friend, a new briefcase from his aunt, a package from his parents that he hadn't opened yet. Unfolding his Swiss Army knife, he pulled the box out from under his desk. In it, he knew he'd find the necessities of life according to Ada Caldwell.

Sure enough, the box was bulging with new underwear—all white—and socks—black of course; a fisherman knit sweater; a warm hat and gloves; a box of stationery complete with self-addressed stamped envelopes; a set of Old Spice toiletries. And carefully packed in a smaller box was a Mason jar filled with his favorite homemade cranberry sauce. Christmas wasn't complete without Mom's cranberry sauce.

With the gifts and wrapping paper strewn around him, Jack picked up Angela's letter and read it once more. At the last paragraph, his mouth quirked at the image of a faceless woman melting a friend for dinner. A chuckle was strangled in his throat as Jack tossed the letter onto the floor.

Obviously, Angela Winters expected an answer. What could he tell her? Dear Angela—I'm a burned-out, bummed-out mess. My wife couldn't stand me. My brilliant career is probably over. I'm planning to find myself as soon as I figure out at which point I became lost.

Jesus! Where was this crap coming from?

He opened the tall foiled box the colonel had given him and glared at the bottle of Scotch. The building was silent with everyone gone but the skeleton staff unfortunate enough to draw holiday duty. Normally, he wouldn't consider drinking at the office, but he was off duty and nothing would be required of him for two days.

Why not? Opening the bottle, he poured two fingers of good Scotch into the water glass on his desk and took a sip, let it trickle down his throat slowly, felt the burn as it hit his stomach.

A framed photo on the desk caught his eye. A picture taken twenty-five years ago of himself and his two brothers. He stared at the image of himself at ten, trying to remember what it had been like to be that young and innocent, that trusting. He'd grown since then—taller, broader, with a body he worked hard to keep in shape—but the basic features were the same: dark blue eyes and dark brown hair that framed an angular, hard-jawed face.

Hard. How many times had Kay accused him of being hard?

Goddam her.

He pushed Kay out of his mind and stared at the photo. Bryan, his older brother by seven years, stood on one side of him, two of his fingers sticking up behind Jack's head. Steve, five years younger than Jack, slouched on the other side, his gaze focused on something no one else could see. In the memory, Jack could even see his father crouched behind his tripod, coaching the boys to "cut the crap" long enough for him to snap the picture. Dad had the shot blown up into a poster for Mom's birthday.

Jack had been scowling. He thought Bryan or Steve should stand in the middle. He was tired of always being in the middle.

Two months after the picture had been taken, Bryan had put him between a rock and a hard place.

To this day, the poster was framed and encased in glass, three boys sealed in a tomb. Three brothers who would never be together again.

He shook his head, poured another drink, drained the glass in one long pull. He wasn't going to do this, he told himself. He wasn't into floating face-down in a bottle of booze. No way was he going to do anything but go on with the rest of his life.

After he got so sloshed that he'd sleep through Christmas.

The first Christmas he'd ever spent alone.

Leaning over, he picked up the crumpled letter and smoothed it out on his knee. Christmas was a lousy time to discover loneliness, the silence of a hollow life. Angela's letter, so full of friendliness and an I'm-not-licked-yet attitude spoke to him with a silent voice that he seemed to hear more clearly than anything Kay had shouted at him.

Outside, a group of carolers strolled through the snow, raising their clear voices against the silence as they sang "O Holy Night." Inside, Major Jack Caldwell covered his face with his hands and grieved, for himself, for an empty future, for the wife he couldn't seem to miss. And he grieved for a woman who celebrated a season of sharing even though she was alone, a woman who was enjoying freedom yet apparently had no one to enjoy it with. Then for good measure, he grieved for a kind young man who was very likely headed for heartbreak and disillusionment.

He didn't want anyone else to learn that you didn't have to stop breathing to be dead.

The carolers silenced, then began another song.

God Rest Ye, Merry Gentlemen.

3

Colorado Springs—December 30, 1990

Now she'd gone and done it.

Not an hour ago, Angie had met with Margot and closed on the sale of the academy. The papers were signed and sealed and Angie was a free spirit. Ready or not, she was going to find out what independence meant without having to look it up in the dictionary. She really should be celebrating.

Life did some strange things to you when you weren't looking—like turning on you just when you thought you had it by the tail.

But when Angie walked out of the academy for the last time today, she'd realized that she had nothing by the tail —not even a comfortable illusion or two. She had everything she could possibly need. She had her health, and she had dreams. She had a whole life ahead of her—years and years worth of future.

Maybe Easy Street had a dead end.

Angie stood on the porch, unable to bring herself to unlock the door. Outside it was easier to believe it was all hers—the house, the future, her life. It was so hard to think of any of it in possessive terms, when she'd lived the last twenty-seven years only on the terms of others.

Outside, the house had her stamp: the windows she'd decorated with tempura paintings of holiday scenes, the Christmas lights she'd strung around the roof and porch and over the junipers hugging the foundation of the house, the handmade wreath on the door, and red velvet ribbons on the mailbox and trunks of the trees. None of it had any order, much less coordination. She'd simply placed the decorations wherever she'd found a bare spot, filling the property with gaiety as she'd tried to fill a lonely weekend with activity.

She loved the neighborhood with its middle-age, middle-class occupants, the permanence reflected in the large trees shading every property, the big, well-kept old houses. The roomy yards had gardens with lush mixtures of barely tamed shrubbery and carefully manicured flower beds. Lawns were piled ankle deep with autumn leaves that seemed to procreate the minute they touched ground. The trees should have been bare long before this, but the weather had been unusually mild.

A rake leaned haphazardly against the wide porch. She could certainly use a few hours of "busy work."

Kicking off her high heels, Angie shrugged out of her Pendleton tweed blazer and laid it over the porch rail with her purse. A cushion of leaves crunched under her feet as she shuffled around the yard, not caring that runners were climbing up her pantyhose or that the ground held a slight chill. Out of habit, she looked down one end of the street and then the other to see if anyone was watching before she rolled up the sleeves of her ivory silk shirt, pulled the tails out of her taupe skirt, and unfastened the button of her waistband. Over the last few months she'd gained ten pounds in spite of her daily practice sessions in the room her mother had refitted with smooth wooden floors, mirrors, a barre, and an expensive stereo system. Junk food and take-out were so much easier than cooking for one.

It didn't matter. She liked the extra weight, and aside from taking care of herself, her appearance was something she rarely thought of. It was no longer necessary to please any critic but herself.

The departures from rules and proper behavior, the defiance of it, were as wasted as her efforts to build her own life. Besides, she thought wryly, what good were all these symbolic gestures if there was no one around to be properly outraged?

And somehow, having no one else to consider or think about just made her solitary state that much more . . . *solitary*.

She picked up the rake and began a lazy rhythm of sweeping leaves into piles, letting her mind wander from troubling thoughts to more pleasant and less demanding paths.

Gena would be showing up anytime now for their annual New Year celebration and pity session. Though she'd expected her at Christmas, it hadn't surprised her when Gena hadn't arrived. Gena's life was ruled by crises and professional obligations that altered her schedule on a daily basis.

From the first time they'd met thirteen years ago, Angie had known that Gena was one of those people who made things happen. Gena had breezed into Angie's dorm room at Collingswood School for Girls as if she'd owned it. From her appearance it was obvious that she could own half the country and probably did.

Two years older than Angie, Gena had an Ivory soap look with wide blue eyes and light gold hair. Dimples and a smile that covered her entire face tricked most people into seeing innocence and an easygoing manner. As she always did when confronted with strangers, Angie had looked at her new roommate and analyzed what she saw beyond the teeth and the smile and featherweight body. In Gena's eyes she'd seen something old and haunted that belied the term *baby blues.* Something she'd recognized.

At some point, life had kicked Gena Collier in the teeth.

After a week of sharing a room with Gena, Angie had developed a passive ambivalence for the girl of boundless energy and mental creativity. She'd resented Gena's ability to translate a thought—no matter how impractical—into tangible results. She'd envied Gena's adaptability. Whatever had put Gena two years behind in school and etched the ages-old knowledge in her eyes hadn't beaten down her spirit or robbed her of courage.

Gena had openly censured Angie for her tendency to react rather than act, and she had been determined to save Angie from herself. She'd said it all in a letter tacked to Angie's headboard at the beginning of their second year together.

Dear Roomie—

You guessed it. We're together again this year. The only way I'll be able to stand it is if you lighten up. I've never known such an intense bitch! We're young. We're expected to be loud, obnoxious, and occasionally irresponsible.

To be fair, I'll try to have more respect for your space. Speaking of which—I've stocked your closet with a few necessities. You're too perfect. "Wannabe" sticks out all over you. If you want to be like the rest of the girls (God knows why), you've got to wear nice clothes that have aged a bit. The designer labels are supposed to look worn, though readable. Cleaned and pressed is good, but geez, Angie, do your blouses have to have military creases? Your dad might be a general, but you're a civilian. Oh, yeah, in case you haven't noticed, you look like a freakin' Barbie doll in pastels and ruffles. If you insist on being a wannabe, at least be subtle about it and, for crying out loud, don't use Barbie as your role model. Ten to one Ken is a jerk—or a cross-dresser.

Angie couldn't help but smile while reading the letter, and then she'd cried. The military creases had been an exaggeration. The rest had struck too close to the bone, as if Gena somehow knew that Angie the wannabe was really a fourteen-year-old has-been.

She and Gena had barely spoken after that—until New Year's Eve, when Gena smuggled some wine into their room. They were virtually alone in the dormitory; the other students were still at home for Christmas break. Angie had returned to school early so her parents could battle out the terms of their divorce, escaping the shouting and the anger as fast as she could. Gena's mother had been called away to straighten out a family crisis.

They'd started a tradition that night.

"You have no life, and I have no date. This is as good a time as any for us to declare our independence by indulging in an immature and irresponsible act."

Angie tipped her head to the side in question, and Gena held up the bottle.

"Frankly, I'd rather lose my virginity than spend New Year's Eve with you, but since that's not an option, I think we should both get drunk, exchange confidences, and see if we can be friends."

"You're still a virgin?" Angie blurted, intrigued.

Gena stiffened. "Are you?" she asked coldly as her gaze skittered around the room and her usual confidence gave way to a sad, vulnerable expression. "Of course you are," Gena said brightly, her mood changing yet again. "Little Miss Perfect couldn't possibly lower herself to be normal."

Angie shrugged. She couldn't tell Gena that she made it a point to be Miss Perfect, that she was too scared to be normal. It was the only way she could escape censure and that horrible look of disappointment in her mother's eyes. There had been a day when Angie was no longer judged the best or the brightest, the most beautiful or the most talented. That day, she'd felt as if she'd finally won. Her mother had been shattered.

"Do you ever think about it?" Gena asked.

"I—"

"Right. You think about it when you're alone, and then you feel guilty for being just like the rest of us."

Startled at Gena's insight, Angie glanced up at her roommate. Unable to ignore Gena's brutal assessment, she nodded.

"Don't sweat it, Angie. We all get initiated sooner or later," Gena said with casual flippancy. "There's nothing wrong with choosing for it to happen later and legally."

"Maybe, maybe not," Angie said, feeling rebellious and knowing it wouldn't last beyond the moment. Still, she had a morbid fascination for the idea of doing the wrong thing, just once.

Sighing, Gena shook her head. "You don't have to be like everyone else, you know," she said softly. "You just have to be yourself."

"I am."

"Sure you are."

Without saying a word, Angie took the lids off of hers and Gena's cans of aerosol hair spray, washed them in the bathroom sink, and held them out to her roommate. "Pour," she managed to say.

Angie could see that it startled Gena, that simple act of decision. Gena poured and spilled some wine onto Angie's hand. With a tight smile she deliberately wiped her fingers on her angora sweater.

"I'll be damned," Gena said as she held up her cap.

They downed the first drink silently, watching each other over the rims of the wide plastic lids.

"After midnight, we'll break into the flask of brandy I lifted from my brother." Gena poured them both another capful and took Angie's arm, leading her over to the bed. They sat down and propped their backs against the wall. Angie cringed as Gena studied the opposite half of the room.

Her gaze darted about the room, at the difference between Gena's side and hers, the color and life Gena had quickly brought, the institutional drabness Angie hadn't noticed on her side until now. Everything from the generic bedspread to the bare walls depressed her, just as the things her mother had furnished her room with at home oppressed her.

"Are you poor?" Gena asked as she gestured toward the opposite end of the room. "That looks like a jail cell."

Closing her eyes, Angie saw her pretty room at home—the lace and satin Dakotah comforter and matching lace bedskirt and curtains, the Monet, Degas, and Edwards posters on the walls, the feminine bottles, atomizers, and music boxes, the host of fluffy stuffed animals, dolls, and porcelain that were too expensive to handle on shelves placed all the way around the room near the ceiling. "Not poor," she said, staring again at her sterile space. "I wonder what it would be like?"

"I wouldn't know. I own Boardwalk, Park Place, and Rodeo Drive." Gena hopped off the bed and grabbed her purse off her dresser, then turned around with a hundred-dollar bill and a pack of matches in her hand. "I've always wanted to do this," she said as she struck a match to the currency.

"I'm not rich enough to appreciate the gesture," Angie said, horrified and fascinated at the same time. The whole scene seemed like those in clever movies from the forties full of sophisticated repartee and jaded observations. Little girls playing dress-up.

"*Are* you aware that you don't have a life?" Gena asked.

"Yes."

"Why don't you?"

"No guts."

"Cowards don't break the rules." Gena held up the bottle of wine, almost empty now.

"This is my first time," Angie confessed. "I never break the rules."

"I'll bet you question them. Not out loud, of course."

"*Never* out loud."

"That's pathetic." Holding up her cap of wine, she tapped it against Angie's. "Here's to Barbie. She has no pubic hair, her legs don't bend, and her boobs look like concrete party hats."

"Really?" Angie asked.

"Don't tell me you never looked."

"No," Angie whispered. She had a whole shelf of the dolls, each an expensive collector's edition that she'd unwrapped at Christmas and dutifully admired before her mother placed it out of reach with the rest of her dolls and stuffed animals. She'd hated them, with their frothy gowns, perfect hair, and painted-on faces.

"Your first New Year's resolution: Use Barbie as a role model for everything you *don't* want to be."

Angie wondered if she knew how to be anything else. "Who's your role model?"

Gena's eyes darkened as she drained her wine. "My mother."

"Oh." The concept confused Angie. She'd heard the other girls describe their mothers as everything from "okay, I guess" to "that bitch" to "stupid." "Why?" she asked.

"Because I'd like to always be right." She turned her head to look at Angie. "You don't like your mom?"

"I love her," Angie said truthfully.

"Uh-oh. Is she the reason you're as stiff-kneed as Barbie?"

Angie said nothing.

"Okay. So tell me, what can you do besides sing, dance, and iron?"

Angie held out her cap for a refill. "I don't—"

"This is an old school, sweetcakes, with real keyholes in the doors, and I'm nosy as hell." Gena poured for them both, draining the bottle. "I've seen you dancing around when you think you're alone, and everyone has heard you sing with your radio cranked up."

Letting the bottle drop from her hand to the floor, Gena turned her head to watch Angie. "Why the big secret? I'd give my eyeteeth to have your talent."

"Take lessons," Angie said bitterly.

"If we keep this up, we'll run out of conversation before midnight. Come on, Angie. For the moment, I almost like you, and I'm in a mood to bare my soul." She reached into her purse and pulled out a large silver flask. "I'll show you mine if you show me yours."

Angie glanced at Gena sharply, then turned her head away from what she saw. There was an appeal behind Gena's flippancy that Angie recognized—her own needs verbalized. In Gena's eyes she again saw the age and weariness, the confusion she could identify with. She saw a defiance that was beyond her experience and had the crazy idea that friendship was a necessity for both of them.

Tongues loosened with the cap of the flask; confidences flowed with every drop of brandy—small drops, because sophisticated Gena knew the proper treatment of rich spirits, virgin stomachs, untried hearts.

"I'm a rebel," Gena stated to get the ball rolling. "My mother is an advice columnist and practices on me and my brothers. Always advice—never orders, or requests, just advice."

"I wouldn't rebel against that." It sounded wonderful to Angie, never being told or coerced or volunteered.

"No? Try it on a regular basis. It's like having to choose

between twenty vegetables you hate and having only one put on your plate."

Angie shrugged. "You can get used to anything."

"Not me. I have choices," she intoned sarcastically. "Big hairy deal. I'm a kid. Once in a while I want to be told what to do, you know?"

Angie didn't know. "What about the rest of the time?"

"I told you—Mom has all the answers. I wanted to find them out for myself."

"What did you do?"

"If Mom 'suggested' one thing, I did another. She's always so *right*. Until my folks got a divorce, I'd just been playing a game. I totally freaked out when I realized that I'd been giving her a hard time when she was going through hell with Dad." Gena shuddered; her eyes closed. "She was so calm and reasonable. Just once, I wish she would have lost it. So I lost it for her. That's why I'm behind in school."

Angie felt as if Gena had walked over her grave with hobnail boots. The parallels were scary. Only Angie hadn't freaked out; she'd simply dropped out.

"My parents are divorced, too," she whispered. "It was my fault."

"That's crap. It was their marriage, their divorce." Gena gave Angie a strange look. "You really believe it's your fault, don't you?"

"I *know* it. I could have made things better, easier for my mother. Then Daddy wouldn't have left. They wouldn't have spent all their time together fighting because of me." Angie drank from her cap to clear the emotion from her throat, to numb the pain and guilt. "I don't see the general much anymore. I don't think he really wants to see me."

"Then he's a jerk."

"No, he's not. He gave up, I guess."

"On what?"

"Me. My mother. They each wanted me to be something different, and I disappointed them both for different reasons."

"You said 'something.' Is that how they see you, as a 'thing'?"

It's over for Angela. Poor thing. How many times had she heard it whispered behind hands, around corners, in the next room?

Feeling the effects of the alcohol after only one capful, Angie nursed the refill Gena pressed on her, holding more than drinking. After a while, she switched to water and felt the burn in her stomach ease with every swallow.

"Okay, enough of this heavy stuff," Gena said firmly.

Angie relaxed against the headboard. It was too soon to strip down to raw feelings, too soon to trust the concept of friendship when it had failed her so often in the past.

"So what do you want to be when you grow up?" Gena asked.

"*Not* Barbie. You?"

"I'm gonna change the world, or at least shake it up a little."

Angie thought Gena was joking and made some absurd remark. Gena shot back with another. They bantered back and forth on the subject of dreams and aspirations, some real, some made up for the occasion. Regardless of the reticence that kept both of them from telling too much, Angie knew that beneath skin and appearances and attitude, she and Gena, for different reasons, were two of a kind, lost souls who, during the course of the night, had found some part of themselves intact.

"Are you gonna barf?" Gena asked, peering owlishly at Angie.

"No."

"What's wrong? The bottle of wine was small, and I drank more than half. You've only had a swallow of the hard stuff."

"I have an ulcer. I shouldn't have had anything to drink."

"Holy shit! At your age?"

Angie nodded.

"Well, it makes my nervous breakdown a little less weird. You'd think life would come with an owner's manual."

"It's scary to think that we were raised by people who didn't know any more about it than we do now."

"It really pisses me off when parents are right," Gena said.

"It pisses me off when they're wrong," Angie said vehemently.

"You said a bad word. I didn't think you knew how."

Angie smiled. "Dad's in the military. Of course I know how—why do you suppose they're bad words?"

"How should I know? Why are apartments called apartments, when they're all stuck together?"

A crease formed between Angie's brows as she thought about it.

"Oh, geez, Angie, it was just a stupid question—nothing to get dysfunctional over."

"Sorry."

"Why do you apologize so much? For over a year, that's all I've heard come out of your mouth."

"Sor—" Angie grimaced at the automatic response and gave no answer beyond a shrug. She'd felt sorry for most of her life for just about everything.

Though it was turned down low, the radio burst with sound as the disc jockey shouted over canned sounds of horns and noisemakers.

"Happy New Year, Angie."

Angie felt the quick, light brush of Gena's lips on her cheek. It wasn't so much the display of affection but Gena's awkwardness that touched her. She'd noticed Gena's discomfort with physical contact before. Angie cleared her throat and with a trace of her normal shyness whispered, "Resolution Number Two: I will decorate my half of the room by the end of the month. Will you help me pick things out?"

"No way."

It happened then, the old feeling of being pushed away, and Angie sagged against the pillow as if she could disappear among the feathers.

"A person's space should be like the cover of a book, giving a hint of what's inside." Gena grinned. "Don't look at me like that, I haven't got a profound bone in my body. It's one of my mom's favorite little 'isms.' "

Angie swung her legs off the bed and stood up. Her body swayed one way while her legs tried to move in another.

Gena jumped up and ran around the bed to grab Angie's arm. "No more booze for you," she said as she led Angie toward her own bed and threw back the covers. "You're not on medication, are you?"

As soon as she settled back on the mattress and stopped moving, Angie began to feel better. She nodded carefully. "I didn't take it yesterday or today, though."

"Great. Okay, sit up. I'm going to pour more water down you and then make some tea. Do you need a doctor?"

"No. My stomach doesn't hurt anymore. I'm just dizzy."

"Okay, but you'll stay awake until we're sure."

Seeing the wisdom of that, Angie slowly eased herself up to sit against the headboard. Gena hovered over her, adjusting pillows behind her and refilling her cap with water, making tea for both of them with hot water from the faucet and the teabags she'd smuggled in with her luggage. Gena always had an assortment of soft drinks, tea, coffee, cookies, chips, and other delicacies squirreled away in the room.

"I'll keep you company while you shop, and buy my own stuff at the same time so the room won't look like an acid nightmare. Other than that, you're on your own."

"What?"

"You heard me. I love to shop. I'll buy my goodies; you buy yours. Just don't ask me to offer any opinions. That's cheating, and the place would look like my cover instead of yours. Face it, Angie. I definitely have the dominant personality."

A shiver of pleasure skittered up Angie's spine as she saw her portion of the room as it could be—an extension of herself, a declaration of who she was, what *she* liked and wanted. "*My* cover," she said, smiling wistfully. "A novel idea."

"Egad! She has a sense of humor!" Gena said to the ceiling. "Methinks there's hope for her."

Angie relaxed against the pillow. Hope . . . for her. Yes, that's exactly what it felt like.

For the remainder of her stay at Collingswood and during college, she'd done exactly that. Gena had been there every step of the way to critique and edit and sometimes approve Angie's decisions.

Except when Angie started the academy. Gena had been remarkably silent then. At the time, Angie had been grateful for that and convinced herself that Gena's reticence was proof that Angie could still think of her life in possessive terms. Now she knew better, and had to admit that her past was nothing but a hollowed-out book that had been filled from time to time with the aspirations of others.

Blinking, she glanced around and saw neat piles of leaves ready to be bagged and disposed of. As she stood in the middle of the yard, she shivered from the chill air wafting over her perspiration-dampened skin. Her feet were cold.

The sun had a fingernail grip on the horizon, leaving soft streaks of color in the western sky. In the east muted gray clouds floated in a deep indigo atmosphere. Rubbing her arms, Angie climbed the steps, collected her purse, shoes, and jacket, and went into the house.

A long bath gave her time to think, to remember her doubts, her regrets. After donning nightgown, robe, and slippers, she gave in to the melancholy that she'd been fighting for days, examining each thought, every feeling. She wandered from room to room, seeing the furnishings as they were: ice blue and frigid white, pretentious crystal, porcelain, and a large still life of perfect flowers, lukewarm splashes of pale rose and dull gold. Her mother's house—now hers in name only.

She felt like a stranger in her own home, her own life.

4

Colorado Springs—December 31, 1990

> *Dear Angela,*
> *I received your letter tonight through the Link International mailbag. Apparently, Lt. Baker, my assistant, saw the postmark and decided to give me the letter. Colorado Springs is home—*

Two short blasts of a horn startled Angie, drawing her attention from the letter she'd just received from an APO in Germany. She glanced up to see an electric blue '56 Thunderbird parked in her driveway and Gena Collier unfolding from the low-slung driver's seat.

Distracted by the angry slashes on a legal-size sheet of yellow paper, she couldn't help but return her gaze to the letter, hoping to read a little more. It was intriguing and strange, hearing from a field-grade officer in response to one of the "blind" letters she always sent out during the holidays. Usually she heard only from new recruits and junior officers. They were the lonely ones, disconnected from all things familiar and safe.

"How appropriate that I arrived with your mail," Gena said as she waved at the departing postman and opened the trunk of her car. Angie's mouth quirked at Gena's camouflage pants, Birkenstock sandals, and "Save Humanity" T-shirt.

Reluctantly, she returned the letter to its envelope. "How appropriate that you've arrived at all. You're only a week late."

"I get better welcomes from the CEOs I hit up for contributions," Gena huffed as she dragged her suitcase up the porch steps. "Didn't you get my message?"

Holding the rest of her mail in one hand, Angie opened the door with the other. "No."

"Oh, hell, I probably thought about it, then forgot to do it." Gena dropped her suitcase on the floor in the entrance hall and turned her face away, hiding her expression. "Mike's been called to arms, and I've spent a week of wild abandonment in bed with him," she said brightly.

"You're kidding."

"Nope. He's on his way to the Persian Gulf, dreaming of dogfights and glory." Gena shook her head and swallowed. "*Dammit!* I might never see him again. War. It seems so strange, you know?"

"Yes, I know." Beyond that, Angie didn't know what to say. In spite of her military background, the mock alerts and drills that supposedly prepared the families on base for nuclear attack, the cloud of fear that hovered over the young children, then dissipated into weary fatalism as they grew older, Angie hadn't considered that she or anyone she knew would be involved. Wasn't this something that always happened to someone else? She should have thought of Mike being called up, what with his previous service record as a pilot and his reserve status. "Gena—"

"Don't say it. Just give me a hug, and then feed me."

The hug was easy. Angie complied, holding Gena and being held in turn. The embrace ended abruptly as Gena pulled away and gave Angie the once-over. "You look disgustingly good."

"And I see that you've forsaken the whales," she said as she gestured toward Gena's T-shirt.

"If humanity gets its act together, the whales will be fine."

Angie smiled. "Welcome home, Gena. I take it you put the world on hold?"

"Just for you, chum. Besides, the world has been on hold since the invasion of Kuwait. No one is spending money, donating it, or making it for that matter, yet Link is busier than ever routing mail, setting up possible entertainment for the troops et cetera, et cetera." Gena turned to give Angie a hard stare. "You look like you'd rather chew nails than worry about the world's cultural and physical health. That letter you're clutching must really be hot."

"Don't be silly, Gena. Tea, soda, or coffee?" Angie asked as she led the way into the kitchen.

"Coffee. Do you have any sweet rolls?" She angled her head to read the return address. "A major. Wow! You're coming up in the world. Who is he?"

"I knew you'd show up eventually," Angie said wryly, ignoring Gena's curiosity. "Homemade cinnamon rolls are in the freezer. You know how to operate the microwave."

"Well, of course I showed up. It's New Year's Eve. Besides, you drop out, I arrive just in time to catch you." With easy familiarity, Gena removed a package of cinnamon rolls from the freezer and plopped the whole dozen into the microwave. "You, sweetcakes, are a meddler's dream."

Gena had made the same comment many times before; they'd even joked about it. Yet this time it irritated Angie, made her feel as if she were shrinking, fading out. But then she was good at fading—into corners, the woodwork, a potted palm, anything handy that might swallow up her presence.

She forced a smile. "You couldn't give me more time to wallow a little?"

"Depends on when you started."

"Since I taught my last class. I celebrated after I made the decision to sell, then started looking around. The job market is pretty grim."

"In that case, wallow away. I'll help." The microwave buzzed, and Gena slid the package of rolls off the tray. "Why were you job hunting?"

"It seemed the right thing to do."

"For who? Charlotte?"

"No. I came to that conclusion all on my own. I'll never make it as one of the idle rich."

"Yeah, I know what you mean. Having money to burn makes me feel guilty, like I have to compensate or make amends to the rest of the world."

"And you're doing it beautifully," Angie said.

A soothing silence fell while they prepared coffee and

buttered rolls, slipping into their friendship as if they
hadn't been separated at all. Angie was content to wait and
let Gena make the first move. It was a given that Angie
thought and Gena acted.

Angie had always felt a little guilty about their relationship, though. Gena had given her so much and asked nothing in return except a listening ear when she'd needed it
and an undemanding silence that she never got in her job
as head of Link International.

Link had grown in leaps and bounds, becoming more
than Gena's mother, an advice columnist, had envisioned
when she'd advised her readers to correspond with lonely
servicemen. Letters had poured into the various newspapers that carried her syndicated column. The management
of said newspapers were at a loss as to what to do with the
mail. They didn't have the staff to handle the forwarding
procedures, and so the Link International Foundation was
born.

Gena's grandfather, a billionaire with more time, wealth,
and visions than he knew what to do with since suffering a
stroke, had listened to Gena's ideas for the foundation and
reveled in helping her put ideas and visions alike into practice.

The blank expression on Gena's face hinted at more private concerns, adding weight to the silence, making Angie
feel inadequate to the task of comforting the friend who
tried to save the world with a unique mix of idealism,
money, and sheer drive. She could force the conversation
toward Gena and her painful week of saying good-bye to
the man she loved, but Gena wouldn't appreciate it. All she
could do was offer Gena a challenging diversion—namely,
herself.

Angie set the pot and two mugs of coffee on the table
and sat down. "Okay, let's get it over with."

Gena closed her eyes and breathed deeply as the scent
of yeast and cinnamon wafted upward on puffs of steam. "I
swear I live for this. It compensates for the rubber chicken
and shriveled veggies on the banquet circuit."

"I'm waiting," Angie said.

"Right," Gena muttered around a mouthful of hot pastry. "You did it again, chum; only this time it makes sense."

"Thank you," Angie said gravely.

"Nobody's here to tell you what to do next. Did you plan it that way?"

"I thought it was good timing."

"Uh-huh. Great timing. So what *are* you going to do next? Any ideas?"

"None that are practical."

"If I did what was practical, Link would be nothing more than a regret." Gena licked icing off her fingers and reached for another roll. "Greeting cards."

"What?"

"Let's face it, Angie. You're a sap, always have been, always will be. You give a whole new meaning to purple prose and sentimental slop. I've seen some of those letters you write, remember? And you've been making your own greeting cards for years. You're also a good artist. Link needs you."

"How did Link get into this?" Angie asked. "Never mind —you and Link are symbiotic. Where one goes the other lurks."

"I won't ask which of us does the lurking." Wiping her hands on a napkin, Gena pinned Angie with one of her bulldog stares. "I need you, chum, and the way I see it, you need Link."

"Interchangeable parts," Angie mumbled.

"Forget the greeting cards for a minute. You're right, I threw Link in there because I have a favor to ask you," Gena said.

The seriousness in Gena's voice caught Angie by surprise. It also kept her from thinking before saying, "Name it."

Gena took a swallow from her mug and sighed. "Not so fast, Angie. You haven't heard it yet."

"So tell me."

This time, Gena stalled by tearing apart a cinnamon roll.

"Ahh. Energy and stimulation." She sat back and held Angie's gaze. "Mom, Grandad, and I created a monster."

"Link."

"What else? We have people of all nations writing letters back and forth, not just Americans to Americans. The cultural exchange through letters alone is phenomenal. Link does more than all the other similar organizations put together." She paused to finish off her roll and reach for another. "Now, in response to a poll we took—you remember the one—we're about to set up an exchange program— students, the elderly, artists, and craftsmen—you name it— only we're not talking about a think tank here. I want hands-on stuff like workshops, classes, performances, concerts. The proceeds will go to promoting more of the same. I have this weird idea that teaching the honestly unemployed and homeless new crafts and skills just might open up new avenues, maybe even improve the economy in some small way."

"I know, Gena. I write the newsletter, remember?" Angie said softly. Too softly, as if she knew the other shoe was about to drop and she didn't want to miss it.

"Yeah, purple prose, and appeals for money that would make Scrooge McDuck shell out a bundle. Well, we're launching a massive media campaign to raise funds—"

"Bottom line, Gena."

"You know that trip you keep saying you're going to take?"

"You mean the trip I keep saying I *might* take? On my own? For pleasure?"

"That's the one," Gena said brightly, then spoke quickly as if to stall any arguments Angie could make. "We want to put out a special book about Link. If one of our board members and *supporters*"—she stressed the word with a meaningful lift of her brows—"went on tour, met some of her pen pals, and let us use her experiences in the book, it would be a nice touch."

"Gena—" Angie didn't like the conversation. Sure, she supported Link. Yes, she was a board member, mainly because she'd helped Gena and her grandfather lay the groundwork—behind the scenes, of course—and she had a knack for keeping Gena from going off the deep end when her intellectual creativity got ahead of her ability to slow down and follow through. "That doesn't qualify me to—"

"Let me finish, Angie. No one would understand as well as I do why you'd want to say no."

"No." Angie suddenly had the urge to lock herself in the bathroom, hide in a closet, anything. "You don't think you've taken on enough? You need to make me a project, too?"

Ignoring the question, Gena finished her coffee in one swallow, thunked her mug down, and leaned over, her eyes bright with excitement. "Think of it, Angie. It would be like Hands Across America, only across the whole world. And Hands was a symbolic gesture. This would be real—people of every culture sharing knowledge, skills, everything. Lost arts would be revived. Histories would be passed on. Ideas would be expanded by different viewpoints. Think of the opportunities in Russia alone! It wouldn't be just hands joining, but minds and hearts. We'd form an international lobby. The world might get smaller in ways that count. And I want to have books published on all of it."

"I heard you the first time, Gena—homeless, unemployed, world peace, economy, save the world single-handedly," Angie said as she refilled their mugs. "I'm not a professional writer, Gena. I'll stuff envelopes, compose letters begging for money—"

"So? We can hire a ghost to smooth out the rough spots —or better yet, we'll railroad one to 'donate' his skill," Gena said as she licked her fingers. "You need this trip, Angie."

"Not like this."

"Why not? All I'm asking you to do is meet some of your pen pals, make some appearances, keep a diary, take some pictures—hell, forget the pictures. I'll hire a photographer with my pin money."

Angie latched onto a single word. "Appearances?"

Gena picked crumbs off her plate with the pad of her finger. "The USO and overseas military newspapers want in on it." She looked up again, her expression challenging. "Well, what do you expect? You've made quite a name for yourself on the mail circuit. We're going to be hip deep in a war. The military needs good PR after Viet Nam. Besides, talent is a terrible thing to waste."

"So is a mind, Gena," Angie said, perfectly serious. "I've spent too many years and too much energy trying to save mine to let myself be manipulated again."

"I'm not manipulating. I'm asking. If you do it, it'll be from choice, not coercion." Gena's stare was hard, truth slamming into Angie. "You need to do this, Angie."

"Why?"

"Because, sweetcakes, sometimes you have to face the demons you know before you take on the ones you imagine."

Angie shuddered, a trembling chill that began inside and grew as it radiated outward. "I'll write you a check," she said, her voice thick.

Gena shook her head and stood up. "Not good enough, my friend—for you or Link. . . . I desperately need a shower. Oh, yeah, I'm parking on your doorstep for a while. Same bedroom?"

"It's always yours, Gena. How long are you staying?"

"As long as it takes," Gena muttered. "I'm having my place renovated, and being alone is hazardous to both of us right now. While I'm pulling myself together, why don't you give it some thought?"

"I already have."

Gena leaned back against the sink, her expression clearly exasperated. "You never make up your mind this fast. Sometimes I wonder if you've ever acted spontaneously in your life." Pushing away from the counter, she sauntered toward the door.

"I sold my partnership on a whim," Angie announced proudly.

Gena arched her left brow, a talent she perfected in her senior year at Collingswood. "So you made the right decision for the right reasons. Don't stop now. Make another decision—fast—or you'll end up in the attic with all the rest of Charlotte's dusty ambitions."

Angie stared down at her hands. "You're asking too much," she said, a lump in her throat. "I can't be on display."

"There's a difference between *can't* and *won't*, chum. Besides, things are on display, inanimate objects with neither brains nor choice. You don't qualify anymore," Gena said compassionately as she picked up her bag and disappeared up the rear staircase.

Angie didn't move until she heard the shower pattering overhead. In spite of her panic, she couldn't help but think about Gena's proposal. It sounded exciting. It would be challenging, productive. She loved Link almost as much as Gena did.

She couldn't do it.

Paper crackled under her hand where she'd laid the mysterious letter from a major stationed in Germany. Opening the envelope, she grasped the letter as if it were a talisman against all those demons Gena had resurrected. The strokes of the major's pen were angry slashes, in some places almost tearing through the paper, as if he had fought against writing the letter as his hand moved the pen. The words, though, conveyed deeper, more profound emotions.

I've wondered why my men haunt the mail room and spend so much time answering letters written by complete strangers. Now I know. Those letters make them feel less forgotten and alone, more significant. I've been sitting in my office thinking about having someone to share the loneliness with, but your letter made me realize that it's a contradiction in terms. If you're sharing, how can you be lonely?

The base I'm on is pretty much like any other—generic government issue—except that there are cobbled streets in the residential section and the buildings are older. Haven't seen much of the country. The only thing I really want to do before going home is to floor my gas pedal on the Autobahn. It will probably be my only chance to speed legally.

*I'm rambling. This is like trying to make conversation on
a blind date, and I don't have anything more to say. I really
wrote this to tell you how much it means to know that
someone cares enough to reach across the distance and fill
the empty hours for men and women away from home.
Much as I appreciate your letter and the work of Link
International, I'll pass.*

*Sorry—I don't mean to come off like an S.O.B., but your
gesture is wasted on me. Thanks for the lift you gave me at
Christmas. I know someone else will welcome your offer of
friendship.*

*Regards,
Major Jack Caldwell*

Well, Angie thought as she dropped the letter onto the
table. Rejection in big bold letters. The question was: Why
had he bothered? In an odd sort of way, she had the feeling
that he'd been trying to confide, to reach out, but didn't
know how.

She knew she had a knack for putting her long-distance
friends at ease. All she had to do was be what they wanted,
sometimes a confidante or a sympathizer, sometimes a
cheerleader or an entertainer, always a friend. It was the
perfect medium for her social life. To date, she'd been accepted in whatever role she played without exception, no
conditions attached.

But not this time. She'd been written to and written off
in one fell swoop by a man who had enough class to deliver
his rejections with a reason why. The major was a decent
man who obviously had a conscience.

It happened, but never like this—overtly, honestly. People who didn't want to correspond didn't bother writing to
say so. It was a contradiction in terms.

Absently, she picked up the single sheet of paper, folded
it, then opened it up again, her smile bittersweet as she
wondered about Jack Caldwell. He was lonely and apparently alone. Why else would he spend Christmas writing to
a stranger? Why wasn't he interested in taking in the sights
and atmosphere of his host country? Unless he was a work-

aholic, married to his job and immune to the lure of a world outside his office.

Unless, like her, Jack was a loner—not the usual species of man to join the largest brotherhood of conformists in the world.

Angie folded the letter and firmly slapped it onto the table. She had better things to do than fret over a man who obviously didn't know what he wanted.

So look who's talking—

"That must be some letter," Gena drawled as she sauntered into the kitchen, her hair damp around the edges, a robe flapping around her bare legs.

"You're not on a whistle-stop tour, Gena. You could take more than five minutes to shower and shampoo."

"I've forgotten how . . . and speaking of tours." Flopping down in the chair opposite Angie, Gena propped her elbows on the table and cupped her chin in her hands. "It's important, chum."

"A noble endeavor, I know," Angie said gravely. "I'm sure you'll have no trouble at all in browbeating some illustrious member of Link to—"

"I don't want illustrious. I want ordinary, down-to-earth—"

"That lets me out. My head is always in the clouds."

"That's your mother talking."

"She's right."

"Angie, that's bull and you know it. Think. You're one of the most talented and creative people I've ever known. You decide to learn macrame, and you've got a twelve-foot plant hanger three hours later. Everything you try, you do well—better than well. I've never seen you fail at anything."

"Then you weren't there, you weren't looking, or you didn't listen."

"I listened, Angie. All those years ago you weren't the one who failed. You did everything asked of you, and you did it better than anyone else." Gena's mouth tightened as she shook her head, clearly exasperated. "You were bound to grow up, you know. Everyone does."

"I have no staying power, Gena."

"Because everything you do is to please someone else— the wrong reason, chum." Gena took a deep breath as she watched her friend warily. Licking her lips, she spoke tentatively, as if she weren't sure if she should cross a boundary or stay diplomatically neutral. "Did it ever occur to you that you've been working so hard to avoid Charlotte's dreams that you never had time to find some of your own?"

"Maybe—in the past, but she has a new life now," Angie said softly. "I'm free to screw up mine any way I choose."

"Yeah, right. The cell door is unlocked. Too bad you've grown so accustomed to the place that nothing outside appeals to you anymore."

"It appeals. You know it does," Angie said wistfully as she thought of all the things she wanted to do, the experiences she wanted to have. But every dream had a pitfall, and the ones she'd have to face were deeper than most. She couldn't go out into the world without plunging headlong into the past and then filling in the hole as she tried to climb out again. "I'll do it, Gena, but my way—not yours or anyone else's, ever again."

"God, to be so idealistic." Gena wearily rubbed her hands over her face as she walked toward the back staircase. "I'm going to take a nap." Abruptly she stopped on the second stair and without turning around said, "Don't change, chum. I'm insanely jealous of you, so you must have something good going for you."

Angie stared at the door, bemused by Gena's parting shot. Jealous? Of her? If she hadn't heard the mixture of envy and resentment in Gena's voice, she might be able to convince herself that it had been sarcasm rather than honesty. Funny how she'd been envious of Gena all these years, how she'd wished she had Gena's courage and resilience.

Was it a normal part of every friendship—that perverse longing for what one had and the other didn't? It didn't make sense. She and Gena were so different, yet so alike. They each wanted so much for the other while coveting what the other had. Gena's strength and purpose. Her courage and ease with people. Angie wanted them all.

She thought of Major Caldwell and wondered what he wanted. There was something tragic about being in a foreign country and only wanting to speed on a highway—

The telephone rang, an unwelcome, yet not unexpected intrusion into the privacy she craved just then. Sipping her coffee, she tried to tune out the muted ring, but it seemed to become more shrill and insistent. She knew who it was, who it had to be. With a sigh of resignation, she picked up the receiver.

"Hello, Mother."

"Happy New Year, darling," Charlotte Winters shouted.

"Mother, where on earth are you?"

"At sea. Isn't technology wonderful?"

"Wonderful," Angie mumbled.

"How are you coping?" Charlotte's voice had become grave and as heavy as doom, as if she already knew the answer.

"Like anyone else," Angie answered, irritated by her mother's choice of words.

"If that were true, you'd be out celebrating with friends. I'll bet you're either reading letters or writing them."

Wryly, Angie glanced at the envelope on the table. "Not at the moment. Gena is here."

"Oh, Angie, what am I going to do with you?"

"Absolutely nothing, Mother."

"But, you need—"

"Absolutely nothing," Angie said calmly. "I'm shy, Mother, not mentally incompetent. I'm twenty-seven, retired from one business and starting another. I'm managing—"

"All right, Angie. I do hope that your ability to manage will extend to developing a social life."

Angie winced and fought the urge to hunch her shoulders, sink down into herself. Her mother's definition of social life, Angie knew, meant finding a husband and presenting her with a grandchild, preferably a girl who might succeed where Angie had failed.

Angie heard her mother's deep breath and cringed. She'd made a rash statement and knew that Charlotte was about to call her on it. Sometimes, her mother was so busy interrupting and following her own thinking that she didn't notice what others were saying.

"You're starting another business?" Charlotte asked sharply.

"Yes, Mother."

"Well?"

"Let it be a surprise."

"I'm not going to like it, am I?"

"You don't have to like it." Angie blinked, surprised at her answer. Why she'd said anything at all was a mystery. Oddly enough, her sudden decision was not. It had seemed right, an accomplished fact rather than a choice to be carefully considered. Gena's on-the-fly suggestion had tapped into a barely recognized idea of her own, a longing to do something that she might truly enjoy. Why not?

"Angie, I want you to be happy."

There it was, the truth Angie had always known no matter what else had gone wrong between them. Her mother loved her, always had. Everything she had done, right or wrong, had been done out of love, deeply felt, sincere, and terribly misguided. Angie closed her eyes, smiled sadly. "I know, Mother, but you're not responsible for my happiness. I am, and I'm doing just fine."

"You're risking your capital on another business when a recession—"

"Mother, stop. It's a good idea, and I'll be working with adults instead of children. Think of the social opportunities." Hating the need to justify herself, Angie bit back the rest of her arguments. "I'm doing fine, Mother," she said firmly.

"But *what* are you doing, Angie? Sitting at home with Gena while the rest of the world goes on without you?"

Not everyone, Angie thought as the letter from Jack Caldwell caught her eye. "What pleases me," Angie said, wincing at the coldness in her voice. Charlotte wasn't solely responsible for who and what her daughter had become.

Angie, too, had to accept responsibility. That was the problem. Until now, Angie had avoided doing exactly that.

She frowned. This seemed to be a day for sudden insights and painful—shameful—revelations. Before the conversation got out of hand, Angie changed the subject.

"Mother, have you been keeping up with the news?"

Even through thousands of miles and a bounce or two off a satellite, Charlotte's sigh eloquently conveyed hurt feelings and the distance she was so adept at putting between them when it suited her. "Of course. That's one of the reasons I called. I thought we might come home early."

"Why?"

"I . . . we . . . didn't think you should be alone if—"

"Mother, our country isn't being invaded or bombed. I'm in no danger of being drafted, and you've already toured the Mediterranean. You are in the Pacific, aren't you?"

"We just left Hong Kong and were going to visit friends in Australia, but—"

Again, Angie interrupted. Her mother's *but*s had a way of multiplying like rabbits. "Do so, Mother. I hear Australia is fascinating."

"But—"

"I'm fine, Mother. Besides, Gena is moving in for the duration, so I won't be alone."

"Oh. Well, maybe—"

Angie smiled. Her mother adored Gena—for her old money, her equally old family name, and oddly, her independence. Before she could drive herself crazy trying to figure that one out, and before she became maudlin over the injustice of it, Angie spoke brightly. "Happy New Year, Mother, and enjoy your honeymoon. I love you."

"I love you, too, darling," Charlotte said after a pause. "And Angie? Don't change too much. Just be happy."

Angie shook her head as she hung up the phone. Her mother understood so little about her. Their conversations were always like this one, avoiding confrontations, raising questions neither wanted to answer. Even that first night when she and Gena had taken the first awkward and wary steps toward friendship, she hadn't felt as much a stranger to her roommate as she did with her mother.

Again Jack's letter drew her, pulling her into a life that had no room for her. Hadn't he said it in so many words? Yet it was what she'd sensed between the lines that gave her a feeling of kinship, a bond she couldn't begin to explain, as if she already knew the man, had known him longer than a lifetime.

Nonsense! Angie didn't believe in such things as past lives, precognition, fate. What you see is what you get: one life, black on one end, white on the other, with shades of gray in between. Jack Caldwell was simply a stranger who wanted to stay that way.

Angie was in a mood to argue.

5

She had reached crisis point.

The soundtrack from *Footloose* filled Angie's head through radio headphones and vibrated all the way through her body as she lay stretched out on Charlotte's ice-blue velvet sofa tapping her toes to the beat.

Her heart refused to maintain a steady pace as she struggled with all the old feelings of inadequacy, panic, the fear of failure. Her mind refused to shut down as she mulled over ideas and possibilities.

Gena always had this effect on her, calling Angie's life the way she saw it, reducing her problems to a choice between solution or surrender.

That was what frightened her—the choices she faced. Gena had voiced what Angie had been trying to avoid. Once it had been necessary to impose limits on herself, to live well within the walls she'd built. Now she had to either tear down her sanctuary brick by brick and go forward, or return to her cell, lock herself in and throw away the key.

It appealed, as familiarity always appealed.

Definitely a crisis.

She sensed a presence beside her. A hand brushed her cheek, gently, then flipped off the switch of her Walkman and jerked the earphones off her head. The unmistakable scent of Knowing perfume wafted in and out of the living room as Gena puttered about, bringing in wine and delicacies for their all-night marathon. Angie immediately recognized that particular combination of warmth and Knowing and impatience. It was the impatience she wanted to avoid as long as possible. And Gena's own brand of knowing— about her weaknesses, the secret that Gena absorbed into her consciousness by osmosis.

Angie was used to Gena the mentor, the "doer," the

meddler. Except that it had become increasingly important to Angie that she do for herself. She didn't mind a little help from her friend, but Gena would see it as her duty to supervise the renovation of Angie's mindset.

Plates rattled and glasses clinked. Kindling crackled, and a dry log popped in the grate as Gena lit the fire. Ignoring Gena was as impossible as ignoring a steamroller parked on your foot.

"Resolution Number One: No more brilliant ideas on the evolution of Angela Winters," Angie said firmly as she swung her legs off the sofa and propped them on the table. She opened her eyes last, reluctant to see any more than she had to any sooner than necessary.

"You started the pity session without me," Gena said as she tossed the earphones onto the table and flopped down next to Angie. "Been at it long?"

"A little before. A little after."

"Before and after what?" Gena asked.

"Before you showed up this morning. After Mother called."

"I knew I should've given her a honeymoon trip to Venus."

"It wouldn't have been far enough. *You* gave her the honeymoon trip?"

"Oops. Forget I said that."

"Why did you do it?"

Gena shrugged. "For all her faults, I like Charlotte."

"Try again, Gena. That was a very extravagant expression of affection."

"I like confused souls. Besides, you're worth it."

"Me? It's not my honeymoon."

"There are honeymoons, and there are honeymoons."

"Great. So what are you? My new caretaker?"

"Not me. You're really down, aren't you?"

"Guilty."

"Well, hell, chum, open the wine, and I'll join you."

Angie noted the bottles of wine and the basket on the coffee table. "A picnic?"

Gena shrugged. "I didn't want to make a dozen trips to

and from the kitchen." Craning her neck, she read the address on an envelope propped against the lamp on the end table. "You already answered the letter you got this morning. Efficient as ever, I see." She squinted and frowned. "Where *did* you find a major?"

"He picked me up in the Link mailbag."

"A field-grade officer who has to be at least thirtysomething? No wife? No kids?"

"No life."

"Ah, a kindred spirit. No wonder you were so fascinated by his letter."

Before Angie could feel defensive about the remark, the phone rang.

"I'm not here," Gena said wearily. "Even the boss is entitled to a vacation."

Angie picked up the receiver. "Hello?"

The voice on the other end was harried, familiar and masculine. "Hi, Angie. I'm stuck between flights and thought I'd call to wish you a Happy New Year."

"Happy New Year to you, too." Through an unusual amount of static and background noise, she heard an impatient sigh, a long pause. "Is—are you all right?"

"I have to talk to Gena."

Angie frowned at the hesitation, the weariness in his voice, the sensation that she was speaking with a stranger. She'd never heard anything but steadiness and warmth from him in the past.

"Gee, I'm sorry, but Gena isn't here, *Mike*."

Gena sucked in her breath, as if she hadn't expected to hear from him. "I'm here," she said, holding out her hand for the phone.

As Angie started to rise, she felt Gena's hand clamp down on her wrist, holding her there, holding on, not letting go when Angie sank back into the cushions. Odd behavior, even for Gena.

"I'm sorry, Mike," Gena said in a choked whisper. "It's my fault for not—"

Any thoughts Angie had entertained of discretion flew right out the window. It was a rare day that Gena apologized for anything, and even rarer for Gena to admit to being wrong. From the expression on her face, the bleakness in her eyes, Angie knew she was worried about more than the impending war.

"I don't need your understanding or your damn nobility, Mike," Gena snapped. "That's the trouble. Everyone understands, and I don't feel the need to do anything to correct the problem. . . . Sure, you care. I *know* that. You showed it the other night. . . . That's not what I meant. It's called Tough Love, otherwise known as a good swift kick. . . . Will you stop being so literal?" Leaning her head back against the sofa, Gena stared upward, her eyes as blank as the ceiling. "We can't do anything about it now, Mike. You stay safe and in one piece. . . . I am not being melodramatic."

Angie turned her head at Gena's short burst of harsh laughter.

"This is funny, really hilarious. I'm delivering all the man's lines. . . . No, Mike, it's time. You have to catch your flight, and I have to . . . Yes, I will, every day . . . You're right, I won't. Tell you what, I'll write once a week and have Angie take up the slack the other six days." Tears slid down Gena's cheeks as she listened. "I know. . . . Yes, bye. . . . Me, too."

Silence seemed to go on forever as Gena held the phone to her ear in one hand, her other still clutching Angie's wrist, as if she were in pain and needed to hold on to something. By Gena's stillness, Angie knew that Mike had already hung up. By the way Gena's knuckles turned white against the receiver, Angie knew that her friend was keeping the connection open as long as she could.

Finally, Gena set down the receiver, gently, her hand lingering on the plastic. Just as gently, Angie pried her wrist loose from Gena's hold and leaned over to pour them both a glass of wine.

Absently, Gena accepted her glass and drank it down as if it were water. Without comment, Angie refilled it.

"I am so screwed up, Angie."

This was one of Gena's teaser lines, thrown out but

never elaborated upon. In all their years together her friend had yet to offer more than a quip here, a random statement there regarding childhood hangups—all academic, since they were delivered with a forced air of flippancy and lack of intensity that discouraged feedback.

Through those quips, Angie knew what Gena's problem was, but Gena had never told her the origin of the problem. For all intents and purposes, Gena Collier hadn't existed before she'd emerged into the world at the age of sixteen.

"It happened again?" she asked hesitantly.

"It *didn't* happen again," Gena corrected. "The bitch of it is that I know why."

"You're a control freak," Angie supplied. Intuition had led her to the answer while she'd been in college—that, and the cockiness of having a minor in psychology. She'd had the skewed idea that she might learn enough to work through her own problems. Instead, she'd learned a more effective way to skirt them while concentrating on everyone else's problems.

"Yeah, an obsessive control freak. I'm healthy, normal, and enthusiastic until—" She shook her head, drank the rest of her wine. "There is such a thing as female impotence, Angie. I'm fine until the crucial moment, then nothing. Nothing! I can't let go except with a vibrator and an empty room."

"Because then you're in control."

"It's disgusting. I hate that lousy vibrator. Sometimes I hate being healthy and normal with no excuses to offer myself."

"Have you tried—"

"Taking the initiative? Being on top? Doing outrageous things to his person? Sure. I'd make a great hooker—lots of imagination and no involvement." She held out her glass as Angie poured. "Except he gets to have all the fun while I do all the work. Sometimes I almost hate him for getting his when I can't even find mine."

"Is that what happened last week?"

"No. I tried something different. I faked it, thought maybe I'd start to believe it if I was good enough at it."

"Faking it doesn't work, Gena. Take it from the greatest faker of all."

"You're telling me? Mike hit the roof." Gena stared at the lights on the Christmas tree Angie had left up for her benefit. "I love Mike. He turns me on, pushes all my buttons. Trouble is, I think I'm missing the big red one that sets off the fireworks."

"Get help, Gena."

Gena slammed her half-full glass down on the table. "That's funny coming from you. The best you can manage is helping yourself a little here, a little there, but never enough to do the job."

"I've been in therapy for over a year," Angie said, her voice deliberately firm, as if she were saying, "Hi. My name is Angie, and I'm an alcoholic." It had felt that way when she'd walked into the psychologist's office for the first time, forcing herself to present her weaknesses up front.

Gena turned her head sharply at Angie's confession. "You didn't tell me."

"No. I couldn't."

"Why?"

There was no accusation or hurt in the question, just curiosity and confusion. It fascinated Angie to know Gena was confused, made her feel as if, for once, she were the stronger one. "You remember what you said to me when I asked you to help me pick out things for my room at Collingswood?"

"Something about book covers and furnishing your own life."

Angie nodded. "You said I was on my own."

"I don't want to hear this, chum."

"Neither did I at the time, but you were right."

Gena's lips slanted into an odd little grin, as if she didn't know whether to laugh or cry, and her mouth had found a happy medium. "I'm usually right."

"Usually."

"I have to change, Angie."

"Wrong, Gena. People don't change; they improve if they really want to."

"To improve, I'll have to admit that I'm not perfect."

"We should both be ashamed," Angie murmured.

"We do it to ourselves," Gena agreed glumly, "because it's easier to wallow than it is to work on the problem."

"When I was seven, I wanted to cut off a leg to avoid learning how to ride a bike," Angie said.

At that, Gena sat perfectly still, barely breathing. "Do I know you at all?" she whispered, then sprang up from the couch and walked to the Christmas tree. "I can't stand this heavy shit. You saved Christmas for me, so let's have Christmas!"

Angie had expected it, was prepared for the quick change in topic and mood, before Gena became too weighted down by advice. Sooner or later, she would come to the right conclusions on her own. Given enough time and space, she always did.

Shaking her head, she rose from the sofa. "It's about time," Angie said as she waved toward the tree, standing within the deep curve of three bay windows set side by side in a towerlike extension of the house. All the packages—from her mother and new stepfather, her father, and Gena's mother—were still wrapped. "I've been dying to open those."

"Liar," Gena said as she knelt in front of the tree. "Gather up the food and wine and get your tush over here."

By the time Angie carried everything over and sat down, Gena had sorted through all the gifts. She accepted a glass and held it up for Angie's toast.

"May we each find something useful in this pile of well-meant and ill-chosen largesse."

"Let's see," Gena said as she shook a box with Angie's name on the label. "This one is from Charlotte. I'll bet it's another frothy debutante special—maybe even some ruffled anklets."

"Ruffled anklets? Never. Mother thought they were tacky." Angie took the box and opened it. Froth and pastel and ruffles. Azure chiffon, with a tiered skirt and modest neckline.

"It's worse than I thought. She sent you a freakin' prom dress."

"Mmm. She still wants me to go to the prom."

"Poor Charlotte."

"Yes."

Gena picked up another gift. "This is from my mother to you. Want to guess?"

"One of her survival kits?" Angie grinned. Gracie Collier saw the world exactly as it was and believed in preparing her offspring and their friends rather than browbeating them. Every few years she delivered said preparation in the form of survival kits.

Expecting items to inspire thought as well as good-natured jokes, Angie ripped into the box and gleefully tossed the contents on the floor around her. "Vitamins, *tastefully* sexy lingerie, audiotapes on stress reduction, a Mace cartridge, and pamphlets on where to enroll for self-defense classes. Cosmetics—" Her eyes widened as she saw the two remaining items in the box.

Gena took over, and reached in to pull out a vibrator and a box of condoms. "What do you suppose the message here is?"

Angie cleared her throat. "That I should use one if I get lucky and the other if I don't?"

Gena rolled her eyes. "If Mom had told me about this, I would have saved her some money. You won't use these. You'd be too embarrassed to help yourself."

Ignoring the taunt, Angie smiled. "I remember when Gracie gave you a pile of the more explicit letters she'd received—minus the names, of course."

"Yep. No rules or sex manuals or heart-to-hearts for me. She just wrote footnotes on those letters telling me: 'If you do this, you'll probably get herpes—or worse,' or some other piece of sage advice she'd already used on the countless confused who wrote to her."

"She gives good advice, Gena," Angie said. "She cares."

"And I'm sure that every one of the 'countless' are grateful." Suddenly, Gena dumped the vibrator and condoms on top of the prom dress and stared at them as if they might retaliate. "God, we're a pair—in our late twenties, and neither one of us knows what sex is all about—me because I can't, and you because you won't. I'll bet you even blush when you're alone."

"I do not."

"Hah!" Gena rose to her feet, her voice hoarse as she muttered, "I need some coffee."

Listening to Gena clatter around in the kitchen, Angie leaned over to fuss with the decorations on the tree. Gena would take her time in brewing the coffee while she pulled herself together into the cheeky, plow-ahead-no-matter-what person she'd spent so many years developing.

Quite a pair, indeed.

She stared at the items huddling in folds of blue chiffon. Gena had been right. Angie would never use the vibrator. Embarrassment was part of it, but beyond that, she just couldn't think of sex in a casual way. She had too many visions of special moments with a special man. To her, physical expression was just that—an expression of love and commitment, a covenant with someone who would value it. Besides, she couldn't miss what she'd never had. It wasn't something she talked about unless she was ready to be ridiculed and accused of being corny and hopelessly out of touch.

A crash followed by an expletive came from the kitchen.

"You okay?" Angie called.

"Fine," Gena called back. "Why can't your drawers stick like everyone else's?"

Leaning back on her elbows, Angie squinted so all she saw were the lights on the Christmas tree winking at her. All her life, she'd been like those lights, not allowed to function unless the control bulb was in place. But no more. Not ever again.

So just what is your problem? she asked herself.

It's just the holiday blues, she told herself. She and Gena had always given in to mild depression at this time of year. That's what their pity sessions were all about: to work it out of their systems on a night when experts said it was okay to feel sadness and regret, to think of what might be and remember what hadn't been. This year, she had a better excuse, since she'd spent most of the holiday season with all the trimmings that had been shared with others before. Until the beginning of the season, she'd been fascinated by the stranger within herself and reveled in making her own acquaintance.

Angie had been alone for years, cut off even from herself, but at first it had been something she couldn't possibly control, and later she had refined the separation by conscious choice—a matter of survival. She had no illusions as to how long it would take or how hard it would be to rewire her thinking. It gave her a vague feeling of unease to know that Gena's circuits were shorting out, too. For the first time in their relationship, she didn't know who was going to do the repairs—

"Fresh coffee!" Gena announced as she sat down on the floor and handed Angie a mug. As she sipped, she examined the room. "It's different. What did you do?"

"What I've always wanted to do—uncoordinate the decorations and *sling,* rather than carefully place, tinsel on the tree."

Grateful for the break from the "heavy shit," Angie gazed at it all in satisfaction—this departure from Charlotte's brand of a color-coordinated holiday to impress onlookers rather than please the principal participants. On Christmas Eve, Charlotte had always entertained a bevy of friends and General Winters's associates during her annual open house. Angie would wear a special dress, specially chosen for the occasion in whatever color Charlotte had chosen to decorate their perfect artificial tree, and she would sit in the window seat, pretty as a picture—a thing to be admired along with the decorations and elaborate buffet.

Now she wore her nightgown and robe, as did Gena. The tree was live, chosen because it wasn't perfect and had a dead branch that had shed its needles all over the floor. She knew that there were places inside herself that would always be like that branch. Places that would never know growth, places that had been neglected by herself and by those who had tried to force her to grow in the wrong directions.

She pulled a gift from under the tree and handed it to Gena. "This is from Mother," she said solemnly.

Gena shook the package, examined and sniffed it. "Gee, she shouldn't have." Ripping off the paper, she glanced at the expensive gift set of fragrance—the same that Charlotte herself wore. "Do you suppose it ever occurred to her that we have our own tastes?"

"Never. What did you send her?" Angie asked.

Gena grinned. "A pastel negligee with lots of ruffles." She rooted through the packages, reading the tags on each. "Open this one. It's from Ben."

"But he already gave me a present."

"What? Where?"

This time, Angie grinned. "Guess."

Gena thought for a moment. "He didn't."

"Yes, he did," Angie said, thinking of her stepfather's gift and the pleasure he had taken in presenting it to her.

"Well, what do you expect from a Cadillac dealer? New or old?"

"Old. A block-long classic, beautifully restored, pink Cadillac convertible complete with tail fins."

"Pink? That had to be Charlotte's idea."

"Mmm. She thinks it used to belong to a cosmetics consultant, but Ben took me aside and told me that it was one of those prizes for Playbunny of the year or something." Angie glanced down at her lap and smiled. "He's having it painted candy-apple red."

Gena laughed. "Come on, let's see what else he gave you."

Angie carefully loosened the tape and unwrapped the foil paper from the elegantly wrapped box her stepfather had sent from Paris. She was reluctant to see what he'd sent, afraid to find out how much more of her the wise newcomer into her life had seen.

The box had the logo of a famous designer printed in the

corner. Angie opened the lid and sucked in her breath. Her hands smoothed over the black lace, delicate as cobwebs, lined with silk faille, then lifted the black dress out of mounds of imprinted tissue paper. It was sophisticated yet utterly feminine, a strapless, knee-length dress designed to flatter the wearer and flirt with the imagination of the beholder. A dress made for a woman of confidence and class. Being the daughter of Charlotte and Bradford Winters, she knew she had the class. What hadn't been bred into her had been fed to her along with her strained carrots.

"Now, that's a dress," Gena said. "If you wear it for anyone but a special man, I'll kill you."

Angie's gaze strayed to the letter propped against the lamp on the end table—the letter she'd written to Jack Caldwell. It was crazy how she kept thinking about him, crazy that she'd answered his dismissal with an invitation, that she kept imagining what he looked like, and what she'd look like in the gown.

She folded the dress back into the box and set it aside.

Outside, the world was empty and silent, time and lives suspended in a single moment before one year gave way to the next. Images and light from the television flickered eerily in the darkness as Angie and Gena curled up in opposite corners of the sofa, each lost to memories of the past, thoughts of now, dreams and apprehensions about the future.

Somewhere outside the walls of her world, Angie knew people were wringing the last drops of pleasure from the waning year. Gena drained the last drops from a bottle of champagne. "New Year's Eve is a bitch," she stated as she held up her glass for yet another toast. "Worse than Christmas. They say it's supposed to be a new beginning, and I keep believing it. Somewhere around twelve-oh-one I realize that new beginnings only happen to babies and amnesiacs. The rest of us just plod along—same garbage, different day."

Not liking the gleam in Gena's eyes, Angie gave her a suspicious look. "Exactly what am I drinking to here?"

"Vacations. Adventure. Who knows? Maybe even a love affair with a mysterious major."

"Forget it, Gena. I know what I'm going to do."

"Yeah? Do tell, chum."

"Greeting cards," Angie said, and clinked her glass against Gena's. "Link can always use another fundraiser, and I'm not too proud to ask for a job."

"You lost me."

"You said it earlier. I'm going to design and produce a line of greeting cards, which Link will buy from me at wholesale cost and sell at retail. The profits, of course, will help fund one of your programs. Aside from that, you can give me a job at Link if you have one available."

Gena tilted her head as she watched Angie's expression, a question in her eyes. "From what I gathered this afternoon, the last thing you wanted was to accept help from me."

"I don't mind help as long as it's for what I choose to do."

"I do need someone to put together a benefit."

"What kind of benefit? When?"

"A Link fundraiser that I intend to become an annual affair. Toward the end of the year—maybe around Christmas."

"You already have a plan," Angie said suspiciously.

"Vaguely. I keep seeing this forties nightclub setting with a big band sound and a torch singer. Do you suppose we could get Madonna to behave herself long enough to donate her time?"

As Gena laid out the rest of her plan, Angie's depression lifted. Organizing the fundraiser would be quite a challenge, but she knew she could do it. Between that and starting a greeting card business, Angie knew that she'd be doing more than testing waters. She'd have to jump in headfirst just like everyone else.

Angie stared at the tree, seeing nothing but images of what the next year could be like. All those random thoughts that had drifted in and out of her mind since Gena had started Link came together and formed a whole.

Why not greeting cards? Why not a forties night club with a big band and torch singer? It made sense in the way that Gena's crazy, idealistic ideas always made sense.

And this time, Angie's involvement would be by her choice. No one would laugh at her or tell her that it wouldn't work, or that it wasn't real. No one would succeed in nudging her into another direction.

In the last moments of an old year and an old life, Angie began to feel as if she really might belong in her own skin.

In the first moments of the new year, she said a silent prayer for Mike's safety, Gena's healing, and that her own new life would indeed be an adventure.

When Gena wasn't looking, Angie turned toward the end table and held up her glass in a silent toast. Maybe, just maybe, two strangers would find friendship with themselves as well as with one another.

6

*G*ermany

Dear Jack,

  Was it something I said?

  It was good to hear from you. I so enjoy meeting new people and hearing about different places. Germany makes me think of cuckoo clocks and old walled cities, Wagner and Beethoven, spotlessly clean doorstoops and Küchen baking in the oven, brooding passions, fire, and dark, stormy skies. I would love to experience it all. Don't take me literally, please.

  The other day I decided to replace the wallpaper in my kitchen. When I got home from the decorating shop, I realized that I'd bought exactly the same pattern.

  I think I'm in a rut.

  Since I'm about to embark on a new career, this will be a short letter. More later. Wish me luck!

Angie

P.S. Happy New Year!

Jack stared at Angie's letter with a black scowl. Didn't she know rejection when she read it? Was she stubborn, he wondered, or was she dense?

Maybe she was desperate.

He swiveled his chair around to face the window. Funny how he'd never minded the gloominess of the climate before. Kay had hated the gray that colored the sky more often than sunlight. She was a sun-worshiper who'd been raised in Colorado where, she'd reminded him often, the sun shone three hundred days a year. He'd never noticed that, either.

Was Angie a sun baby, too?

Angie again.

He turned back around and glared at the letter lying flat on his desk, a long thin sheet that women used for their grocery lists. It was decorated with a random array of stylized snowflakes, obviously drawn with the same pen she'd used to write the letter. Opening the middle drawer in his desk, he pulled out the letter he'd received from her at Christmas. It had a whimsical border of Santa's elves tumbling over half-finished toys. Those elves had filled some empty moments for him as he'd studied the individual expressions and tried to figure out what was missing from each toy. When he'd written back to her, he'd meant to comment on the stationery, which had entertained him almost as much as the letter itself. But he'd written his answer in a hurry, knowing—hoping—that such insanity was temporary.

With the feeling that he was severing his last link with humanity, he'd written Angie, saying thanks, but no thanks. As soon as he'd dropped it into the mail, he'd known that it was the most asinine thing he'd done in his life. That letter had been sophomoric, like adolescent missives that began with "How are you? I am fine. My dog Spot is fine, too."

Then she'd just had to write back, with a question no less. Did she know how hard it was for a man like him to leave questions—any questions—unanswered? He was in intelligence, for crying out loud. It was his job to find answers, even if he had to cover them up afterward.

No, there was no way she could know that.

She had to be young, and a romantic, writing about brooding passions and fire. The German people were direct and efficient and cheerfully brusque. He'd never seen one hint of brooding anything.

Still, he couldn't help but envy her ability to dream about passion, to believe it lasted long enough to develop moods.

He'd spent a lot of time wondering why her handwriting looked like a row of baby spiders crowded nose to butt, why she doodled on everything in sight including her grocery list paper, why an outgoing woman with an obvious sense of humor would write to a complete stranger. Only someone with a sense of humor would start a new business with recession and war running neck and neck for the lead position.

And he wondered about a woman who wanted to change her wallpaper, yet wound up with the same pattern.

What was wrong with that? It meant order, familiarity. It meant that in one place, at least, there would be no surprises.

No change.

Jack pushed away from his desk and began to pace his office. She was probably some bored, flaky, poor little rich girl who used business as a hobby and took nothing seriously, least of all a poor sap she'd written to on an empty Saturday night.

Obviously, he had nothing in common with her.

Except that they both seemed to be occupying the same rut.

Compressing the letter into a ball, Jack lobbed it at the wastebasket. It rebounded off the rim and skipped back toward him like a friendly puppy. Bending over, he picked it up, bounced it in his hand. Friendly, he wondered, or lost? Suddenly the answer was important to him.

"Bullshit!" he muttered; then, almost as an afterthought, he scrawled a short note on a clean sheet of legal-size paper.

> *Dear Angela—*
> *Can't you take a hint?*
> *Major Jack Caldwell*

Evidently not, Angie answered silently as she leaned on the counter at the print shop and reread Jack's note. The printer was in the back at his computer, working up the estimates she'd asked for a week ago. He, too, had hinted that her presence was not welcome until she actually had a job for him. She'd made it equally clear that there would be no job until she had an estimate.

The object of her quest had changed since she'd plunged headlong into preparations for her new business. She'd ap-

proached only the suppliers and tradesmen who were
known to deliver quality work, so that was no longer an
issue. She was too aggravated to worry about small price
differences. Whoever could manage to deliver an estimate
promptly would get the job.

It was, she'd discovered, going to be a long, slow haul
gathering estimates from competing printers and the companies that made color separations. She was still waiting
for the paper suppliers to provide her with sample chests
and price books.

Impatience ruled every move she made these days.

Now Major Jack Caldwell was determined to add to her
aggravation.

Her gaze caught on a basket full of pens that ironically
promised "Tomorrow's job delivered yesterday!" A stack of
memo pads repeating the message listed against a sign inviting her to "take one."

Hearing the proprietor argue with his press man, she
sighed and helped herself.

Obviously, tenacity was the only way to get things done.
She'd might as well add Jack to her list.

Dear Jack,
   Which hint are you referring to?
   *I washed the paint off my windows yesterday. Why is it
that everything that seemed so bright and warm and magical before Christmas looks like so much clutter afterward?
I guess some things just aren't meant to become ordinary
parts of life. Christmas wouldn't be special if it lasted all
year long, and heaven knows how parents of small children
could survive if it did.*

Jack glared at the letter—written on memo paper no less
—and cursed himself for not throwing it away, unopened.
The last thing he needed was to become involved with her
disillusionment, especially when she apparently invited it
year after year.

It was his own fault. He shouldn't have written back to
her, shouldn't have left the door open for a reply. Obvi-

ously she had problems. With a flick of his wrist he bounced the letter off the wall. Who gave a rat's ass about her problems?

The whole world had problems, none of which he was prepared for. At least not emotionally. His generation had a cynical view of the concept of war and mass destruction in one blinding millisecond of light, but that was in the abstract. Being educated by Uncle Sam had prepared his instincts and mind for quick thought and quicker action—a joke, considering all the red tape he had to unravel before he or anyone else could "act quickly."

He bent over the newest satellite photos, his gaze sharp, analytical, searching for the proverbial needle in the haystack. He checked out the Soviet Union, a large land mass on the photo that showed nothing of the splinters breaking away from the main body. History in the making—new countries being born, old ones reclaiming their heritage like adopted children searching for their roots. Only in two dimensions did the world seem whole and solid.

Another sheet showed the latest trouble spot, another land mass in the Middle East, a body of water that was both playground to the rich and famous and battleground for the dissatisfied and power mad. The countdown had started. January fifteenth, the president's deadline for peace endorsed by the United Nations.

Was it that easy? he wondered. Did man deny himself peaceful settlements because he insisted on complicating matters and adding conditions that were impossible to meet? Or was it because there weren't enough ultimatums that gave only either/or choices?

His attention wandered to the photo of Kay on the desk. Maybe he'd missed something. Kay had given him exactly those two choices more than once, and he'd ignored them, looking for alternatives, offering compromises, empty promises, assurances that things would be better *when* . . .

Maybe too much negotiation invited self-deceit and provided too much time to slip back into old habits. Maybe all negotiation did was put people on the defensive, inviting justifications, excuses, accusations, discouraging the simple act of saying, "I was wrong."

Jack raised his head and leaned back in his chair, still staring at the picture of Kay. They'd negotiated themselves into a corner, each talking about his own needs, not listening to the other, and letting frustration escalate the problem into a battle for power.

Just as the world was doing.

War was coming. How it would turn out was anybody's guess. What would be lost or gained was less a question than what would be left—the same thinking that had accompanied the Bay of Pigs, the Six-Day War, and countless other conflicts. Somehow he kept equating the world situation with his marriage, with Kay. They hadn't tried hard enough, committed enough, given enough. They hadn't listened to one another. His mouth quirked. If they had, they probably would have called it quits a long time ago.

Sighing, he raked his hand through his hair. He'd never called anything quits in his life. No matter what, he'd seen things through—every goal, each commitment, all the obligations, real and imagined.

Until Kay.

More and more lately he'd been thinking about Kay, what they'd started with, what was left besides anger and a sense of failure.

Nothing.

Maybe.

He really hated unanswered questions. He reached for the phone, punched in a long series of numbers, and listened to the silence, followed by clicks and static and finally the first ring. He let it ring again and again, until he heard her husky voice. He had to *know* what was left.

He swallowed, said the first thing that came to mind. "Did you quit smoking yet?"

He listened to her indrawn breath, the silence, and wondered if he shouldn't just hang up before she did. But the silence drew out, and he waited—for the old feelings he'd had for her, the smile that he'd always had when he knew she was near, the catch in his throat, the stirring in his groin.

Nothing happened.

"Hello, Jack," she said quietly, calmly. "Trying to settle unfinished business before the world goes bang?"

It startled him—that bulls'-eye she'd always had on his thinking. That quiet tone of hers meant she was holding herself tightly checked, trying to hang on to a little control. Kay was volatile, undisciplined, her emotions always on a short fuse.

"How are you?" he asked.

"Just ducky. And you?"

"Did you see a doctor when you got back?"

She released her breath sharply. "I've been back for months, Jack. Is this concern an afterthought?"

He pinched his fingers together on the bridge of his nose. "No. I've been keeping track."

"So what did the doctor tell you?"

"He said that you were doing fine."

"There you have it. You didn't need to call at all. Why did you?"

He wished he knew. Belatedly, he realized that it was an arrogant assumption on his part to think she was trying to hold herself together. She simply didn't care enough to have any feelings. He grimaced as he gave her the truth. "You were right—unfinished business."

"You want forgiveness, Jack?"

Did he? For what, exactly? "I—"

"Is this where I'm supposed to admit that it was my fault, too?" she asked, interrupting him. "Sorry, Jack, it doesn't work that way."

No, it never did, Jack thought as he listened to the long pause, the silence at the other end of the line.

"I should have left a long time ago, Jack," she said, echoing his earlier thought. "Love isn't enough, sentiment goes only so far, and you're not the only good lay in town."

He winced.

"Look, Jack, rationally I can admit to my part in all of it. I can even say that you're really a good man, when you remember that you're not a government issue robot. But, dammit, I lost a baby. I can't have any more. I've gone through hell, and I want you to go through hell, too. I didn't deserve what happened, and I don't want to forgive you."

"Kay—" He could barely get her name out, much less anything else. He was too angry. Too caught up in feelings he thought had been a temporary aberration. He didn't know how to deal with aberrations. Aside from that, Kay wanted him to feel like a class A bastard. All he could think of was that she was a class A bitch.

He felt nothing at all for her. Not a lingering fondness nor regret at her absence.

Her voice came over the wire, firm, almost fierce. "I don't want to forgive you, Jack. I need the anger. I need to blame you for what happened."

"All right, Kay," he said. Oddly, he understood how she felt. A long time ago, he'd felt the same way with Bryan, because of Bryan. He shook his head to clear away the thought.

Like Kay, he preferred anger to guilt.

"It probably is," Kay said with a touch of dryness. "You're so good at picking up other people's crosses. You probably won't even notice mine after a while."

He could have told her that he wasn't carrying her cross. He was too busy dealing with his own actions that last night to take on the responsibility for hers.

She wanted guilt. Somewhere, deep inside, he knew it existed—guilt for more than what had happened between himself and Kay. But consciously, he knew that it was a purely selfish emotion that did nothing but fool you into thinking that you were suffering as badly as the one you'd hurt.

His stomach clenched, and he tasted the bitterness of something old, unresolved. "Good-bye, Kay. Take care of yourself," he said softly, and lowered the receiver.

So now he knew what was left: regret and emptiness, the memory of two people who had lived together as strangers, and a guilt neither of them was willing to face, much less name.

Strangers in the beginning, and strangers in the end.

He glanced at the framed photograph sitting on the desk —himself and Kay walking under crossed swords after their wedding ceremony at the Academy chapel. He didn't recognize the happiness on their faces. Hell, he couldn't even remember it.

The memory seemed so distant, part of some other life. A life that had belonged to someone else, someone he didn't know. A life that *should* have belonged to Bryan.

Maybe that was really the root of his anger—not Kay herself, but the way thoughts of her inevitably resurrected other memories.

He focused on the green desk blotter as he reached for the picture, folded the stand flat, and rose from his chair. Without a second look, he carried it across the room. Without a second thought, he bent over to pick up Angie's letter, then dropped the last of his old life in with the rest of the trash.

7

Colorado Springs

Dear Angie,

The base seems divided into two parts tonight. The living quarters are lit up, though it's one in the morning. Earlier, when kids should have been playing in the snow, the playgrounds were deserted. The others in my building speak in whispers as if they're afraid of spooking the enemy. No one I've seen looks like he knows where he is or where he's going. Even though we've been working on this for months, I don't think any of us believed we'd actually do it.

I didn't think war would be like this.

The office buildings are all lit up, and several of the duty officers brought in portable TVs to the offices. I can see the flash and light of shows on the Armed Forces European Network through the windows. It's strange that we're all watching TV for news when we're the ones making it, as if there might be someone doing things behind our backs. A bunch of kids shipped in this week from the States—National Guard and reservists. They look scared and excited, and some are obviously disappointed that they're not closer to the action.

I feel like that.

Everyone is restless, including me. I feel as if I'm straining to see through a crack in the wall. And I'm rambling again.

I don't know why I'm writing to you, except that everyone seems to be sealed off, and I needed some kind of a connection with home. There's no point to this. I've been trying to figure out who's the crazy one—you or me.

I know this isn't fair, but don't bother writing back. I can't think of a single reason why this should continue.
                                    Major Jack Caldwell

Angie chewed the nail of her little finger as she read the letter, and grimaced at the taste of nail polish. Her television was tuned to CNN, as were all the sets in the city. Jack could have been describing every neighborhood in America: the hushed atmosphere and sober expressions, the quiet discussions and apprehension that hung in the air more heavily than pollution. Though people went to work every day, it seemed that business had virtually stopped. Decisions were being put on hold, and expenditures were shelved except for the necessities.

Twice, she'd seen her father on television being interviewed as an "expert." He was, of course, having been involved in one way or another in Cuba, Viet Nam, Grenada, and Panama, and now that he was retired, he served as an advisor for several government agencies in the District of Columbia. She'd watched him dispassionately, as if he were someone she didn't really know, like Peter Jennings or Bernard Shaw, familiar yet still a stranger.

I feel like them. She read the passage in Jack's letter over again and remembered how her father had chafed when he was isolated from the actual theater of war, remembered, too, the element of fear she'd sensed in him when he was about to join the action. Of course she hadn't been around for most of it, but she'd heard the stories, the battles being fought over and over again over a game of cards or an official function.

I needed some kind of a connection with home.

How many times had she read that in a letter? Too many to count, yet this was different. Jack didn't seem like a stranger. He never had.

"Anyone I know?" Gena asked as she walked in the front door.

"Hm? Oh, the major."

"Yeah? For a man who didn't want a pen pal, he's sure using up a lot of postage." Tossing her coat on the window seat, Gena slipped off her shoes and flopped down in a chair.

Gena hadn't been kidding when she'd said she was staying a while. She'd moved in for the duration. Angie didn't mind. It was good to have the company, though Gena went to work at Link every morning and didn't always leave at quitting time. Link was busier than ever, and Angie found herself working at the office more and more often as she set the preliminary stages of the benefit in motion.

Gena's smugness grew in direct proportion to the hours Angie clocked at Link.

The smugness didn't bother Angie. She enjoyed working at Link. The greeting cards were fun and a challenge, but it was solitary work. It felt good to have a place to go, a place where she felt she belonged, full of people she enjoyed working with.

Self-consciousness wasn't allowed at Link; shyness wasn't tolerated. Every person on the staff was driven by their own ideals and the goals Gena set in their lives like flags at a finish line. If Angie didn't move fast to join in with Gena's team, she'd simply be left behind and left out.

Link, with its creative atmosphere and constant surprises, was simply a place and a group of people to which she wanted to belong.

When Gena was around, they spent time researching computer equipment for Angie's fledgling business, poring over designs, and laughing over some of Angie's sappy verses. Angie didn't want to think about the steps she was taking so impulsively, and Gena was trying to outrun thoughts of Mike. Their lives, like so many others, were on hold for the duration.

Jack was right. It didn't seem real.

Germany

Dear Jack,

It's been pretty much the same here, too—all hushed and slowed down, as if the whole world is holding its breath. Actually, there is an air of elation here because of the one-

sided battle. It's been a long time since we won anything. I wonder, though, exactly what we're winning, or is it all an illusion? Don't answer that—I'm sure it's classified information. Dad used to get all wrapped around the axle when I asked questions of a military nature.

My friend Gena has moved in with me until renovations are complete on her own house (and I suspect, until Mike comes home from the Gulf). I don't have an oak tree, but I do have a scarlet maple. When Mike was called up, we tied a huge yellow ribbon around the trunk. As more of our friends were sent overseas, we began to write their names on it. Yours is next to my neighbor's—a history teacher whose reserve unit was activated. It's a lovely tradition that should be employed in peace as well as war.

Mother and Ben are in Australia, guests of friends who own a sheep station. She hasn't once complained about the dust, though she's having trouble adjusting to high summer in January. When they've had their fill of the outback, they'll resume traveling—Hong Kong, Japan, Hawaii, and if I know my stepfather, Tahiti. Ben is all but retired from his Cadillac dealership and claims he's scoping out possible locations for his golden years.

I should be ashamed of myself for being relieved that they were waylaid in the outback. I like the freedom of being able to indulge myself. I'm a night owl. It's marvelous being able to work till dawn. The phone doesn't ring, and there's no one to care if I change into my robe and slippers at six o'clock in the evening.

I find myself envying Mother lately. It's the wanderlust left over from my beginnings as an Air Force brat, I guess.

In fact, after I sold my share of the school, I considered taking a trip or two until I became involved in other things. So now I'm working at Gena's office and railroading her resident genius into teaching me everything he knows about computers.

I'll spend this time learning what I need to know, and when the war is over (it's strange to mention war so casually), I'll be ready to set up shop.

Anyway, I've made friends all over the world—S.O.B.'s

included—and there are places I'd like to see again as an adult. All work and no play have made me a very dull person. I'm enjoying a slower pace for a change, doing my own thing and playing mother hen to Gena.

This isn't a letter—it's a book. Now look who's rambling. I'm off to learn how to interface!

Angie

P.S. You write; I write back. Sorry, that's the way it is. If you insist on there being a point to everything you do, try this: I like making new friends. Don't you?

Did he? Jack wondered. Funny, but until this minute he hadn't given it much thought. He'd had casual acquaintances, but actual friends? Not in years. It hadn't seemed necessary, or practical, since he moved every one to three years.

Kay had friends she'd kept in touch with for a while after each transfer to a new base, but it never lasted. He was beginning to think that nothing lasted. Not even ambition.

He tried to remember when he'd last had a real friend. When he'd been ten. In spite of the seven years between them, he and Bryan had been closer than brothers. They had been friends. At least that was what he'd thought, until Bryan had shared a last secret with Jack before he'd checked out of life.

It's okay to tell now.

Bryan had put him in the middle, forced responsibility on him that he hadn't known how to handle. Sometime after that, Jack had decided that friendship and trust led to betrayal. The more you trusted, the worse the betrayal when it came. He hadn't made a conscious decision to avoid that kind of involvement, yet he had made it just the same—inside, where thoughts are obscure, unexplained. As he blindly stared at Angie's letter, he acknowledged that he hadn't had a real friend in twenty-five years.

Oh, God.

Blinking once, Jack squeezed his eyes shut, breathed deeply, harshly. Did he need friends? Did he want them?

No, he didn't want them. He could get by without them.

But need?

He wasn't sure anymore of what he needed. Whatever it was, he didn't have it yet. Hell, he didn't even know what it was.

He opened his eyes, his gaze automatically focusing on Angie's letter, his mind focusing on her, on anything but himself and the mess he'd made of his life.

No wonder he couldn't help but write back to her. Angela Winters had a nasty habit of saying a lot without telling him anything. What school? What new career? Who in the hell were Gena and Mike?

Why did he care?

Laying back on his bed, he crooked an arm behind his head and studied the design on her stationery—Pike's Peak and Cheyenne Mountain and the graceful silver peaks of the Air Force Academy chapel.

She'd sent him a little glimpse of home and written his name on a giant yellow ribbon.

It was an odd feeling—being part of a war, yet not being actually *in* it. He'd been trying to come to terms with that without much success. Of course he'd had training in combat, survival, and the art of resisting his captors should the need arise. It had scared the hell out of him. He'd seen the reactions of the other men in his class range from fear to excitement to macho posturing. In his opinion the ones who were scared were the sanest.

The war seemed anticlimactic, as if the training were real and everything else a carefully staged game. But what did he know? He was sitting in a comfortable office trying to concentrate on satellite pictures and bits and pieces of intelligence.

It wasn't right, him being safe in Germany, a trained soldier, when weekend warriors were actually fighting the battles. Angie's neighbors, the history teacher—his little brother.

That didn't seem real, either, not when Steve hated the military, hated any form of discipline that wasn't convenient. But the phone call from his mother had been real. It had shaken him all the way to his bones.

"Jack, is that you?" she'd shouted into the phone.

"What's wrong?" he'd asked immediately.

"Oh, Jack, Steve is gone."

He'd turned cold at the sound of tears in his mother's voice, at the memories, and then his insides had cramped up until he could barely speak. Not Steve, too. How? *Why?* The calmness and authority in his voice surprised him, as if someone else had moved into his head and taken over his end of the conversation. "Mom, where has Steve gone?" he asked reasonably, while visions of hospital beds and tubes and wires and flat lines on a monitor haunted him. Not Steve.

"He's in the Gulf, Jack. Since October. Flying bombing raids. He was one of the first. We thought he was on a job. He didn't tell us."

He couldn't have heard right. His stomach relaxed a little. It had to be a mistake. Steve had served six years in the Navy after college and then taken advantage of a Reduction in Force and resigned his commission. Jack knew that the Navy hadn't been sorry to see Steve go. Steve was a hot dog pilot who bucked the system every chance he got. More than once, Steve's butt had been caught in a wringer and then, true to form, had found a way to pull it out again none the worse for wear. Because Steve was brilliant in the cockpit of a plane, he managed to get away with being a renegade.

The thoughts ran through his head at fast forward, a mental review of the facts as he tried to figure out what was going on. It just didn't add up.

"If he didn't tell you, how do you know he's in Saudi?" Jack asked.

"We saw him on television—interviewed by Charles Jaco, I think it was—then a letter came. Jack, he's been in the reserves all along. We didn't know!"

Reserves? Jack shook his head. That didn't sound like Steve. It did explain Steve's frequent weekend jaunts to "parts unknown." They'd never questioned his desire to take off and do "whatever." His job as a hot dog pilot took him all over the country at a moment's notice to fight forest fires, drop relief packages in disaster areas, run rescue missions. "What did the letter say?" he asked.

"He said that he'd done it on a whim." Ada Caldwell's voice caught on a sob and frayed into gulps and ragged breaths.

Now that did sound like Steve. Whims and spur-of-the-moment adventure were what he lived for. But a commitment?

"Mom, put Dad on for a minute." He listened to the silence, the shuffle of hands passing the receiver, his father's voice boom over the wire.

"Dad?"

"It's true, son. Steve is there, flying off a carrier in the Mediterranean. You didn't know about any of this?"

"As much as you did," Jack answered, his voice strained. "I haven't heard from him in a while." Again, a shuffle, then his mother's voice, calmer, but still thick, grieving.

"I don't understand, Jack."

"Neither do I, Mom."

"Can you reach him? Can you get him out?"

"I might be able to patch through a call—"

"Get him out, Jack. I can't lose all of you."

"Mom, calm down. You're not losing anyone—"

"It feels that way, Jack. It feels as if I've lost all of you and I can't find a way to get you back."

The chill had come back after that, making Jack feel brittle and stiff. He'd hung up the phone, knowing something important had been said, yet not understanding what, exactly, it was.

His attention had snagged on one thing: Steve was fighting, flying an A-6 Intruder off of an aircraft carrier, more than likely searching out and destroying SCUD missile launchers. Steve—keeping up his training one weekend a month and six weeks in the summer. Why had he done it? Why hadn't he told his family?

Sweet Jesus, why aren't I fighting instead?

He'd been asking himself the same question ever since. It had been abstract before. Now it was immediate, personal. No matter how much training Steve had, no matter how good he might be in the cockpit, he had no business being in the action.

Not when Jack, a career officer with career training, was flying a desk in a comfortable office, interpreting intelligence that others had risked their lives to gather.

He hadn't been able to get through to Steve, hadn't been able to do anything but keep tabs on his brother. It didn't help to know that it was more than he'd done for Steve in over twenty years.

Steve had always been separate from Jack and Bryan, marching to a tune no one else could hear. After Bryan had gone, he and Steve had cut the cord permanently, each dealing with tragedy in privacy and silence, each easing his parents' pain in his own way. Even at Bryan's funeral, Steve had stood apart from the family, preoccupied by things unknown while Jack had taken care of the details, taken care of their parents. It had never occurred to him to find out if Steve needed someone to take care of him.

They'd never fought or disagreed. They'd never shared. Jack had been busy pursuing a goal. Steve was too much an individual to share more than his energy and craziness with his family.

And for all Jack's connections and the resources available to him, he couldn't call his brother and tell him to be careful, that at least one of the Caldwell boys had to make it.

At least one of them had to do more than exist.

It was driving Jack crazy, wondering why Steve had "jumped in bed" with the enemy, as he'd called it. It couldn't be for any reason other than Steve liked flying A-6's.

It couldn't be because he was trying to prove something, or maybe because he, too, felt an obligation.

Dammit, Steve, isn't one of us enough?

Jack reached over to pick up his tablet of paper and a pen. He had to turn off his thoughts for a while. He needed to think of normal things—of Colorado Springs, even though his parents were rarely there. For a few minutes he wanted to concentrate on questions with easy answers.

So he thought of Angie, living alone in a big house. She didn't get phone calls at night, and she liked to putter around in her robe. It would be the thick, baggy kind, loose and worn in a dozen places. Her slippers were probably fuzzy. He liked the image. It was comfortable and warm, as he imagined Angie to be.

As he might never be.

Colorado Springs

> *Dear Angela,*
>
> *I always have an excuse for writing—like being alone at Christmas, or being maudlin over a war where nobody fights back. And, yes, there should be a point to what I do. It isn't fair to you. Are you so young that you can't see past your ideals? If you are, I'll spell it out: I've been using you.*
>
> *About the yellow ribbon—thanks. You do know that I'm not in the action? My younger brother, Steve, is on a carrier in the Gulf. Haven't been able to connect with him, except to make sure he's still in one piece and raising hell as usual. I think he's avoiding me.*
>
> *I hope that Mike (whoever he is) is okay. Your history teacher, too. It amazes me that we can uproot civilians from their sane, normal lives and stick them right in the line of fire while—never mind. The thought is inappropriate.*
>
> *Lieutenant Baker informed me that it's Valentine's Day. I guess that explains the flowers I saw on several of the women's desks. It slipped by me this year. Good thing I don't have anyone to give a valentine to.*

The man had serious problems. Worse than her own, Angie decided as she read Jack's letter. All the hype and hoopla generated for every holiday, and he still had been unaware of Valentine's Day. No wonder he was alone.

She couldn't believe that he wanted it that way. Not when he tacked on friendly little paragraphs to his disclaimers that he didn't want to continue the correspondence.

There was a poignancy to Jack's letters that reached down deep inside of her and grabbed something vital, pulling it out in the open, exposing her own needs, the bareness of her life.

Valentine's Day was another killer, a day that really brought her low because it was a day for two, and she didn't even have the courage to be complete in herself.

Gena didn't count. Especially not when she was upstairs crying buckets into the flowers Mike had somehow managed to send via a friend stationed in England.

Shaking her head, Angie read on.

This is it. No more letters. I'm busy and so are you, though you've left out the details.

Best,
Jack

P.S. *When you buy a computer, make sure it's upgradable. Damn things become obsolete almost before they hit the stores. Don't know what you're going to use it for, but the more RAM (memory) you have, the better performance you'll get. Your friend's resident genius has probably already covered this.*

Angie smiled at the transition from "Major Jack Caldwell" to simply "Jack." Obviously he was curious about her. Details, indeed. Why should he mention the lack thereof or offer advice unless he was interested?

At least he was having as hard a time ignoring her as she was trying not to think about him.

She didn't understand her reactions to him. Why Jack specifically? Why did she relate to him so strongly? It had never happened before with her other pen pals. She'd always felt like an observer of their lives, a curious bystander rather than a participant. She was taking everything about Jack Caldwell personally—and seriously.

So what *was* the point? she asked herself.

8

Germany

Dear Jack,

Happy Easter—early!

I couldn't resist a bit of madness. I passed a candy display and went crazy. Why does Easter candy taste so much better than other kinds? It has the same ingredients. It must be the cute little bunny shapes. In an act of pure regression, I bought a couple of those dye kits and destroyed my kitchen. Dye everywhere. The eggs are no problem, but what am I going to do with all this candy? I know this will arrive early for the holiday, but I can't eat it all. Bon apetit . . .

I drained the meat out of your Easter eggs before sending them, or something would have definitely been rotten in Germany. Sorry. They are pretty, though, aren't they? I hope they arrived intact.

Angie

P.S. Thanks for the advice. I'm now the proud owner of a 486 with 16M of RAM. I've discovered that computerspeak is a lot like military lingo. By the way—I'm old enough to interface. If you want details—ask!

Jack stared at the postscript. Surely she hadn't meant that last bit the way it sounded? It had to be like that remark about brooding desire or passions or whatever—naive and meaning something else entirely.

Either Angie Winters was a smartass, had hoof-in-mouth disease, or she was unbelievably naive. Maybe she was one of those homely women who couldn't interest a man in "interfacing" in person.

Maybe she was shy or lonely. He read the letter again.

He'd never met a shy smartass.

A large box sat on his desk, ignored as he tried to talk himself out of being curious, out of wanting to see what lay beneath the Styrofoam peanuts and green tissue paper. Once he did, he'd be obligated to thank her.

That meant another letter.

So what was one more?

His hands were gentle as he lifted his gift out of the carefully packed box. His throat felt as if it had a giant egg caught halfway down. Angie had not only gone to the trouble to drain the eggs and paint some pretty elaborate scenes on them, but she had put together an Easter basket for him, complete with cellophane grass and a fancy bow tied around the handle. The kicker was a stuffed toy version of the Tasmanian Devil with rabbit ears tied on its head and a sign around his neck that said: s.o.b. IN DISGUISE. He leaned back in his chair and held the Devil in his hands, staring at it. It was so ugly, it was cute.

Was that how she pictured him?

"Uh, sir?" Baker stood in the doorway, his gaze swinging from the basket to Jack and back again.

"What is it, Lieutenant?"

"I've been trying to patch that call through for you, sir. Still no luck."

Still no Steve. Jack put a clamp on his frustration. At least he knew that Steve was alive, all in one piece, and raising hell as usual. What was it like, he wondered, to raise hell?

Shuffling papers on his desk, he glanced up at Baker. "Anything else?"

"Uh, DCA is sending over the reports from DOD. The colonel wants to see you ASAP. He's on his way back from the O Club."

"I'll be there by the time he arrives," Jack said, keeping his amusement under wraps. Baker had a real fascination for the acronyms the military attached to everything and used them whenever he could. Angie was right. It did resemble computerese.

"Yes, sir." Baker hesitated, staring now at the toy. Privately, he thought that it bore a striking similarity to the major first thing in the morning. "Uh . . . Major?"

"Spit it out, Lieutenant," Jack said mildly.

"Well, sir, unless you're of a mind to share that candy with every man in the building, you'd better hide that basket."

"Thank you, Lieutenant."

"Yes, sir."

"Lieutenant," Jack called as Baker turned to go. He searched the basket for a bag of milk chocolate eggs and tossed them over. "Heads up."

Baker caught the bag and grinned. "Happy Easter, sir."

"Oh, Lieutenant . . ." Jack paused to clear his throat.

"Sir?"

"Just thought you should know that the German police are making authorized raids on the base."

Baker's skin paled, and his perpetual grin dropped off his face. "What for, sir?" he asked quietly.

"Immigration problems. Some of the nannies on post are in the country illegally. The police are checking credentials and rounding up anyone who even looks suspicious." Glancing up from his papers, Jack pinned the lieutenant with a probing stare. "I thought you might want to tell your girl that—"

"I understand, Major," Baker interrupted. "She'll want to make sure she has her papers handy."

His eyes narrowed, Jack stared at Baker a moment longer. The young man wasn't looking back, and Jack could almost see the wheels turning in his head. If he didn't miss his guess, Baker would be requesting leave to take his girl on a little vacation. The family she worked for would be more than willing to let her go until things died down. A heavy fine was levied on Americans found harboring illegal aliens. He cleared his throat again.

"I don't suppose it will do me any good to tell you that the odds of things working out for a serviceman and one of these girls are slim to none?"

"I understand," Baker said stiffly, "but you should tell it to someone it applies to, sir."

Jack shook his head as Baker walked out of his office. Baker was as stubborn as Angela. With a sigh of defeat, he propped the Tasmanian Devil on his desk where the picture of his ex-wife used to be.

Colorado Springs

Dear Angela,
You're right—bunny shapes do taste better. Thanks. In fact, everyone in J-2 thanks you. Baker warned me to hide it, and I didn't listen. Good thing I'd already eaten the hollow rabbits and marshmallow ducks.

Chocolate doesn't seem to agree with Baker. Poor man has been using Clearasil by the pint—the tinted kind that's not supposed to show, except that it does. I wish I had the heart to tell him. Hell, I wish I had the heart to tell him a lot of things. Where Baker is concerned, I'm afraid the course of true love is going to be forty miles of bad road.

But who am I to talk? I'm still trying to figure out what "irreconcilable differences" means. . . .

Unable to wait to read Jack's letter, Angie stood just inside the front door, her coat still buttoned against the chill outside. She forgot about her feet, sore from a long day of trudging from one specialty shop to another displaying her sample line of cards. A large bag containing Colonel Sanders's extra crispy chicken sat on the floor cooling and soaking up the puddle of snow melting off her boots.

She'd sent Jack the gift on an impulse and had suffered a million bad moments ever since. Was it too forward? Too silly? Too juvenile? He was a man of the world with heavy responsibilities. J-2 was the intelligence arm of the military. Whatever his actual job, she knew it had to be sensitive and demanding, guaranteed to keep a man on the sharp edge of stress. Despite his disclaimer, he was part of the action —a vital part regardless of how far removed he was from the sound of bombs falling.

The job had to add to his loneliness. With the kind of classified and top secret information he must deal with on a day-to-day basis, he didn't even have the luxury of talking shop over a beer at the Officers' Club after work.

He was divorced.

More relief, disturbing in its significance.

Gena's voice made her jump as the door bumped her from behind. "Let me in, Angie. It's colder than a well-digger's behind out here."

Stumbling over the bag, Angie lurched into the wall. Gena burst into the entryway. "What are you—food!" Gena said, picking up the bag and kicking the door shut. Leaning over, she peered at the envelope Angie held with the letter. "I should have known. The mysterious major again. How is he?"

"He likes hollow rabbits and marshmallow ducks," Angie said absently.

"Well, that's a load off my mind," Gena said dryly, then sighed as she picked up the bag of food. "Read your letter, chum. I'll cook."

"Okay," Angie said as she unbuttoned her coat and struggled to pull it off one-handed. "Thanks." Turning the page over, she continued reading as she wandered into the living room and plopped down in the window seat.

> *Glad to hear about your computer. Depending on what you're going to do with it, you should have plenty of power and speed. The thing I'm working on is one step above a hammer and chisel and pictures on the wall of a cave. By the time I go home next year, the machines will probably activate directly from thought waves.*
>
> *Time to go. Thought I'd spend the afternoon taking some pictures in the Black Forest outside the perimeter of the base. Thanks again for the ducks and bunnies and the "Devil." He's leering at me from a corner of my desk.*
>
> *Jack*
>
> *P.S. You got me for one more letter, but I still can't figure out why. There's no future in it.*

Angie grinned as she stared out the window. The moon was a luminous fingerprint behind light gray clouds. Yellow ribbons tied around any stationary object in the neighborhood flapped in a strong breeze, their ragged and frayed edges glistening with moisture as snowflakes fell in a diagonal line from sky to ground.

"What are you smirking about?" Gena asked as she walked in, her arms laden with a large silver tray neatly arranged with china, crystal, and silver flatware.

"He has a sense of humor."

"Do tell? What else does he have?" Setting the tray on the coffee table, Gena began unfolding two TV trays. "Since there was a very fine wine in the Colonel Sanders bag, I assume we're celebrating?"

"He *doesn't* have a wife."

"So?" Gena said, then paused. "Oh. Is *that* why we're celebrating?" The TV trays up, Gena headed back to the kitchen without waiting for an answer.

So nothing. It was simply a tidbit of information, Angie told herself. An explanation for his loneliness. An excuse for being an S.O.B.

She wondered if he'd loved his wife.

Angie flipped through the rest of her mail and tossed it aside, her mind wandering between thoughts of Jack and the lieutenant he seemed so concerned about, wondering what it would be like to be in love. And then, she remembered her parents and how love hadn't been enough to keep them together.

Neither had their daughter. Because of her, they had ceased to like and respect each other.

Irreconcilable differences. What a convenient term that was, designed to cover what couldn't be explained to protect those who preferred discretion to honesty.

Evidently he had loved someone and married her. Evidently, it hadn't worked out.

So what?

Love and the commitment it required were a dream she couldn't deny, yet they weren't on her list of priorities. Her mother loved her, yet didn't know her. Her father loved her, and though he'd never said so and hadn't shown it in any tangible way, she sensed that he resented her. She loved them both, yet it had never been enough to satisfy them. Gena, too, had suffered from loving and being loved by a mother who gave advice instead of structure and discipline, by relatives who had indulged their needs by literally smothering Gena in affection but had never listened to or seen Gena's own needs.

And surely, Jack cared about his brother, yet from the tone of that letter, he wasn't surprised that Steve might be avoiding him.

So much for love.

Germany

> *Dear Jack,*
>
> *Life has settled down again, and it's as if the war never happened, although I know that the birds dying on oil-slicked beaches and the people who can't breathe for the smoke shrouding their country would disagree with me. For all our high-tech communications and ability to literally plug in to live action in other parts of the world, we really are insular in our thinking. If it isn't happening to us, it can't be happening.*
>
> *So much for philosophizing. It always makes me relate in uncomfortable ways. See what I mean? Insular.*
>
> *The night I received your letter Gena and I celebrated my first success in my new business venture by feasting on extra crispy fried chicken and biscuits and gravy. I even splurged on corn on the cob and wine. I got eight orders! Last night I bounced off the ceiling. Today, I face the reality of deadlines and a thousand details I'd rather not think about. Don Quixote will have his trial by fire. (Don is my computer.)*
>
> *I've added to my education by mastering Paintbrush and fonts and text wrap. Postscript is the most amazing thing! You didn't, however, tell me about full-page monitors. Shame.*
>
> *I hope that you have finally reached your brother. We added his name to our ribbon. Also, I hope Lieutenant*

Baker's problem has cleared up. Too bad love can't be treated medically with concealing cream.

Mother and Ben are in Japan. Now I really am envious. We were stationed there when I was very young, but I still remember—mostly the wonderful little toy shops and how when we went into the country, it seemed like a different world from the cities. I used to poke my finger through the rice paper in the shoji screens, fascinated by having paper walls that slid back and forth to change the shape of the rooms.

Well, deadlines loom. More later.

Angie

P.S. As for the future you're so worried about—I proposed friendship, not marriage. Nothing to get dysfunctional over.

The paper was plain white bond with a border of every symbol from stars to check marks to bullets. The writing was neat, perfectly spaced Times Roman in one paragraph, Helvetica in the next. Obviously, Angie had practiced using her fonts on him.

Jack missed her little spidery scratches. He was also missing a lot of information, and it was driving him crazy. She had to be an airhead. Reading Angie's letters was like reading the middle four pages of a book—a mystery where you walked in after the murder and left before it was solved.

She'd named her computer, for crying out loud.

He didn't need this.

Colorado Springs

Dear Angie,

I give up. You win. Uncle!

What business? Deadlines for what? Orders for what—corn on the cob and wine?

Who are Gena and Mike?

What school?

> *What made you so cynical about love, and how old are you?*
>
>   *Jack*
>
> *P.S. Sorry about the full-page monitor. I have a sudden yen for fried chicken and can't cook worth a damn. Think I'll go to the O Club and see what's on the menu.*

It felt so strange, confusing, like losing the battles, but winning the war.

For once Angie didn't have the urge to immediately answer a letter from Jack. All of a sudden, she wasn't sure she wanted to answer him at all. The mixture of elation, satisfaction, and unease provoked uncomfortable thoughts, difficult questions.

Against every insecurity she'd harbored in her emotional repertoire, she had plunged right into a one-sided relationship with a man she didn't know, pursuing him as if gaining his capitulation were a milestone she had to reach. Now that she had her way, she didn't know how to respond.

Friendship—remember, Angie?

It didn't feel like friendship, exactly. Fascination? Yes. Liking? It would seem so. Kinship? From the first. But what else? she wondered.

Try honesty.

She didn't want to try honesty. She cringed to think about how much of herself she'd revealed to Jack or how comfortable and natural it seemed to talk to him without mulling over every word. Without trying to be someone she wasn't. Without focusing entirely on him and ignoring her own needs to reach out, to be real.

A two-sided relationship. How quaint. How awkward.

How provocative.

Refusing to listen to the nagging—and sarcastic—voice in her head, Angie glanced up at the computer screen, blinked, and stared. It was all there, every thought, every question, every answer. She'd been typing her entire conversation with herself, as if the computer played devil's advocate to her foolishness.

She smiled at the screen. Foolish indeed. What was she

so worried about? The major was simply a lonely man afraid of the responsibility of *not* being lonely. Afraid of losing the anonymity that went with a silent life.

She could relate to that.

Pulling out a drawer in the workstation she'd installed in the study cum workroom, she retrieved all of Jack's letters. . . .

Her hand paused over the unopened box she'd stowed under the letters. She'd put the vibrator there rather than in the more logical locations in her bathroom or bedroom where she might be tempted to indulge herself, to take the fantasies she'd been having lately a step farther. Fantasies of Jack and her together.

Curious, she pulled out the oblong box and opened it, studied the vibrator. Heat climbed up her face. Gena was right. She did blush when she was alone.

"Enough, Angie. Throw the darn thing away before it gets you into trouble," she said firmly as she laid the box on top of her desk and picked up Jack's letters, reread them, studied them, tried to remember her responses.

They were like an ongoing conversation between two people in the same room.

An otherwise empty room, isolated from the rest of the world.

Something fluttered in her chest. A chill skittered up her spine and spread to her arms, her neck, the back of her skull. It was so simple, really. She and the mysterious major were half a world away from one another, yet in she felt a universe away from anyone else. In a wary, blind way, she and Jack Caldwell *were* talking to one another. Somehow, she had found another person living in her dimension. He'd certainly been living in her dreams.

Her gaze found the box. She really should throw it away. She certainly shouldn't be suffering from mal de hormones over a man she'd never seen and didn't know—not really.

Yes, she did know him. Really.

Staring down at the letters stacked in her lap, she smiled. Somehow, half a world didn't seem so far away.

Germany

Dear Jack,

Specialty greeting cards and stationery. (I got eight orders the first day out!) The wine and chicken and corn on the cob were to celebrate. I won't ask what your job is—I already know about J-2.

My closest friend and her fiancé—maybe. How is Lieutenant Baker, by the way?

The Winters-Haley Academy of Dance, of which I was a founding partner.

The same thing that made you cynical about love—irreconcilable differences (not mine, but everyone else's).

Twenty-seven going on twenty-eight. How old are you? Have I covered everything?

Mike has finally returned from the Gulf, and Gena has moved back into her newly renovated house. I fear that, like your Lieutenant Baker, their road to love is paved with good intentions and little else. I've said too much.

Mother is in Hawaii, and, yes, on to Tahiti. How strange that I seem to know my new stepfather better than I do a parent I've spent my life with. Truth to tell—he seems to know me better than mother does, though I suspect it's because he raised a daughter of his own and has decided that I need a father.

The house is quiet without Gena, and after a week of solitude (and peace), being alone is beginning to pall. There are only so many ways to dress up a TV dinner, and who wants to cook every day for one? That sounds horribly grim, and of course, it isn't. Do you have any idea how many menus are available in TV dinners nowadays? I have a checklist. There just isn't enough incentive to cook or clean up afterward.

Enough! Suddenly I'm hungry for take-out Chinese. Thank heavens they deliver.

                                                         Angie

If Jack had doubted it before, he was sure now—Angie *was* crazy. As far as he was concerned, TV dinners were not a laughing matter, nor was adapting to loneliness. Yet Angie was adapting, cheerfully it would seem. Freedom, she'd called it—an odd word to use in this day and age. The last time he'd checked, women had been unchained from their pedestals and let out of their ivory towers. He had the feeling that Angie was just now finding that out.

She seemed to have the ability to see the best in every situation and joke about it. On some level, he resented that ability. On another level, he thought she must be a permanent resident of La-La Land.

Checking his watch, Jack decided he had time to make it to the commissary before it closed.

He had a sudden craving for egg rolls.

9

Germany

Jack,

I'm in the hospital in Ramstein—no big deal, just a blown appendix. Be out in no time.

Would appreciate it if you didn't tell the parents. They worry enough without this. I'm going to see the sights in Europe after I blow this pop stand. I'd ask you to come along, but doubt the Air Force can function without you or vice versa. Don't bother coming up here to see me. Feel free to call, though, if you have time. We should get together as soon as I get out of here. The parents expect it. Make it easy on yourself. I've got nothing but time.

Steve

No big deal. It's only pain. Don't tell . . . they'd worry.

Jack's hands shook as he pushed the memory away, a memory he'd kept away for over twenty years. His throat felt tight, clogged. Steve had been sick, and had somehow circumvented standard procedure to keep his family from knowing what was going on. It was just like his younger brother to dispense information like a controlled substance.

If Jack hadn't called the hospital as soon as he'd read the letter the first time, he would have been on his way whether Steve liked it or not.

Steve was okay—a case of peritonitis notwithstanding. He'd be under treatment for another two weeks, then another four weeks for convalescence.

No big deal, hell. A ruptured appendix was nothing to fool around with, and the infection could be deadly. Hospitals didn't keep a patient around long unless he was in trouble to begin with.

Jack wasn't okay. It was taking all his energy to fight the sheer fury brought on by Steve's request. It hit too close to home, made him feel ashamed somehow. He should have tried harder to keep in touch with Steve, pulled strings, called in favors—whatever it took to connect with his brother. But instead he'd respected Steve's wishes to be left alone. It had been safer.

Quit messing with my head, Jack.

His head had been in the sand about a lot of things. Things he was just now beginning to think about as he adjusted to seeing life as it really was rather than how he wanted it to be.

Or how he'd *thought* he'd wanted it to be.

It really ticked him off that Kay, the U.S. Air Force, and now Steve, were forcing him to take a reality break.

With slow controlled movements, he laid the letter down, smoothed it out, then picked up the phone and dialed a series of numbers that would link him with his parents.

He'd sworn off secrets a long time ago.

Rothenburg ob der Tauber, Germany

What in the hell was he doing here?

A city built in the Middle Ages, Rothenburg ob der Tauber was an anachronism. It still functioned, still had a population that lived and worked within its high stone walls. With few concessions to the modern age, the city was much as it had been when the aristocracy strolled in the castle gardens and enemies fought to breach the ramparts. It was almost like stepping back in time.

Modern cars rolled down the cobbled streets and indoor plumbing graced the dwellings and hotels. The people wore contemporary fabrics and tennis shoes, and most of the women tourists wore slacks or jeans.

Remembering Angie's questions about his host country, he'd gotten a wild hair and decided to "do" Germany and maybe take some pictures to send her. So now he was play-

ing tourist, a camera slung around his neck, an equipment
bag over one shoulder, his tripod sheathed in its case over
the other like some medieval weapon. His jeans and cham-
bray shirt felt funny, and he tried to think back to how
often he'd been out of uniform lately.

He was an anachronism.

He didn't want to see Steve, yet he'd called him and told
him that he had some leave coming and would meet him at
Lake Constance. Why he'd scheduled his leave so he'd
spend one week on his own and one with Steve was a mystery. Lately, he was as uncomfortable with his own company as he knew he would be with Steve's.

Either way, he'd be putting in some hard time with a
stranger.

He and his brother had zilch in common except that they
happened to come from the same gene pool. His younger
brother had never been an active part of his life, not like
Bryan. Steve had been too quixotic for Jack to relate to,
and the youngest of the Caldwell brothers hadn't understood Bryan's and then Jack's preoccupation with their future as adults rather than milking adolescence for all it was
worth.

They hadn't even been raised alike. Steve was the baby,
five years younger than Jack, their parents' chance to relive
Bryan's childhood, to correct the mistakes they'd made in
raising Bryan—real or imagined. Steve had been their
chance to build a new past, while Jack had been their hope
for the future as it should have been.

Standing on the catwalk that ringed the walls, he raked
his hand through his hair and forced his concentration on
the arrow slits carved out of the rocks, the grooves in the
stone beneath his feet where guards had walked back and
forth century after century, watching for danger, fighting
for their homes and families. Standing there, he almost felt
a part of it, could almost imagine what it had been like
living in another time, another place.

Not so different from now, except for the outer trappings of war. Back then, soldiers had been born into their

profession, just as blacksmiths and peasant farmers had been born into theirs.

He supposed that he had been born into his profession, too, the day that Bryan had left behind an unfinished dream.

I'm counting on you to make good.

It must have been easier in the fourteenth century, knowing your future before you'd even started with a present. Maybe to his ten-year-old mind, it had been comforting not to have choices.

He left the catwalk, turning sideways to accommodate his size on stone steps too narrow for the enemy to storm more than one at a time. Below, he saw the contrast between past and present, felt his bearings shift a little. He'd been feeling a lot of shifts lately—inside, like a hairline crack that was being strained by pressure. Something was pushing hard behind that crack, trying to get out. He had the odd idea that it was a ten-year-old boy.

Someone named Jack, who rarely had been without a camera in his hand since his big brother had given him a clunky, brightly colored Fisher Price replica of the real thing.

It's only pain.

The royal gardens didn't seem quite right with their winding paths, ancient trees, and irregular stone embrasures set into the wall. Yesterday, he'd looked for the castle and finally discovered that it no longer existed—the only part of Rothenburg not still intact—destroyed not by war or decay but by an earthquake. Without the castle, the setting was like an amputee that had survived devastation and continued to function though its primary purpose was gone.

Like him, the old city was incomplete.

He headed for a book shop that had travel brochures and guide books in English. Angie had really been the reason he'd chosen his itinerary. He'd thought of the Easter basket, the yellow ribbon, and the drawings of Pike's Peak and decided to send her a little bit of Germany. Yesterday, he'd picked up his cameras, those forgotten friends that had been a part of his little-boy fantasies. He would be like Ansel Adams—better, even—maybe win a Pulitzer for that one special photo that really was worth a thousand words.

The first shot had been hard, his handling of the equipment awkward, but as he exposed roll after roll of film, the cameras became a part of him, as if he'd never packed them away with his dreams. And as he exposed roll after roll of film, his world became texture and contrast and depth, and the last twenty years faded into a two-dimensional blur.

With a bag full of books, postcards, and brochures, he left the shop and walked back to his hotel, the cameras at rest until another image caught his imagination.

Dear Angie,

I'm on two weeks' leave and decided to see some of the sights. I'm in a medieval walled city called Rothenburg ob der Tauber (on the Tauber River), and it's almost like it was centuries ago. The walls are high and there are towers and tall-spired churches and a museum of torture devices. Everywhere I felt the contradictions: horses wearing flower wreaths and straw hats and cars chugging down cobbled streets, old houses and public buildings and electric lights, shops with stone floors and cash registers sitting on the counters. The smells are timeless: Küchen and potato pancakes and cabbage, damp rock and flowers and musty corners. The sounds are completely modern: mothers calling their children in a dozen different languages and those same children begging for a replica of a warrior's sword or a lady's dagger or a giant pencil with the name of the city printed all over it.

There's one building—a bakery that was a bakery centuries ago—and it has a round tower with a leaded-glass window. Late last night, I wandered around after all the tourists were gone from the streets and saw a single candle in the tower window, shining gold against the dark blue sky and black shadows of the buildings. Today, I went into a shop that had original copperplate prints (I thought that was a lost art). They had one of the tower at night, in shades of dark blue with that gold light coming out of the window. A lost art and a reminder of a lost time, and maybe someone waiting inside a room without corners. To coin a corny phrase: it spoke to me.

I'm sending you a calendar with removable postcards of this place so you can see what it's like. If you ignore the tourists in some of the shots, you can imagine what it was like hundreds of years ago. As I stood on the battlements, I could have sworn I heard strains from Wagner's Die Walküre.

I finally got to speed on the Autobahn, though it's not considered speeding here. Knowing that took some of the fun out of it. I passed a Gypsy caravan, twelve cars long (new Mercedes-Benzes, no less), each hauling an Airstream trailer with white lace curtains in the windows. So much for romantic legends.

Tomorrow I'm going to Triburg, where they make the Black Forest cuckoo clocks, and I meet my brother at Lake Constance next week. They have a city there that celebrated its millennium a couple of years ago.

I've been taking a lot of pictures. At first my cameras seemed foreign to me after being semi-retired for so long. But once I played with them for a while, it was as if I'd never put them down. I don't think I'll be able to forget them again. As soon as I develop the film, I'll send you photos. You're the reason I brought the cameras in the first place.

Thanks, Angie.

I had a couple of beers (no relation to the stuff back home) and can hardly keep my eyes open. I'm still looking for your brooding passions and fire.

                                                              Jack

Jack saw him sitting at a table on a small verandah of *Altes Schloss* that overlooked Lake Constance and the Swiss Alps beyond. As always, Steve was smiling—this time at a waitress. As always his brother's charm and easygoing manner held the young Fräulein's attention long after she should have moved on.

Jack wanted to turn around, walk away fast, before his brother saw him, before he'd have to talk to him and remember other talks, other times—with Bryan.

All three of the Caldwell brothers had looked alike, with the same tall, lean builds that never seemed to gain anything but muscle, the craggy faces with prominent bone structure and dark blue eyes. The girls that gravitated toward Bryan had called them "bedroom eyes." Later, Steve had attracted the same kind of attention.

Though his eyes were the same as those of his brothers, Jack hadn't attracted any of the same frankly sensual appraisals from girls when he'd reached high school. He hadn't attracted girls period. Too serious, they said. Too intense. Too cold.

"Jack!"

He held up his hand in acknowledgment as he walked toward the table, turned sideways to fit in the narrow aisle, and sat down in stages in the cramped space. His smile growing wider, Steve held up his hand to signal the waitress, who was all too eager to return and even more eager to linger as she took their order. As soon as she left, Steve's smile faded as he studied Jack. "So, what's up? I'm surprised that you took the time off to see me," he said. Leave it to Steve not to bother with social protocol.

"I'm surprised you came," Jack countered. "I know Mom and Dad called you in the hospital."

"I wish you'd have left it alone, Jack. I went to a lot of trouble to keep them from knowing I'd been sick."

Jack chewed the inside of his cheek as he stared out at the lake. "You were out of line, Steve."

"Why? It was only an appendix—nothing vital."

"You went sour for a while. Mom knew I was keeping tabs on you—"

Steve plowed his hand through his hair, a trait that had been handed down from father to sons. "It would have been my responsibility—"

"Damn you, Steve. Responsibility is for the ones who are . . ." Jack's voice trailed off. He couldn't say it, couldn't face the old nightmare.

"The ones who are left to pick up the pieces?" Steve finished for him. "Bryan is dust, Jack—*his* choice, *his* decision, *his* responsibility—"

"Leave Bryan out of this, Steve."

"I didn't bring him into this," Steve said softly. "He's everywhere—at home, here sitting across the table. How does it feel to be a living shrine, Jack?"

Jack's chair collided with the railing as he shoved it back and tried to stand in the cramped space. "Nice seeing you, Steve," he said through clenched teeth, then fumbled in his pocket and dropped a key on the table. "Here's your room key. Enjoy your trip." The table kept him from straightening, and the chair rebounded to catch the back of his knees. He felt like a fool, half standing and half bending over the table, the people at the next table watching as if they expected him to jump over the rail.

Steve stared at the key and sighed. "Damn *you,* Jack, for being so arrogant."

Arrogant? Was he? Jack wondered. It stopped him, held him suspended between leaving and staying. He'd been accused of being a lot of things, but not that. Bryan had been the arrogant one, with everything in his life falling into place, everything coming so easily that he expected it to always be that way. Nothing had come easily for Jack. He'd had to work his butt off to get where he was today.

In Bryan's shoes.

Lifting his gaze, Steve grimaced. "I'd hoped that maybe we . . ." He shook his head, looked down again. "You look like an ass, Jack. Either sit down or leave."

Jack felt like an ass—probably, he thought wryly, because he was acting like one. He never lost his cool, never walked away from a problem until it was solved. People counted on him to make things right; they expected it.

He, on the other hand, expected nothing from anyone.

Except that the bleak expression on Steve's face raised a question he couldn't ignore. The note of sorrow he'd heard in Steve's voice echoed his own feeling that he was facing an opportunity that hovered between life and death. Slowly, he lowered himself back down into the chair and told himself that he had no choice. The cramped space notwithstanding, he knew he couldn't get out unless Steve walked away first.

Silence followed as he avoided Steve's gaze and Steve avoided his. His breath whooshed out in a frustrated sigh when the waitress appeared with their coffee and *Küchen*. Now what? he wondered. It had always been like this between them—two brothers who didn't know how to be brothers.

Was that what Steve meant about hoping?

Jack cleared his throat. "Where did it happen?" he asked, switching to a more neutral subject.

Steve shrugged and grinned, his pensive mood gone as if it had never been. "There was this WAF, blond hair and big bumpers. We were in bed, and I doubled up. Thought it was just the creepin' crud from the change in water or something—told her not to get hyper over a few cramps. She went to sleep and I passed out."

"Last time I looked, WAFs weren't stationed on carriers. Where were you?"

Steve's grin faded, and he stared down at his coffee. "Here in Germany. I had some leave time coming, and the parents asked me to look you up after I was released from duty."

"Otherwise you wouldn't have," Jack said flatly.

"Probably not."

His mouth tightening, Jack stared out at the water, its surface rippled by a breeze.

"They're worried, Jack."

"I write. I call. What's the problem?"

"Your letters. Your calls." Steve added sugar to his coffee, then drank half of it in one gulp. Steve did everything like that, gulping life before it cooled.

"They don't say anything, Jack—just facts and details. Kay leaves you, we fight and win a war, and you carry on as if nothing is different."

"Life goes on."

"They keep remembering—" Steve paused, finishing off

his coffee as if it would wash down what he'd been about to say.

"Yeah. Well, I'm not Bryan."

"Not for lack of trying."

He couldn't look at Steve, couldn't look anywhere but down at his hands, clenching and unclenching. Good, strong hands that he was beginning to think did nothing useful or important. At least not to Jack Caldwell.

"I saw Kay before I left the States," Steve said casually. "I'm having a hard time believing what she told me."

Jack wrapped his hand around his cup. "How is she?"

"Taking it a lot better than you, I think."

"I'm not taking it at all," Jack said flatly.

"What really happened?"

"Back off, Steve," Jack warned.

Steve's gaze sharpened on Jack. "Kay never was any good at accepting responsibility. You made it easy for her, Jack. The way I see it, she made her choices; she just can't live with the results, so she's letting you do it for her."

Jack glanced away from Steve, his jaw set as he wondered why he hadn't walked away while he had the chance.

"You haven't talked about this with anyone, have you?"

"No point. It's over."

"I can see that," Steve said. "It was over the day Bryan died. You sold your soul for his life. Now you're both dead."

Jack nearly doubled over at Steve's words, but he sat straight and still in his chair, barely breathing, feeling more than he wanted to feel. "No," he said, hearing it come from somewhere else, someone else. Someone who didn't want Steve to be right.

Steve shook his head as he played with lumps of sugar in a bowl. "Three weeks in a hospital did a number on my mind—nothing to do but think. The shit in your head gets pretty deep when you're not sure if you'll make it or not. You think about all the things you should have done and said, all the mistakes you made. You think about second chances and what you'd do with them."

Another blow. Another memory. Jack didn't want to talk

about second chances, couldn't consider that they really existed. Lately, he'd spent too much time convincing himself that lives couldn't be recycled and made into something else. He forced his hands to relax on the table, forced his voice to an even timbre. "You're right, Steve. This is crap."

Again Steve sighed. "Humor me, Jack. I need to make things right."

"What have you got to make right?" Jack asked harshly. "You've never answered to anyone."

"I've chosen my own battles," Steve said as his mouth widened into that mocking slash of a smile that Jack hated. "Even when they were the wrong ones and even when I lost, they were mine."

"Right or wrong, no matter who it hurts."

"You can't please everyone, Jack."

"Only yourself."

"What would you know about that?"

Jack knew he should have an answer, but he couldn't find one.

After signaling the waitress for more coffee, Steve shoved his empty cup aside and stared at the rough grain in the table. "I told you I had a lot of time to think." His eyes narrowed as he glanced at their surroundings. "Have you ever wondered why we always meet in public places?"

"Never thought about it." But Jack was thinking about it now. The answer wasn't hard to find: he and Steve had never had anything private to say to one another.

"How did we all get so fucked up?" Steve asked. "We had a healthy family life. We had love. What happened?"

Jack's head snapped up. "You tell me, Steve. Are you normal? Do most sons and brothers go to war and have surgery without telling their families?"

"Is it any less than you expected?"

It threw Jack to hear the bleakness in his brother's voice. He stared at Steve, seeing what he'd heard—loneliness and pain in a face that had never shown anything but stubborn independence, isolation. The same isolation and pain he'd seen once before on Bryan's face. Except that Steve wasn't staring at a blank ceiling. Steve still knew how to hope. "Shit, Steve."

"Exactly. For all my hell-raising, I always managed to get out of the ringer before anyone found out, and I only wrecked the car once. The parents don't expect me to screw up, therefore they wouldn't know if I did."

Jack felt uncomfortable, itchy. "They expect what you lead them to expect. We all assumed that you had what you wanted." His voice trailed off. Something clicked in his brain, painfully, like when you turn your head suddenly and crack your neck. "Oh, God."

"I'll second that," Steve nodded at the waitress as she served fresh cups of coffee.

Jack looked out over the town below and watched as the crowd thinned to a trickle of sightseers. Merchants stepped outside their shops for a moment of peace. The terrace was quiet, unoccupied except for himself and Steve. He had the feeling that they were no longer in public, but in a time and place that existed for a single moment. A moment that would pass unnoticed if he didn't recognize its value. Out of the corner of his eye, he saw Steve playing with the sugar cubes he'd scattered all over his side of the table. Like Steve, scattering the moments of his life as he tilted at windmills. He turned his head, watched Steve line them up in a neat row, heard Steve's voice as if it were in the air all around him, saying things he didn't want to hear.

"It's some kind of trap that we set for ourselves, Jack. A dumb kid does something that gets a reaction, then keeps doing it to get another reaction. I could make the parents laugh, distract them from thinking about Bryan. You kept them busy with your ambitions. You made Bryan live through you." He shoved the cubes into a pile and brushed it aside. "No wonder we didn't get along. We canceled each other out."

"You rebelled, Steve. The secrecy, the risks—what were you trying to prove?"

"Can't have my brothers show me up," Steve said flippantly.

"Is that what you're doing? Competing?"

Leaning back, Steve balanced his chair on two legs, the high back resting against the table behind him. "You've been trying to walk in Bryan's footsteps, and I've been running myself ragged trying to stay out of them. The only thing I couldn't do was stay out of the jets, but I did that for me, Jack—not Bryan."

Jack felt as if the blood had drained out of his body. He sat stone still, felt the breeze all the way to his bones, heard the words echoing in his head over and over again.

Bryan's footsteps. Bryan's life. Bryan's choices—

"You really have been thinking."

"Yeah." Steve's grin reappeared, crooked and mocking. "I came up with some pretty interesting conclusions." The grin faded as he stared down at his hands. "It seemed important to talk"—he cleared his throat—"to reconnect with the family."

Jack didn't know how to handle this. If it had been one of his men—no problem. It would have been ephemeral, coming and going without touching him in any personal way. But this was Steve, his brother, a stranger whom he loved and was suddenly beginning to like.

"You don't get it, do you, Jack? You started out wanting to follow in Bryan's footsteps. Then the folks were proud of your ambition, so you kept right on going. The prouder they were, the more you tried not to disappoint them."

Again Jack stared out at the lake and felt like jumping in. "You don't want their pride?"

"Sure, but not until I know I'm proud of myself." Angling his body, Steve dug in his pocket and pulled out the proper amount of deutsche marks. "You don't want to hear this, and they're going to throw us out of here."

Jack rose carefully in the small space. No, he didn't want to hear any more of Steve's conclusions, didn't want to get personal. He thought of Angie, her question about friends. Did he need them?

Did he need to hear the truth according to Steve?

Without another word, Steve followed suit and walked inside to pay the bill. They left the *Schloss* and walked to their hotel in silence, but Jack didn't notice the quiet until he found himself alone in his room with memories he'd rather forget. Memories of Bryan at seventeen, of himself at ten, of lives mangled by a freak accident.

10

It's no big deal, bro.

It had been a big deal to ten-year-old Jack as he'd run into Bryan's room and seen the beer in his hand—not the first of the day, if the empty bottles meant anything—and the bottle of prescription pain-killers Bryan held. He'd come in to see if his brother was ready to go to Jack's championship playoff game. He looked from the beer to the pills and knew that Bryan wouldn't make it, that he'd be out for the count before the game ever started.

"Don't do it, Bryan," Jack had said, angered by what his brother was doing. "You can't mix—"

"It's my life, Jack. I need this."

"Why?"

Bryan tipped his head back, stared at the ceiling while he swallowed. "So I can get through what's left of my fucking life."

Jack might have only been ten at the time, but he felt responsible for Bryan, responsible for helping him to go on. He wanted to make it better. "You have to try, Bryan. Your hand will heal, and they'll let you into Annapolis after all. You'll see."

Bryan squeezed his eyes shut as he flexed his hand. Jack watched the movement and winced at the memory of what had happened to Bryan eight months before, saw it all as if it had happened to him. In a way it had. He'd been there, urging Bryan to hurry so they wouldn't be late for the Bronco game. The tickets were too rare to waste.

But they'd had a flat tire and Bryan tried to hurry. The jack hadn't held, and the weight of the car had shattered Bryan's hand, destroyed nerves. The wheel completely severed one of his fingers, and it still wobbled as if nothing connected it to him but skin.

Jack ran for help, two miles to Castle Rock, but not fast enough. Bryan had passed out by the side of the road, and no one stopped to help. The finger had been without blood too long.

Bryan had told Jack that running didn't matter. It was all over, his dreams, his plans. He'd never fly a plane. He'd be lucky if he could manage a chin-up unless he did it one-handed.

At the time Jack hadn't understood. Real life was about things that could be fixed—by their parents, by doctors, and by teachers. But as he stood there in Bryan's room eight months later he saw the destruction and hopelessness that life parceled out with prime seats at a Bronco game and once-in-a-lifetime opportunities. He saw pain as more than a skinned knee or a missed fly ball. He saw it, but didn't know how to deal with it. He heard the misery in Bryan's voice but didn't know what to say to make it better, so he repeated himself, "You'll see, Bryan. It has to be all right."

Opening his eyes, Bryan looked down at his hand. "Sorry, short round," he said softly. "You'll have to find another hero. Shut the door on your way out."

Bryan wouldn't be going to the game. That more than anything else shattered Jack's control. He clenched his fists against the anger, but it wasn't enough. "You're chicken, Bryan," he shouted as he backed toward the door. "All you do is lay around and snivel, like—like a *girl.*"

Bryan didn't look up from the bottle of pills in his hand. "You'll be late for your game," he said, then sighed and glanced up when Jack didn't move. "It'll be okay, bro. It's only pain. Don't tell the folks. They'd worry and drive me around the bend."

"I won't tell, but—"

"Don't mess with my head, Jack! Everybody's always messing with me." Bryan tossed two more pills into his mouth, emptied his beer, and threw the bottle across the room.

Jack backed out the door and ran all the way to the park where his teammates were getting ready for the biggest baseball game of the year. He'd had to play that day. He couldn't let anyone down.

He couldn't rat on his brother. As usual, he thought sourly, he was in the middle.

His team won, and there had been a party for the team and their parents afterward. Bryan was sprawled out on his bed when they arrived home. Only Jack noticed that his eyes were open.

But still he didn't tell. He'd promised not to tell, just as he'd promised his teammates that he'd show for the game. Besides, Bryan lay on his bed a lot, staring at the ceiling. Nothing weird about that. What was to tell?

Jack found the note Bryan left tucked beneath his pillow, just as he'd found other notes from the brother he idolized, giving advice, relating a dirty joke, telling him of a party or game. Too busy accepting the successes and glories that he'd taken for granted, Bryan was seldom home, yet to Jack, he was always *there*.

Jack slid the note out from under the pillow and thought that everything was fine. Nothing had changed. He unfolded the sheet of paper and a shiver started at the top of his skull and moved down his body. He read the note slowly, unaware that he was shaking his head, unaware that he was crying. It wasn't like other notes Bryan had written, but a note from someone he didn't know at all, a stranger.

Dear Jack—

Sorry to check out on you like this, bro, but it's the only thing I want to do now. Guess you're right. I am a chicken. Tell the folks I'm sorry.

I know you and Steve will keep them too busy to think about me for long. Give the little rugrat a kiss for me. He's not so bad when he's asleep.

I'm counting on you to make good, make the folks proud of you. I screwed up, but you won't. Do me a favor and let someone else change your flat tires.

—Bryan

P.S. It's okay for you to tell, now.

He sat up, read it again as he walked, then ran, to the door connecting his room to Bryan's.

The distance seemed to grow with every step he took, but he finally made it through. Pausing inside Bryan's room, Jack stared at the bed, at Bryan's eyes still fixed on the ceiling, at Bryan's chest moving beneath his T-shirt.

He watched Bryan breathe, watched him stare, and told himself that it was a joke and Bryan was getting even with him for hassling him over the pain-killers and beer. Hadn't Bryan taught him all about practical jokes?

In the morning, Bryan would wake up with a headache, and Jack would yell at him for scaring him like that. Bryan would groan and throw his pillow at Jack to shut him up. He'd probably even barf, Jack thought with satisfaction as he returned to his own room, leaving the door open so he could watch Bryan breathe. Seeing Bryan puke his guts out and hold his head as if it would crack at the next noise was all the revenge Jack would need.

Jack decided that he wouldn't tell. The parents would never know, and Jack could get some mileage out of the secret, like Bryan taking him to the next Bronco game.

But Bryan didn't wake up, and he didn't barf or throw his pillow at Jack. At ten the next morning, he was still staring at the ceiling, and Jack knew that the connection between him and his brother no longer existed, even though the door was still open.

Somehow he knew that it was too late. Maybe it had been too late when he hadn't run fast enough for help, when he'd yelled at Bryan and called him a chicken, when he'd decided to keep the note a secret, even though the doctors said it had been too late before they'd come home from the game the evening before.

He heard the sirens then, and his father's voice directing someone into Bryan's room. Someone pulled the connecting door shut, closing Jack into his own little world where all he could do was lie on his bed and listen to his mother's cries.

Still, he didn't tell. And the next day, he demolished the tree house he and Bryan had built.

Bryan wouldn't care. For all intents and purposes, he was gone, his heart and soul trapped in a decaying shell as he lay comatose in a nursing home for five years.

Jack wandered around his hotel room, a room as impersonal as his quarters on base. The mirror hanging above an old dresser stopped him, held him fascinated as he stared at the image of himself. In that image he saw the Caldwell features, so consistent from generation to generation. He saw parts of Bryan at seventeen, parts of Steve as he was today.

He leaned closer, searching for his individuality. Steve had fine lines radiating out from his eyes, etched by smiles and burned in by working outside. Steve had creases alongside his mouth that deepened with frequent laughter. Steve's face changed from one emotion to the next, displaying the essence of the person he was.

Jack searched for those same qualities in his own face and found little resemblance beyond structure and coloring. The only lines he had were carved across his forehead —no smile lines, no creases etched by laughter, only the marks of stress. There were twin furrows between his eyes, engraved by concentration and serious thoughts. Only his face, legs, and part of his arms were tanned from his daily jog around the track, while Steve's skin was a deep all over tan. And though he was older than Steve, Jack looked younger, less touched by life.

Maybe because Steve had lived more.

The thought came out of nowhere. So did the twinge of resentment and envy.

Not for Steve. It couldn't be.

He leaned closer to the mirror, focused on his eyes.

Steve's were a lighter shade of blue, and they had a shine to them, a depth that reflected an innate curiosity, the ability to see life in three dimensions. Jack's seemed dark and empty in comparison.

Empty, like Bryan's eyes, as he'd stared at a blank ceiling year after year.

He turned his back on the mirror, but the memory stayed with him, dogging him as he stretched out on the bed and folded his arms behind his head. He stared at the ceiling and remembered how long it had taken for Bryan to be free from the artificial life he was forced to live, remembered that last day and how he'd been the last to go into Bryan's hospital room, the only member of the family who could bear to wait and watch for the end.

He'd been fifteen that day—just a kid in high school, yet he'd felt old and beat-up inside.

He'd felt cheated and betrayed.

The hospital room was almost bare of life with its white walls and white sheets and white blinds on the window—a place of defeat and hopelessness. Bryan lay still beneath the sheet, his body curled into itself as if that were the only way to keep his soul from drifting away.

Machines perched like scavengers on tables and stands, their talons curved toward Bryan, sinking into his skin to monitor the signs of life, to screech when it was over. This was what hell was like, a place devoid of color and texture, a place of ceaseless waiting and an existence that couldn't recognize itself.

How many times in the last five years had Jack stood by Bryan's bed, watched him, and howled inside where no one else would hear? He'd wondered why his parents wouldn't let Bryan go. He'd wondered if God was so mad at Bryan that he wouldn't take him. He'd wondered if God was mad at him and that was why he had to see his brother like this and remember that he hadn't told when it might have done some good. And he'd yelled at Bryan, daring him to wake up. He'd sat at the bedside and cried because Bryan was in hell and Jack didn't know how to pull him out. Once he'd even reached for the controls of the machines, so tempted to switch them off that he had howled out loud and the nurse had led him away.

After that he'd stopped coming to the hospital so often. He told himself it was because he was too busy "making good." Because he was keeping Bryan alive in another way that he could control.

Because his parents were proud as hell of him, and they were becoming a family again.

Jack stood there feeling the labored beat of his heart, the breaths that he forced, living and breathing for his brother as well as himself. And he closed his eyes as he prayed, because even now, he hoped for a second chance for both of them, a miracle.

But he knew that Bryan wasn't going to suddenly sit up and take on responsibility for what he'd done. He'd copped out, left Jack to do what was best for everyone in the family. Somehow, Jack knew that he had to keep quiet, make sure that the truth would never come out. Somehow, he thought it would be easier if their parents could go on believing it had been an accident of youthful bad judgment.

He heard the final hiss of the respirator as they disconnected it, saw Bryan's head turn slightly as he was freed from the bondage of tubes and chemicals. Jack stared at the monitor, watching the last of Bryan's life become a thin, flat line, and then blackness as the last claw was removed from Bryan's body.

"It's done," a voice said in the silence of the room.

Jack nodded and said good-bye to his brother, his hero. He'd thought Bryan was larger than life, but he'd been wrong.

Bryan had pretended to be a winner, just as he'd pretended to be alive for the last five years.

Just as Jack had pretended to hope.

Jack held his body rigid as the nurses and doctors left the room, wheeling their machines away. Squeezing his eyes closed, he bent his head, clenched his hands over the side rail of the bed to keep from smashing everything in the room. He clamped his lips shut to keep from shouting at Bryan for not fighting, at his parents for hoping, for keeping Bryan in hell, at himself because all he could do was thank God that it was over. It *was* over, Jack thought as his eyes drifted shut and sleep blacked out the memories.

It happened over and over again—a few minutes of dozing, then a jerk of his body waking him up, making him think about second chances and a brother who had life written all over his face. A brother who should be a stranger, yet seemed to know him better than he knew himself.

A hell of a way to spend a vacation.

A pile of sacks on the desk caught his eye. He rolled to his side and rose from the bed. One was filled with souvenirs for his parents, another with postcards, and the third with the items he'd bought for Angie.

Angie. A friend. Someone who didn't care about how many laugh lines he had or even whether he was real or not. In a way, he supposed that to her, he wasn't real beyond the words he put to paper. She wasn't quite real to him, either. Maybe that was the attraction. Maybe because they didn't seem like flesh and blood to one another, the growing friendship seemed more real.

More comfortable, less threatening. Illusions usually were.

The thought chilled him. Abruptly, he shook it off and sat down at the desk.

Dear Angie—

I'm in Meersburg on Lake Constance and met up with my brother this morning. We'll spend a week bumming around if we don't kill each other first. He's different, older, and full of the kind of wisdom that comes from almost dying and having too much down-time to think about it.

Germany is an enlightened country, as you can see from the picture on the front of this card. The statue is of a woman who was revered for her poetry a couple of centuries ago. They even gave her a suite in the castle. Looks like women's lib happened here before we knew what it was about.

More later.

Jack

He didn't know what to do with himself.

Jack rubbed his eyes and stared blankly at the postcard, the words running together, making nonsense to his tired mind. A stack of finished cards lay on the desk, cards to his parents, his aunt, a cousin, even to Lieutenant Baker and the various clerks at the office who worked with him.

Postcards. God, he was desperate.

The sun was just coming up, washing the horizon with pastel hues of pink, lavender, and gold. He'd been sitting in the same position for hours, writing postcards, reading guide books—anything to keep his mind off himself and the isolation of a moonless night and sleeping world.

Like a coward, he'd avoided Steve since they'd arrived at the hotel and stood a few feet apart, unlocking the doors to their respective rooms. They had stood there after the doors were opened, both reluctant to walk in, to shut themselves in separate worlds. How Jack knew that, he wasn't sure. It seemed like a bond of mutual feeling, a connection where there hadn't been one before.

He'd forgotten how to reach out in twenty-five years.

Muttering under his breath, he grabbed a sweater and pulled it over his head as he left his room and headed for the promenade that rimmed the lake.

Across the water, the Swiss Alps were crowned with a glittering crust of snow. Behind him, the village was splashed with the color of early spring flowers in tiny courtyards and vividly painted window boxes. Water lapped below him, harmonizing with the gentle ripple of waves in the morning breeze.

Just ahead, a man stood, his hands clenched around the railing, his head bent, his legs braced wide apart, as if he weren't strong enough to support his thoughts. In the dawn light, he was a shadow, indistinct, yet Jack knew him, saw the burden of his own thoughts in the bowed body. He paused, unsure of whether to go on or retreat, avoid confrontation or invite it.

His feet moved. He rested his elbows on the rail, his hands clasped as he focused on a sailboat rocking idly in the lake.

Steve said nothing, did nothing to acknowledge his presence.

"When did you grow up?" Jack asked.

Steve shrugged. "Maybe I haven't."

"What's going on, Steve?"

"Is that a rhetorical question?"

Was it? Jack wondered. "I don't know. Maybe."

"Then I can't answer you."

Could anyone? Jack's mouth twisted in a parody of a smile, bitter and melancholy. They were brothers who wanted to *be* brothers. That much he knew after yesterday. They'd talked more, *said* more, than in the last twenty-five years put together. Maybe it was enough to start with. Maybe—if one of them was willing to take the next step. It was his move. He said the first thing that came to mind, the first thing that came to mind a lot lately.

"Know what I did?" His smile relaxed as he heard himself sounding like a boy inviting secrets by offering one of his own. A boy of ten, before his life had somehow become that of another.

Steve angled his head to look at him. "You took a vacation."

"From sanity. I have a pen pal." He paused, feeling stupid, feeling heat climb up his neck and into his face. "I got a letter last Christmas through Link. From this girl—woman—in Colorado Springs. I still don't know why I answered it."

Steve sighed. "I answered a few of those myself while I was in the Gulf. It's called loneliness."

"Yeah."

"Yeah."

They straightened at the same time and walked toward the village.

Jack felt Steve's hand cup his shoulder and squeeze, just once, then fall away. "I need some sleep," he said.

A small smile creased Steve's cheeks, deepened the lines around his eyes. "Me, too. This male bonding crap is hard work."

"Yeah."

11

*D*enver

The restaurant walls were covered with old posters, pictures of movie stars, and other memorabilia. The dining area was divided into several nooks and levels, giving it an intimate atmosphere. The late lunch crowd talked about business, sports, and social plans, their tables filled with plates of everything from quiche to hamburgers and large cups of cappuccino.

Gena stretched out her legs on the seat of the booth and leaned her head back to study a photo of Marilyn Monroe.

"So when is the big day?" Gena asked as she watched Angie cut into a slice of cake.

"What big day?" A drop of chocolate syrup dribbled at the corner of her mouth. Angie wiped it off, then licked her finger.

"Charlotte is coming home."

"How did you know?"

"You've gained five pounds and you're eating a whole piece of that cake instead of sharing it with me. I'm surprised you haven't hauled out more than one crutch."

"Thanks, Gena, for making me sound like such a wuss."

"Angie, you're twenty-seven. You make a good living for yourself. Charlotte finally has a life of her own. What is your problem?"

"Mother is arriving today, at Stapleton."

Raising a hand, Gena beckoned for their waiter. "Wine," she ordered. "One glass. Chardonnay." As the young man left, she glared at Angie. "So that's why you invited me to come to Denver for lunch. *I'm* your other crutch."

"Only for a couple of hours," Angie said with forced lightness. "Besides, you haven't seen Ben's house."

"Angie, it's not high on my list."

"Wait till you see it. He designed it himself."

"Right. And it's in Gennessee, which means we go to Stapleton, then drive to the foothills, then drive all the way back to the Springs. Just what I needed to do for relaxation." She grabbed the glass of wine right from the waiter's hand and took a gulp. "Okay. Tell me. You're having anxiety attacks again?"

Angie lowered her head. "Not really. Not bad, anyway. A twinge now and then."

"What are you afraid of? She can't make you do anything you don't want to do."

"She doesn't have to. I've always made myself do it—for her. It was easy when Mother was gone, but now . . ." Angie finished off her cappuccino and felt the familiar beginnings of panic, the surge of anxiety, the clench of her insides as if they were curling up in self-defense. "It's a hard habit to break." Her hands shook, and she lowered them to her lap as she breathed in through her nose, held it, then let it out through her mouth. Thankfully, the moment passed.

"I never understood, you know, always thought it was neurotic," Gena said.

"I know. Most people do." Angie laughed, a short, self-deprecating sound that grated on her nerves. "In spite of what the doctors and the therapists and countless books on the subject say, I'm still not entirely convinced."

Gena swung her feet off the bench and leaned forward. "Angie, those doctors say that I'm healthy and have all the right pulse points and erogenous zones, but look at me. It's buried deep, you know? It takes a lot of hard work to dig problems like that out. Believe me, I'll never shrug off your little bouts of anxiety again."

"They don't seem so little."

"Sweetcakes, I used to have to carry a brown paper bag around to get your breathing back to normal. A minute ago, I watched you beat it down in sixty seconds. I'd say you've come a long way."

Was it true? Angie wondered. It didn't seem that way in the wake of losing control, even for sixty seconds. It seemed weak and stupid and neurotic. Yet she'd been dismissed from therapy with the advice to find a better way to spend her money. A clean bill of mental health. Was there such a thing?

"Sometimes, it seems that the farther I go, the longer the road gets, but thanks, Gena—" She focused on Gena, her smile fading before it began. Gena's eyes were distant, her expression lost. It wasn't the first time. "Mike?"

"Took a hike."

"But last night—"

"Last night, he told me all about the lady doctor he met in Saudi and how he realized what love was all about. I got the classic line about how we could be friends and he loved me but he wasn't 'in' love with me." Tilting her glass, Gena swirled the remaining liquid around and around. "I'm sure in time I'll be grateful. Who needs a man who only wants a pair of boobs and a—"

Angie reached over to take the glass from Gena, set it down, stilled Gena's hands with her own. "I don't think that's all Mike wanted."

"No? Well, my mind and sparkling personality sure as hell weren't enough for him—and don't you dare give me any sympathy, or advice," Gena said fiercely, then whispered, "Just someone, for once in my life, please tell me what to do."

"Pay the bill, so we can get out of here."

Gena's head jerked up. "You sound like my shrink."

"You're seeing one?"

Fumbling in her purse, Gena pulled out some bills and laid them on the tray the waiter had left on the table. "Yours. She's good."

Angie said nothing until they reached her car, a candy-apple red Cadillac complete with tail fins. As she fastened her seat belt, she glanced over at Gena. "But?"

Blond hair fell over Gena's face as she leaned forward to put her purse on the floor. "Dammit, Angie, if I can't talk about it with you, how am I supposed to talk about it with her?"

"That's the easy part," Angie said, remembering all too

well the process of denial, the giving in to fear. "I'm not sure that telling me or Mike or Dr. Landon is what's important." She paused to organize her thoughts, the insight that had been vague until now. "Talking about it with yourself, admitting it, is when you really begin to sort it out."

"I know what the problem is. I know why and how and when."

As she turned the key in the ignition and shifted to drive, Angie stared straight ahead, seeing more than she had in a long time. "Yes, but have you ever asked yourself what is the worst thing that can happen if you do what comes naturally instead of fighting it?"

"Fight the past? How do you fight something that isn't here to fight back?"

"It's here, Gena, always, until you can put it in a box and tuck it in the attic. Even then it's with you, influencing you because it made you what you are."

Gena didn't answer but turned her head to look out the window as Angie negotiated the Hampden Avenue traffic, then later the more hectic snarl of cars and buses and taxis on Stapleton Drive. The closer they came to the airport, the more her own thoughts jammed up. Denial was such a convenient form of self-deception.

Evidently Gena had come to the same conclusion as they sat in one of the "watering holes" scattered in the airport, drinking cola while waiting for Charlotte's and Ben's delayed flight.

"So have you heard from the mystery major lately?"

"You make him sound like something growing mold in the back of my refrigerator." The corners of Angie's mouth turned up. "A letter two weeks ago. He's on leave—touring with his brother."

"You're hung up on him."

"I like him. He's a friend, just like all the others are friends," Angie said firmly, though she couldn't quite look Gena in the eye. She had come to terms with having a degree of friendship with Jack that she had neither wanted, invited, nor welcomed with her other pen pals. It was okay, she'd told herself over and over again, because he was half

a world away, a fantasy that would never become solid or
real.

He seemed frighteningly real at night and at odd moments during the day when a simple thought of him
brought hot flashes of sensation, awareness of her femininity, graphic dreams that were more appropriate to adolescents.

"Has your 'friend' told you anything interesting about
himself?"

Angie ran the tip of her forefinger around the rim of her
plastic glass. "He's from the Springs, and his parents travel
a lot in a motor home. He has a brother who flew bombers
off a carrier."

Gena cupped her chin in her hands. "Fascinating," she
said in a droll voice.

For some reason, Angie took offense. "He's lonely,
Gena."

"Isn't everyone, in one way or another?"

"Yes. But it's more with him. In spite of his family, I
think he feels cut off." She shook her head. "I get the
feeling that he just woke up and doesn't recognize the
world around him. It's stupid, I know—"

"Great! You've hooked up with Rip Van Winkle. Does
he have a long white beard?"

"I don't know what he looks like."

"Why not? You usually exchange pictures with your pen
pals."

"Not this time."

"Uh-huh. It wouldn't do to disturb our fantasies."

Angie glanced up from her study of the ice chips melting
in her Coke. "No, it wouldn't," she said softly.

Gena opened her mouth, then closed it again as an arriving flight was announced.

Smiling ruefully, Angie stood up and smoothed her skirt,
straightened her collar, ran a hand over her hair. "That's
us. I guess we should go."

"Don't they have to go through customs?" Gena asked
as they walked down the concourse.

"No. They stopped in California."

"Angie!"

The voice stopped Angie in her tracks. The past she'd been thinking about suddenly changed from abstract to real. She wanted to hunch her shoulders, crawl inside herself, pretend again that she was someone else, something else.

Just as she focused on her mother, she was enveloped in silk and perfume and spray-stiffened hair. The hug lasted longer than usual, seemed tighter, and she could swear that she heard a sob.

"It's so good to see you, darling," Charlotte said as she released her and stepped back to give her a critical once-over.

Gena stepped between them, effectively cutting off Charlotte's inspection and kissed her cheek. "Welcome home, Charlotte."

Ben Patterson, wearing khaki shorts and a Disneyland T-shirt on his tall frame, stepped forward, towering over Angie. His head was completely bald and shiny enough to cast a glare. The cut of his face was patrician and solemn, except for the twinkle that never left his bright blue eyes. He opened his arms to Angie as if he'd been doing it forever.

Shyly, she took the step toward him and stood on tiptoe to kiss his cheek. He gave her a quick hug and let her go, as if he knew how uncomfortable she felt. "How's Gypsy Rose handling?" he whispered so his wife wouldn't hear.

Angie glanced down at the floor, took in his pump action Nikes, and smiled. Gypsy Rose was the name he had given her car. He named all of his own cars, just as Angie had named her computer.

"He's wonderful—until I have to parallel park," she said.

"He?"

"Angie decided that the car was just too brawny to be a she," Gena said loudly. "And he's too impractical to be a woman."

They were walking down the concourse, and Angie was

swept along without knowing when or how they'd left the crush of passengers on the jetway.

"So what's his name?" Ben asked with a lift of his brows.

Angie blushed.

"Dracula," Gena announced. "For the way he sucks up premium."

"It's ridiculous the way you name everything," Charlotte said, but with a smile that startled Angie.

"Angela, if you'd rather have something more economical, I can arrange it," Ben said.

"Don't you dare," Angie interrupted, surprising herself. Maybe it was her mother's smile. Maybe it was Ben's placid expression that instantly soothed and said that it was okay for her to express an opinion. "I love that car."

"Mmm. It makes her feel powerful, gives her an edge over the other drivers on the road," Gena offered.

"Angie, you don't speed or anything—"

"No, Mother. I just like having all that steel around me."

"And," Gena added, "she likes all the flash and flamboyance."

Angie shot her friend a warning glare. Why hadn't she remembered how Gena liked to jerk Charlotte's chain? "It's getting so I can't take you anywhere," she muttered.

Gena widened her eyes in feigned innocence.

Ben winked at her. "Um, Angela, I know you and Gena were planning on taking us up to the house, but your mother is worn out, and I just wouldn't feel right carrying her over the threshold with you girls looking on. What say we take a rain check?"

"Now there's a hint that's broader than a barn," Gena said happily.

"But how will you get home?" Angie asked.

Gena jabbed her with an elbow and whispered, "Don't look a gift horse in the mouth."

"I called for a limousine from the plane." Again Ben winked.

Those winks were like Morse code, Angie thought. A code that she seemed to understand. Her mother didn't look tired at all, and Angie was reasonably sure that, after their long honeymoon, Ben wasn't dying of unfulfilled passion for his new wife.

The idea stunned her, stopped her cold in the middle of the concourse. Passion? Her mother and Ben? It hadn't occurred to her until now.

"First, let's stop in here and have a drink," Ben said, taking Charlotte's elbow in one hand and Angie's in the other, leaving Gena to bring up the rear as he guided them into a restaurant.

"Great idea. I'll have white wine," Gena said.

After seating first Charlotte, then Angie and Gena, Ben stood in the aisle. "Angela?"

He'd always called her Angela, the only person to do so, and it made her feel as if he saw something in her that no one else did. Like a woman who would enjoy wearing a grown-up dress. "I'll have a Coke, please."

"Make that diet, Ben," Charlotte said. "Angie looks as if she's putting on weight. I'll have coffee."

"Angela?"

"A regular Coke, Ben," Angie said, wondering where the defiance had come from.

Before Charlotte could argue, Ben walked up to the bar to give the order.

"Have you given up dancing altogether, Angie?"

"No, Mother. I practice every morning."

"She looks good, Charlotte, and as long as she can fit into that spectacular dress Ben sent her from Paris, why worry?"

Angie kicked Gena under the table. She had a feeling her mother didn't know—

"What dress?" Charlotte looked up as Ben slid into the banquette beside her. "You sent her a dress? From Paris?"

"Just an LBD, as my daughter would call it," Ben said cheerfully. "According to her, no girl should be without one."

"A *what*?"

"A Little Black Dress, Charlotte," Gena supplied. "And she's right. They're even wearing them to proms nowadays."

"Ben, you're spoiling her."

Angie wanted to slide beneath the table. They were all talking around her as if she were too young to speak for herself, as if she couldn't possibly have an opinion. As she tore the top off the wrapper on her straw, she had an urge to blow it off as she'd seen teenagers do.

"Daughters are meant to be spoiled," Ben said. "Especially by new stepfathers trying to make points. Do you like the dress, Angela?" he asked.

She put the exposed tip of the straw to her lips and blew, watching with interest as the wrapper sailed past Gena's ear. "It's beautiful. And yes, I love it, though I don't know when I'll have a chance to wear it." *Or the guts.*

"What about the social life you kept telling me about?" Charlotte asked in a weary voice as if she'd known all along that Angie had just been paying her lip service.

"She'll have the chance soon enough, Ben. Then she'll wear it, and I'll take pictures," Gena cut in. "She's saving it for a special occasion, aren't you, Angie?"

Angie had to think about it, so she sipped Coke through her straw, her eyes widening to discover that it was not diet. "Yes, I'm saving it for a special occasion, and yes, I'll definitely wear it."

"Ben, not the dress we saw in that little boutique—the one that I wanted to send to . . . ?"

"That's the one, honey. It wasn't made for Cara. She's straight as a stick. That dress had Angela's name written all over it, so I switched the boxes and sent Cara the frilly one."

"How can you say such a thing about your own daughter?"

"The same way you can tell yours that she's gaining weight, Charlotte." Ben took a sip of his coffee, ignoring the deadly look his wife shot him. "Don't get me wrong. My daughter is beautiful and classy, but she likes a little more frou-frou on her clothes to fill her out."

A crease deepened between Charlotte's brows. "I hadn't noticed."

"That's because she wears her clothes and not the other way around."

"Angie, I'm sure Ben's feelings won't be hurt if you don't want to wear the dress."

"All this shit for a dress?" Gena mumbled.

"I most certainly will wear it, Mother. Ben has excellent taste."

Clicking her tongue, Charlotte signaled her annoyance, and her defeat.

Angie stared at her mother, bemused by the easy surrender. Charlotte met her gaze for a moment, then, her face flushing, looked down at her hands, as if she were embarrassed.

How odd.

"How was the honeymoon?" Gena asked.

"Best wedding present I ever had," Ben said, his arm around his wife, his hand caressing her shoulder.

Angie had noticed that a lot—the touching, the flare in her mother's eyes as she looked often at her husband.

"It was, Gena." Charlotte's eyes softened, and her flush deepened. "Thank you so much."

"My pleasure." Holding up her glass, Gena clicked it against Ben's, then Charlotte's coffee cups. "May it never end."

Ben cleared his throat and stood. "On that note, I think it's time I carried you over that threshold, Charlotte. The limousine awaits." With Old World courtesy, he helped his wife rise from the banquette and bowed to Angie and Gena. "We'll see you girls next time we come up for air." He leaned over and quickly planted a dry kiss on Angie's cheek before hustling his flustered wife out of the restaurant.

Angie exhaled and felt as if a weight had been lifted off her chest.

"That man is incredible," Gena said.

"Yes," Angie said, distracted. Incredible that he had accepted her as a daughter so easily. Incredible that he seemed to know her so well, as well as if he'd raised her himself. Incredible that with a few calmly spoken words, he could silence her mother when shouting and accusations and condemnations hadn't worked for the general.

Still, it felt strange to be the object of such open and harmless affection from a man who had been a relative stranger until two years ago.

"Did you notice that Charlotte was less vocal than usual?" Gena asked.

"Yes."

"Ben really turns her on. Funny. Have you ever thought of your parents as being sexual?"

"No. Are you finished, Gena? We should start back."

"Sure."

They left the restaurant, then the airport, and made the long journey through the parking facility to Angie's car.

"Come on, Angie. Charlotte's fifty years old—not exactly over the hill. Obviously she loves Ben. You didn't think they played Tiddly Winks in bed, did you?" Gena said as Angie turned onto the freeway.

"I guess I didn't think about it at all."

"Maybe because you don't think about sex at all."

Smiling mirthlessly, Angie switched lanes to pass an eighteen wheeler. The older she became, the more she thought about sex, until she wondered which would be worse: dying of frustration if she didn't, or dying of mortification if she did and then didn't get it right.

"Does it bother you—knowing your mom and Ben do the 'wild thing'?"

Angie thought about that, too. "No, not really. It just surprises me that she's really in love."

"I can't believe all you got was one remark about the weight you've gained, and no remarks about your life."

"Ben didn't give her much of a chance."

"Since when has that stopped her?"

"Since Ben. She really does love him, doesn't she?"

"Obviously. And he's nuts about her. He'll keep her busy, chum. Too busy to worry about you."

At Gena's observation, it struck Angie that she truly was free, that a crutch had fallen away. She could no longer count on her mother to make her choices for her, give her the easy way out.

From now on, she was on her own—for real.

She didn't know whether to be relieved or scared.

She did know that if Ben Patterson had wanted to score points with her, he'd surely succeeded.

12

*D*ear Jack,

I just received your postcard. How wonderful that you're soaking up the atmosphere. Never mind the brooding passions, etc. I suspect that's an impression I got from listening to Wagner and has no basis in fact anywhere in the world. Please tell me more about your travels, assuming of course that you and your brother have refrained from killing one another. You describe everything so eloquently, and shame me in my efforts to write "sweet everythings"—that's my trade name—for my greeting cards. (I'm supplying fourteen shops—not a living, but an encouraging start!)

How is your brother? You didn't say what had happened to him. Was he wounded? I'd heard that some of the injured were air-evacuated to Germany. I hope he's all right now.

I can't help but wonder at your not getting along with him. I know it happens, since Gena and her four brothers constantly bicker, but it's also obvious they love and watch out for one another. What I wouldn't have given to have a sibling.

Gena and I drove to Denver today to meet Mother and Ben. They might be home, but the honeymoon is definitely not over. Suddenly, I look at my mother and don't see my mother. Suddenly, she's Ben Patterson's wife, a new bride complete with flushed cheeks and secret looks at her husband, and I'm not at all sure about my place in it all.

Ben seems to have no such doubts. I'm trying to adjust to the realization that he has—when I wasn't looking—become the father figure in my life. It's awfully sad to know that he is more interested in me than the general. I can't help but wonder what I've done—

That's strange, too—having Ben accept me so readily as

his daughter, to know that he wants to, rather than having no other choice. I've been thinking about choices a lot lately. They open up a whole new world of problems, don't they? What on earth do we do with the ones we don't understand?

I've been staring at Don Quixote for twelve hours, and frankly, I'm sick to death of him. Our honeymoon is definitely over!

Angie

P.S. I can't wait to see the photographs you've taken!

Dear Angie,

Steve and I managed to restrain ourselves. In fact, he's still here, exploring Europe and showing up on my doorstep every now and then to disrupt my life. He's bored with convalescence and needs me to be his current challenge. I can't figure out what that means.

Last night we went to this restaurant that used to be an old monastery. The dining room is in the cellar, and we were served on wooden trenchers by costumed staff—all very medieval. We ate pork and dumplings and red cabbage and drank honey wine brewed on the premises. They gave us daggers instead of forks and told us the highest compliment we could give the chef was a loud belch. Like the crass teenager he thinks he is, Steve complied. Everyone applauded.

No, Steve wasn't wounded. His appendix ruptured while he was on his way to pay me a surprise visit. No Purple Heart for him.

Maybe your stepfather can see more of you than your folks because to him, you're brand-new—no emotional clutter obstructing the view. We should all be so lucky. I know that my folks see in me only what they expect to see—wisdom according to Steve.

We all have mirrors of one kind or another, and we see the emotional clutter in our own faces.

Funny you should mention choices. There's going to be a major cutback (no secret there—I know it's been in all the papers back home), and I find myself wondering what I'm

going to do. The Reduction in Force probably won't affect
me, and I won't have to worry about doing anything except
my job, but something is changing—me or the job, I don't
know which, and I feel displaced. It's crazy for me to consider leaving the service when I can retire in a few years.
How many men can do that by the time they're forty? Still,
whatever had me fired up about this particular career so
many years ago just isn't there anymore. The job bores the
hell out of me, and I'm restless. Could be I'm just going
through a premature midlife crisis.

Steve would call it a second chance.

I guess that I should be considering it, just in case. The
service is top-heavy, and you never know who might get cut.
That's just an excuse. I can't help thinking about cutting
the cord and striking out on my own regardless of what the
service decides. It'll pass, I'm sure. Who's crazy enough to
throw away a life? I wish I knew exactly what I'm trying to
convince myself of.

It's time to convince Steve to go home. He's big on
choices, and I wouldn't know one if it came up and intro-
duced itself. He keeps saying I should "find myself." That's
all well and good for hippies and people who know at
which point they became lost.

I need to get lost in some sleep. That honey wine has
more staying power than straight Scotch.

                                                            Jack

P.S. Photographs are on the way.

Dear Jack,
    Your package finally arrived yesterday! I love the calen-
dar with the days marked in German. At the end of the
year, I think I'll frame the postcards. What a beautiful place
Rothenburg is. And thank you for marking the pages in the
guide books to show where you'd been. Most of all, I love
the photographs. They're not just shots snapped by a tourist, but works of art taken by a professional. Why didn't you
tell me what a gift you have? Later, I want to discuss having enlargements made that I can frame.
    There's a certain amount of convenience in living vicari-

ously. You have to worry about counting out the right amount of money and being disillusioned by all the floral-shirted tourists, while I get to see the good parts. Still, it's not quite the same.

Your second postcard and latest letter just this minute arrived. Meersburg and Lake Constance are enchanting— so many flowers! It's almost like a village in a Walt Disney fairy-tale movie with all the pastel houses and stone walls and cobbled streets. I can almost hear the cuckoo clocks. We had one—given to my parents by a friend who had been stationed in Germany—but Mother took it with her to Ben's house. It was large, with little wooden people dressed in lederhosen (did I spell that right?) that slid out of the doors to dance while music played different tunes for the hour and half-hour.

Mother and Ben still haven't come up for air except to call and assure me that all is well. He has officially retired from his Cadillac dealership and installed a hot tub in an enclosed atrium in his home in Gennessee Park. Looks like he decided to bring Tahiti to the Rockies. I may never see him and Mother again. I don't think I took the idea of a new lease on life seriously until now. Don't ask me whether that applies to me or Mother and Ben. Maybe all of the above.

I'm not so naive that I don't realize that it will come to an end. Sooner or later, Mother is bound to decide I need her guidance. I cannot believe that honeymoons last for-ever.

This letter might, if I don't close. I have twenty new or-ders. I convinced several companies that they had to have cards specially designed for Christmas. Who would have thought I had it in me? Aggressive isn't really my style.

Thanks again for the "goody bag."

Angie

P.S. Have you ever speeded illegally—like when you were an irresponsible teenager? Did you ever belch in public just to be gross and obnoxious? Neither have I.

As for tossing away a life—I guess it depends on whether it's what you wanted in the first place or just a half-life.

Sometimes, it's hard to tell what was your choice and what wasn't. I can, as of last year, speak about this with authority. I chucked six years of work and twenty years of training on a whim and can't regret it no matter how much Mother tries to convince me I should. I have come to the conclusion that a half-life is not better than no life at all. Again, I speak metaphorically rather than literally.

If you need a second chance, I think you should take it.

A half-life.

Or no life at all.

Was Angie right? Jack wondered as he walked toward the gate to meet Steve. It beat the hell out of sitting in his room staring at the copperplate print of a tower room.

A room without corners, with everything in plain view. The safest place in a castle.

Once again, Angie had managed to touch his thoughts, share them.

The idea of chucking it all didn't strike him as being bizarre anymore. Suddenly, everywhere he turned, he saw corners, full of shadows and questions. Corners he could turn, not knowing what waited for him just out of sight.

Like a second chance.

Why was he taking Angie's letter so seriously? he wondered.

She was ages younger than he felt, too naive to be real, too insecure to be handing out wisdom as if she'd invented it. *"Aggressive isn't my style,"* she'd written. What a crock. She'd been aggressive enough in getting him to write to her. She was aggressive enough to run her own business.

But Angie wasn't his problem. She was simply a silent voice that made him feel better in some indefinable way. An illusion, like an imaginary friend, offering comfort and distraction when he needed them most. A fantasy, like heroes, that couldn't possibly live up to the image.

He kicked a rock and turned around to gaze at the base where so much of his life had changed. It was just another American military installation, just another assignment.

Yet here, the straight and narrow road he'd mapped out for his life had taken a series of hairpin turns and switchbacks.

This was where Kay had left him to struggle with a whole new set of questions—about his dreams, about the kind of man he was.

No matter how hard he tried, he couldn't dismiss what had happened that last night. He couldn't explain or excuse it. He couldn't seem to live with it, either. And deep down, where he'd fooled himself into believing he could bury anything, he knew that he didn't hate Kay for leaving him.

He hated her for letting him back her against a mirror, for forcing him to take a good look at himself.

Jamming his hands in his pockets, Jack watched a car pull up to the guard station with Steve behind the wheel. He stuck his head out the window. "Let's go, Jack," he called as he honked the horn.

Still holding Angie's letter, Jack nodded to the guard and strolled over to the car. "Where?"

Steve shrugged. "Around. See the city. I hear there's a *Fest* later."

Before he could think of an argument, Jack opened the passenger door and climbed in. Why not? It was Saturday, and he wasn't on duty again until Monday night.

"Nice car," he said, settling into deep leather seats. "A rental?"

"Nope. I bought it, ordered it months ago."

Inhaling the new car smell, Jack took in the instrument panel, all digital displays and dials and a stereo system that would make any kid drool all over the plush carpeting. It was a Mercedes, a car that he would forever associate with Gypsies and more than a year's pay.

"I'm heading home next week," Steve said.

"Back to the job?"

"Nope. I quit over a year ago."

"To do what?" Jack asked suspiciously. He'd never liked the risks inherent in Steve's job, never liked to think about the consequences of just one accident, one miscalculation. At the same time, he knew Steve, knew his brother's pursuit of risk and challenge. And Steve had earned more in one year than Jack made in three.

"Thought I'd turn wrenches."

"Just like that?" Jack shook his head. Steve had always been fascinated with mechanics, but he had no formal training. "Who's going to hire you with no experience?"

Steve's mouth quirked as if he'd recalled a private joke, shared only with himself. "No one. I bought a shop of my own."

"When?"

"Before I met you in Meersburg."

"You lost me."

"The guy Dad sold his garage to let the place go down the tubes. Dad repossessed, and I'm buying it from him."

"Steve, working in Dad's garage on weekends isn't the same—"

"I'm certified, Jack—went to school and everything." Steve shifted again, fussed with the gadgets on the dash, clearly impatient with having to explain himself. "I also hired an Ace mechanic. He's taking care of the place until I get back. I'll learn a lot from him."

Jack raked his hand through his hair, not understanding, even though Steve had anticipated and answered the pertinent questions. "Your Ace will have to be good."

Steve grinned. "Dad's the best there is."

"Dad?" Jack said sharply. "Dammit, Steve, he's retired."

Steve turned off the street that would take them into downtown Stuttgart and drove through a residential section. "Not everyone sees retirement as a relief, Jack. It was driving him and Mom crazy. Now Dad can work without the responsibility and pressure, and they can travel for vacations instead of as a way of life."

Swallowing, Jack stared out the window. They were discussing family. His family. Yet he hadn't known that Steve had learned a new trade or that their father wasn't happy in retirement. He hadn't known the little, everyday details.

Displaced. He knew just how Angie felt.

The garage had been their father's pride and joy, and

he'd hoped that Steve would want to take it over. But it hadn't happened that way, and Dad finally sold out.

Now, it seemed, life had come full circle for Steve, for their father.

"The folks didn't know you quit firefighting or that you went back to school, did they?"

Steve sighed. "Not until it was a done deal."

"What happened to not following in someone else's footsteps?"

Steve pulled off the road and stared out the windshield at a pasture filled with sheep on the fringe of the city. "I'm not doing this for Dad, Jack. It's what I want to do."

"Since when?"

"Since I discovered that I've been trying so hard to avoid being a victim of family tradition or family expectations or family guilt that I was making the same mistakes. Bryan was a coward, giving up because it was easier than starting over. You picked up where he left off, because you thought it was expected of you." His fingers tapped against the steering wheel. "I've had a hell of a good time, Jack, but no matter what road I took, I always found myself back where I started. I like wrenching. I don't care if Dad thinks I'm following in his footsteps. I don't care if you think I'm giving up. I just want to stop running in place."

Jack opened the car door and stepped out. With his hands in his pockets, his feet planted wide apart, he stood on the edge of the pasture watching the sheep, then swept his gaze over the surrounding buildings. More anachronisms. No one at home would think of pastures and vineyards in the middle of a large city.

Displaced. Somehow Steve, the renegade of the family, was more of a family member than he was. He heard the slam of a door, felt Steve's presence beside him.

"You're giving up and going on, Steve," he said quietly, wincing as if each word he uttered were a slap in his own face. "I can't argue with that. It makes too much sense."

"What about you?"

"I can retire in five years."

"Do you want to wait that long? Are *you* happy?"

"It's the life I wanted."

"It's the life Bryan wanted."

"I chose it."

"Did you?"

I'm counting on you to make good.

Steve held out his hand. "You dropped this when you got out of the car. Your pen pal? The woman back home?"

Jack took the letter, saw his footprint on the plain computer paper. It had been a while since she'd decorated her letters, used off-the-wall paper. He missed her funny doodles. "Yeah. I feel like an idiot."

"How long has it been going on?"

"Since Christmas." Since the night he'd begun to realize that he'd been running in circles for so long, he'd forgotten where he wanted to go.

"What's she like?"

"Crazy. Gutsy. Lonely. Creative. An optimist." Jack turned back toward the car. "She's a survivor."

"You going to look her up?"

"Hadn't thought about it."

"Want me to do it for you? Sort of a recon mission? That way if she doesn't match the fantasy—"

"No." Jack knew that Steve was joking, but it bothered him, put him on the defensive. He didn't want to lose the magic of having something private, wholly his. A person who knew only him, a man, an individual, rather than a mirror image of someone else.

Now all he had to do was figure out who "himself" was.

"Look over there," Steve said, pointing to a lone sheep wandering away from the herd. "A rebel."

"He'll get lost," Jack mumbled, his gaze straying back to the herd, the members huddled so close that they seemed to turn into one another, becoming a single entity, indistinguishable as separate beings.

Oh, God.

13

*D*ear Angie,

Steve is back in the States by now. As relieved as I was to see him go, I miss him. We've never been close, and I'm not sure if we are now, but at least we understand each other. Communication has never been one of my strong suits. It was uncomfortable talking to Steve, yet it felt good. I can't explain. It's been a while and takes some getting used to. My little brother grew up and became smarter than I am. It's a matter of pride that I do my best to catch up.

My tour in Germany will be up this year, and several possibilities have presented themselves. The safest thing I could do with the RIF escalating is to take a teaching position at the Academy, but I can't shake the feeling that I'd be right back where I started and not much better off. Don't ask me why. I haven't figured it out yet. Maybe I'm just bored with "safe."

No, I didn't speed when I was a kid. Playing it safe was a way of life even then. As for belching—I don't remember. I think my peers considered me obnoxious because I was boring.

There's not much happening at this end. For a change, the world is relatively quiet . . . today.

Lieutenant Baker just came in. He's been wandering around with a black eye and acting as if he just saw Old Yeller die. I've been keeping my nose out of it but have the feeling that Baker needs to talk. Can't figure out who died and made me Dutch uncle. Still, I think I'll do a little discreet probing and hope it doesn't come back to haunt me.

Jack

"Shut the door, Lieutenant."

Baker complied, then stood stiffly in front of Jack's desk. The shiner surrounding his left eye had turned yellow, and his expression was as blank as it had been for the past three days.

Why was he doing this? Jack wondered. Whatever problems Baker had, they weren't affecting his performance on the job. Raking his hand through his hair, Jack told himself that he'd done all he could by warning Baker. It was none of his business. The base had a chaplain, and the hospital had a psychiatrist.

And Lieutenant Baker had a problem that was best left off the record. Any record.

At least that was what Jack told himself. The boy had a promising future that meant something to him. Glancing at his watch, Jack smiled. "We're officially off duty, Lieutenant, so you might as well sit down."

Baker's lanky body slumped as soon as his butt hit the seat.

"Several of the nannies are missing," Jack said, and winced as Baker's face paled. So much for discretion.

"Yes, sir." Baker's eyes looked like Old Yeller's just before he breathed his last—wide and soulful and completely trusting.

Pushing away from his desk, Jack rose and stood at the window behind his chair. He was out of his element and more than a little arrogant to think he could help. "Your girl?"

"I can't find her, sir. I found one of the sweathouses that the illegals go to, but she wasn't there."

"That was a damn fool thing to do. The people who run those places are—"

"Yes, sir, I found that out."

"Is that where you got the black eye?"

"Yes, sir."

"You're lucky that's all you got."

"Yes, sir."

Jack shoved a hand in his pocket and stared out the window. The sweathouses were grim places that harbored illegal aliens in Germany, giving them menial and often hard labor to earn their keep while promising to solve their problems. As far as hideouts went, Jack guessed that the Hole-in-the-Wall Gang had it easy compared to what these people suffered at the hands of their supposed saviors.

"You don't know where she is, but have you heard from her?"

Baker squirmed in his chair.

"She called and asked you for money," Jack said, resigned.

"Someone stole her clothes, sir, and she has to go to another base until—"

Jack slammed his palms on his desk, and leaned forward. "Until you can get married? It isn't going to happen, Lieutenant. She's illegal. Poison. Off limits—" Jack clamped his mouth shut before he could call the girl an opportunist and a dozen other names that didn't sound as nice.

"She loves me, sir," Baker said defensively.

That told Jack a lot. Not "I love her" or "We love each other" but "She loves me," as if Baker had doubts of his own and was trying to convince himself.

"She's looking for a one-way ticket to the States, Baker, as in marriage certificate," Jack said harshly. "If she goes to another base to work, I guarantee you that she'll hook up with someone else inside a week."

Baker shot up out of the chair, his fists clenched, his chin thrust out. "No, sir! She said she wouldn't."

"You asked her? Why?" Jack asked softly, gently.

A flush climbed from Baker's neck to his hairline, but his body remained belligerently stiff. "I needed to know, *sir*!"

"You didn't trust her?"

"I love her!" Baker said, his gaze avoiding Jack's.

"You love her, but you don't trust her," Jack persisted.

"I only wondered—" Baker's voice cracked and splintered as he lowered his head. His shoulders drooped. "I don't know, sir. I just feel kind of responsible."

"Was she your first, Lieutenant?"

As he barely nodded, Baker's shoulders began to shake. "Pretty special, that first time."

Again, Baker nodded.

Jack wanted to zero in, hit Baker with statistics and horror stories from others who had been in similar predicaments, but he couldn't bring himself to do it. Maybe it was time for tact.

"You weren't her first, were you, Bobby?" Jack asked, though he already knew the answer, just as he knew that he was out of line by asking.

"No, sir."

Jack nodded as Baker looked up at him, his eyes bright with moisture. "The first time can be special, but it won't always be if your feelings aren't special, too."

"How do you find out, sir?"

Jack asked himself the same question. He wasn't too familiar with "special." He had no business doing this—talking to Baker, advising him, when the young lieutenant probably knew more about relationships than he did. All Jack could do was wing it.

"Because love really is blind, Bobby. It doesn't see problems as doubts but as things you can work out together. You don't give a shit how many problems there might be. They don't matter as much as being together. And you know that something that good shouldn't be wasted on anything less than a whole relationship—a future." Frowning, Jack wondered where he learned that. It damn sure hadn't come from personal experience.

"But, sir, Mary—she—"

"Was pretty? Helpless? She needed you, or maybe what you could give her?"

Swallowing, Baker nodded and looked down again.

With a sigh, Jack ran his hand around the back of his neck. His stomach did a slow roll, and he felt a restless urge to get out of this situation before he said too much, thought too much. "Every man dreams about having a woman depend on him to take care of her, protect her. Every man wants to feel like a white knight—"

"You, sir?"

Jack cleared his throat and shifted to glance out the window. "Yeah. It feels good once in a while. But if it went on all the time, a man might feel like he was a babysitter or a caretaker. Macho tendencies notwithstanding, Bobby, I think a man needs someone who is willing to take care of him every now and then. Do you think Mary could have or would have done that for you? Do you think that maybe knights might get tired of having to take what they want or fight for what they need all the time? Maybe knights would like to have something given to them—just because." *Oh brother,* Jack thought as he swallowed, shifted his feet, tried to figure out what to do with his hands.

"She was everything I'd ever dreamed about, sir."

"*Was,* Bobby?" The air seemed to become heavier, settling around Jack, stifling his energy, surrounding him with grief. "Like the dream you had about being a fireman or a train engineer?"

Baker frowned as he stared at his hands twisting around each other. "Every boy wants that when he's little."

"And when he's an adolescent he wants a good lay," Jack said bluntly, tired of tact and his own dimestore philosophy. He cleared his throat. "I wanted to be a photographer."

"Why aren't you?"

"Because sometimes we're stupid and let things get fucked up."

"You're telling me that I've . . . uh . . . screwed up?"

Yes, that's what I'm telling you—with tact and discretion. A corner of Jack's mouth slashed upward in a mocking smile. "What I'm telling you is that maybe you're hanging on to the tail end of that particular dream, Lieutenant. Maybe it's time for a new one."

Lieutenant Baker straightened in his chair up as a sheen of moisture blurred his eyes, and his voice shook as he whispered, "I think that's what my dad would say, Major Caldwell."

"I think it's worth your while to call your dad and listen to what he has to say."

"He's on a camping trip, sir—no phones and no mail," Baker said thickly.

No wonder the lieutenant had been going off the deep

end, with no one to go to, no one to share in his desperation, his confusion. Jack was willing to bet that this was the first major crisis Bobby Baker had ever faced alone. Jack knew where Baker was, a bleak and empty place where there was no doubt that he was alone, where there was no one to turn to but himself for answers.

He'd been there since he was ten.

"I still feel responsible, sir."

"Responsibility isn't always a good thing, Lieutenant, unless it's really yours. Is it possible that you feel responsible because you think she loves you? Because you slept with her and thought you loved her?"

Baker nodded miserably. "She needs help, sir."

"Is that your responsibility?"

"I don't know."

"Is it worth risking your career and future?"

Baker raised wide, stricken eyes to Jack.

Sighing, Jack walked around his desk, sat on its edge.

"Bottom line, Lieutenant. If you're not willing to make major sacrifices for this girl, then you don't love her and probably never did." Jack felt a chill as he spoke. *You don't love her and probably never did.* As he hadn't loved Kay— not the way he should have. Not the way he'd thought he had.

Not enough.

"No, sir," Baker choked out. "I just couldn't admit it, I guess." Rising from the chair, Bobby Baker faced Jack squarely. "But, sir, it's not right to—to—"

"To make love with a girl, then drop her?"

Baker nodded.

"You're right, it isn't—if you took advantage of her. If you lied to her or deliberately used her."

"No, sir. She . . ." Swallowing, Baker dropped his gaze again.

"She knew the score?"

"Yes, sir."

"She started it?"

Baker stared out the window.

"I don't want to know the details. They're your business. But I do want you to think about it, Lieutenant."

"Yes, sir. Thank you, Major Caldwell."

Jack reached into his back pocket for his wallet and pulled out some deutsche marks. "When you *send* her some money, add this to the pot. Advise her to go home and try getting into the States legally."

Swallowing hard, Baker nodded. "Why, sir?"

"Because, Bobby, she needs help." *Because you need to learn that all she wants is a payoff.* "And in your shoes, I think I'd do the same thing."

As Baker saluted, then walked out of the office, Jack slumped down in the chair Baker had vacated. He thought about his father, a man who had made no secret of his pleasure in the role. Then he remembered the day he'd left home to become a resident at the Air Force Academy, and his father had come into his room with a jar full of change.

"This is for the phones, son. You call anytime, for any reason. You want to come home, I'll come and get you."

"I won't," Jack had answered.

"Nobody's going to fault you if you've changed your mind, Jack. This is the time to do it, before you get trapped—"

"It's what I want, Dad," Jack said defensively as he averted his gaze, deliberately blinding himself to his own doubts.

"Keep the money, son," Joe Caldwell said as he backed out of the room. "Nobody would blame you or be disappointed."

Nobody but himself. The blinders were gone, lifted because of a "duty talk" with a subordinate who had more heart than common sense and maturity. Jack had never allowed himself to wonder what his father meant about being trapped. He hadn't dared ask the nature of the trap, yet at gut level he'd always known. Baker had, indirectly, brought Jack's own problems out into the open.

The letter he'd been writing to Angie lay folded on his desk, ready to be mailed.

It was so easy to talk to her, tell her things he wasn't

consciously aware of. It was easy to confide in someone who didn't seem real except in his mind. Angie was a fantasy. A friend. A thought that never failed to comfort or fill a corner with warmth. He didn't want to think of her any other way. He was beginning to think that their long-distance closeness was the only kind he was any good at, a closeness that kept the parties involved out of hurting range and kept their emotions reasonably detached.

Only it wasn't working in this case. Angie seemed to be getting closer, becoming more tangible. There were times when his thoughts of her went beyond platonic.

Without exploring that thought too closely, he unfolded the letter, picked up his pen and began to write.

I'll never make it as a Dutch uncle. As I think back on my conversation with Baker, I wonder where the words came from and what exactly they meant. I cringe at all the wisdom I dispensed—wisdom that has no relationship to my own life—about dreams and white knights and every other corny cliché in the book. Given enough time, I probably would have tripped myself up with a spiel about honor.

That's the problem—Baker was trying to do the honorable thing, and I had to find a way to talk him out of it without saying some ugly things about the girl he'd hooked up with. It just isn't that cut-and-dried. The girl was desperate rather than unscrupulous. Possibly she even feels something for Baker and would have tried to make him happy. Baker might have tried to be happy, even though he's already figured out that he feels more responsibility than love for her. Thank God the government wasn't about to allow him that choice.

Did I mention that the girl is an illegal alien?

It set my teeth on edge, knowing that the kid was willing to build his life on a misplaced sense of responsibility.

I can't believe that I was spouting off about dreams and white knights and handing out advice as if I knew what I was talking about.

If I'd known that trying to talk through someone else's problems would lead to reminders of my own, I would have

*kept my nose out of it. At least I had the sense to advise
Baker to talk to his father. That inspiration came after
Baker compared me to his father. Ouch.*

Jack raised his head and stared blankly at the opposite
wall as, once again, he saw and heard his own father trying
to reach out, trying to help, though all he'd succeeded in
doing was to make Jack uncomfortably aware of an anger
he thought had burned out in an uncontrollable expression
of anguish and loss years before.

And when it was done, nothing was said by his parents. It
might not have happened at all. Jack had worked damn
hard to believe it hadn't. It was easier than accepting the
fact that his feelings had been ignored—overlooked, more
likely—because no one had the emotional energy to deal
with them. It was a fine point that he was only now beginning to understand—too late to douse an anger that had
been simmering for longer than he cared to think about.

He'd been so good at control, so patient, and quietly
patronizing when his father had reached out to him with
that jar of small change. No one would have guessed at
how close he'd been to throwing the jar across the room
after his father had left. No one, including Jack, would
have guessed that the anger still burned.

You get used to anything if you live with it long enough.

No wonder that last night with Kay had caught him by
surprise. All of a sudden the fury had just *been there*, consuming him.

He took a deep breath as if to cleanse himself of the
memory, to eradicate the guilt and resentment that
hovered in his mind like a cloud of smoke. He told himself
that he had managed to control it—barely. But "barely"
had never been good enough for Jack.

For five years, Bryan had been "barely" alive.

For twenty-five years, Jack had been "barely" living.

14

*D*ear Jack,

Poor Lieutenant Baker. I can imagine how difficult and confusing first love must be. I'm assuming that it was his first love and it went sour? I'm not at all sure I'd want to experience any of it. Certainly not the heartbreak.

Were you discreet with the lieutenant? Never mind. I'm sure you were. From your letters I have the impression that you're a sensitive and caring man.

Still, I know it's difficult. When I talk to Gena about her problems, I feel like a midget trying to play basketball. Of course, I imagine that in your position you sometimes have to counsel your men. Dad did. I always resented the fact that he had advice for them and not for me. Is that what Gena calls a "man thing"?

Mike finally returned from extended duty in the Gulf and stayed long enough to tell Gena that he'd met a woman there—a doctor in the Army—and will be joining her at her new duty station. Though Gena refuses to talk about it, I can see the signs clearly enough. She's shattered enough to have gone underground for the healing process. I know she'll work through it in her own time. She always does, but still it's hard having to watch without being able to do anything to help her.

The one time she did talk about it, I know I wasn't particularly tactful or sensitive to Gena, I'm afraid. Frankly, I don't think I've been anything at all. It's hard when I haven't any experience on the subject. Oops. I suppose I shouldn't be admitting such a thing, but since I'll probably never have to look you in the eye, I will be spared embarrassment at having done so.

Sometimes, I wish I did have some firsthand knowledge of what Gena calls the "man/woman thing" but I'm not at

*all sure such knowledge is worth the inevitable price. Love
strikes me as being conditional. Most relationships are, I
think, but good, solid friendships seem to be less so.*

*As you've probably noticed, I'm in an odd mood. Mother
and Ben are on their way over as I write this, and I shudder
to think what she will say about what I've done with the
house. At almost twenty-eight, I have finally committed an
act of total independence. Yes, I know that's a rather pathetic admission, but for the moment (until Mother walks
in the door) I can't help but feel smug.*

*Let me know how Baker is holding up. And how you are
holding up after your session with him. You really shouldn't
worry about your abilities in that quarter. Your letters to me
are perceptive and eloquent. I can't imagine that you are
any different.*

*A car has just pulled up in the driveway. Can you believe
Ben, the retired Cadillac dealer, is driving a Jaguar XJ-
something-or-other?*

Time to face the lions. Wish me luck.

"What have you done?" Charlotte demanded the minute
she walked in the door. Ben stood behind her trying to
peer over her shoulder.

"Redecorated," Angie replied, wishing she could hide in
the attic behind the old furniture. But she'd resolved to be
brave, to not let her mother intimidate her.

Ben gave his wife a gentle push forward and helped her
slip off her coat. "Looks good to me," he said brightly.

"Why?" Charlotte asked.

With her arms wrapped around her middle, Angie
shrugged and turned away to stare at the room. "The carpet was beginning to wear. I stored your furniture in the
attic in case you wanted it." Her voice trailed off as she
glanced over her shoulder to see Ben shake his head and
gesture wildly.

"Angie," Ben said as he sauntered toward the study door
next to the staircase, "why don't you show me your office
while your mother looks around?"

Torn between wanting to accept Ben's offer of temporary

relief and needing to ease the transition for her mother, Angie followed him into the large room she'd converted into an office and workroom while watching Charlotte over her shoulder.

"So what do you use the drafting table for?" Ben asked.

"I . . . uh . . . do paste-ups there," Angie said as she hovered in the doorway. "You know, position type on overlays, produce camera-ready art for the printers."

"Mmm. You need a better lamp for that. This thing will blind you with glare." Ben scanned the books and software manuals on the shelves that ran floor to ceiling along one wall. "What's this for?"

"That's a desktop publishing program for the computer for doing layouts and type." She worried her bottom lip when her mother disappeared into the kitchen. "I've even learned how to generate some original art on the computer."

"Looks like a good system—a scanner, too." Ben wandered over to the large arrangement of computer furniture that wrapped around a corner of the room.

"Yes. With that, I can scan drawings and input them into Don Quixote and refine them. . . ." Her voice died as Ben jammed his hands into his pockets and stared up at an oblong box perched on top of the hutch. Her face burned and mortification seemed to lodge in her throat.

Why hadn't she just thrown the darn vibrator away?

Ben kept staring at the box. "I've done this before," he said musingly. "Only I came across Cara's under the bathroom sink while I was looking for the Charmin—"

"Uh, Ben?" Angie interrupted in a strangled voice. "Could you please forget about this? Now?"

"Honey, I can't forget the first time this happened. I still don't know what to do or say."

"It's not what you think." In the next three seconds, Angie thought she might find a way to be clever and modern about the whole thing.

"Of course it isn't," Ben said as he cleared his throat, wiped a hand over his face. "You spend a lot of time at the computer. The newspapers are full of warnings about stiff necks and lower back pain. This model is a honey—easy to hold and—"

"Ben, shut up," Angie said, then slapped a hand over her mouth.

"Good idea, honey."

"Um. Are you really interested in all this, Ben?" Angie asked for the sake of saying something.

Ben shook his head as the ruddy flush subsided from his face. "Only in how interested you are in all this. Angela, are you happy? Do you enjoy what you're doing?"

"I . . . yes, of course I am."

"That surprises me. It seems to me that it would bore you silly working by yourself every day."

"I like 'by myself,' Ben."

"Mmm."

That *mmm* said far more than she wanted to hear in a tone that reflected as much dissatisfaction with her answer as she'd been feeling lately. "It takes a while to get any business going, Ben."

"I know. Still, it seems to me that after the newness wears off, this particular job would be pretty monotonous for someone like you."

"Angela. Ben. I've put on a fresh pot of coffee," Charlotte called from the living room. "It will be ready in a few minutes."

Angie sprang for the door, glad for once to face her mother's displeasure. Charlotte never called her Angela unless she was upset.

"Angela," Ben's voice stopped her in her tracks, "I'll go ahead. Maybe you want to pick up a little in here, just in case Charlotte decides to—"

"Uh-huh," Angie said, and whipped past him to reach for the vibrator and stuff it in the nearest drawer.

"You know, honey," Ben said as he paused on his way out, "from what I've heard and seen, you've spent a lot of years sticking to things to justify yourself in someone else's eyes. And from what I've heard and seen, your heart belongs to Link. I'm a big believer in following your heart.

Think about it, Angela, before you get caught in your own trap."

Angie knew her mouth was open, but talking was impossible when you'd just been zapped with a ray of truth you'd been dodging for several weeks. Later, she knew, she was going to feel like a hypocrite for even considering giving Ben a denial or argument. Since she'd been jabbering to anyone who'd listen—Jack included—about instinct and second chances, her professional future was an issue she would have to deal with soon.

Third chances were harder to justify.

She would think about it—later.

Smoothing her slacks, she raised her head and followed Ben into the living room, like the condemned taking a stroll down death row.

"How can you afford such expensive carpet, Angela?" Charlotte asked as she examined the thick plush.

She couldn't help but throw a quick glance at Ben. His eyes gave nothing away except for a surreptitious wink that somehow made everything okay. Then he nodded toward her mother, a message that there were far worse things to face than getting caught being a normal, contemporary woman.

"I'm not exactly poor, Mother, and it matches the furniture I wanted." Her gaze swept over the floor, admiring the carpet that was almost iridescent in its richness, sometimes a rosy beige, sometimes a pale peach, depending on the light. She loved the unique quality of change in the luster of the fibers.

"Yes, the furniture," Charlotte murmured. "What possessed you to buy such large pieces?"

"I like to sprawl, and I like soft." Angie swallowed and told herself not to explain, not to defend.

"But it's so dark."

Dark? Angie wondered as her gaze fell on the twin sofas upholstered in a luxurious tapestry fabric in shades of bronze, gold, green, peach, teal, and deep burgundy that seemed to merge into one another, picking up the burgundy velvet of an overstuffed chair and ottoman. Maybe they were dark, but she saw beyond that to the large room that gathered and held the sunlight in jewel tones reflected through stained-glass panels set into the bay window. She saw richness and warmth, space and intimacy and comfort.

Except now, with her mother in the room, she felt closed in, trapped.

"Where are my draperies?" Charlotte asked as she eyed the natural wood shutters covering the conventional rectangular windows. The three bay windows had been made into one large alcove where stained glass reached from the circular window seat to the ceiling.

"In the attic, Mother." Again Angie followed Charlotte's gaze and lingered on the stenciled art she'd painted in the molded woodwork on either side of the window. Small pillows in the same shades as the sofas were scattered on the spattered watercolor-velvet upholstery of the window seats like so many jewels that picked up the light in the lustrous texture of antique satin.

"What happened to good taste, Angela? This is much too flamboyant."

"Good or bad, Mother, this is my taste."

"How about coffee?" Ben asked as he rubbed his hands together.

Gratefully, Angie escaped to the kitchen before her mother could object to the occasional tables that had oriental lines or to the lamps scattered around the room, none of which matched the others but had been chosen simply because Angie liked them.

Her hands shook as she filled the silver coffee service with French roast, real cream, and sugar—a sop to her mother's sense of propriety. Carrying the tray into the living room, Angie stopped three steps in, shocked by what she saw.

Emotions assaulted her, too fast to sort through, too strong for her to ignore or control. "What are you doing?" she asked as she set the tray down on the chinoiserie desk against the wall.

Charlotte stood back, a lamp in her hand, her gaze

sweeping the room. "That's better. And put this thing in the attic."

"Put it back, Mother—all of it."

"Really, Angela, I've taught you how to arrange furniture—"

Too outraged to speak, Angie began moving her furniture back into its original positions. As she brushed by Ben, she waved in the direction of the tray, an invitation to help himself. If she picked up the coffee server, she was afraid she might throw it.

"Angela, don't act so hastily," Charlotte said as she followed behind Angie, moving things again. "Angela, stop this. It's understandable that you wouldn't know about these things. I've always taken care of it."

The anger dissolved as if it had never existed. Angie's face burned and her throat felt tight. She blinked against the pressure building behind her eyes. She turned her back and walked toward the tray, but Ben was leaning against the wall, watching her, seeing her defeat, her cowardice, her failure.

Pushing away from the wall, he poured a cup of coffee, loaded it with sugar and cream, and pressed it—sans saucer—into Angie's hand. She couldn't see his expression through the blur of humiliation, but she imagined it would be one of pity or disappointment.

She'd give anything to be back in her office with Ben, trying to explain away the vibrator.

"Put it all back, Charlotte," he said quietly.

"She'll be much happier with it this way, Ben."

"Put it back." In spite of his even tone and soft voice, there was steel and command in his order.

"Stay out of this—" Charlotte said, her voice rising.

Angie cringed and moved blindly toward the doorway.

"I think you need to practice what you preach, honey," he said.

"I will not be told what to do in my own house!"

"This is Angela's house now, and it's her furniture. You don't live here anymore."

Angie wanted to run, to curl up on the back stairway, as

she had when her mother had fought with the general, because it was the smallest, most enclosed area of the house. She could touch the walls there, pretend to pull them around her, escape the shouts, the ugliness. But she stood rooted in the arched threshold of the kitchen, watching Ben calmly move a table here, a chair there, precisely fitting legs into the indentations in the carpet until the room was exactly as Angie had arranged it. And she waited for the shouting, praying that it wouldn't happen. Not because of her. Not again.

"It's hard to let go, honey," Ben crooned. "Believe me, I know. I still see Cara in pigtails and braces, still feel her sticky hands when she'd give me a hug."

"Angie never had sticky hands."

Dimly, Angie noticed that her mother wasn't calling her Angela anymore.

"No? Too bad. A sticky hug stays with you a while." Gently, he took the lamp from her hands and steered her toward the overstuffed chair, lowered her down, lifted her feet onto the ottoman. "Relax, honey. I know you're worried about Angela. You've depended on each other for so long. The thing is—she doesn't need babying anymore. You'll have to wait for grandchildren for that." He walked to the tray, poured another cup of coffee, and carried it to his wife.

Angie caught his wink, that code he'd developed just for her, a message that told her not to worry. Everything would be fine.

No shouting. No recriminations. No contempt.

Charlotte took the cup from Ben, stared up at him. Her chest rose and fell with a shuddering breath. "You don't understand."

Angie saw the expression on her mother's face, lost, desperate . . . afraid.

"Nope. I never could understand why little girls have to grow up. God knows I did my damnedest to protect my daughter, to keep her wrapped up in ruffles and lace and safety. You were better at it than I was." Ben held out his arm toward Angie as he sat on the edge of the ottoman.

"Cara still likes the ruffles and lace, but she's moved on to grown-up things, whether I understand or not."

Angie wasn't so bewildered that she mistook his gesture for anything but the order it was. She moved toward him, felt his hand take hers, pull her down on the other side of Charlotte's feet. The ottoman was more than large enough. Then she registered what he'd said, the message he'd been giving her as well as her mother.

It really was all right. Even the vibrator.

Charlotte raised her hand as if to touch Angie's cheek, then lowered it again. "Angie is different."

"Sure she is," Ben said. "She's serene where Cara takes on all comers. I can't tell you how much trouble it gets Cara into. And Angela thinks about things. Cara always has a wild hair about something. More trouble."

"Angie has never been any trouble. She was perfect," Charlotte said wistfully.

Fascinated, Angie listened to the exchange with no desire to interfere. Her own father had shouted and accused and cursed her mother. He'd thrown whatever was handy, and then he'd started in on Angie, listing her weaknesses, letting her know in no uncertain terms what a disappointment she was.

"Well, then maybe it's time to let her be imperfect if she wants to be. Angela's lucky, honey." With his finger, Ben guided the cup to Charlotte's lips as he directed a pointed glance at Angie. "Most of us have to wait until we're old and don't have the energy to turn our mistakes into experiences rather than disasters."

Angie received his smile, his expression that shared mischief and secrets and a less than subtle reminder of his earlier advice. Angie shot what she hoped was a respectful warning look at him. This was not the time to do anything but soothe her mother, to try to make her understand. It was time she learned to fight her own battles.

Angie inhaled deeply and met her mother's gaze head on. "Mother, I don't like ruffles and pastels. I don't want my house to look like anyone else's."

"Of course you liked them, Angie. You've been the

daughter every woman dreams of." There was a note of hysteria in Charlotte's voice that alarmed Angie.

"Mother, tastes change. Little girls grow up."

"But to just pack everything away in the attic—all that I've done."

Angie's shoulders drooped, feeling the weight of all her mother had done, all she'd allowed her mother to do. All of it upstairs, hidden away, yet remembered and hated. "Yes, Mother—all that *you've* done," Angie said softly, almost to herself.

"Angie—the trophies and photos and reels of film . . . you didn't—"

"No, Mother. They're yours. I know how important they are to you."

Ben's hand found Charlotte's, squeezed it gently. "Honey, it's just old furniture Angela stored away."

"I didn't pack *you* in the attic, Mother." Angie sucked in her breath as she heard what she'd said, saw her mother's face drain of color, heard the wobble in Charlotte's voice as she spoke.

"I'm behaving like a child."

Clenching her fists in her lap, Angie leaned forward, knowing she had to speak, had to make her mother understand as she was beginning to understand. "No, Mother. I was. I did all this for myself, but not just because I didn't like your furniture. I wanted to prove something to you, and I wanted to rebel." She laughed, a strangled sound cut short. "It's hard trying to be perfect all the time. I can't do it anymore."

"Who asked you to be perfect?" Charlotte demanded.

Angie wanted to laugh hysterically at that, shout out a lifetime of anger and frustration, but she couldn't raise her voice, couldn't free the emotions as easily as that.

Ben stepped into the charged silence. "Honey, you want to see what's up there and have it moved to our place?" he asked with dread in his voice.

"No, not now," Charlotte said wearily. "I would like to go home."

Angie bit her lip as she reached over to her mother. The

air of defeat disturbed her as it always had, as if she alone were responsible for a loss only Charlotte understood and it was up to her to make up for that loss. "Mother—"

Charlotte rose from the chair. "This *is* your home now, Angie. And you *aren't* a little girl any longer. I'm not such a silly woman that I *can't* recognize your right to change anything you choose to change. I *do* understand." She straightened her spine a little more with every word she emphasized, as if she were trying to convince herself rather than reassure her daughter. "I'll get used to it."

Angie hugged Ben and kissed her mother's cheek, then stood in the doorway as they drove away. Over and over again, she heard Charlotte's voice, echoes of accusation and hurt and confusion.

Her mother didn't understand. How could Angie expect her to, when she was just beginning to see the truth herself? She hadn't changed all that much. She was simply learning to be herself, growing up and growing out in new directions—growing into herself.

Like the house. Fantasies didn't always center around desert sheikhs or Superman. She'd had what she'd thought were vivid images of the house as she wanted it, not realizing that it might become a translation of a part of herself she wasn't ready to acknowledge. Now, as her gaze swept over the room, she saw the reality and wondered if she could live up to it, wondered if she was using it to express what she never would.

She had wanted her own space, a sanctuary where she could hide, yet she'd created a place where everywhere she looked, she saw herself. And every time she looked around herself, inside herself, she had to wonder which image was real, which part of her was the honest one.

Sighing, she turned her back on the room she'd taken such pride in and walked into her office. Only when she was writing to Jack—talking to him—did she feel honest.

I know this letter was supposed to be finished, but I was feeling awkward with myself and thought I would find more pleasant company. Does that ever happen to you?

Mother and Ben left early. She was horrified by my choice of decor, and poor Ben was afraid that she would want to take the old furnishings to his home in Gennessee. Her spindly antiques and cool colors would look ghastly in Ben's log home. It's a wonderful house and I know Mother likes it (or at least she's getting used to it), but drawing room elegance would definitely be out of place there.

Truth to tell—I'm just a tad horrified myself after seeing it through Mother's eyes. I remember being so pleased after the last piece of furniture was in place and the last cushion plumped. It was late afternoon, and the sun slanted in through the stained glass. I had Yanni playing on the stereo, a piece called "First Touch," and I whirled through the living room and felt as if I were dancing in the middle of a jewel and touching, for the first time, hidden facets of myself.

Goodness but I'm getting punchy. Gena is forever warning me about purple prose and sappy sentiment.

I was so happy with it all, and now I can't help but wonder why. Did I do it for myself, or because I wanted to make a statement to my mother? I suppose I'll have to come up with an answer. This time I have truly confronted myself. I was much more comfortable when "myself" wasn't so much of a mystery.

How could I have believed that changing furniture and wallpaper would clear up a lifetime of misunderstanding and confusion? How on earth can stained glass and carpeting make a statement when even I don't know what I'm trying to say or to whom I'm trying to say it?

Gena accuses me of thinking too much. Possibly, I spend so much time thinking just so I'll be too busy to pay attention to myself. I've gone and done it again. It's said and duly admitted. Memory is a tricky thing. It latches on to the most unsettling moments and the most disturbing thoughts and doesn't let us forget them.

Speaking of memories—I don't know what to do with all those antiques, but I just realized they'll have to go, along with all reminders of my childhood. There is a lot of emo-

tional baggage literally hanging over my head. Having them in the attic is too much like living in a haunted house.

Are you confused? Join the club. I thought that once we hit eighteen we were supposed to be all grown up.

If that is true, then I suppose I'd better be mature and keep my promise to Ben to think about a certain issue he brought up today. I'll explain later after I've thought about it.

I may never forgive Ben. Talk about sensitive and caring men—they're suddenly crawling out of the woodwork.

The more Jack read, the more he worried. He wasn't sure what worried him the most—Angie, or the fact that he was worrying about Angie.

The woman had serious problems. What twenty-seven-year-old woman in this day and age gave a diddly damn what her mother thought about furniture? What woman—or girl, for that matter—past the age of fifteen could honestly claim ignorance about love and sex, yet still have such a jaundiced view of both?

Yet, she was whimsical, a dreamer who obviously had the guts to buck the systems her mother and upbringing had established, and the sensitivity to feel bad about the repercussions.

Sensitivity. He found the passage in her letter. She'd actually accused him of being sensitive and caring. That was supposed to be the ultimate compliment for a man in this day and age. No doubt about it—Angie was whimsical, all right.

Obviously, he'd done a better job of fooling Angie than he had of fooling Kay.

Impatient with memories he refused to dwell on, he glanced down at the letter.

Dancing in the middle of a jewel. He had to smile at that. Purple suited Angie. Just as a baggy robe and fuzzy slippers suited her. He saw her more and more clearly in his mind, an average woman, nonthreatening in her plainness, cheerful yet shy, a mother-hen type who went through life with her wings wide open and ready to shelter anyone in her path. He thought of her as plump, because he couldn't imagine her with a dancer's body that was no-frills bone and sinew. It just didn't go with purple sentiment and bright and lively letters.

And dancers had to have enough confidence to play to a crowd, to make that crowd believe they were the best even when they tripped up. Angie had no confidence in herself or her decisions.

Angela Winters was, he decided, one big contradiction.

He should be confused by the scattered parts of herself that she revealed in her letters, but oddly enough, he understood what she was talking about. He and Angie had a lot in common. They weren't strangers to each other anymore, yet with each passing day, they became less familiar with themselves. They both were caught in a transition, yet Angie seemed to be handling her personal crisis a hell of a lot better than he was handling—or not handling—his.

That was scary.

15

*D*ear Angie,

Change seems to be on the agenda for both of us. I did something I still can't explain or understand—I handed in my resignation, and it was accepted. That was a low blow to the ego. Uncle Sam could have at least made a token protest, offered me a promotion to stay in, instead of showing me just how expendable I am. But that's pride talking.

The Air Force is giving payoffs to officers who are willing to resign—the government's version of early retirement for expendable minor executives, I guess. Still, money is better than a gold watch. I had to face facts. Promotions are frozen, the defense budget is shrinking daily, and I'm going nowhere in a hurry.

Time is getting short. I'll be officially out in six weeks. I've got to be crazy to give up everything like this. Funny thing is that I don't feel crazy. No regret or second thoughts. Yet. I think I'm still shell-shocked at having everything happen before I had time to change my mind. The government is never fast.

You advised me to take a second chance if that's what I wanted. Well, ready or not, that's what I have, and it's too late for second thoughts.

Right now, I'm still feeling irrational and am believing I might actually be able to plug into an old dream.

That's funny, too. I thought I had my dream, but I'm beginning to discover that all I've had are ambition and goals. Not the same thing. With one, you're successful because you're happy in what you're doing. In the other, you're driven to be successful with the hope that you will be happy. I think.

Well, I'll have plenty of time to figure it out. I'm a lame duck now, with more and more of my duty being split up *and eliminated. How does a world go from red alert to condition green so fast? Frankly, I don't buy it. From what I can see, the planet is still a cannonball with a short fuse.*

Anyway, I'm not sure where I'll go from here. A couple of East Coast companies have approached me, so I might set up some interviews before I make any permanent plans. The folks will be on the road again for a family reunion so probably won't make it to the Springs for a while. Even Steve is going to join them there, so the old homestead and family business will be closed up. There doesn't seem much point to hitting Colorado yet. Still, I might change my mind and check out the job possibilities there. I don't really care to settle elsewhere. Do I sound indecisive? Well, I am. I've never had so many choices before. I've never had any experience at being a free spirit, and it's intimidating as hell.

It had happened before—letters full of future plans rather than the loneliness of the present. Letters that spoke of good-bye even when it wasn't said outright. It was never easy, knowing that a friend was moving out of her life, outgrowing her and moving on, but she'd always expected it and had been prepared to tuck away the memories like sachets that lost their scent as time passed.

Sooner or later they all found the flesh and blood companionship of on-the-scene friends more satisfying than a monthly letter. She'd always been happy for them. She tried to be happy now, but a lump grew in her throat and her eyes burned with suppressed tears. Blinking rapidly, she focused on the paper in her hand, the words that slashed across the page, reminding her of the first time he'd written, the anger that had ripped the paper in places.

Angie walked into the kitchen, put water on to boil, and dropped a teabag into a mug, deliberately putting off the moment when she would read the letter more carefully and have to think about the implications.

There would be no more letters.

She would never forget him.

Carrying her mug of peach tea into the living room, Angie curled up in the window seat to sort through her mail

and tossed the various envelopes into piles on the floor—
bills in one, junk in another, magazines and letters into a
third—until only Jack's letter remained on her lap.

She'd developed a habit of that lately—approaching his
letters warily, suspicious of her own response to what he
might say. It had become complicated and frightening, this
relationship with Jack that seemed to evolve so naturally,
as if it were meant to be. This kind of friendship was supposed to be static, contained by the boundaries of time and
distance and lives that branched out into new directions. It
wasn't supposed to create on-the-fly fantasies and hours of
anxious anticipation for the next letter.

Pretending it was the first time, she read the letter again,
carefully searching between the lines for hidden meanings,
any hint that he planned to look her up.

Hidden meanings eluded her. His life was changing—by
choice. He was moving on. There wasn't a word that hinted
at a desire to see her.

It had happened so many times before.

This time, she wasn't prepared.

> *I've thought about traveling the country and give the
> cameras a workout, see what develops. (No pun intended.)
> Don't know how to handle being a thirty-five year old ado-
> lescent who's trying to find himself. Hell of a way to con-
> duct a life.*

Angie couldn't have agreed more. Finding yourself was a
massive—and disturbing—undertaking at any age. It had
been obvious for quite some time that Jack was restless
and dissatisfied with his life. Equally obvious was the fact
that this was the first spontaneous act he'd indulged in in
years. She didn't count his response to her first letter, or
the ones that came after. Permanence and commitment
weren't a part of that scene.

She should have remembered that.

Spontaneity was living by trial and error. Too late, she
realized that corresponding with Jack had been one long
chain reaction of emotions never felt, sensations never ex-

perienced, creating an atmosphere of anticipation and romance in her life. In those fantasies, she was everything he wanted and needed in a woman, never disappointing or dull, and never shy. In those fantasies, he was hers.

She'd begun to believe it.

Anticipation was nice, she decided. Romance was wonderful. She'd lived in extremes for so long that she appreciated the subtlety of taking steps one at a time, slowly, so she could savor each new experience, each hard won victory. Meeting Jack would complicate her life, become a matter of extremes.

She swallowed hard, tried to fill the emptiness she felt inside with happiness for him, for the second chance he needed so badly.

Actually, his timing was brilliant, she told herself as she ignored the tightness in her chest and throat, the pressure building behind her eyes. She, too, was going forward in new directions. Available time for writing scores of letters every month was dwindling. Because of military cutbacks, so was the number of pen pals who needed a temporary friend.

She couldn't isolate herself forever. She had already made some major changes in her life, made some major discoveries about herself. It was going to take time to sort through the confusion those discoveries brought, make them count for something. Angie rolled her eyes. One of these days she might find the courage to live more than a few inches at a time.

And if she couldn't find the courage . . . well, she would fake it. She was an expert at faking it.

Jack was the only person in the world who would see through her. It was one thing to share confidences with him in a letter and quite another to expose herself to him in person. She didn't want him to discover that she was a fake.

Angie frowned and stared out the window. Sunset melted the sky, lighting embers on the underside of the clouds, and dripping orange and rose and deep, rich gold over the snow capping Pike's Peak. Another day over, dying with a flare of brilliance, refusing to steal away passively.

Leaning her head against the window panes, she allowed herself to wonder—just once more—about the man who had come into her life through a trick of fate. Always, she saw him with a serious, thoughtful expression, his eyes deep set, his brows drawn together as he said little. Always, she saw him watching, observing, seeing what was beyond the notice of most people. And always, she thought of his eyes as blue, deep enough to hold a thousand private thoughts where no one else could find them.

She would never know for sure.

Dear Jack,

Congratulations!

I know you probably don't feel like celebrating right now. It's frightening to suddenly find your life turned upside down, even if you're the one who did the turning. Somehow that makes it worse—and a lot harder to adjust. If you're laid off or the company goes bankrupt, you can blame it on circumstance, take a pragmatic "I will survive this" attitude, and go on. It's no less shattering, but at least you know you weren't responsible.

When I sold my partnership in the school, I suffered major anxiety and thought I probably should check myself into Mount Airy for psychiatric evaluation. If I hadn't felt so relieved, I might have done just that, but the relief saved me. Remember when I told you that Ben had asked me to think about something? Well, that's all I've been able to do. I may never forgive him for making me admit (to myself) what a mistake I've made.

Now I'll admit it to you. In a nutshell—I don't want to be a greeting-card person. Not for a living, anyway. It's fun as a hobby, but as a living, it's boring and lonely. You'll have to admit that specially designed greeting cards and stationery is a unique gift for friends, and it saves them a bundle not to mention the aggravation of deciding whether they want funny or pastoral or religious. Gena can spend hours in a store searching for just the right cards.

As I was saying—it was fun and seemed like a good idea at the time, and getting the business rolling was a challenge. But ever since then, I've been working hard to convince myself that I made a good choice. Now really, it doesn't take a genius to figure out that if you have to work that hard to convince yourself of something, then ninety-nine to one it's a lie.

It's been eating at me for a while now that I was more excited over new orders rather than the design and production process. I was bred on the value of material success. New orders, you see, validate what I'm doing. The fun is gone. I hate spending so much time working alone.

Bottom line? The creative process was simply a way to fill the empty hours when I wasn't working for Gena. Now, that is fun! I resent the time I have to spend away from the office, and I feel as if I'm accomplishing so much more there.

So I admit it. I made a mistake. I'm about to become a quitter—again—and you know what? I am absolutely thrilled about it—again. Ben said that I was mature enough to turn mistakes into experiences and young enough to profit from them.

Well, so are you!

So there!

In several of your letters you've mentioned your cameras. You also mentioned plugging into an old dream. I have to believe there's a connection between the two. Thank heavens you have an old dream. It has to be easier than building a new one when you have no idea how to go about it. It has to be much better than living on the secondhand dreams passed down to you by others and trying to convince yourself that they're yours as well.

Since you do have that dream and you've given seventeen years to the service for whatever reason, I'd say it's definitely your turn.

The purpose of this boring little lecture is purely selfish. Having said all this, I must now practice what I preach. Pathetic, isn't it—having to force oneself into grabbing one's life by the tail?

The lesson I find most difficult to learn is that I no longer have an excuse for being a wuss. Instead, I have an obligation to myself. So do you, Jack. And you have a great deal more courage than I. That's what it takes to find happiness within yourself.

You also have a great deal of talent. Your images are truly eloquent—each one worth more than a thousand words.

With that, I will shut up and wish us both the best of good fortune. Don't you dare let anyone tell you that you don't deserve it.

I guess this is the last letter, since I doubt there's time for more. I'm sure you're busy packing and wrapping up your old life. It's just as well, I suppose. The next few months are going to be frantic around here. Take care, Jack. I'll miss you.

                                              Angie

So this was good-bye.

Jack told himself that he was relieved, that Angie had made it easy for him by taking it out of his hands. He'd been wondering how he was going to cut the cord between them since he'd struggled with that last letter he'd written to her. He'd meant to say it then—good-bye and good luck and it's been great—but instead he'd rattled on about God knows what like a guest who didn't want to leave the party even after it was over.

If he'd been transferring to another assignment, their relationship once removed could have gone on. No problem. But he was going home—and Angie lived five miles from home.

She was dead wrong about his courage. If he had any guts at all, he would have told her flat out that he was going home rather than implying otherwise. He could have simply said good-bye and have a nice life. He could have been blunt as a crowbar and told her that the letters were great but no way did he want to meet her in person.

He could have done anything but stall for time.

Time for what? To develop some character lines on his face?

It didn't matter. She'd kissed him off. Life was a lot simpler now that she had taken it out of his hands. He sure as hell wouldn't miss her. He didn't have to worry about hurting her.

And no way had she hurt him with that friendly, supportive ration of manure she'd given him.

If you have to work that hard to convince yourself of something, then ninety-nine to one it's a lie.

TOO EARLY

Too early awakened
By the gnawing sound of metal
Scraping against metal.
Footsteps traipsing,
Voices raping,
Dreams fading,
The cowardly clock hangs accused
By the rich glare of the sun . . .
A stiff warp across my cover
Jogs my memory.
Time to wash my face,
Time to take my place,
Half eaten, half made.
My God how I must look!

—Jennie Cissell Thompson

16

September

Nothing was worse than being on the wrong side of a locked front door when your phone was ringing, Angie decided as she balanced her briefcase and a large paper bag and tried to fit her key in the lock. It was too late in the day for a business call, and the only social calls she received were when a neighbor was desperate for bodies at a home demonstration party.

The phone stopped ringing just as she turned the lock. Great. She couldn't help but wonder if it had been Jack. It was driving her crazy to know that he was on the same continent. She'd figured it all out: probable accumulated leave time and the sketchy timetable he'd given her. He could be stateside by now.

She kept trying to tuck him away with other fond memories without success. Jack refused to stay tucked.

She looked over her shoulder at the surrounding houses. No telltale overflow of cars lined the street. Thank goodness. She had enough jewelry, cosmetics, and handcrafted gift items to see her into the next century. The word *no* didn't exist in her vocabulary when it came to misfits, lonely souls, and hostesses desperate enough to wield guilt like an automatic weapon. She knew all about not belonging, being lonely, feeling desperate. And she couldn't stand the thought of letting anyone down. Guilt always brought her to her knees.

A gust of wind accompanied by a barrage of snow hit her back, urging her into the house.

"Bad weather on Fridays should be outlawed," she grumbled as she kicked the door shut and dumped the bag of take-out Chinese onto the table flanking the stairway. Snow in September wasn't unheard of, but this early in the year it was rare. No one had expected the early winter storm to stall in the foothills and grow in intensity. She'd had big plans for the weekend, namely putting together a storage shed in the back yard. The crates had been an eyesore, leaning up against the back of her house since June.

"Oh, well," she said to empty air as her gaze automatically zoomed to the telephone. She'd been hovering near it for over a week, wishing he'd call, hoping he wouldn't, *knowing* he wouldn't. Jack had made plans for his future, in which she had no place.

"He is not going to call. He is not going to show up on my doorstep," she repeated for the thousandth time that day. More than once, Gena or someone else at Link had caught her muttering to herself, chanting the same words over and over again.

Why should he? If the situation were reversed, she certainly wouldn't. She absolutely did not want a change in the status quo.

Did she?

Maybe. Maybe not.

"Give it a rest, Angie," she said as she hung up her coat and set her boots on the mat by the door. She walked over to the table to retrieve the dinner she was too keyed up to eat, deliberately patted the phone, and jumped as it rang.

Before she could stop herself, she snatched it up, then stared at it as if she'd forgotten what it was for. Did she want to talk to him? What could she say? Taking a deep breath, she released it on a sigh and brought the receiver up to her ear. "Hello?"

"You made it home safe and sound?"

It was Gena. Only Gena. Angie swallowed a lump of disappointment. "Yes. I stopped off for Chinese."

"Crabmeat wontons?"

"Yes."

"Dumplings and fantail shrimp and beef and broccoli?"

"Yes, and fried rice and hot and sour soup and lo mein."

"Who are you feeding?"

"Me, myself, and I."

"Some party. If it wasn't so nasty outside, I'd crash."

"Why don't you?" Angie asked. Company would be nice. Gena's company would be welcome. "It's been a while since we buried our sorrows in cholesterol and MSG. I even have plum wine."

"My car is buried in a snowbank three blocks away. No way am I stepping foot outside again."

"Are you okay?" Angie asked.

"I'm fine. Icicles become me."

"I'll come there," Angie blurted.

"You stay put. I know how much you hate driving in snow."

"I have the Bronco, Gena."

"Don't gloat. There's something obscene about being a two-car person—what's wrong? Afraid he'll call, or afraid he won't?"

Angie sighed. It sounded so silly, so *high school.* "Yes," she answered truthfully.

"You're better off if he doesn't."

"Definitely."

"He's bound to be a disappointment."

"Yes," Angie said.

Gena sighed. "You have to know, don't you, chum?"

"I'm not sure that I want to know, Gena."

"You *have* to know," Gena said firmly. "Personally, I hope he does call so you can stop wondering and thinking of him as some kind of Prince Charming. Besides, you've been absolutely useless to me since you got that letter."

Angie knew that Jack wasn't a prince, charming or otherwise. He was an ordinary man, sometimes an S.O.B., sometimes sensitive and vulnerable, always lonely, a lost soul trying to find himself. When he did, he wouldn't be interested in finding her. "I like him just the way he is, Gena—at a distance, nonthreatening, safe. Besides, I'm not exactly Cinderella."

"I had in mind Sleeping Beauty."

"After I've had time to think about that remark, I'll probably be offended."

"You still don't have a life, Angie."

"Could have fooled me," Angie said, feeling uncomfortable and restless and anxious to end the conversation.

"What'd you do—write him off with some breezy little note?"

"Sort of."

"Right. Do it to him before he can do it to you—dammit, Angie, why don't you just admit that you're hurting?"

"Okay, I'm hurting—chronic but not terminal."

"Do you remember when we doubled on a blind date in our senior year?"

"I've successfully blocked it out."

"Try to revive the memory, chum. Dredge it up every time you wonder about Jack. If that doesn't make the stars in your eyes fall, nothing will."

"Right."

"And if he does call, arrange to meet him in a public place," Gena advised.

"He won't."

"Mmm. Well, if he does, be careful. He's still a stranger to you, chum."

"That's what I'm afraid of," Angie admitted.

"You lost me."

Angie was a little lost herself. How could she explain her fear that if she did meet Jack, they would become strangers as they never had been while writing to one another? How could she explain that for the first time in her life, she was worried about being disappointed rather than the other way around?

Absently, she plucked a wonton from the bag and bit into it. "Speaking of strangers . . ."

"Go right ahead."

"I've missed you, Gena," Angie said softly. She'd never said it before when Gena had retreated. She'd never pushed before.

"Good," Gena said without hesitation or feeble excuses. "You'll appreciate me that much more when I surface."

Angie took a deep breath and plunged into forbidden waters. "Gena . . ." She tried to say what was on her mind, voice the anxiety she felt for her friend, but she couldn't seem to break the code of silence that Gena had always required of her.

"Spit it out, Angie," Gena said, her voice heavy with resignation. "I'll even help you: It's been three months."

"Now that you mention it, it's been closer to four."

"And you're worried."

"Yes."

"Must be a slow year," Gena muttered. "Four months isn't too long to languish with a broken heart, chum, and I'm happy to report that my period of mourning is almost over. I'll survive."

Another deep breath, another dive into dangerous waters. Angie forced herself to speak slowly, naturally, as if she were simply passing the time of day. "Gena, if you crawl too far inside yourself, you might not be able to get out again. You might get confused about what you see in there."

"You should know."

Closing her eyes, Angie tried not to listen to the sarcasm in Gena's voice, not to build scar tissue around an imagined blow. "Yes, I do know." She opened her eyes, smiled wryly at the paranoia that was never far from the surface. "*Don't* fall into the same trap I did. *Don't* let yourself become so obsessed with protecting yourself from hurt that you—"

"Forget how to be myself? If I did that, sweetcakes, who on earth would remind you of who you are?"

"True. I'd be a lost cause, and we both know you consider that particular term an oxymoron," Angie said as she smiled.

"Mmm. Thanks for reminding me."

"You're welcome."

"I guess that means we're both going to make it."

"Can't quit now."

"Nope, and if you're going to sit around waiting for a call that will never come, I suppose I should quit tying up the line."

"He isn't going to call."

"For your sake, I hope he does . . . I think. Oh, hell,

who am I kidding? I don't know what I hope. You coming in tomorrow?"

"Unless they close the roads."

"Or he shows up on your doorstep and you're both carried away by instant and blinding passion."

"Sure, Gena," Angie said, feeling a blaze of embarrassment in her face. Gena couldn't possibly know how many times that particular daydream had popped into her mind lately.

"Angie? Have you thought about what you'll do if he does contact you?"

"Say hello?"

"Funny—how do you feel about some advice?"

"I can always take a page out of your book and ignore it."

"I take advice. I'm seeing Dr. Landon."

"True. Okay, shoot with the advice."

Silence spun out as Gena paused. "If he does show up, Angie, please be yourself."

"Who else would I be?"

"I'm not kidding, Angie. You're like Lily Tomlin, with a persona for every occasion. That's okay for your other pen pals, but not for the major. He's too important to you. If he comes, it'll be because you're important to him, too."

"This is too complicated, Gena."

"Yeah, I know. Who ever heard of falling in love by mail?"

"Your mother. She publishes at least one letter a year with a variation on that theme."

"You're not denying it?"

"I haven't decided yet."

"Uh-huh. And you won't unless you meet him. You're right—this is complicated."

Finishing off the wonton she still held between her fingers, Angie mumbled a quick good-bye and hung up, then picked up the bag and headed for the kitchen. The food was cold, and so was she. A shower was in order, then a good roaring fire. She'd heat up her dinner in the microwave and curl up in front of the fireplace and listen to the snow fall.

She would not think of Jack and wait for the phone to ring.

Jack turned the defroster of his rental car on high and squinted to see through the windshield. The roads in Colorado Springs were a nightmare of ice and drifting snow. Jack's mind was a nightmare of indecision. Dammit! He ought to be at home rather than driving around in zero visibility, his palms sweating over the idea of meeting a woman.

But Angie wasn't just any woman. She was his friend, his confidante, his fantasy. What, he wondered, do you say to a fantasy? *Hi, Angie. It's me, Jack. Nice weather we're having.* Or how about: *I was in the neighborhood—*

Sure, Jack, you were driving around in a blizzard just for the hell of it.

Angie was a very comfortable fantasy—perfect and flexible, meeting the needs of the moment. Realities had needs of their own. So did Angie. From that first letter, he'd wanted to rescue Angie from loneliness, protect her from life's little glitches, buy her a dozen kinds of wallpaper and candy for every occasion. He was beginning to believe he was the only man who could do it right.

Sure, Jack. Just like you did the last time around.

When—if—he met Angie in person, he wanted to have it all together—his future, his goals, his feelings. He had to be ready to handle disappointment. He had to be sure he was in control, sure that he wouldn't—couldn't—hurt her in any way.

That he wouldn't hurt himself any more than he already had.

He wasn't so screwed up that he couldn't acknowledge what bothered him most of all. He liked the Angie he knew on paper. The possibility existed that he wouldn't feel the same way after meeting her. Maybe in person she was a whiner, or maybe she nagged and clung. He couldn't handle a clinging vine. Everybody knew that he was a hollow man with a hard shell. The mirror told him that said shell had developed no character lines, no texture. Nothing to cling to.

The whole scenario was crazy. She wasn't Roxane, and he wasn't Cyrano. Real people didn't fall in love by letter. Things like this didn't happen in real life. Maybe he *should* see her just to prove his point. Who ever heard of a carnal friendship? How could a grown man be turned on by a woman he'd never met?

Because, Jack, you've got too much beach and not enough sand.

He braked at the corner and stared at the lighted phone booth. What would it hurt if he called her? It was a Friday night. Angie probably wasn't home. At least he'd be able to walk away without kicking himself for not trying.

He counted the rings, knowing she'd had time to get to the phone from Siberia, yet still he let it ring one more time, and then another. He hated the thought that she might be out with another man. It was crazy how territorial he'd become when it came to Angie. There were nights on base when the men around him were reading letters from their pen pals, speculating about the strangers who wrote to them. Sometimes the speculation became downright raunchy. He'd had a few X-rated dreams himself lately.

It was curiosity and loneliness, he told himself. No way did he feel any of the finer—or baser—emotions for Angie. He didn't know how. He hadn't felt anything when his wife had told him she was leaving. Later, he'd felt too much of a bad thing, shown it in all the wrong ways. Just as he had with Bryan.

A ground blizzard kicked up snow and piled it against the phone booth. Jack waited for one more ring, then clenched his jaw and dropped the receiver in the cradle. Okay, so he'd tried. Now he could head for home, enjoy the peace and quiet of an empty house. Hunching against ̶ ̶wind, he ran to his rental car.

̶ ̶ ̶the hell was Angie doing out on a night like

̶ ̶ ̶king toward his destination,

guided by a homing instinct that had nothing to do with rational thought. Right now, he needed to see a friendly face, hear a voice with genuine warmth in it, more than he needed silence and empty rooms.

The house was big and old with a roofed front porch and dormer windows jutting out from the attic. The largest bay window he'd ever seen curved out from the side and extended up to the second floor like a tower—bright with the light pouring through stained-glass windows and bleeding onto the weathered stone face of the house, welcoming him with color. A yellow glow flickered on the glass, promising the warmth of a fire. He saw a shadow move from window to window, adjusting blinds and closing drapes.

She was home.

His palms were sweating again. With a wry twist of his mouth, Jack pulled out his comb and ran it through his hair. The next thing he knew, he'd be checking for zits in the rearview mirror. A glance in said mirror showed no such imperfections. The glance lengthened into a critical examination of his face.

Yep, it was the same one he'd awakened with this morning, complete with whisker shadow and faint circles under his eyes. Shaking his head, he purposely ran his hand through his hair and saluted his image with false bravado. *Okay, ladykiller, go in there and show her what a man of the world you are.*

He didn't move. This wasn't right. He had no business here, inviting disappointment, maybe even rejection. "If it ain't broke, don't fix it," his dad had always said. Everything about his relationship with Angie was perfect as it was. It worked. He should be satisfied by that.

Except that he wasn't. Whenever he thought of Angie, he felt as if something were unfinished, as if a question had been left unanswered.

This was asinine. Maybe some questions were meant to remain unanswered, some good-byes meant to be said.

The neighborhood seemed deserted. Street lights were faint, eerie blurs against the brightness of the snow. Jack felt as if he were closed in a world absent of color, without life, except for the trees, stark in their bareness, rigid in the cold, their branches dark, emaciated arms outlined against luminous gray skies.

God, he was lonely.

17

The night was silent, empty with snow drifting against the house, insulating it like the individually wrapped springs of a mattress. Angie wound a towel around her just-washed hair, pulled on a robe over her nightgown, then wandered through the house shutting draperies and pulling blinds.

She couldn't stop thinking about Jack, feeling the loneliness magnify with the knowledge that he might be relatively close, yet too far away to see, to talk to, to touch.

For so long now, she'd wanted to touch him, be touched by him. It had been worse since she'd received his last letter, since she'd been forced into thinking about him as being more than emotions and words on a page. Now she knew what the girls at school had found so fascinating about men, why they'd been preoccupied by sexual speculation.

Fine. So she'd finally caught up with the rest of American womanhood. Had she thought it would never happen? And Jack was such a convenient no-risk, no-fault hero. It gave a whole new meaning to safe sex.

But it was more than that. It was regret and sorrow for something that would die before it had the chance to live.

The doorbell chimed, startling her. One of the awful things about living alone was the anxiety of having someone unexpectedly pop up on your doorstep, especially on a night fit only for polar bears and people who didn't have the sanity to stay in out of the snow. Maybe a friend who had suddenly decided to brave the elements for a wontons and fried dumplings.

The bell chimed again, and she caught room, avoiding the windows on he stood on tiptoe to peer throu

The general had installed it at his eye level, as if he hadn't thought that she and her mother might need that little measure of security.

All she saw was a large, dark shape blocking any other view of the street. The shape of a man with frost coming from his mouth with every breath, fogging the peephole. She hung back, trying to decide whether she was a woman or a wimp.

"Yes?" she called through the wood.

"I'm looking for Angela Winters."

If Jack's letters could have a voice, it would be that one: deep and a little angry, like his handwriting. She forgot her state of dress, the towel on her head, the misgivings she'd tried to convince herself she had just a few minutes ago. Without thoughts of caution and her state of dress, she slipped the chain and pulled open the door.

The porch light cast shadows over the top half of his face, emphasizing the deep set of his eyes beneath thick, blunt brows. The lines creasing his forehead appeared engraved in stone. He looked so grim and forbidding, so cold. In her visions of him, Angie had never seen grim or forbidding, had never envisioned a man as imposing as this one with his hard jaw and Air Force "blues" beneath the government-issue parka.

"Angie?" he said, his voice soft and deep, this time a rich whisper ᵗʰ ᵗ went all the way down, like a warm soothing drink   ic receded. "Come in," she whispered as she st   pull the door open. She couldn't stop sta⸱

⸱⸱⸱ you're cold," she mum-
⸱ips threatened to stick to her
⸱ssons in etiquette and hos-
⸱erience in faking it was

⸱s the threshold, feel-
⸱d and he needed a
⸱as a picnic com-

pared to the tightness that gripped him everywhere. If his mind rejected the possibility that the knockout gorgeous woman standing before him was Angie, his nose had no trouble identifying the vanilla and spice scent that clung to her letters.

She was real.

She had the kind of face that was both innocent and earthy, porcelain delicate, yet open and expressive. Dammit, he'd never cared what she looked like and was almost disappointed not to find plump, warm, and comfortable.

He shut the door and frowned as Angie took a backward step at the same time. Her hand clutched the collar of her robe around her throat and she looked as if she'd bolt if he so much as breathed.

An end of the towel wrapped around her head plopped against her cheek. He'd be willing to bet that under that towel, there was a head full of hair to match the single auburn strand that had been tangled in the elaborate bow on his Easter basket. Only her eyes matched his images of her. They were dark brown and wide, soft and expressive.

He hadn't bargained on them expressing panic.

Impulsively, he raised his hand, tucked the stray corner of the towel back in. Her breath caught, and she shivered as his fingers brushed her cheek. Her skin was cold, clammy. Her gaze darted up to his face, her eyes wide and unblinking. He felt like a hunter staring down his sights at Bambi.

"You always open your door to complete strangers?" he asked gruffly. He had a strong urge to wrap himself around her, protect her from the world.

She swallowed, skimmed her tongue over her lips, swallowed again. "You're not a stranger."

"You're sure about that?" he asked, and frowned at her slow, timid nod.

Good Lord, Angie of the bright and lively letters *was* shy.

Jack shifted uncomfortably under Angie's gaze. Shyness seemed to be as catching as a yawn. Next to Angie, he felt awkward and oversized, and he wasn't sure what to say that wouldn't send her shrinking into the nearest corner. He cleared his throat. "A fire, you say? Great."

He couldn't get into the living room fast enough. Once there, he yanked open the fasteners on his parka, practically tore it off, then just stood there holding it like a coat hook. He'd forgotten the cold as soon as he'd smelled the perfume, seen a reality that exceeded his fantasies. So many of those fantasies had included a thick robe and fuzzy slippers.

The robe was soft and loose, but it was a raw silk kimono with the traditional chrysanthemum embroidery in vivid blues and yellows. The slippers were fuzzy, all right—yellow satin with a sprout of fluff on top. He'd caught a glimpse of a silky yellow gown beneath her robe.

Exotic nightwear did not go with meek and shy. Neither did the face and body of the woman wearing it. Five foot four might be an exaggeration of her height, and with every step she took into the room, the silk draped and caressed her full curves. If he didn't miss his guess, her legs started at her armpits. Angie was the girl next door from the neck up and centerfold material everywhere else. He needed a good stiff drink.

"Would you like some tea?" Angie asked, forcing the words out, forcing herself not to stare.

"What?"

"Um . . . peach. The tea is peach," she stammered.

His smile was quick, a flash of expression that didn't quite make it past his clenched jaws. "Peach tea. Sure. Sounds good." He cleared his throat and looked into the fire. *Peach tea?* Now, that matched his visions of Angie.

A corner of her gown caught on the toe of her slipper as Angie literally tripped into the kitchen. She tossed a quick glance over her shoulder to make sure he wasn't watching just as his gaze jerked back to the fire. Cursing herself for a clod, she made the tea in fumbling, unconscious movements while her mind lingered in the living room, with Jack.

She thought of his voice, and the teakettle overflowed onto her hand. Shutting off the faucet and pouring out half the water, she thought of his mouth and the cleft in his squared-off chin and had to stoop to catch the lid to her porcelain teapot before it shattered on the floor. She stared at the mound of loose tea she'd spilled on the counter. With an impatient shake of her head, she reached into a canister for teabags, then pushed the pot aside in favor of two sturdy mugs.

From her first glimpse of him, she'd suffered more shock than shyness. She hadn't imagined him as being tall with wall-to-wall shoulders. Never in her wildest dreams had she conjured a man with such thick, brown hair and well-defined mouth with a sexy curve to the lower lip. That mouth could get a woman into all sorts of trouble.

But his eyes were exactly as she'd pictured them—dark blue and serious, as if to him the world was a dark and serious place. In his uniform, he looked like a man infinitely capable of defending his country, a man who could be the ultimate threat to the virtue of its daughters.

She felt . . . something, a disturbance of her senses, a stirring of energy in the air that drew her gaze to the window above the sink. His image reflected back at her from the glass, blurred, like a dream, less imposing, more manageable. The electricity charging her nervous system was pure reality. Turning around, she gripped the edges of the counter behind her and smiled self-consciously. "I . . . hope teabags are all right?" Why, she wondered, couldn't she be writing a letter? Reasonably intelligent conversation never eluded her on paper.

"It's fine," he said as he walked farther into the large country kitchen, his gaze riveted by the decor. Two porcelain unicorns—one white, one black—each with a golden horn rising from the center of its forehead, reared in battle in the center of an oval table made of mellow wood. The counters dividing the room into two sections were covered in dark blue Formica. He walked right up to a papered wall and stared. The background was a deep, rich red. Unicorns and white-gowned maidens frolicked between trees crowned with leaves of forest green, and glimpses of a night dark sky showed through the branches. He blinked.

Unicorns and jewel colors. "I expected pink and blue flowers—in baskets, maybe—or geese with bows around their necks," he said musingly.

"Flowers in baskets," Angie confirmed. "I exchanged it."

His hands in his pockets, Jack stared a moment longer, then turned to look at her. "My rut is grayish green with brown carpeting." He smiled whimsically. "I like yours better."

"I've been accused of having rather flamboyant taste," she said, her smile soft as the brush of snow on the window panes as she cocked her head. "Welcome to my rut, Jack," she whispered.

"You do know me," he said, his eyes narrowed in concentration—on her.

"Of course." She smiled self-consciously, then dropped her gaze to the mugs as her fingers rearranged the teabags. "How?"

"Um . . . your eyes, and . . . the uniform." Again, she moved the teabags to another spot inside the mugs. "And your voice—it sounds like your letters."

"Colorado Springs is full of uniforms," he reminded her. He wasn't about to ask why she would recognize his eyes or how his voice could possibly be a clue. Uniforms made sense—sort of. "I wouldn't have recognized you," he said gruffly.

She felt his gaze all the way to her bones as she turned to watch the teakettle, waiting for the water to boil, waiting for him to quit staring at her. Awareness held her spellbound: of her silk nightgown caressing her skin with every breath, sensuously, light as air; of the scent of peaches and spice permeating the air like an aphrodisiac; of her blood turning to liquid fire.

She snatched the teakettle from the stove and poured water that had just began to simmer into the mugs, then spoke quickly as she faced him. "Cream isn't very good in peach tea, but I do recommend sugar, or Equal, if you prefer."

Jack took a step toward her, and then another, his gaze another kind of silk, sliding over her, acquainting her with her own femininity, her own sensuality. Her lips parted as she raised her head. The end of the towel slipped over her right eye, and she tilted her head so it would fall away from her face.

He didn't know what he was about to do until he brushed the towel out of the way, closed his hands around her arms, bent to touch his mouth to hers, softly brushing back and forth, then drawing away. The little moan coming from the back of her throat cut the threads of his control. He enfolded her in his arms, felt her body sway and mold against his as if they'd been together like this a thousand times before. Her response was anything but shy.

Barely damp hair, as silky as her gown, brushed his hands as it tumbled down her back. In his dreams of Angie, he'd never felt the textures of hair and skin and silk, the heat of her mouth, the pressure of her body against his. In dreams or reality, he'd never felt the merging of emotion and desire as he felt it now.

She stood against him, her hands fluttering at her sides, her mouth beneath his, being shaped by his. He opened his eyes, saw that hers were closed, her lashes fanned against flushed cheeks, and steam was rising from the mugs on the counter behind her.

Peach tea and unicorns.

Reality.

He tore his mouth away from hers, jerked his arms from around her—fast, like ripping off a Band-Aid so it wouldn't hurt as much. It wasn't fast enough. He felt as if a part of himself had torn away and become a part of her. Straightening, he backed away, before he lost control, before he believed that they really weren't strangers, and kissing her was the most natural thing in the world.

"I'm not ready for this," he said without thinking as he jammed his hands in his pockets and paced back to the wall, trying to elevate the level of his brain.

"It's scary," Angie said, her voice breathless. "I didn't expect it to be so overwhelming." She bit her lower lip and averted her gaze, knowing she'd said too much. Maybe he'd miss the implications. She wanted to hide behind something—anything—just in case he did. "I think I'll go change into something less . . . comfortable." The quip came out all wrong, her airy tone as obviously forced as her smile, her deliberately light step toward the back stairway too stiff and careful to pass for casual. She just wasn't any good at this sort of thing.

Jack's voice—controlled and flat—caught up with her as she raised her foot to the first step. "You were expecting this?"

She thought about pretending she hadn't heard him, but the neutrality in his voice compelled her to stop, to answer honestly. "I've thought about it—wondered what it would be like." She shrugged. "Maybe it was the mystery."

"Yeah, the mystery. Well, now we know."

There was something final about his statement. The panic was back, acute and paralyzing, followed by a desperate, reckless courage she hadn't known she possessed. "Are you going to leave while I'm changing?"

His brows lowered, and his eyes clouded, reminding her of dark, gloomy skies. "I hadn't thought that far ahead yet," he admitted.

Angie's ability to bluff reasserted itself. She squared her shoulders, lifted her chin, stared directly at him with every bit of false pride she'd developed through years of practice. If only she were taller. "If you leave now, I'll follow you."

Jack sighed heavily and shook his head. "I don't think you've ever done anything like that in your life." He saw her gaze waver, then fasten on him with a challenging glint.

"No? Whatever gave you that impression?"

He might have believed that challenge came naturally for her if her voice hadn't faltered. "You're shy." It was an accusation and he knew it, but dammit, the truth of it had hit him like a fast ball right between the eyes. He could have handled anything but her particular brand of shyness.

She had unicorns in her kitchen, for crying out loud.

"No, I'm not," she protested vehemently. Her shoulders sagged. "Yes, I am—painfully so." *And never more painful than at this moment,* she thought. Forget taller. She'd rather be extroverted, brave, and so darn seductive that he wouldn't have been able to end that kiss if his life depended on it.

Maybe in the next life.

"Why aren't you shy in your letters?" he asked.

She shrugged again. "Because no one expects more than a letter. It's like being an imaginary friend."

What could he say to that when he knew exactly what she meant? Imaginary friends played the game according to your rules, without complaining, without cheating, without expecting more than you could give. Imaginary friends were for lonely children who needed challenge and variety for lively minds, for children who had no other way to express themselves, or weren't allowed to do so. He frowned, felt the creases in his forehead deepen, felt the pressure between his eyes. "We *are* strangers, Angie," he said harshly.

"No."

"Yes, dammit!"

Her expression changed, as if she'd just discovered something important, something shattering. "I've always known you, Jack."

At her admission, Jack forgot about making a quick getaway. The word *mystery* didn't quite describe Angie. She was a paradox, self-conscious one minute, forthright and revealing the next, sparkling and gregarious in her letters, yet subdued and skittish as hell in person. And she wasn't just painfully shy, she was painfully honest. On the outside, she was an exotic blossom, but inside she was a shrinking violet. Or was it the other way around? He needed to figure that out before he left—

"I was about to heat up dinner—it's take-out Chinese. There's more than enough for two."

Jack rubbed the back of his neck and scowled at the unicorns on the table.

"I guess I thought you might come if I bought enough for two," Angie blurted, revealing the hope she had refused to acknowledge earlier.

He turned sideways, toward the door, moved one foot forward. Angie glanced down at herself, with one foot on the first stair, the other on the second, her hand high on the rail, anticipating the climb. It all struck her as being tragically funny. Before she knew what she was doing, she heard her voice, grave and a little mocking. "It's only dinner, Jack. If we're both going to run away, we'll need our strength."

His head jerked up as his gaze shot to hers, then traveled down to her hands, her feet. A corner of his mouth lifted as he stared down at his own body, poised to walk away. "Is that the food?" he asked, nodding toward the bag next to the microwave.

"Yes." Forgetting all about changing her clothes, she lowered her hand from the rail and walked toward the counter. "As you can see—a lot of food."

His posture relaxed and he took the steps to join her, helped her remove cardboard cartons and styrofoam cups from the bag. She smiled up at him, suddenly feeling light and free and reckless.

Opening the refrigerator, she pulled out the bottle of plum wine, then unceremoniously dumped out the mugs of tea before reaching into a cupboard for two stemmed glasses. The cork left the bottle with a little whoosh and pop. The wine splashed into the crystal stemware with a whimsical gurgle. The microwave beeped in counterpoint as Jack slid in cartons of food and set the timer, then watched the seconds count down on the digital display.

Angie rushed around the kitchen, collecting plates and utensils, then paused in indecision between the dining area and the smaller table set into a large breakfast nook surrounded on two sides by floor-to-ceiling greenhouse windows. No, she decided, the nook was too intimate, with snow whispering against the glass and collecting in the corners of the square panes. Above the smaller table, the luminous silver night shone through, and the moon was a platinum medallion, smudged by moisture. With the skeletal trees and long tapered branches of juniper shrubs frosted in glittering white, it seemed too much like a different world, frozen in time and silent of everything but dreams.

She walked over to the larger table, where a buffet stood beneath a window bordered by a calendar on one side and a clock on the other. Carefully, she set out stoneware and stainless steel utensils, wine glasses, folded paper napkins by each plate, then left a pile at one end of the table. The first thing she'd done when her mother left was to replace the Kutani china, old Gorham sterling and damask napkins with more ordinary tableware. It had seemed so important to be ordinary.

The microwave buzzed, startling her from her contemplation of the table. Lifting her head, she watched Jack open the door, reach in, then snatch his hand back. His gaze searched the kitchen as he sucked on two of his fingers.

"Potholders above the stove," she said absently.

He nodded and reached for two. Angie started toward him to help but stopped herself, afraid that if she got too close, he would leave, afraid that if he got too close, she would run.

Once all the food was transferred to the table, she sank into her chair with a sigh and felt Jack's foot brush hers, then quickly draw away as he sat across from her.

Her hand hovered over the array of food. She had bought a variety, but out of habit she'd ordered each quantity for one. She was such a good customer that the owner of the restaurant automatically gave her half an order of each item. What were Jack's favorites? she wondered. Did he want the egg roll, or would he prefer the wontons? If she asked, would he be too polite to state a preference and leave the decision up to her? Quickly, she pulled her hands back and grabbed her napkin, unfolded it, set it just so in her lap.

Jack watched Angie's hands flutter as they passed over each carton without stopping, then fiddle with her napkin, then her wine. Her sudden smile was wide and strained, her eyes wide, a little unfocused. He reached for his own wine and drained half the glass, then twirled the stem between his fingers as he waited for her to serve. Her gaze darted from him to the food and back again.

The moment was awkward and as strained as the smile Jack returned to her. He needed something to occupy his hands and his mouth until he felt more balanced. But one minute stretched into two, and Angie had refilled both glasses with wine. She looked like a little girl, afraid and fidgety, as if she weren't sure what a fork was and the food might be something she wouldn't like.

Well, she'd asked him to stay for dinner and he'd agreed. Maybe they'd both made a mistake, but it was made, and he couldn't think of a graceful way out of it now.

Obviously, the only way they could communicate was through letters.

Absently, he patted his pocket, then pulled out his pen. Smoothing out the napkin with his other hand, he wrote out a message and slid the paper across to her.

18

Hi!

Angie glanced down at the napkin he'd nudged under her hand and read the single word. Something gave inside of her, a pressure that had been building since she'd heard his voice through the front door.

She felt as if warmth were being squeezed through a million tiny holes inside her, slow and easy streams of relief that eased her tension and carried away anxiety. Suddenly, she recognized him again as if there had never been a clumsy moment, and he was once again the man with whom she'd spent more time than anyone she saw at Link.

A man for whom new dreams had been created.

She reached over to the buffet, picked up the pen by the phone and wrote on her own napkin: *Are you as nervous as I am?* She saw his smile as he read—a real smile, wide and relaxed and more than a little relieved rather than the stiff grimaces he'd shown before.

He grabbed another napkin off the pile and wrote: *It's only a meal—nothing to get dysfunctional over.*

She bit her lip as she glanced at the cartons of food, remembering her dilemma and wanting to laugh. The solution was so simple. Again her hand hovered above the table. "Help yourself," she said, then reached for the dumplings with a knife in her hand.

At the same time, Jack reached for the egg roll and frowned. There was only one. Why hadn't the courses in etiquette and protocol at the Academy covered egg rolls and an odd number of wontons? No wonder Angie had hesitated. He saw the knife beside his plate and picked it up, cut the egg roll neatly in two, and slid half onto each of their plates.

Angie served up two and a half dumplings to each of

them while Jack divvied up the wontons—one and a half each, meticulously scooping up the filling that had squeezed out. His half flew across the table as their hands collided, the knives they each held crossing like swords.

Her gaze flew to the mutilated tidbit spilling its insides onto the tablecloth, then to the knives locked in mortal combat over the lo mein.

Jack could have sworn he heard her try to swallow down an indelicate snort of amusement. Biting the inside of his cheek, he dropped his knife and leaned over to scoop up the mess, but he turned at the last minute to look at Angie. "Should we let it die in peace?" he asked solemnly.

Suddenly her laughter filled the room, a sound that came from deep inside, full and throaty and punctuated by sputters as she tried speak around it. "I'm so glad . . . that you . . . did . . . that. I'm usually . . . the . . . one to . . ." She shook her head as she raised her hand to cover her mouth.

Jack sank back down in his chair, ignoring the wonton, focusing instead on the dimple that peeked out at him from between her fingers. He cleared his throat. "The next ice-breaker is on you," he said darkly.

Her eyes widened and the smile slipped as she lowered her hand. "I really hope we won't need another one."

"Amen," he said as he occupied himself with splitting the rest of the food between them and heard Angie's sigh blend with his when it was done.

Another napkin with tiny crowded handwriting in one corner appeared by his plate. *Thank you.* His gaze shot to Angie, but she was staring down at the table, and the towel she'd rewound around her head was dangerously close to falling off onto her plate. He wrote one final message.

We can't keep meeting like this.

Angie read the napkin and reached for her wine, taking a succession of sips before meeting his gaze and beginning the small talk that seemed inevitable. Her imagination had deserted her, and without a layer of paper between them, she could no longer be anyone but herself, grabbing for the first subject to pop into her mind. As usual the first subject was Jack. "You're back for good?" she said as she dropped her hands onto her lap and crossed her fingers.

"Yes."

"Since you're in uniform, I take it you flew in on government transport?"

"Yes," he said, "and I've been at Cheyenne Mountain all afternoon. A former commander of mine is stationed there."

"And he wanted you to transfer to Space Command after Germany?" Angie guessed.

"Something like that. I owed him a visit and explanation."

"So you haven't been home yet."

"The last time I was home, I'd just made major."

"Below the zone?" she asked, using the term for a recommended early promotion.

"Yeah," he said flatly.

"You're regretting your resignation," she stated.

"It was a damn fool thing to do."

"No, it wasn't, Jack," she said earnestly, forgetting how awkward she'd felt just a moment ago. "Not if the service isn't what you want."

Until lately, he hadn't thought of it that way—as something he wanted or didn't want. As if it were a choice he'd always had. "It's a little late for me to think, period," he said to himself as well as Angie.

"You haven't been happy. I could see it in your letters."

"Midlife crisis."

"You need a reason for everything you do," she quoted from one of his letters as she served equal portions of fried rice and beef and broccoli and lo mein. "But midlife crisis isn't it, Jack. You want to be a photographer. That's what's important to you."

"I'm on the wrong side of thirty, Angie. I need a stable career, not a glorified hobby."

"Lots of people make a good living in photography. The sky won't fall if you do what you want to do, Jack."

He glanced over at the breakfast nook and the snow covering the transparent roof. "It feels that way," he said wryly. "It was crazy enough to give up a retirement and benefits this close to the wire." Uncomfortable, he bent to his food. He hadn't meant to voice his unease, the second thoughts that wouldn't change a thing. Problems shared in a letter were one thing—sort of an intimacy once removed —but voicing them was quite another. It was too immediate and personal this way.

"You said that the Air Force was giving a payoff to officers who were willing to take an early out, and you have only yourself to take care of. Why don't you take some time and explore the possibilities?"

He said nothing in response to her but scowled and concentrated on his meal, cleansing away each different flavor with wine. Angie followed suit, and all too soon, the wine bottle was as empty as the conversation.

"How is Lieutenant Baker?" Angie asked as she rolled the stem of her glass between her fingers. "What happened with the girl he was seeing?"

Swallowing a bite of food, Jack drained his glass. "He sent her some money, and she moved on to another base. When I left Germany, Baker was being eyed by a cute little second louie who's got more energy than a platoon of Marines. I heard her asking Baker if he'd go into Stuttgart with her for First Saturday." Tilting her head to the side, Angie looked at him in question.

"Baker said yes."

"Well, thank goodness." Angie smiled. "What's First Saturday?"

"All the stores and shops in town stay open all day the first Saturday of every month instead of closing at noon."

"That's tomorrow. I wonder how they'll make out," Angie said.

"Judging from the gleam in her eye, they'll make out plenty," Jack said with a smile.

Despite the color rising in Angie's face, the way her gaze dropped to the table, she spoke vehemently, as if Baker were a personal friend and she had suffered through his trials right along with him. In a way, Jack supposed she had. "I hope they have a wonderful time."

He cleared his throat. "What did you do about your greeting card business?"

Angie frowned and looked confused as if she weren't accustomed to having anyone ask about her life. "I'm honoring my present commitments, then closing up shop. I guess we're both in the same boat—admitting to a mistake and doing something about it." She grinned mischievously, her eyes shining with pride. "Isn't it a great feeling?"

"What?"

"Escaping your own trap."

Put that way, Jack couldn't argue with her logic. He had been in a trap of his own making.

"Tell me about Gena's company—what you do there."

"Link? It's wonderful. Everyone there is a free spirit and wonderfully creative. The energy is amazing."

"Link," Jack said. "As in International? And Gena as in Collier?"

"I didn't tell you, did I?"

"No." His mouth quirked. "But then I didn't ask."

"Ah." She smiled back. "Well, now you know."

"I take it you've been connected with Link for a long time?" he asked, somehow knowing that her involvement went far beyond a job. She and Gena Collier were old friends, and everyone knew that Link had been started by a close group of family and friends.

"From the beginning, in one way or another," she answered. "I've always written the newsletter and filled in whenever, but it's organized and official now, with a full-time staff."

"And a board of directors."

"That, too."

"You're on the board."

"Yes. I helped put Link together. It's been the most exciting thing, watching it grow and being a part of its development. Working with Gena is an adventure in itself."

Jack forgot about eating as he watched her and learned all about shyness. It wasn't about stammering and hiding behind the nearest large object and having vocal chords suddenly freeze up. It was about eyes that flickered every time she spoke, as if she were taking an oral examination and weren't sure about her answers, and it was about Angie hunching up to fit herself in the smallest possible space, like her handwriting. It was about self-conscious blushes and uncertain fits and starts of movement—

Except when she talked about Link. Then her eyes came alive with tiny golden flares of light in soft brown depths, while her hands danced in the air, punctuating her enthusiasm as her voice found a steady pitch and her words vibrated with energy.

"Jack, you can't be full. There's too much food left."

He was full—of Angie, her life, and the world she'd created within walls built of native Colorado stone. Clearing his throat, he picked up his fork and dug into the lo mein, frowned as the slippery noodles slid through the tines. "So what do you do there now?"

"Lo mein is as bad as spaghetti, isn't it?" she said sympathetically. "Right now, I'm in charge of organizing a black tie benefit we're holding in December—a forties-style night club with a big band and torch singer."

"Sounds like a big job."

"Mmm. I still don't remember volunteering for it."

"You're having a ball," he guessed.

"I'll let you know after I give Gena my report." Angie placed her napkin on the table and reached for her wine. "All I had to go on for models was a lot of old movies."

"Sounds like fun."

"I hope so. Since the Davises don't give the Carousel Ball anymore, Gena is hoping to tap into that market."

"Are you going to perform?"

The shyness returned full force, complete with red face and skittering gaze. "Heavens, no. I'm an amateur."

"You must be good to be a teacher."

"Technically, but I'm not a performer. And I haven't sung for an audience in—" She broke off the sentence and shook her head. "No. I'm an amateur," she repeated.

Something told Jack that he'd struck a nerve. Angie's hands were shredding her napkin, and her shoulders were hunched again. Her forehead scrunched up, and if she weren't careful, she'd bite her lip clean through. The liveliness in her eyes changed to something else, to a steady burn of old pain, raw and bitter emotion.

Maybe she wanted to perform at the benefit and the idea had been nixed. Maybe she didn't have the courage to volunteer her talents.

"Do you keep up with it—the dancing and singing?" he probed.

"Only for myself," she said fiercely, as if she were trying to convince him and maybe herself.

"You enjoy it."

"I . . . yes." Suddenly, she snapped her head up and crushed the tattered napkin in her hand. "I have a studio behind the kitchen. It's a great stress reducer to crank up the music and just let go." Her gaze slammed into his, challenged him in some way he didn't understand. He did understand that the subject was closed.

He leaned back in his chair and surveyed the large kitchen, finding something new every time his gaze swept the room. Above the stove hung quilted potholders that were thick and colorful and shaped like the unicorns and trees and flowers in the wallpaper. "Did you make those?" he asked.

"Some of them. Others I found at craft shows and church bazaars. I collect them."

So much for that subject. He'd heard of some strange hobbies, but collecting potholders? It wasn't exactly a topic for stimulating conversation, and without that, he knew he would spend the time looking at her, cataloguing all the differences between baggy robes and clinging silk, chubby plainness and a vibrant sensuality that seemed to change with every moment. Angie was everything he hadn't expected. She stimulated his imagination without saying a word. She stimulated his libido just by sitting there.

He searched the corners and crannies of the room. A bulletin board hung just inside the arched doorway. Photographs covered every inch—of children and adults, some in what appeared to be costumes, others standing outdoors in front of a variety of architecture. He focused more clearly and saw men in various uniforms, either in casual, friendly poses or the more formal ones of studio shots. There had to be at least fifty different faces on the cork board.

His mind shifted gears, lurched, then raced back to something she'd said earlier. *No one expects more than a letter.* "Quite a collection you have there," he said, feeling the food in his stomach congeal into one big lump. "Old schoolmates?"

"My other pen pals."

"Other pen pals?" he asked in a too-soft voice. "How many others?" He gritted his teeth, knowing he sounded as if he were asking how many lovers she had rather than how many letters she wrote.

"Probably about twenty at any one given time. It depends. During the Gulf War, I had sixty."

Probably. She didn't even know the exact number, as if they *were* part of a collection—as if *he* were part of a collection. "In the service?"

"Most of them," she answered with a puzzled frown. "Why?"

Good question, he thought. Too bad he couldn't give her an honest answer. How was he supposed to tell her that it hurt, like losing an illusion hurt? They were pen pals, for crying out loud, *not* lovers. But he'd thought he was the only one she'd shared herself with, not one in a cast of thousands. For nine months and countless letters, he'd felt special, important to someone, as if he belonged to someone besides his parents. His parents had to like him. Angie didn't.

Bits and pieces of casual conversations he'd heard over the last few years drifted through his mind. His eyes narrowed on her as he spoke, the words feeling as if they might choke him. "In Germany?"

"A few."

"Which one are you—Angel or Baby or Our Girl?"

"Angel," she admitted reluctantly. "I hate that nickname."

"I'm impressed." Jack said flatly, as he pushed back his chair and rose. He strode over to the corkboard, his jaw clenching and unclenching as he studied the photos of the men in uniform—another collection that she'd hung on the kitchen wall. "You're a celebrity on the mail circuit—everything from saint to siren."

She raised her head with a jerk, her gaze stricken, shocked. "I don't . . . I'm not—" she stammered. "What do you mean?"

"I mean that you entertain the troops in more ways than one," he grated. "You send cookies and sympathy and . . . stimulation. Barracks are worse than locker rooms, and most of the men in them are still boys. While they're sharing your cookies, they wonder how you look undressed, how you'd be in bed."

"No, that can't be," Angie whispered, shaking her head as she stood and began carrying plates to the sink, her gaze everywhere but on him. "Their letters are so sweet."

"You can't be that naive."

"Yes, I can," Angie said evenly, and gripped the edge of the counter, feeling slightly sick at the implications of what he'd told her.

Rationality deserted him like a fair weather friend. "Uh-huh. I could tell that by the way you acted earlier. Is that how you welcome all the pen pals who drop in on you?"

Angie felt his anger like a blast of flame, burning her. She backed away instinctively, putting distance between them. Other than that step, she didn't blink or move a muscle—nothing to show the pain his words inflicted, the panic that anger always invoked. More than anything, she feared anger, shouting, ugly words. But more than that, she feared the destruction of what had become the most important thing in her life. She couldn't let it happen, couldn't lose one inch of the ground she had gained over the past few months.

Conditioned response took over, a response that had seen her through other times when she'd been judged, evaluated, dismissed. Her shoulders straightened and her back stiffened as she forced herself to stand still, to keep her hands at her sides, her head up, as she had when she'd stood in line with the finalists and felt the nightmare close around her. "I've never met a pen pal before," she said. "I've never wanted to."

Jack clenched his hands on the table and struggled with an anger that he'd never encountered before. Anger that hurt and kept him from swallowing and made every breath feel like ten pounds of lead. He felt the tightness in his chest, willing it to let go, willing himself *not* to let go. "Why do you do it?" he asked to give himself time. None of what she said or did should bother him. He couldn't let it bother him.

"They're lonely, Jack," she said, her voice becoming softer with every word. "And they're lost—"

"Charity cases," he mumbled as he swiped his hand around the back of his neck. "We're all freaking charity cases." He strode toward the living room, then stopped abruptly in the doorway, turned halfway, not quite facing her. "If I'd wanted charity, I would have contacted the Red Cross."

"If I'd wanted to make a charitable contribution, I'd have adopted a whale. I understand that they're more intelligent than man," Angie snapped, an unfamiliar feeling of outrage chafing her nerves. How could he believe what he was saying, as if she had used him because she had too much time and not enough imagination to fill her life in any other way? And then realization hit her, a devastating jolt of truth. Jack had stated the facts as he saw them, as they were. Imaginary friends—no real commitment, no risk, no growth, no confrontations with the monsters under her bed. A shallow existence. And now, when it really mattered, it had caught up with her.

She faced him then, because it was important that he see the truth. "You weren't charity, Jack. None of you were," she said, her voice barely above a shaky breath. *I'm the charity case,* she wanted to add, but the sudden calm in his expression stopped her.

A dead calm.

Jack glanced into the living room, at the ceiling, the floor beneath his feet, anywhere but at her. "None of us. All of us," he rasped. "When you wrote to me—were they variations on a form letter?" He shook his head with a jerk. "Don't answer that." Out of the corner of his eye, he saw her take another backward step, as if she were being pushed farther and farther away by his anger. Her expression was stricken, her skin pale against the vivid colors of her kimono, like the contrast between illusion and fact.

His mouth quirked in humor, a note of discord with the bleakness eating at him like acid. "Now I know what it means to feel lonely in a crowd." He walked away, grabbing his coat on the way out the front door.

Jack climbed into the rental car and stared through the windshield. Light slanted out onto the street from the open door of Angie's house. He hadn't shut it tightly on his way out. Gripping the steering wheel, he turned his head toward the house, waited for her to close the door, lock herself in.

Except that she'd already locked herself in before he left.

He hadn't missed the way she'd backed herself into a corner in the kitchen, her hands behind her as she pressed herself into the smallest space she could find. She'd seemed to fade, the light in her eyes dimming, her expression losing the animation that had been there even during the most awkward moments. She'd looked more like a broken doll than a person.

Good going, hot shot. You knew how fragile Angie was the minute you laid eyes on her.

"Yeah, fragile," he said as he jammed the key into the ignition, gave it a vicious twist. "She really did a job on me."

Did what, Jack? Written letters? Reached out to people who are as lonely as she is? Since when is that a crime?

He revved the motor unnecessarily while the car was warming up. Hadn't loneliness been the initial attraction? Hadn't she told him in a lot of little ways that her life was as hollow as his? He remembered her shyness, her panic, the way she'd responded to him, hot and desperate, as if that response had been waiting a long time to come out in the open.

Waiting for him. Wasn't that his fantasy all along? He

wasn't so different from all the other barracks Romeos, each reading her letters and pretending that she was waiting at home—for him. Only him.

Only there was a difference. Beyond their fantasies, the others knew better. But not Major Jack Caldwell. He'd read the letters and believed each and every fantasy, living from one to the next, pretending that through their correspondence, Angie had become his, just as he had become hers. His instincts had been right. He'd needed to see her, to get his head screwed on straight and remember that fantasies never last and people are never what they seem.

They were never what you wanted them to be.

Who cared how many letters she wrote? He reached over to switch on the windshield wipers and realized he hadn't turned on the lights. Stomping on the gas, he shot away from the curb, the rear of the car fishtailing all over the street. He acted on instinct, turning into the skid as he talked himself into a more rational state of mind. Except he couldn't get past his feelings. Strong, overwhelming feelings of disappointment, jealousy, even guilt at the way he'd talked to her.

He felt betrayed.

19

He felt like an ass.

The car was perched on a four-foot pile of snow, the rear end pointing toward the sky, the front burrowed in a mound of fresh powder. Landing in a snowdrift was a reasonable end to trying to burn rubber on snowpacked streets. Every time he tried to run on instinct, trouble was the natural conclusion. Complications were an inevitable result of confronting a fantasy.

At least he'd had the sense to get away from Angie before he'd let fly with his temper. He hadn't hurt anyone but himself. He knew better than to let his emotions get ahead of his control. It was stupid, adolescent—and dangerous.

He'd felt like an adolescent since he'd scrapped every plan he had to meet a woman he damn sure had no business meeting.

Jack punched the steering wheel with a clenched fist. Reason had nothing to do with his reactions to Angie. Nature had everything to do with his responses. It didn't take a genius to figure out that when a good excuse to leave hadn't been forthcoming, he'd made one up in the form of her "other" pen pals, and his place among them. It was more comfortable to believe that he occupied last place on her list.

Deep down inside, he had a nagging fear of just that.

He shrugged into his coat and left the car to survey the damage. The car was in as deep as he was. "Shit!" he muttered as he glanced around, looking for a lighted house, but the street was silent and dark. Checking his watch, he cursed again as he saw that it was almost midnight. Who would open their door to a stranger crazy enough to be out in a blizzard at this hour? Who would he call? Steve was out of town with the parents. The car rental office was closed. He'd let his auto club membership lapse while he was overseas.

Angie's door was still open, the light still a bright wedge against the gloom. Shaking his head, he again scanned the neighborhood, seeing nothing of the winter scene—the stark outlines and contrast of texture in black and white and shades of gray that had always challenged and fascinated his photographer's eye. There had been a time when he would have reached for the nearest camera, disregarding his predicament to capture the moods of a winter storm. But he wasn't seeing moods right then. He was feeling them—one after another, beating him from the inside.

He closed his eyes as if blindness would make the memories of his own actions cease to exist. But in that enforced darkness was the imprint of an open doorway, spilling light like promises into the night.

"Total bull, Caldwell," he muttered to himself as he dug into his pockets for his handkerchief, then spread it out under one of the rear wheels. He got back in the car and sat in a pile of snow that had collected on the seat. "Brilliant. You haven't screwed up enough tonight? Now you have to freeze your balls off?"

Now he was talking to himself. Studiously, he ignored Angie's house as he shifted into gear and eased his foot down on the gas. The tires slid forward six inches and dug into another drift.

The open doorway beckoned. It would be so easy to walk up to the door and ask to use the phone. He could call for a tow truck, then wait in the car.

But he wouldn't do that. He couldn't risk losing his temper again. At the same time, he couldn't risk losing the anger that he felt. He couldn't risk being around Angie, seeing her, touching her, feeling as if, in Angie, he would find himself.

More bullshit.

A shadow interrupted the light slanting out from her doorway, a dark cutout of curves and soft edges with dimension and substance and a color all its own. Jack didn't realize he'd been staring at that light. He didn't register that the shadow reached out onto the snow as Angie walked toward him.

Her face appeared on the other side of the car window, and she tapped on the glass next to him. Angie stood in the iridescent light of a veiled moon, her face so close to his, sparkling all over with the snowflakes showering onto her hair, her shoulders, her eyelashes, and the tip of her nose.

Her hand slowly spread out over the glass as if she were caressing his cheek, comforting him. And then he saw her shiver.

"Sonofabitch," he said under his breath as he opened the door and stepped out of the car. The wind whipped around him and froze the wet spot on the back of his pants where he'd sat in the pile of snow. Icy flakes stung his face, and he tucked his ungloved hands under his armpits to keep them warm.

"You're all right?" Angie asked as she took a step back.

"I'm fine," he said tersely, and noted that she had pulled on knee-length fur boots, insulated arctic mittens, and a red quilted ski jacket over her kimono and nightgown. She looked funny as hell, like a little girl whose mother had stuffed her into cold-weather gear over dress-up clothes. He was fine all right, if he didn't count cold balls and a pecker that was sore from doing situps all evening.

Her lips were turning blue. "Go inside," he ordered.

She backed up, then stopped as if she weren't quite sure what to do. "I tried to call a cab for you. They won't come out in this," she said in a voice as small as her handwriting. "The tow trucks are booked until at least tomorrow morning." Staring down at her feet, she added, "You should come back into the house."

"Dammit. I should have known better," he said, more to himself than to Angie as he realized that he wanted to go with her, to have a chance to make things right again. "Are the roads closed?"

"No, but you need a four wheel drive."

He needed a miracle. "I'll figure something out."

She put one foot forward and crossed her arms over her chest as if she were trying to withhold her next statement.

"I have a Bronco," she said through chattering teeth. "I'll drive you—"

"No, thanks."

Angie took a deep breath, shifted her feet to a wider stance, and lowered her arms to her sides. He could swear that her hands had tightened into militant little fists. Her mouth opened and closed, then opened again. "Darn it!" Pivoting on her heel, she leaned into the wind and stomped toward her house.

He lowered his head and bit the inside of his cheeks to stifle the laughter that Angie always seemed to inspire at unexpected moments. If he didn't miss his guess, she'd just lost her temper, a guess only because her voice hadn't climbed by one note but remained calm, conversational. Still, the rigidity of her posture and the way her clenched fists had made her mittens look like boxing gloves was a clue. So was the impact of something cold and hard against the top of his head. Raising his hand, he felt clumps of snow sticking to his hair. She'd thrown a snowball at him.

She had a good arm.

She was stomping back toward the house again.

He slammed the car door shut. At the sound, he saw her pause, then shuffle slowly up the walk, her head bent, her hands shoved into her pockets, as if she thought something had ended and there was no reason to hurry or to escape.

She had another think coming.

Jack stopped thinking altogether and followed her. The smooth soles of his regulation black shoes slipped on the packed snow of the street, and he slid three steps for every one, his free arm outflung for balance.

On the sidewalk, loose snow crunched beneath his feet and gave him better purchase as he scooped up a handful of snow and caught up with Angie. "You want to play, Angie?" Oddly enough, *he* wanted to play. He wanted to wrestle her down into the snow and roll around with her like a kid who had no concept of safety and the dangers of a winter night.

But she was freezing, and she looked as brittle as the icicles hanging from her porch. His balls were so cold, they'd probably shatter at the slightest touch, and he felt as if he'd left his feet back at the car.

She glanced up at him. "I'm not in the mood," she mumbled.

"Isn't it a little early in our relationship for a statement like that?" he asked lightly as he plopped the handful of snow on top of her head. How easy she made it for him to scrap Major Jack Caldwell and be who he wanted to be, who he was.

Oh, God.

"I can walk on my own, thank you," Angie said, ignoring his comment as she swiped at her hair and twisted her arm to free it from his grip.

He held on. "I can't. With these shoes, I'll fall flat on my face if I don't hold on to something."

She stopped dead in her tracks halfway across the porch. "If you need some*thing*, Jack, there's a rail that leads down the steps. There are hedges you can grab, and a tree near the curb." She didn't look at him but stared straight ahead.

Somehow, he'd pushed the wrong button, hurt her again, but he couldn't figure out how. "I'd rather hold on to you," he said quietly, and realized he'd been doing just that for over eight months.

Sighing, Angie stepped into the house and nudged the door shut with a swing of her hip that struck him as being an unconscious habit, as if she often entered the house with her hands full.

This time, he let her pull away from his hold.

Everything changed with the closing of that door. The light seared his eyes after the absence of color outside. Sudden warmth felt like a blast of reality on his cold skin, burning the nerve ends after the howling wind and bitter cold that numbed his senses and kept his thoughts centered on the moment.

Never had he been so painfully aware of a closed door, of the seconds that seemed eternally long as he and Angie faced one another, silently staring, barely moving, breathing carefully as if they had entered the wrong room and discovered in one another the presence of the dreaded tiger.

But who was the tiger—Angie or himself?

Reality came back into focus as Jack's eyes adjusted to the light. An electric light. Heat from a gas furnace and logs burning in the hearth of the living room. Rooms formed by wood and sheetrock and plaster. A flesh and blood woman, who was shy and nervous as she watched moisture spread down his trouser legs.

Her gaze skittered away from him altogether as she pulled off her gloves, shrugged out of the ski jacket, bent over to tug off her boots, and talked a mile a minute. "There's a list of numbers by the phone—towing companies, garages, Triple A." She held out her hand for his coat and hung it up next to hers.

"You already tried."

"Yes, but maybe you want to make sure. Maybe I missed someone."

"Anxious to get rid of me?" he asked.

Finally, she stopped buzzing around and met his gaze with an expression that went from sudden frown to deadpan serious. "If you're still angry, I'd just as soon take you home. If you're not, then I'd like you to stay." She nodded as if she were satisfied with what she'd said, then flicked a glance at his pants.

Letting her take him anywhere in this weather, at this time of night wasn't an option, not when she'd have to drive back alone. "I don't know what I am, Angie," he said quietly.

He really should get out of there before he found out.

"You're wet, Jack. Take off your shoes and socks, and stand with your back to the fire. I'll make some hot chocolate or something," she said, sounding a little like a general herself.

Hoping she'd opt for "or something," he raised one foot, then the other to untie his shoes and ease them off. His soggy socks landed in the shoes with a plop, and he carried the lot over to the mat, where Angie set them next to her boots, then spread out his socks to dry. There was something very intimate about having a woman handle his socks.

Slowly, Angie straightened up, and her gaze homed in on his wet trousers.

He sighed as he rubbed his forehead and explained, "I sat in a pile of snow and would like nothing better than to stand in front of the fire. And thank you, but hot chocolate isn't going to do it, Angie."

Her gaze roamed all over him, everywhere but on his pants as she blushed a bright red that clashed with her auburn hair. "I didn't think—it just looks funny—"

"I know what it looks like. It feels even worse." His facial muscles thawed and ached as he smiled. "There's nothing like being caught with wet pants to give a person perspective."

The corners of her mouth tipped up as her lips parted in a hundred-proof smile. "You mean like meeting someone important for the first time with a towel wrapped around your head and no makeup in sight?"

He barely heard her for staring at that smile, and wondering about that "someone important." Was he important to her? Wasn't that what his show of temper had been about?

His smile faded as he strode into the living room and bent over to add a log to the fire. "Ah, you mentioned a drink?"

"A toddy?" she asked. "I used to make them for the General. He says they're the best thing about . . . coming home." Her smile slipped, but she pulled it back up as she threw him a quick glance on her way to the kitchen.

As soon as she was out of sight, Jack presented his backside to the fire. Beyond Angie and unicorns and dancing maidens, he hadn't really noticed much about the house earlier. To him, one room was pretty much like another— furniture on the floor and pictures hanging on the walls.

Nothing about this room was ordinary: not the golden glow in the air, nor the wisps of color that reflected off the bay window and danced on the walls with every sway and leap of flames in the fireplace. Not the uncoordinated decor and jewel tones that seemed to peacefully coexist in spite of their differences, nor the illusion that wherever he looked, he saw her reading or watching television or listening to music.

In this room, he *sensed* her presence, felt as if he'd slipped inside a special place that held him close, surrounded him with sensuality and the excitement of discovering something he hadn't known existed. Like the fantasies of Angie that had soothed his restlessness night after night, as if she'd somehow known that he needed soothing. Like a very real understanding on a level that didn't need explanation.

He inhaled the lingering scents of her perfume, peach tea, woodsmoke, the fresh flowers on the low cocktail table —her own world created to keep her safe from the one outside.

He, on the other hand, didn't feel safe at all.

He did feel the burn on his backside as the fire heated the moisture in his pants, scalding his skin, warning him that he was standing too close to the flames.

"You're steaming," Angie said as she returned from the kitchen carrying two crockery mugs. "I think you're probably dry."

As he stepped down off the hearth, he accepted a mug and watched the shimmer of a hundred shades of autumn reds and golds and browns in the loose spiral curls that framed her face and cascaded down her back. He heard her slow careful breaths as she stood facing him, saw the signs of uncertainty and wariness in her expression.

He *was* an ass.

"Angie, I had no right to go off like that," he said quickly before the awkwardness took over again, before he could talk himself back into anger. "I had no right to think—" He stopped himself from saying something he didn't want to hear and raised his mug, breathed deeply the aroma of lemonade, honey, and whiskey. Lots of whiskey, he hoped. He needed anesthetizing. After taking a cautious sip, he gazed down at the toddy. "Hell, I wasn't thinking at all."

Angie nodded, then took a large swallow of her own drink. "Well, that explains it," she said brightly. "Every time I stop thinking, I put my foot in my mouth." She walked over to the bay window and sat down as if the sofa hadn't been closer, and the circular alcove were her natural habitat, her sanctuary. "I never know the right thing to say or do until it's ten minutes too late," she said in a rush. Gradually, her eyes seemed to lose their depth, becoming distant, blank. "Letters are a great way to communicate. I have hours or days to think up a response, to say what my pen pals want to hear."

"What about what you want to say?"

"No." Her voice was curiously flat, as if she were reciting a lesson and knew she'd be censured because it was the wrong one. "That's not what they want from me. It's not what I want to give."

"Angie," he said gently, "you weren't paying me lip service in the letters you wrote. You were honest."

Her eyes widened and her head jerked, as if he'd surprised her by telling her something she didn't know. Then she nodded and shrugged her shoulders. "You're different. I thought maybe you'd understand . . . that maybe you wouldn't think I should change the way I am."

"What about Gena?"

Her hair danced around her face and fell against her cheeks as she shook her head. "Gena knows me, but she wants me to change, too. She wanted me to go on a sort of tour to meet some of my pen pals, but that wasn't what I wanted to do, just as you probably didn't really want to see me." Suddenly she thunked her mug down on the ledge beneath the stained glass window and rose. "I'll see about your bedding," she said as she hurried into the foyer and climbed the stairs.

Deep in thought, he sank down on the window seat and sprawled with his back against the wall, one leg raised on the seat, his elbow supported by his upraised knee. He stretched his other leg out on the floor and massaged the bottom of his foot on the nap of the plush carpet. The toddy did its work, warming and relaxing him, neutralizing his ambivalence at being here.

He noticed for the first time the soft, curved edges of the interior of her house—arched doorways and rounded corners, a curved staircase and bay windows. Even the walls met the ceilings on a curve and the fireplace was hemispherical, like a sun rising on the horizon.

It was a place where he not only saw Angie in every nook and cranny, but himself as well, beside her, talking to her, sharing comfortable silences—

The whole thing was getting a little too metaphysical for comfort.

"The bedrooms are all empty—I'm renovating—except for mine and one other, and the sofa is larger than the spare bed," she said breathlessly as she returned with an armload of bedding and dumped the lot onto the sofa before he could get up to help her.

"It's been a long time since I've had the luxury of sacking out on a sofa, Angie. I'm looking forward to it, especially if I can fall asleep with the TV on." He studied the sofa, its thick cushions, just one more thing he could sink into, be absorbed, as he was being absorbed into the house, into Angie's presence.

She nodded. "Mm," she said.

She reached across him for her mug and took several gulps, her gaze fixed on him over the rim of her cup. Where her eyes had been a bright, clear brown a moment before, they now seemed to fade, lose their animation. Her expression smoothed out as if she could leave herself at will. As if she had found a place out of harm's way.

It was an old defense tactic, one he recognized with intimate familiarity. It bothered him to see it in her, to know she felt she needed it enough to develop the technique, to use it with him.

"You have to understand, Jack," she said, her voice devoid of inflection. "I'm what you call a friend in need. My pen pals are all transients in my life, coming and going as the need arises. When they don't need me anymore, they go on."

"Without you."

"Yes, of course." She sank onto the seat beside him, holding her mug in both hands. "I had no reason to believe that you'd be any different. Yet I did believe it. I still do."

That "of course" unsettled him. Her crazy mixture of idealism and fatalism scared the hell out of him. Her closeness was driving him nuts. He doubted that she was aware that she had leaned back against his leg or that her kimono had fallen open, just a little bit. Just enough for him to see the glimmer of dusting powder on her neck, her collarbone, the rise of her breasts. So close that he could smell her shampoo and see the faint sprinkling of freckles across her nose. Too close for him to ignore her unsteady breaths, the way she had to control her mouth to keep it from trembling when she spoke.

"When your letter came, I really believed that I did not want to see you—ever." She kept on talking, explaining, as if she were reciting a speech and wanted to get it over with as soon as possible, as if she expected ridicule or criticism. "Leaving town seemed like a good idea, and I even considered Gena's tour idea—for about five minutes. Instead, I counted the weeks and then the days, and when I thought the time was right for you to come home, I spent a whole day at a salon getting a facial, hair styling, manicure, pedicure, and working out in my studio—the works. I bought five new outfits and wore one today, then I almost didn't go out in case—"

"You're beautiful, even with a towel on your head and no makeup," he said, surprising himself. *Compliments, Jack? Since when?*

"I know," she said, the light in her eyes fading even more. "I also have a great figure—since the age of eleven. That's something else you need to understand." She paused to drink the last of her toddy.

Right then, he knew he should break in, change the subject, plead the call of nature—anything to stop her. He shouldn't want to understand anything about Angie. He shouldn't be sitting so close to her, needing to understand. "Angie—"

"No, darn it! You're here, Jack. You're the one who asked about what I want to say. Now you'll have to hear it while I have the courage."

"Angie—"

"I know I'm pretty, Jack. I know I have a great figure. It's all anyone ever saw about me. But those weren't my choices, and I haven't given any of that much thought in years. Then you came along, and suddenly I was glad about the way I look."

Jack frowned. Why wouldn't she have been glad before? Other women could only envy . . . Suddenly, he understood. Envy. Jealousy. Maybe at the age of eleven, the kind of attention she got from boys was more than she could handle. Another question had nagged at him since he'd first seen her. "You haven't always been shy, have you?"

She hesitated and squeezed her eyes shut, and he saw the shudder she tried to suppress. But then it was gone— all expression, any hint of emotion. "No. At the time, it seemed the only choice I had."

He didn't understand how someone could choose to be shy, to climb into a rut and stay there, yet it didn't matter— not then. He reached over and took the mug from her hands and set it on the window ledge next to his own. Nothing seemed more natural than to wrap his hand around her shoulder and pull her back against his chest, to cradle her knees with his arm and lift her legs to rest on the cushion, to shift her body so that she was nestled between his thighs.

Hints of Angie came back into her eyes as she looked up at him and sighed. He waited for protest or signs of unease, but instead her body flowed and conformed to his between one heartbeat and the next. He knew he shouldn't be doing this, but he'd been breaking a lot of his own rules lately. There didn't seem to be any reason to stop now.

Gently, he squeezed her shoulder with his hand. "Tell me," he ordered softly.

Again, she sighed as he urged her to rest her cheek against his chest. If she faded out again, he didn't want to see it. "You had a great body at eleven," he prompted.

"Yes, but nothing that went with it. I never felt what the other girls did. Boys didn't interest me. Later, neither did men—not that way. I was the worst case of arrested development in history. At least, until your letters."

Her head moved on his chest, and he looked down at her face tilted up to his. She hadn't withdrawn again, but gazed at him with all the uncertainty he'd seen when he'd first walked into her life. And he saw determination and forced courage.

He had a feeling that shy or not, self-consciousness notwithstanding, Angie was going to mess with his head but good.

"I don't know why I answered your first letter. Normally, I wouldn't have considered following up on a rejection," she said.

Something was coming—maybe a freight train or a tidal wave—something he wouldn't be able to stop or avoid, that would rearrange him from the inside out, scramble what was left of his common sense and reason. "Angie—"

Obviously, Angie was in a mood to flirt with trouble.

"I've never wanted to see anyone in my life as much as I wanted to see you, Jack. I never wanted to be held by anyone as I've wanted to be held by you. I don't think I'll ever regret anything in my life more than I'd regret not being touched by you."

She'd been thinking about sex. With him. Maybe she was talking about more than sex. With him.

He was thinking about it, too.

That did it. All the discipline and order he'd worked so hard at setting up in neat formations scattered in full retreat. Inch by inch, he'd been willing his body to relax—some parts more than others—while his mind had given up any hold on rationality. Now was the time to sit Angie up and set fantasies aside for good. Now was the time to take the easy way out. "Angie—"

She wouldn't shut up, and a gentleman never walked out while a lady was talking.

"I know, Jack. It's not supposed to happen this way—

through letters, for heaven's sake. It's crazy, and risky and impractical to fall in love—"

He didn't hear any more for the roaring in his ears. *Love* —the magic word guaranteed to make him disappear, preferably in the next two seconds. *Love*—a convenience store word that offered a little bit of everything without stocking enough of anything for more than a snack at an inflated price. *Love*. He tried it out anyway—in his thoughts, as he had when he'd heard from Angie, thought about Angie, dreamed about Angie.

"Angie, we're strangers."

"No. We met a long time ago," she said, still whispering. "We've seen so much of each other—more than most people see when they're standing in front of each other." She bit her lip, frowned. "I'm *not* sorry I said that."

Jack was. He didn't want to hear it, but it was too late now. He had heard it and felt it. She'd answered questions he'd barely acknowledged to himself, and now that she had, it was there, a part of him.

He was hooked, and he knew it, but he wasn't about to admit it. Maybe he was splitting hairs. Maybe he didn't really mind being hooked. Except that he knew he couldn't give in to it. Being one of two wasn't for him. Being close with a woman—or anyone for that matter—meant personal involvement. For him, that meant trouble. It meant two-way hurting and eventual loss, the potential for betrayal and losing control.

He had to leave. He had to do something besides tighten his arms around her, rest his chin on top of her head, inhale the coconut fragrance of her shampoo, feel the satin softness of her hair. He needed to go back outside and sit in a snowdrift.

Jack tried to ease away from her, forced his hands to be gentle, tried to think beyond his crotch. He'd never felt so full and heavy as he grew in direct proportion to the emotions he experienced for the first time. It wasn't possible. He'd been married. But he'd never gotten a hard-on just by looking at Kay, just by hearing the sound of her voice. Their relationship hadn't been that spontaneous. Want and lust were easy to understand, but not so easy for him to accept. Not with someone he'd just met. Not when his feelings kept getting in the way.

She was crazy. He'd known that all along. He knew that he'd come here because he wanted to be a little crazy, too.

Dammit, he still did.

The room was warm and mellow with color and welcome. The woman was so close, reminding him that she'd become a part of his life a long time ago. They were enclosed and insulated, protected by thick walls and special emotion. There was no way to leave.

No way to escape the magic.

At his continued silence, Angie twisted around to look at him, to splay her hand over his chest, nestle her head on his shoulder. She saw his mouth tighten and twin grooves mark the space between his eyebrows. She wanted to smooth it all away, to somehow make it better. Jack worried too much. She'd seen a hundred subtle clues in his letters. "Have you ever been completely selfish, Jack, and done something you really wanted to do without thinking about it or worrying how it might affect someone else?"

"Yes," he said roughly as memories flashed through his mind—of Bryan and Kay and even Steve. Each time he'd been thinking only of his feelings, his pain.

"Me, too. But others *were* involved, and they were hurt," she whispered. Chewing the inside of her lip, Angie stared at the way her fingers were nervously pleating the fabric of her kimono. She clamped her lips firmly together, trying not to say more, reveal more.

She didn't make it. More words tumbled out, fast, pushing past her self-consciousness. "We were friends first, Jack. For a while now, I've felt like maybe there's more. I . . . need to know for sure."

She took a long, deep breath, swallowed, licked her lips, then raised her hands to either side of his face, arched her neck, stretching until her mouth reached his and nibbled in tiny biting kisses.

His arms tightened around hers, and his lips parted without breaking contact. His tongue traced the seam of her

lips, coaxed them apart, sneaked inside, as if he were desperate to absorb as much of her as he could. He tasted like
lemon and honey and strong whiskey—all warm and intoxi-
cating. Sensations sharpened as her eyes drifted shut. Her
body was heating up from the inside out.

His tongue explored the corners of her mouth, dipped
inside—barely—for quick little tastes as he held her fast
against his body. All of his body, bold and hard and *needy.*
That had been her first impression of him so long ago—
that he was as needy as she was, as empty.

His hands grew bolder, his touch more firm as she followed his lead, met each kiss, once, twice, three times. The
teasing nibbles were over. His mouth covered hers with
firm pressure, insistence, hunger. Their tongues mated and
parted and played. He drew her into his mouth, consuming
her with sensations she'd never felt before.

She knew what to do, thanks to *The Joy of Sex* and Lon-
nie Barbach and erotica by the Kensington Ladies. Didn't
she have a full complement of healthy instincts? Wasn't
this what she'd been asking for?

And she'd done this before—sort of—late at night, when
she'd dreamed of a renegade major appearing out of nowhere to make slow, tender love to her. She'd felt the restlessness and need, but it had never been this desperate and
dangerous rush of craving and sensation. She'd never felt
reckless with the phantom lover who had brought her hormones out of hiding. All she'd really known was that those
nights left her wanting more.

She wanted more now.

It was difficult to think rationally with Jack so close, his
breath fanning her cheek, the hard and hot reminder that
he was a man pressing against her bottom. Difficult but not
impossible. She had no inclination to think.

Beneath her, she felt the hard ridge he couldn't hide,
hard with insistence and desire.

She'd done this to him.

Wow!

She'd dreamed of a moment like this dozens of times,
only the dreams were silent. In the dreams she'd never

been shy and awkward and worried when her phantom lover drifted out of the shadows, took her in his arms, caressed her breasts with deft, sure hands.

Hands that were flesh-and-blood warm, with a slight calloused roughness. Hands that sent a shock of pure energy through her as they skimmed the sides of her breasts, rotated over her nipples.

She'd asked for it blatantly.

Jack was responding—blatantly.

She'd wanted him for such a long time, regardless of what he looked like—short or tall, homely or handsome. It just hadn't mattered. Handsome was a bonus. So were muscles and height and a kiss that lasted forever.

She wanted another just like it. She wanted to stop feeling so restless, as if she were about to jump out of her skin, as if her nerves were on fire.

Everything was fine, Angie told herself. She knew what she was doing. It wasn't so hard, taking that first step into an unfamiliar experience.

All she had to do was grow a backbone. Quick.

20

She'd asked for it.

Angie knew she had, babbling like an idiot, saying things to him that shouldn't be said, blindly acting on instincts she wasn't familiar with. She was running fast and loose on instinct again, running a race, catching up with herself as she discovered a whole new Angie who operated independently from the one who believed in safe conduct at all times.

No book in the world could prepare a woman for a man's erection. No manual ever written could adequately describe the sensations that crowded one another, like the clumps of air that lodged in her throat.

The books hadn't said anything about the current of feeling that arced from her breasts to her belly as he looked at her, visually exploring her body through the silk. The books never said that there were times when breathing wasn't necessary, nor did they hint that the skim of a man's hands on the inside of her elbows might make her feel like warm butter.

Clearly, Jack wasn't one to go by the book.

"It's easy for a man to be selfish, Angie," Jack said, his gaze locking on to hers, holding it. "There's a point where selfishness is a given, and it's too late to stop."

She understood the warning. That much had been in the more technical manuals she'd read. The look in his eyes willed her to listen, to make another choice now. His hands delivered a different message. He didn't want to stop. Her gaze darted to the bulge beneath the zipper of his pants. Or maybe wanting had nothing to do with it, and he just couldn't stop.

It was a shock to think she might have that kind of power

over him. Power meant responsibility, the possibility of failing—Jack as well as herself.

What was she doing?

Jack's hands became urgent, his eyes heavy-lidded as his gaze roamed over her body. She wanted to raise her arms, cross them over herself, but she couldn't seem to move. Her heart skipped and skidded in her chest. A chill rippled over her, inside her.

Abruptly, she jerked upright, dislodged his hands, separated herself from the drift of his breath on her skin. Her throat clogged up, trapped breath in her lungs, and her heart thumped in panic. No matter how much she wanted this, she couldn't do it. She wasn't sure how, but she'd conned him, conned herself. She'd set them both up for disappointment, failure, rejection—hers, his, she didn't know and wasn't in the mood to analyze it right then. The fear was enough.

Jack had been married. In spite of all the reading material Gena's mother had provided for her, Angie was still inexperienced and hung up on her ability to perform. Obviously, men weren't the only ones to suffer from that particular insecurity.

Bending her knees, she tried to scoot away from him and slid off the seat altogether, jarring her teeth as her rump met the floor.

Mortified, she buried her face in her arms and forced herself to inhale, hold for the count of twenty, and exhale slowly. She desperately needed a paper bag.

"Angie?"

He was there, sitting next to her on the carpet, his elbows crooked on his upraised knees, not touching her, but close enough to remind her of the heat of his body, how easy it would be to lean into him again.

"I am so embarrassed," she said, her voice thready and a little strangled.

"Yeah," Jack said gruffly.

"Our first instincts were right, Jack," she said before she could think about it. Impulse had landed them in this mess. Maybe it would get them out. "We shouldn't have met.

You've been driving me crazy for months, and seeing you, well, it's making me more crazy." She knew she was babbling again, but he had to know it wasn't his fault that her arrested development had suddenly made parole. "I'm *sorry,* Jack. You *didn't* want to hear what I said. You didn't *need* to know how I feel. Usually, I'm so good at faking it. But this isn't the time. For once I have to be honest."

She wove her fingers together, separated them, and repeated the process. "I wanted to be selfish, Jack, and *dammit,* I still do—but that doesn't excuse my putting you in this position."

"You're scared, Angie?"

"No, not exactly—well sort of . . . but not . . . actually, I'm—"

"Scared," he repeated flatly.

"I really should have practiced," she blurted, then horrified, she buried her head in her arms.

Jack blinked as he stared at her. "Practiced? How?"

"Please forget I said that." She turned her head just enough to peek at him.

A corner of his mouth slanted upward in bemusement. He cleared his throat. "Exactly what is the problem here, Angie? Second thoughts?"

She shook her head. "No. It's just that . . . well . . . I was thinking about what we were doing, and then I couldn't help but think past that—you know, all the way. I really didn't think that it would be so overwhelming. That I'd be so vulnerable." She licked her lips, swallowed, tried for a whole, uninterrupted breath of air. "I thought I was so enlightened, Jack, and I am, but I didn't really believe that men were so—that they . . . you . . . responded so . . . that I would be so *thoughtless.*"

She dared another peek at him, saw his eyebrows drawn together as if he were concentrating very hard on what she was saying. So far, she knew she'd said nothing that made any sense, but she couldn't seem to stop talking. "It's so easy for men. I guess maybe your instincts are more detail-oriented or something. And you don't really need to feel anything to—" She shook her head, tried again. "I'm sorry,

Jack. I didn't mean to fool you. Enlightenment is a long way from experience."

Crossing his arms on top of his knees, he rested his chin on one balled-up fist. That meekly voiced confirmation of what he'd suspected should have scared him off, but somewhere between last Christmas and now, he'd guessed the truth, adjusted to it.

She was a virgin. But she was also twenty-seven years old —an *enlightened* woman who thought things out a hell of a lot better than he did. "You're right, Angie. It's easy for men. I didn't have a chance against you. We're all mindless idiots whose brains drop at the sight of a pretty woman. Haven't you noticed how we all walk around in an almost constant state of arousal?" he asked wryly, hearing the amusement in his voice, feeling it and wondering why. He was frustrated and hard and annoyed and . . . hard. Painfully hard. "We are so easily fooled."

Jack knew he was talking to buy time, to give himself a chance to elevate his thoughts a little, to wait for the old sense of caution to kick in. Nothing happened. Caution might never have been a part of his makeup. The person he'd been for twenty-five years had just broken ranks. He was simply a man—sans rank and serial number and weapons against the world. He was Jack Caldwell, who, once upon a time, had believed that heroes really did exist, that dreams could be real.

"I didn't mean that," she protested.

He dragged in air, ran his hand over the back of his neck.

"Angie, it's all right. You don't want to . . . go all the way." He almost choked on the old-fashioned term, a term he suspected Angie used because it sounded a lot nicer than more modern phrases.

"Yes, I do," she said softly, her voice muffled by her arms. "I want very badly. I just didn't expect to need quite so much, or to feel so vulnerable."

It wasn't what Jack wanted to hear, yet her statement brought a sense of relief that crowded out the last of his doubts. He wanted, too. Badly. He needed even worse. The

truth was that since she'd opened her door to him, he'd
had nothing to rely on but emotion. "Angie," he said, his
throat feeling like a bed of gravel, "you don't think a man
is vulnerable?" Twisting his body, he sat facing her as he
grabbed her hand, pulled it down to his lap. "At least you
can think. I might be able to dredge up a thought or two—
if I wanted, but you took that choice away from me."

He eased her fingers open, flattened her hand over his
erection. "Feel this, Angie. This is vulnerability. It's almost
like a separate entity, knowing where it wants to go, and
not particularly caring how it gets there." His voice died as
pleasure speared through him at the pressure of her hand,
the way her fingers kneaded him through tight cloth and
the textural ridge of a strained zipper. "It only cares about
physical relief, not human satisfaction."

"Then it all boils down to mutual trust, doesn't it?" Angie's voice stumbled on the question.

"Blind trust," he corrected.

"What do you care about, Jack—relief or satisfaction?"

Yesterday he wouldn't have known how to answer that.
He wouldn't have understood the difference. He might
even have had better sense than to reach out to her, touch
the tip of her breast, roll it between his thumb and forefinger, revel in her staggered breath. "I care about this, Angie. About the sounds you make when I touch you, and the
way you change in response."

Tomorrow, he'd probably kick himself all the way back to
Germany for what he was doing. But not tonight. Tonight
was his, as the moments he'd spent reading Angie's letters
had been his. Tonight he'd found a dream he couldn't pass
up, a dream worth doing.

Tonight he was going to be a hero.

Long, slender fingers wrapped around his wrist, held his
hand still on her breast, held it more firmly against her soft
flesh until he met her gaze, saw the brightness of her eyes,
the certainty of her expression.

"I think we should both be selfish, Jack." Angie's panic
receded as she said the words that made his eyes flare, his
body shudder.

The room tilted suddenly, and she found herself staring at the ceiling before Jack's head eclipsed the colors dancing on textured ivory plaster. The thick carpet cushioned her back as he framed her face with his hands, held her still as his mouth covered hers in a hard, fast kiss.

She couldn't pull away again regardless of the risks—of not meeting his expectations, of being disappointed herself, of maybe losing him.

She knew what Jack was doing. He was taking over, exercising his own power over her by pinning her wrists to the floor on either side of her head, lowering the full force of his body over hers, showing her that her need was mutual, that power was mutual.

She wondered why she'd panicked in the first place.

His eyes closed for a bare second, and he shuddered once as he raised up on his elbows. His hands touched hers, massaged them over and around and down into the crevices between her fingers, over her palms, lingering in the soft center, then lifting her hand to his mouth to do the same with his lips, his tongue.

Against her belly, she felt him grow harder and, well . . . grow. It was amazing, that growth. Beneath her gown, she felt her nipples tighten, her breasts swell, felt her senses come alive in a chain reaction, join together until she became sensation itself.

His hand wrapped around hers, guided it between the buttons of his shirt to touch bare, hot skin, springy hair, male nipples as stiff and puckered as her own. She found firm muscles, tensing at her touch, responding to *her* touch.

The kimono fell open on either side of her, and he traced the straps of her gown where they bit into her arms just above her elbows. He tugged to slide them down further, but they wouldn't budge. Pushing them back in place on her shoulders, he soothed the creases they'd left in her skin, then lowered his body over hers.

He was strong, and his skin was hot through his clothes. His hand found her breast again and stroked the peak through her nightgown. Another electric charge shot through her, creating friction with silk on skin, feeling better than she had ever imagined. None of this was a mystery to her—not his hands that were roving from the soft spots beneath her ears to her neck, her collarbone, her chest, and down, as his fingers wandered, homed in on the inside of her thighs.

"I care, Angie," he rasped, "that you like what I'm doing, that you're wet and ready and trust me enough to show it."

She was melting inside. To prove it, she shifted, opened to his caress, felt the air like a shock on the heat and moisture Jack had discovered in her. In the last few moments—minutes? hours?—her body had changed more drastically than when she'd been eleven, and she realized that she wasn't undersexed. Maybe she never had been. Maybe she'd simply been waiting for the right touch, and the right man to deliver it. "I trust you, Jack," she said on a sigh.

At the sound of her voice, Jack's breath grew harsh, his heartbeat beneath her fingers heavy, pounding. He felt like a hormone milkshake in a cracked glass. All because of a few words. Words that were another kind of caress. He hadn't known that the brain was an erogenous zone, that sexual response could be soul deep.

Suddenly, he realized that selfishness meant more than the relief of pleasing himself. It meant finding satisfaction in pleasing Angie. Suddenly he was acutely aware of her rather than himself, of her responses, her needs, her dependence on him.

He gazed down at Angie, her flushed cheeks, her eyes open and dazed, watching him, following every move he made. He wanted closed eyes. He didn't want her to witness his helplessness, his sudden uncertainty. He'd only been with one woman—his wife. They'd followed a pattern with no variations. It had been good sex. Satisfying sex. Only now did he understand that there was a difference between having sex and making love.

He knew that he wasn't having sex now.

He was laying himself on the line—all of himself.

He almost went limp at the thought.

Angie wouldn't allow it, not because of anything she did,

but because she was right there, responding to him, his partner in insanity.

Angie reached up to caress his cheek, curl her hand around his neck, draw his head down to meet her kiss. A sweet kiss that might have been timid if it weren't for the trembling of her lips, the heat of her skin, the catches in her breath. Only her hand, the one clasping the back of his neck, was pure ice.

She was nervous.

So was he.

Something had to be done.

Reaching up, he claimed that hand and guided it down to his chest, tucked it back between the buttons of his shirt, stroked it until her skin became warm on his.

Her fingers began to wander inside his shirt and a button popped open, then two and three, and then all of them were freed. He felt her gaze on his bare skin, touching him, evoking a response of puckering flesh and expectant muscles. She watched her hands as they explored his neck and collarbone, his chest, the spatter of wiry hair that pointed downward over his stomach, around his navel. Her hands stilled, and her head bent just a little more, and he felt the heat of her gaze on the bulge beneath his trousers.

She was curious.

So was he.

Somehow, he'd slipped the kimono off her shoulders, but it caught beneath her. The straps of her nightgown criss-crossed over her back, preventing him from sliding them down over her arms. Undressing a woman was foreign to him. Kay had been efficient in all things, including using nudity as a signal that she was in the mood. But Kay wasn't important now. Angie was. Only Angie, with whom he was learning about eroticism and sensuality and a seduction that had nothing to do with planning or routine.

He felt like a hero, powerful, primitive, able to make a woman surrender simply by arching a brow, crooking a finger, lowering his eyelids to a drowsy half-mast. He felt ten feet tall and ten inches long every time Angie gave one of those little moans, every time her body trembled and arched at his touch, every time she gasped in surprise.

He raised up again, stared at her body swathed in silk, and wondered how he was going to get it off of her without making a fool of himself. Weren't heroes supposed to be able to undress a woman with the bend of a finger, the twist of a wrist?

It was the eggrolls and wontons all over again.

Her strap dropped lower to bare the center of a full breast—a peek, an unconscious tease of what he would find, what he wanted to taste. She ran her tongue over her lips, a nervous response that demanded reassurance. Lowering his head, he took advantage of her open mouth, became intoxicated by the flavors of honey and lemon and potent whiskey . . . and Angie.

Only Angie. It felt like forever, holding her, as if he always had, touching her as if the world held nothing else worth touching, needing her as if need was new to him.

It shook him, the stunning emotion he felt, the sense of becoming himself, the desire to be only himself. Her touch made him know, in that moment, what selfishness was, that it wasn't always wrong. That sometimes it was necessary. With Angie.

Only Angie.

He needed to hear her sigh, so he lowered his head as his hand gathered folds of her gown, slid it up over her long, sleek legs, her flat stomach, her breasts. Finally, he sprinkled kisses on her bared breasts. He wanted to feel her tremble, so he stroked the length of her legs, the back of her knees, the outside of her thighs, around her hip, down again to cup her, to press against her, and to feel the moisture, the heat.

He craved her touch and shifted to shrug out of his shirt, congratulating himself on the smoothness of the operation until the buttoned cuffs caught on his hands. His groan of frustration alerted Angie. Pushing the folds of her gown away from her face, she watched him struggle. He groaned again as she sat up, and the gown fell over her body. Heat climbed up his neck, into his face, and he gazed up at the ceiling as he held out his arms to her, silently asking for help.

Her fingers were like a whisper on his wrists as she tried to work the buttons free. He heard her tongue click against the roof of her mouth, saw a button fly across the room as she jerked at one cuff, then the other. The second button bounced off his chest.

Startled, he glanced down at her, saw her staring at the button that had fallen into his lap, balanced on the hard ridge beneath his pants.

Her gaze jerked up to his face. "I can sew," she assured him.

Pressure built in his chest. He ran his hand over his mouth. The muscles in his face felt strained, tight and painful as laughter erupted, almost choking him.

Sweet Jesus, had it been that long?

Out of the corner of his eye, he saw Angie's smile. Tossing off his shirt, he hauled her close, felt her own laughter vibrating against his chest, felt her breath whooshing past his ear, heard the sound of shared amusement.

Shared.

Yes!

He laid back on the carpet, taking Angie with him, holding her, holding her laughter just as close.

It ended gradually, giving way to stronger emotion. She raised up to stare down at him, the lingering smile slowly fading from her face. He stared back, noticing for the first time that her thick lashes were tipped with a hint of gold, that one of her eyeteeth slightly overlapped one of her front teeth, that her forehead had faint lines that spoke of too much tension in her life.

His hands found the back of her thighs, skimmed up to cup her bottom, dragging the nightgown in their wake. She whimpered in her throat, her hands clutched his shoulders, her legs moved restlessly alongside his.

The clothes had to go.

Finesse didn't matter anymore. He pulled at the gown as he mumbled directions to her, rolled over so they both lay on their sides facing each other. The nightgown was off if he didn't count the strap still clinging to her arm trapped against the floor.

He wanted to touch her, but not yet. His hand fumbled at his belt, freed it, then searched for the tab on his zipper. He couldn't find it.

"May I?" she whispered.

His hand fell to his side as her fingers probed beneath the placket, found the tab, eased it downward. He felt every tooth separate from its mate, felt himself swell even more with the gradual release of fabric, prayed his erection wouldn't jump out at her.

It didn't.

Pleasure shuddered through him at the brush of air on vulnerable skin. He groaned at the touch of Angie's hand tracing his length, testing his hardness. He used her preoccupation to surreptitiously kick off his shoes, then unable to wait any longer to touch her, he eased her onto her back, lowered his head to her breasts. His hand wandered over her ribs, languidly tracing each one, moving ever downward.

He demanded more than sighs and trembles—with his kiss that drank from her, with his teeth as he took her nipple into his mouth, bit gently, then explored the crushed velvet texture with his tongue, with his fingers that penetrated her and found a place of incredible delicacy. Everywhere he touched, he found resilient muscle, satin skin, sensitive nerves. So sensitive, responsive, alive.

She cried out, trembled, sighed. And she grew bold with her hands as they clumsily groped inside his shorts, cupped him between his thighs, grazed his length, then wrapped around him and stroked, up, down, up again to sift through the hair at his groin.

She was killing him in more ways than one. Her hands were too tight around him; a fingernail snagged on sensitive skin. He reached down between them to grasp her hands, to stop her from disabling him, from ending the moment prematurely.

Shyness had disappeared—his and Angie's. He knew she wasn't thinking anymore. His control was slipping fast.

That vague thought jolted him, cleared the sensual haze from his mind.

He knew that heroes were expected to always be in control, to be aggressive yet always honorable. Whatever it cost, no matter how much he wished that he could be a villain instead, he wanted to be a hero more.

Holding her hands still, he gulped in air, forced out the words. "Angie, it's time."

"Yes."

Rolling to his back, he kicked off his pants, underwear and all, not caring if he looked clumsy rather than practiced. He knew she was watching him, knew that her gaze was roaming from his size fourteen feet, over his hair-sprinkled legs and lingering on his erection.

He hoped it looked heroic.

"You want to think about this for a minute, Angie?" He almost strangled on the question. What would he do if she said yes?

"No. Do you?"

"Not now," he said as he executed the one smooth move of the evening, rolling over, raising himself above her, settling between her legs, entering her a bare half-inch.

He clenched his teeth as her legs tensed on either side of his. He dipped his head to take her mouth, absorbing her as she absorbed him, slowly, drawing him into her, allowing him power over her vulnerability, even as she began to close around his own.

He met resistance and paused . . . only he couldn't just hover there wondering whether it should be slow and easy or hard and fast. If he hurt her, he'd shoot himself. He rested his forehead against hers, tried to gain some control over the urgency that was driving him—too fast, too hard —into her.

He was going to blow it.

Her hands splayed over his chest, and she thrust upward, meeting him, helping him penetrate her more deeply. He felt a spasm of pain and knew it was hers as well. Her nails dug into his shoulders as she held on and knew she'd drawn blood. But then, so had he.

Poetic justice.

Her muscles clenched around him. She caught her breath and met his plunges again and again. She bathed him in heat and moisture, soothing them both as she rolled her head from side to side, lifted her hips, matching his rhythm, as if the pain meant nothing, as if he were all that mattered.

Her body stilled, and he heard her voice through the roaring in his ears, the beat of his heart, the rush of blood in his veins. "Jack . . . look . . ."

He turned his head, shuddered as he saw their shadows on the wall, still now, as if the fire had burned their images into the textured plaster.

"Shh," he whispered in her ear, then laved it with his tongue. She had such small ears. Such tender skin. So tender that everywhere he touched her seemed to be alive with exposed nerves.

"Shh," he whispered again, feeling stronger and more powerful than he'd ever felt in his life with every sigh she gave, every cry, and every breath that drifted across his skin.

He rotated his hips, and she matched every move, every stroke and thrust, every caress. And through it all he watched their shadows dance on the wall, writhing together, then apart in a primitive ritual . . . as he rose above Angie . . . as she lifted to meet him, accepted his plunge into her body, arched her neck and raked her hands up his back . . . as Angie rotated her hips, held him tightly, greedily, sealing him within herself as she stared at the shadows.

He caught her fingertip between his lips, drew it into his mouth, held it there as she held him within her body. Her eyes were slumberous, misty as her mouth parted and her hips matched the tempo he set with his tongue.

He heard the pop of wood burning, felt the friction of their bodies creating fire, breathed the scent of fevered skin and passion.

Forever became reality as the moment came, as he came and knew she followed. It wouldn't stop—the spasms, the dampness that slicked their bodies and melded them together, the feeling that he was the center of ever-tightening ripples in a stream engulfing him, drowning him in Angie, her essence, the hot rain of her own orgasm. He wrapped his arms around her back, held her close, felt her heartbeat pounding against his, listened to her ragged breathing echo his, savored the climax that trembled inside them both.

Climax—the end of a fantasy he couldn't mourn for the reality of feeling, experiencing, sharing.

With Angie. Only Angie.

Careful not to separate their bodies, he rolled to his side, taking Angie with him, keeping her close, knowing that she wanted to be close. He savored the luxury he'd never enjoyed during marriage—that of being connected, of *feeling* connected to another human being.

He exhaled, a sound of satisfaction and exhaustion, an expression of relief. Nothing terrible had happened. He hadn't let Angie down. He hadn't let himself down. She'd been with him to the end. Bodies didn't lie.

He still felt like a hero.

Thank God.

She sighed, and her feet languidly rubbed the sides of his. She slid down a fraction to seat him more firmly within her, holding him, caressing him in a way he hadn't thought possible. She had the most incredible muscles—in her legs, in her arms, in her stomach, *inside* her. Muscles that didn't bulge, but seemed to flow and conform. He could imagine her dancing, drifting and floating with her feet barely on the floor, dancing as she had danced beneath him and their shadows had echoed their movements in the firelight.

Now he knew the meaning of "special."

21

Is that all there is? Angie wondered as she lay on her side, curled up and wrapped to her chin in blankets. Flames had died down to embers, tiny pinpoints of fire smothering in a bed of ash. It was three A.M., the deepest part of the night, thick with silence, heavy with loneliness. The air held the faint and ghostly glow of a winter storm, blurring the edges of the furniture, leeching out color and life. Not the best time to be awake with nothing but her own insecurities for company.

She'd taken a lot for granted—like a happy ending to a night of lovemaking.

Obviously she'd been reading the wrong books. Why hadn't it occurred to her that *The Joy of Sex* would focus on just that—the joy. Naturally it wouldn't have a chapter describing the difficult moments—hours—afterward, the uncertainty that went with inexperience, the memory of those moments when she'd been stripped bare of defenses and dignity. Naturally the books that glorified the act of love wouldn't mention how vulnerable and frightening it was to respond so uncontrollably, to give so much emotion without knowing what would come next.

She'd expected tenderness and closeness in the aftermath. Maybe there would be a hushed conversation, or maybe just simple, quiet affection. She should at least feel relaxed, satisfied, fulfilled. She expected to be all warm and squishy inside, glowing on the outside.

She closed her eyes and tried to view it all objectively, to see making love with Jack as something less than she remembered. She really hadn't expected it to be so good—not the first time. She'd been prepared for discomfort and clumsiness, which there had been. She hadn't really thought that fireworks would burst, that sensations would explode, which they had. Never had she dreamed that such an act would make her feel so free, so . . . *found*.

Sometime during the night, they'd stumbled around, hastily unfolding the bedding she dumped on the sofa, arranging it in some kind of order. They'd chuckled in low, private voices as they fumbled and tripped in the dark, then they'd collapsed on their makeshift bed and everything changed.

The laughter died. She had nothing to say. Neither did Jack. She didn't know what to do. Evidently Jack didn't want to do anything. She'd lain by his side, staring up at the ceiling, barely breathing, not moving, suddenly terrified that he would acknowledge her presence, her nakedness.

Finally, she'd heard his breathing slow and felt his body relax beside her in sleep. She'd turned to her side but couldn't find comfort or rest. Sleeping with another person wasn't something you adjusted to automatically. She was too aware of him beside her, too conscious of the distance he seemed to want between them.

She had to do something . . . anything.

Jack's eyes snapped open at the chime of the grandfather clock in the foyer. Four chimes. Disoriented, he focused on the light in the room, the silence, then the solid, flat surface beneath him, the table leg pressing into his shoulder.

He was sleeping on the floor with a woman—with Angie. He'd lost control. So had she. They'd made love.

It had been better than sex.

And then something went wrong. They'd both become awkward, embarrassed, like panicked strangers thrown together in a stalled elevator, neither knowing what to do next.

He'd fallen asleep.

No one would ever accuse him of being a Sensitive Male.

Carefully, he turned his head, found her sitting on the edge of their pallet, her head bent over as if she were reading.

He still didn't know what to do, what to say. It shocked

him to realize how inexperienced he was in spite of a thir-
teen-year marriage. Kay had hated what she called "coital
conversation," before, during, and after. That had been
fine with him. He'd never been much with dialogue for its
own sake. He'd felt comfortable with the routine they'd
established.

A few hours with Angie, and all the routines he valued
were shot to shit. He'd wanted to hold her. He'd wanted to
talk. But he hadn't known about Angie's preferences, and
by the time he'd worried about it for ten minutes, he'd
fallen asleep.

Thoughts of Kay disappeared as he stared at Angie, the
sleek line of her bare back where the sheet she'd wrapped
around herself had slipped and her skin was pearled by the
otherworldly glow of a snowy night and a fire in the hearth.
Her hair had no order; tangled curls surrounded her head
like an unruly halo backlit by the flames feeding off of
fresh logs.

She'd been awake long enough to rebuild the fire.
Maybe she had never fallen asleep.

Maybe he was still asleep. Maybe the whole thing had
been a dream. Maybe he just wasn't ready to face facts yet.
Some dreams were worth hanging on to.

He reached out, traced the line of her spine from the
nape of her neck to below her waist.

"Ouch!" she said as she jerked, then sucked on her forefinger.

Jack raised up, peered over her shoulder. A needle was
stuck in the carpet, and his shirt lay crumpled in her lap.
He grasped her hand, pulled it away from her mouth, and
saw a drop of blood on the tip of her finger. He glanced
back at the shirt and the spool of matching thread on the
floor next to her right foot.

She'd been sewing the buttons back on his cuffs.

At four in the morning?

"Why?" he asked.

Angie shrugged, then laid the shirt aside, her movements
slow and precise as she placed the needle and thread into a
small plastic pouch on the coffee table. The shrug drooped

into a slump, and she hugged her knees, curled into herself, the picture of misery.

He sank back down, supporting himself on one elbow. He'd screwed up big time and he knew he'd have hell to pay when he really thought about it, but that didn't matter right now. The world, life, his attention, all centered on Angie.

Raking a hand through his hair, he watched her, willed her to face him. "You want to give me a clue, Angie?"

She said nothing.

"You're not happy?" he prompted.

Silence.

"Angie, I don't know what to do here."

"Neither do I," she said on a sigh.

Frowning, Jack digested her reply and thought back to everything that had happened: the wildness, the laughter, then the sudden shying away from each other, the stiffness as he'd wondered whether she wanted to be held or left alone. He'd fallen asleep wondering how heroes always knew exactly the right thing to do. . . .

He'd fallen asleep. Some hero.

He inhaled sharply and reached for Angie, pulled her down, tucked her against his side, coaxed her head into the crook of his shoulder, and got a mouthful of her hair. It took him a minute to remedy the situation, to stifle the urge to sneeze away a few wayward strands that tickled his nose.

She was still stiff, her skin cool and unresponsive to the gentle stroke of his hands.

Maybe a little conversation would help.

He took a deep breath, concentrated on keeping his voice low and soothing. "I saw the gen—your father on TV last week." *Good, Jack. Get her to talk about herself.*

"Yes. Me, too."

"Does he come around much?"

"No."

"You don't get along?"

"He's . . . just busy."

Damn, but this was hard work. "How long since your parents divorced?"

"I was fourteen."

"And the general's been busy ever since." Jack remembered General Winters, retired, as he'd last seen him, medium height, tight build, ruddy complexion, and shrewd, brown eyes. The media had tracked him down while he was deep-sea fishing off the coast of Cabo San Lucas. His khaki shorts had been starched and creased, his hair unruffled by the breeze; even his stark white T-shirt looked as if it had been pressed. It had taken Jack a full ten minutes to realize the man wasn't in uniform.

"He always took care of me, Jack," she said defensively with a trace of resignation. "He deeded the house to me and set up a trust fund. He remembers my birthday and calls when he can."

"Mmm." Conscience money, Jack thought. Duty calls. It was no secret that the man lived for the military, for patriotism and honor and duty. Angie had run a poor fifth. She accepted that. It was evident in her voice.

So was the tight note of pain.

If anything, her body had grown more tense. It wasn't natural. Not for Angie, who approached strangers as if she'd always known them and filled pages with easy conversation and casual intimacy. Angie, he realized, never expected her problems to be addressed by anyone but herself. She didn't even talk about them as if they were problems. Earlier in the evening, she'd explained some of them to him in broad terms—facts of life only. In her letters he'd seen glimpses of more facts, but never complaints, never pleas for help. Maybe the letters themselves were as close as she could get to reaching out for something she needed.

At some point in her life, she'd buried herself alive.

He'd never been comfortable with insight, particularly his own. Especially when it concerned Angie. Dammit, he did not want to feel protective—toward anyone.

His arm tightened around her, drew her closer. The cool skin and stiff body and restrained conversation had to go.

He wanted results. And he needed to know that he was responsible. Tonight, he felt like indulging in arrogance, ego boosting, in the need to be a hero, to be a hero for Angie. If only he knew how to go about it.

"Jack?" Angie said, breaking the silence. "It's been a comedy of errors, hasn't it?"

Her question made him sick. His ego was down for the count. He needed protection more than she did. He had to do something—fast.

Raising up, he angled his body over hers and framed her chin with his hand. Her mouth opened as if she were about to protest. He took advantage—fast—and landed a hard kiss on her lips, sealing in whatever she'd been about to say. He didn't want to hear it. He had the impression that she didn't want to say it, either.

His tongue homed in on hers, initiated play and mutual exploration. She didn't argue. Her temperature climbed. Her hands fluttered on his back, then kneaded and skimmed. Finally, her stiffness dissolved and she seemed to flow around him, into him. He tasted her sigh, drew on her tongue, asking for more sighs.

She obliged with a whimper or two for good measure.

She opened for him, that fast, that soon, and he was inside her again, growing with every heartbeat, feeling her stretch and conform around him as he tried to slow down. Heat intensified between them, slicking flesh and sensitizing nerves. Moisture flowed from her, inviting him like a warm, rainy day when the sun still shines in the distance.

It didn't happen this way. He'd always thought it was ridiculous when other men bragged about how many times they could "perform" in one night. He'd sure as hell never had the inclination. Sex for him had always been a release of natural urges, a physical need met by a physical action. It had never been an experience . . . an adventure . . . a *discovery*.

Angie's hands were busy exploring his shoulders. Her eyes were equally busy searching his, their color clear and bright. Wayward strands of hair tangled around her face and caught on her swollen and rosy lips.

He raised his hands to comb through her hair, to feel the vibrant spring of her curls, the rich texture, to absorb the fragrance into his own skin. Glancing down, he traced the place where her breasts met his chest, a barely discernible line where their bodies joined, where her softness seemed to melt around him, become a part of him.

A few minutes ago, he might have told her that, yes, it had been a comedy of errors. He might have admitted that he'd felt inept and clumsy, and there had been an element of trial and error to their lovemaking. He could tell her that he'd always avoided spontaneous actions for just that reason. No one wanted to look like a fool. But not now. It was still night, and the scent of passion was heavy in the room. His. Hers. *Theirs.*

And he was too busy feeling like a hero.

22

"When the cock gets hard, the brains get soft." Jack had heard the old proverb from his father years ago and laughed about it. It wasn't so funny now.

Neither was waking up on a carelessly made bed on the floor, wearing nothing but a woman he'd met less than twelve hours ago.

The fire had died, and he could hear the low hum of the furnace, feel the warm air being forced into the room. A table leg dug into his shoulder, and Angie's hair kept tickling his nose. Outside, the sky was gunmetal gray, drab, with no hint of the iridescent shimmer of a veiled moon, no sense that they were insulated from the outside world, two solitary people living out a fantasy.

An illusion he'd actually believed in for a few selfish moments.

Angie had wanted to be selfish, yet all she'd done was give.

All he'd done was let go, uncontrollably hard and fast—not once but twice.

It had been her first time.

He hadn't used any protection.

Shit!

Sex had never been a driving force in his life. He'd been too busy, too focused. He'd never indulged in affairs, much less one-night stands. He'd been with one woman—his wife —after the official engagement. They'd both been satisfied with establishing a routine. Imagination hadn't been a part of their intimate relationship. Neither had spontaneity or the kind of overwhelming response he'd experienced with Angie, forgetting restraint and finesse and forgetting himself, completely.

It gave Angie power over him. Too much power.

"What would you like for breakfast?" Angie asked as she lifted her head and gave him a sleepy-eyed stare.

"Coffee." He glanced at her, barely, and tried to smile and had a funny feeling that it didn't take.

"In a minute. I have to wake up first," she said, her voice slightly slurred.

"Are you all right?" he asked.

"Uh . . . Jack? I'm a tad cranky in the mornings. Just don't ask me to talk for a few minutes." She turned to her side and lay still for half a second, then murmured, "Coffee," as she twisted into a sitting position. For someone who wasn't a morning person, Angie streaked through the living room with remarkable coordination, wrapping a sheet around herself like a toga with one hand while scooping up her nightgown and robe from the window seat.

Angie stumbled into the kitchen, clutching her clothes, and leaned against the counter in relief when she saw that she had set the timer on the coffee machine the night before. Usually, she had to take her mornings in stages with at least two cups of coffee, the newspaper comics, a workout in her studio, and a written schedule to remind her that life was waiting outside the front door. She had a feeling that she wouldn't be so blessed today.

She'd awakened too fast, to the sound of Jack's voice, the feel of it vibrating in his chest. Her mind had been working double time ever since.

Jack was here.

She'd acted impulsively, without a single thought to back up those actions.

They'd made love.

Heat climbed up her face as she remembered how awkward she'd been, how completely ridiculous she must have seemed. The corners of her mouth tilted upward in a half-smile. Jack had been just as awkward and nervous, and just a little bit shy.

He'd been wonderful.

Her smile grew as her face flamed hotter. She hadn't been so bad herself. Who needed instruction books and practiced moves? It was so much more fun when two people had to muddle through the mechanics together.

Oh, dear Lord, but it had been fun.

Absently, she checked the coffeemaker and frowned. It was half full and dripping steadily. She shot a quick glance at the doorway to make sure Jack was still safely in the living room, then fumbled to slip her nightgown over her head while still trying to hold on to the sheet. Somehow it all worked out, and she managed to get one on before the other fell to the floor. A sleeve on her robe twisted before she finally pulled it over her shoulders.

She didn't want to be away from Jack for too long. He didn't need time to think any more than she did. The lives they'd left behind the night before would catch up with them soon enough.

As she gathered mugs from the cupboard and poured the coffee, her hands began to tremble. What would happen next? Gripping the edges of the Formica to steady herself, she closed her eyes, willed herself to follow the instincts that had served her so well since Jack appeared on her doorstep. Every time she'd given in to the urge to think, the moments with Jack had become heavy, clumsy, miserably strained.

She grabbed the mugs and took determined steps back into the living room. Back to Jack.

The bedding was neatly folded and stacked on the sofa. Jack was dressed and standing in front of the bay window, staring at the stained glass, at the murky gray light that wasn't strong enough to make a respectable showing through the scattered pieces of rippled clear glass set in the design. Then his head bent and his gaze focused on the carpet at his feet—carpet mashed down by their bodies and marred by a quarter-size reddish brown stain.

The frown on his face told a story she didn't want to hear.

"How are you feeling?" he asked, the back of his neck and the skin on his cheeks darkening.

"I'm feeling lovely, thank you," she said brightly, and handed him a mug of coffee.

"Lovely," he repeated dully as he took the mug and drank.

Angie took a sip of coffee, then spoke in a sober tone, realizing that he didn't appreciate brightness at the moment. "Not pretty or beautiful, Jack. *Lovely.* Inside."

"Great."

"Yes." She tilted her head and suddenly felt weak in the knees. "Can we sit down?"

He grasped her elbow, guided her to the burgundy chair, and eased her down. "Good idea," he said as he strode back to the window across the room from her, putting distance between them. His gaze zeroed in on the stain on the carpet.

"Regrets are inappropriate, Jack."

"How the hell would you know?"

Her eyes narrowed, and she felt her brow scrunch up. No! She hadn't thought last night; she wouldn't think now. "I can—finally—speak with some authority on the subject."

His hair stood on end as he plowed his fingers through the military-short strands. "Are you on the Pill?"

"No."

"A diaphragm?"

"No." She sighed. She was blushing again. She could feel it.

"Anything?"

She gulped down the last of her coffee.

"Damn!"

"That's one thing I should have thought about, especially since I have a box of . . ." Her voice trailed off as the blush extended to her finger and toenails.

"One of us should have."

"It's . . . not the right . . . time, Jack."

His brows arched as he turned his head, gave her a hard, questioning stare, and vaguely noticed that her gown and robe were on wrong-side out. "Excuse me?"

"You know—fertility cycles . . . and uh . . . ovulation." Now she was too embarrassed to blush.

"Oh. A box of what?"

"Um . . . condoms." She forced herself to smile, to nonchalantly wave her hand. "Extra large, lubricated."

"Oh, God." Rubbing his hand over his face, he returned his gaze to the window. "You were planning this?"

A chuckle came out of nowhere, shoved its way past her throat. She couldn't help it. "Obviously," she choked, "*we* didn't plan anything."

His frown would have stopped a clock.

"They were a sort of gag gift from Gena's mother," she explained.

"From a *mother*?"

"Mmm. Gracie believes that independence, enlightenment, and preparation belong together."

"I don't believe this."

"We need more coffee." Angie jumped up from the chair, grabbed Jack's mug, and disappeared into the kitchen.

Jack *didn't* believe it—any of it. What had he gotten himself into? A crude answer popped up in his mind, and he slammed it down again. Last night had been incredible in more ways than one. Incredibly awkward and embarrassing. Incredibly stupid and irresponsible. Incredibly intense and special.

Incredible.

He didn't want this. Angie had shown him in a thousand ways—through her letters, through her actions—that she needed closeness. He'd stumbled on that particular bit of wisdom purely by accident and had played out a whole hero fantasy around it. But that was last night. That was a fantasy.

Major Jack Caldwell was no hero. Not even close.

In reality, closeness wasn't his thing. Not since he'd last run into Bryan's room in the throes of a nightmare. Not since he'd experienced its sudden absence and reacted with a fury that had scared him. He'd learned that closeness bred dependence, so he'd buried that part of himself, covered it with layers of control and discipline.

Buried alive.

He straightened his shoulders, lifted his head. So why

was he worried? It wasn't as if he'd be around long enough to become dependent on Angie.

"When are you leaving?"

He almost jumped out of his skin at the sound of her voice—so close, so matter-of-fact.

"Today. I've already called for a tow truck." The sooner the better. He accepted the fresh mug of coffee and paced to the other end of the room. He dragged in a breath, forced it out. "Angie, my dad used to quote an old proverb every time we went out on a date. It's a little raw, but true."

She said nothing as she sat on the window seat and tucked her feet beneath her gown.

"When the . . . uh . . . when a man gets hard—"

"I heard you the first time," she said quietly, seriously. "Either you talk in your sleep, or you wake up every morning beating yourself for something." Her manner had changed from flippant and breezy to soft and sober. "Don't beat yourself over last night, Jack. We're both adults. We knew what was happening between us and did it anyway. I liked it."

"Most people do," he mumbled, remembering how much he had liked it, too. It might have been a comedy of errors, but even the fumbles and groping had seemed significant, special. Angie was a throwback to a time when women were less sophisticated, approaching a new experience as if it were a surprise package she couldn't wait to open. He'd acted like a throwback, too, approaching Angie with primitive instincts and a swollen ego.

She wrapped her hands around her mug, fixed her gaze on him, steady and sure. "Were you afraid that I'd forgotten you're leaving? I didn't, Jack. Not for one second."

"I don't like one-night stands, Angie."

"Is that what it was, Jack? Are you going to leave here and push me out of your mind and forget that this ever happened?"

He plowed a hand through his hair. "I don't know." Push her out of his mind? Not likely. Forget about last night? He wished it were that simple. He wasn't lying to her exactly. He didn't know what came next.

"I see. Well, at least you're honest. I should appreciate that." Her voice was a monotone. Her expression was blank, empty, as if she'd stepped out of the room and left her body behind. "For the record: I don't like wishing I'd done this and regretting I hadn't done that. It's been the story of my life—taking the easy way out, playing it safe. Last night was a risk I'll never regret taking."

"Dammit, Angie! I'm sorry as hell about last night. It was—"

"It was an experience, Jack," she said smoothly, as if she were reciting a well-rehearsed speech. "I told you I've always been undersexed. For a while I even questioned my sexual leanings—not because I was attracted to women, but because I *wasn't* attracted to men. The closest I ever came was when I'd see Tom Selleck or Mel Gibson in a movie, but that didn't count. It wasn't real."

"Neither was last night," he said harshly, and willed himself to believe it. "Watch the old movies sometime, Angie. They're full of lovers caught in a storm, full of *'brooding passions and fire,'*" he said, and winced at his sarcasm. "They even have happy endings if that's what you're looking for."

Angie backed up to stand in the arched doorway to the kitchen. She turned around, began to walk away, then paused. "I'm going to take a shower and get dressed. If . . . your tow arrives before I'm finished, please lock the door on your way out."

He watched her disappear into the kitchen, heard her slippered footsteps fade. She'd made it easy for him. Easier than he deserved, but hell, how did other men handle sticky situations like this?

Sonofabitch!

He strode through the living room and kitchen, caught up with her at the foot of the back stairway, grasped her arm to stop her. "Angie."

She didn't look at him but stared at his hand on her arm. Still he could see her eyes, wide and glazed with moisture, and her mouth, closed tight and pale. "I came here out of curiosity, Angie, not to use you, but that's what happened."

"I don't think so, Jack."

At a complete loss as to deal with the situation, Jack snorted and shook his head and snatched his hand away from her as he pivoted on his heel and headed for the counter to put down the mug he still held in his hand. Outside a horn honked, signaling the arrival of the tow truck.

Inside, snow spattered against the glass-enclosed breakfast nook, and maidens frolicked on the walls with unicorns. Jack carefully set the mug down and gripped the edge of the counter, waiting for Angie to climb the stairs.

"Jack?"

He stayed where he was, unmoving.

"I'm not asking for more of a happy ending than you've already given me."

As exit lines went, it was a killer.

Feeling more hunted than he had at any other time, Jack made tracks for the front door. Angie had made it so easy for him to walk away, without guilt, without responsibility. Why, he wondered, did he feel so damn guilty and responsible? Why did he want to follow her up the stairs?

For the same reasons he put off setting up interviews on the East Coast. The same reasons he drove through a blizzard to see her.

He heard the answer in the back of his mind, a whisper of truth that was going to give him no end of grief.

Hell.

FULL CIRCLE

My life once again has come full circle.
Today, I see the mountain from the underside.
Where now is that glimmering truth I trusted just a few days
*   ago?*
Is it up there beyond my dreams,
Where reality has kneaded itself so neatly into my thoughts.
Or is it down there below,
Where my dreams have not yet the audacity to emerge.
Or is it here,
In the midst of the ruins of my life come once again full
*   circle.*

—*Jennie Cissell Thompson*

23

Jack drove home on automatic pilot, as if he hadn't been gone for years and the city hadn't changed. He didn't think about where he was going or what he'd do when he got there—not too bright, considering the condition of the roads and his questionable state of mind.

But then heroes were reckless, and desperate situations rarely gave a man time to think. He'd read enough on the subject in the history books in school and the military journals at the Air Force Academy to know. During his years in an organization that hailed heroism even as it promoted a team mentality, he'd rubbed elbows with the valiant few, heard their stories, learned the nature of the breed as well as the eventual fate of the majority.

He'd learned that heroes usually earned that distinction by accident. They were also easily replaced by the next man who was high on adrenaline and short on survival instincts. He really should have remembered that.

Last night he'd been high on testosterone, and survival had been a relative term, depending on which body part was hurting the most.

He swung into a right turn and blinked at the familiar cul de sac, the sprawling ranch style house that sat back from the road, the basketball hoop attached above the garage door.

Home.

He parked in front of the house because the driveway was full, then sat there, feeling lost, misplaced. It had been a long time—flying visits notwithstanding.

Home. Where he could cry in a beer or two in peace.

He stared at the house with its faded red bricks and dark green shutters and the big tree in the back yard that had once held the treehouse he and Bryan had built. He blinked again.

Home—where the motor home stood in the wide driveway, flanked by the family Volvo and Steve's Harley. The rear of a Mercedes stuck out from the open garage, and a face peeked out from behind the curtains in the living room.

He would have turned around and driven to the farthest hotel if it hadn't been for that face. If he had remembered that he couldn't be seen or recognized through the smoked glass windows of his rental car. If he still didn't halfway believe the propaganda his parents had fed him that they had eyes in the back of their heads and they knew everything.

Home, where the refrigerator was always stocked with Coors and peace was in short supply.

He set the emergency brake and opened the car door. The draperies fell shut, and the front door to the house was thrown open. Ada Caldwell burst out of the house, her arms open wide, tears already gushing from her eyes. Joe Caldwell sauntered in her wake, his iron gray hair standing on end where he'd leaned his head against the back of his La-Z-Boy recliner. Steve was probably still in bed.

"Jack!" Ada wrapped her arms around his waist and looked up at him through shiny wet robin's-egg-blue eyes. Her white hair was still long, still in its bedtime braid, and she smelled of fried bacon and Chanel.

"Son, come in out of the cold," Joe said as he pumped Jack's hand while pulling the combined mass of mother and son into the house. "Didn't think you'd show up for a while. Didn't you have some interviews on the East Coast?"

"I haven't set anything up yet—"

"I told your father that it would all work out when we couldn't go to the family reunion. Some things are just meant to be. Now we can have our own party."

"Why aren't you at the reunion?" Jack asked.

"Steve got pneumonia. We just couldn't leave."

Jack's stomach rolled into a knot. Of course they

couldn't leave. Since Bryan's "accident," the parents had hovered over their remaining sons for everything from a hangnail to hay fever. "How's he doing?"

"Coming along," Ada said as they walked into the kitchen.

"Ornery—and he's just fine, son." Joe said as he took his place at a fully loaded breakfast table. "Sit down and eat."

Before he knew it, Jack was staring down at a plate of bacon, eggs, home fries, and toast. Ada poured him a cup of coffee, leaned down to kiss his cheek, and sniffed at Jack's collar.

"You have a girlfriend, Jack?"

"He's barely in the door, Mom," Steve said as he strolled into the kitchen and sat down next to Jack. "Why don't you take off your coat and stay awhile?" He reached behind Jack to help him shrug out of the parka and drape it on the back of the chair.

Joe reached for the jelly. "Ada, sit down so we can eat."

"I smell Shalimar, Joe. He has a girlfriend."

"Good. Pass the salt."

Ada passed the salt. "You were with her last night, Jack? Who is she? I know that Kay doesn't wear Shalimar."

"The pen pal," Steve murmured.

"The *what*?"

"Ada, I need the pepper."

Jack spread apple butter on a slice of toast and dug into the pile of scrambled eggs. His mother wouldn't allow talking with a full mouth.

Sure enough, she frowned and bit into a piece of bacon. Steve chuckled and jabbed Jack in the ribs. Joe sighed in relief.

No doubt about it—he was home.

"You look worse than I feel." Steve sauntered into Jack's bedroom an hour after breakfast and looked around as he flipped the cap of a bottle of Coors with his thumb and handed it to Jack.

"Tired," Jack said as he unpacked clothes from his suitcase. "How did you get pneumonia?"

Steve shrugged. "I guess I'm still a little run down, and going from the Gulf to Germany and back here confused my body." He sprawled out on Jack's bed. "I'm recovered, but it'll take Mom another week to accept it. Mom isn't going to let you off easy, you know. She'll pry information about your pen pal out of you with her can opener if she has to."

"Nothing to tell."

"Uh-huh. So who wears Shalimar?"

Jack raised the beer to his mouth and took a long pull. In all the years that they'd lived under the same roof, he and Steve had shared nothing more than small talk. They'd done better than that in Germany, but it was still too new for Jack to feel comfortable with it.

"What's she like?"

"Crazy. Gutsy. Lonely. Creative," Jack said repeating the description he'd given Steve in Germany.

"Homely as a mud fence," Steve guessed.

"No." She was beautiful, sexy.

"She's boring?"

"No." She was funny and shy and full of surprises.

"She can't cook."

Jack set his beer on the dresser and began hanging up his shirts. He didn't know about her talent with food, but he felt as if he'd been boiled and pushed through a strainer.

"Okay. What does she do?"

"She works at Link International," Jack said, relieved that Steve's questions had taken a less personal direction.

"No kidding?" Propping himself up on an elbow, Steve held up his beer. "They have an ad in the classifieds—for a photographer. Mom cut it out for you."

Jack frowned at the bottle in his hand and wondered why he was drinking right after breakfast. He checked his watch; it was one in the afternoon. They must have talked around the breakfast table longer than he'd thought.

"Kay showed up about a month ago," Steve said as he drained his bottle. "She wanted to get the piano Mom was keeping for her."

Jack didn't pause in hanging up his shirts. "Is she okay?"

"Fine. She really blasted you to the parents—handed 'em a crock about what you did to her."

Bile threatened to choke Jack as memories jockeyed for position in his mind. Somehow, he managed to swallow down the bile, slam the door on the memories, keep arranging his shirts and trousers in the closet.

"Mom told Kay to—"

"I believe the term was 'suck eggs,' " Joe interrupted as he walked in and shut the door. He, too, held beer—several bottles' worth. "Closest I ever heard to swearing come out of your mother's mouth."

"Yeah." Steve grinned. "Who'd of thought Kay would turn out to be such a bitch?"

Jack braced his hands on either side of the closet and bent his head. "Maybe Kay was right."

"Not likely, son. Maybe you lost your temper, but no way would you hurt a woman, especially a pregnant woman."

"Was it yours?" Steve asked.

A body slam from Godzilla couldn't have taken Jack more by surprise. He jerked upright and turned around, forced himself to continue unpacking as if nothing had been said and he hadn't been reminded of what happened that last night with Kay, as if a question hadn't been asked. He had an aversion to discussing personal matters with anyone. Joe Caldwell had drummed it into his sons that "real men" didn't discuss their wives, their dogs, or their money with anyone. The two men waiting for him to speak might be family, but Jack had learned early to keep things from family. Especially family.

"She was my wife at the time," he said, and felt the bile rise again.

"You're a credit to the uniform, Jack—a real officer and gentleman." Steve rose, his mouth slanted mockingly as he saluted Jack with his empty bottle. "I'm going to find a recent issue of *Playboy* and read myself to sleep."

Joe waited until he heard Steve's bedroom door shut before he spoke again. "Can't imagine where he got his attitude." He spread his knees, leaned forward, and stared down at the bottle of beer he held in his hand. "But he's right, Jack. Far as I'm concerned, all bets are off with Kay, and you're carrying honor and loyalty too far."

Sighing, Jack drained his beer and tossed the bottle into the waste can. A large beanbag cushion occupied one corner of the room. He used to love to flop down, sink into the vinyl seat, and feel the beans shift and slide under him. A dozen places sported patches of tape where he'd worried the bean while he studied until he'd poked a hole in the covering. He flopped down as he always had and sank lower than he remembered. He could just see his father over his knees.

Joe threw him another bottle of beer. "Don't tell me you bought that bull about it all being your fault, Jack."

"It was." Jack flipped off the cap and gulped down half the bottle. He'd never felt comfortable with father-son heart-to-hearts. His father had a way of slipping under the surface of a subject, prying secrets loose. Some secrets needed to be kept under wraps where they couldn't hurt anyone else, couldn't make him think too much about the price he'd paid for them.

"Half of it was, son. Don't kid yourself that it could be more." Joe opened his second beer. "There's an old saying that if you want to know how a woman will turn out, just take a good long look at her mother. That can go for more than appearances." He slid off the bed onto the floor, meeting Jack at eye level. "You remember Kay's mother, don't you?"

Though she'd been dead for six years, Jack remembered Kay's mother well. Louise Williams had been self-centered, shallow, and—according to her—never, ever wrong. If she made a mistake, it was someone else's fault. "Dad, you don't know—"

"You're right about that, son. Not likely I'll ever know since you're not the best talker in the world."

"Does it matter?"

"Depends on whether it matters to you."

"Dad, child psychology won't work on me anymore."

"Have another beer, son."

Catching the bottle one-handed, Jack couldn't help but grin. The scenario would make a great commercial: father and errant son tossing breakable bottles across the room, flipping off the caps with their thumbs, guzzling brew, and talking around each other. It was every stereotype known to modern man, right down to the bedroom that hadn't changed since Jack graduated from high school. Pink Floyd posters, a stackable stereo system, and a mylar poster with a cutaway view of the Starship Enterprise were still in their original places, along with a desk, a bureau, a stationary bike, and various articles of sports equipment. It occurred to him that he was noticing the room more now than he had at eighteen.

His gaze found the model airplanes arranged on a shelf, the stainless-steel chest that held camera equipment, the battered leather case—

"I took the Hasselblad to Waxman's in Denver for a good going over," Joe mentioned. "Thought you'd want to break it out now that you're home. Still can't figure out why you didn't take it overseas with you."

"I haven't had much time for hobbies, Dad." Jack stared at the case. He could almost see the lines of the medium format camera, feel it in his hands, hear the shutter click. The parents had given it to him when he'd graduated from high school. He'd used it a few times, then put it away after he'd had a sudden urge to throw it at the nearest concrete wall.

"I remember how you handled it when we gave it to you, Jack—like other boys your age handled a Mustang or Camaro."

"It's an expensive camera," Jack said carefully. He had handled it as if it were a part of him. Once, a camera like that had been all he wanted from life. Once, before he'd traded one set of priorities for another.

"Sure as hell was, son—too expensive to sit in a case for seventeen years." Leaning his head back against the bed, Joe closed his eyes. "I remember looking in on you one night. You were so wrapped up in that camera, you didn't see me, but I watched you clean it and check it and pack it up. Later that night, I heard you crying as if someone had ripped out your left nut."

Jack swallowed, drained his bottle of beer, stifled a belch. "I was eighteen, Dad."

"So? You think only kids cry? You were a grown man long before you should have been, son, but that night I realized just how grown you really were. I'm glad you've at least used your Nikon," Joe said. "Your mother cried when she saw the pictures you sent us from Germany." Another bottle streaked across the room.

Jack barely caught it, fumbled to open it. His head was starting to buzz. He needed to sleep the clock around. Except that he wasn't sleepy. He couldn't afford the buzz, either. His father was working up to something, making Jack feel as if he had Glad Wrap for skin and his father could see all the way through him.

But Jack couldn't seem to move, to end the talk, to block his father's insights. Instead, he wanted to hear what Joe had to say, what he thought. He even had the urge to ask, but the concept was foreign to him.

There was a brief knock on the door, then his mother's face peeked in. "I thought you might need refills." She walked in, holding a cooler. As she pulled off the lid, Jack saw that it was stocked with beer and sandwiches. "It's been five hours since we sat down to breakfast. You both know better than to drink on an empty stomach," she said while she distributed food and drink, then sat down on the floor next to her husband and began to eat.

Jack stared. Obviously his mother had no intention of leaving—an unprecedented action in the male-dominated household.

"Jack, I converted Bryan's room into a library/sewing room for me. I thought we'd wall in the connecting doorways between these three bedrooms. There are a few of Bryan's things I kept in case you wanted them."

"No," Jack said harshly.

"No," Ada repeated. "Your father said that you might already have more of Bryan than you really want."

Frowning, Jack bit into his sandwich. He had to check

under the bread to see what it was. Ham. He could've sworn it was sand in his mouth. He washed it down with beer. Once he might have wondered what she meant. The treehouse was gone; he'd seen to that. The Kodak Instamatic that Bryan had given him had been smashed to pieces. So was the Fisher Price toy camera. The last note Bryan had written had gone up in smoke a long time ago.

Still, Jack knew what she meant. He had all of Bryan that mattered. Bryan's life. Bryan's dreams.

Suddenly, he remembered something she'd said to him on the phone not so long ago. "Mom, what did you mean when you said that you'd lost all your sons?"

"If you have to ask, Jack, then I think you already know."

"Tell me, Mom," Jack said. It was important that he hear it, have it confirmed.

Ada stared down at her lap and picked crumbs off her khaki slacks. "I lost you and Bryan at the same time, Jack. You closed up, separated yourself from us. Then Steve lived his life as if we had no place in it. I've always been overly dramatic where my sons are concerned."

"Guilt trips—Ada style," Joe offered.

"I never, *never,* laid guilt on my boys, Joe, and you know it."

"No, but we've both damn near beat ourselves to death with it, honey," Joe said gently.

"Well, we have a lot to answer for," Ada said wearily.

"Uh, I think I need to walk off some of this beer." Jack tried to haul himself out of the beanbag, but he seemed to sink in deeper. His legs felt like licorice sticks. How many beers had he had? he wondered.

"Yep," Joe agreed, as if Jack hadn't said a word, hadn't tried to escape the seat that held him like a cocoon. "We gave all our energy to Bryan when Jack and Steve needed it more."

"We didn't have the sense," Ada continued, "to say anything when Jack took an ax to the tree house."

Joe nodded. "Should have grounded him for a month of Sundays for breaking the rules about dangerous tools."

"Maybe we should have helped him," Ada said thoughtfully, slanting a look at Jack. "We were angry, too. Did it help, to tear down your memories, Jack?"

"No," Jack answered, caught off guard by suddenly being included in the conversation.

"We couldn't have helped him, Ada," Joe pointed out. "We didn't notice the tree house was gone until I hauled out the trash. Those boards were mighty heavy. Should've made Jack carry them out to the curb."

"I suppose we should be grateful he didn't do the same to the Hasselblad." Ada sighed.

Jack's body jerked as his mother repeated his earlier thought.

"I wish he had," Ada said. "Maybe it would have made us think, ask the right questions. Instead, we were relieved to see that you didn't seem to have any trauma to speak of. Do you know how proud we were of how you handled it all, how you stepped right into the breach?"

That called for another swallow of beer. "Yeah, Mom, I knew."

"That was the problem all along, wasn't it? Our pride in you for all the wrong reasons?"

All Jack could do was frown.

"We didn't understand until it was too late, Jack," Ada said. "By then, your mind was set and you had too much pride of your own to back out."

"We should have known what you were doing," Joe added. "We should have stopped you."

Ada nodded. "We assumed that you'd know we were proud of you no matter what you chose to do with your life."

"We assumed," Joe said, "that you wanted to go into the service. It was easier than dealing with another problem."

Jack leaned his head back, stared at the ceiling. A pattern was emerging. A pattern that picked up where he and Steve left off in Germany. "I'm going to kill Steve," he muttered, his tongue feeling as if it had tripled in size.

"You think we can't figure all this out on our own, son?"

Joe asked. "I knew when I watched you pack away that camera. I just didn't know what to do about it."

Jack remembered the jar of change.

Ada sighed again, a heavy, grieving sound. "Is it time now, Joe?" she asked her husband.

Joe squinted at Jack and nodded as he pulled a split of champagne out of the cooler. "Guess so."

Ada held glasses as her husband poured, then carried one over to Jack. Joe rose to his feet, held out his glass, waited for Ada to do the same. He cleared his throat. "Congratulations, son. You are now a free man."

Huh? Jack peered up at his parents, saw apprehension on their faces. His head cleared marginally. "For what, Dad?"

"For getting out of the service before it was too late."

"Too late for what?"

"To live your own life," Ada said.

"To bury Bryan," Joe said as he stared into his glass.

The images stared at him—three boys, ages seventeen, ten, and five, in shades of black and white and gray preserved behind glass, faded into shadows of what they had been, merging with the half light of a winter storm that seeped through drapes closed against the night.

Jack prowled around the living room, unable to sleep in spite of the beer chased by champagne that had blurred his thoughts, numbed the pain from resurrected memories and regrets that had aged into acceptance.

In Germany, it had been easy to file away Steve's observations. He had been too young to understand what had happened to his brothers. It had been easy to chalk up Steve's opinion as fancy guesswork that would stay that way as long as it wasn't confirmed.

Jack had never confirmed it, even to himself.

He heard a soft shuffle on the carpet, caught the scent of Chanel, turned his head, and saw the tall, angular shape of his mother glide up beside him.

It had been like this all day, family members coming and going, stepping into his thoughts as if they shared them, intruding into the quiet moments he'd thought he wanted. They seemed more like connections being established rather than intrusions. And they brought relief from thoughts of Angie, memories of Angie. Several times he'd started for the shower, only to wander into a room full of voices and activity. More than once, he'd yawned and told himself he had to get some sleep, only to wander some more.

"Can't sleep?" Ada asked.

"My internal clock is off, I guess," Jack said as he absently raked his hand through his hair.

"You boys were something," Ada said softly, wistfully, as she stared at the framed poster. "Each of you so different. I was a little disappointed when you began to follow in Bryan's footsteps."

"Mom—"

"You look so put out in that picture, Jack. I'll bet it was because you were in the middle."

Jack smiled. "It was a pain."

"Mmm. Not easy being neither the oldest nor the baby. Bryan used to complain at always having to babysit and take all the responsibility. Steve was so overwhelmed by his brothers that he set his path as far away from yours as possible—or so we thought."

Jack jammed his hands into his pockets. "He's back to stay this time, Mom."

"Yes, thank God. I was afraid that maybe your father and I had done too much damage. It's so difficult knowing that your children are lost and you're powerless to find them." She twined her arm through his, squeezed his wrist. "Who would have thought that parental pride could be destructive?"

"It wasn't," Jack said, his throat tight.

"No? Tell me, Jack: if we hadn't been so proud, would you have kept driving yourself to do what you didn't want to do—just to please us?" Her voice lowered, caught. "Just to compensate us because our oldest was gone?"

"I don't know," Jack said, and winced. He hadn't meant to say anything, admit anything, but his parents were determined to make things right, to understand. Something inside of him needed that understanding, that measure of healing.

He freed his hand from his pocket, hooked his arm around her shoulders. "Mom, it's all right. I had my own confusion to deal with. It's not your fault that it took me so long."

"Have you dealt with it, Jack? You and Bryan were so close, closer than normal for brothers with so many years between them."

"He liked being a hero," Jack said. "I liked having a hero. It worked for us."

"And Steve?"

Jack's mouth quirked. "He was a rugrat."

"A monster," Ada agreed. "I shouldn't have said that about my own son."

"Every family needs one," Jack teased, and wondered how long had it been since he'd teased anyone.

Ada's body trembled. "I need my family, Jack. I need us to close ranks, fill in the empty space Bryan left."

Turning his head, Jack lifted his hand, swiped at his eyes. "I need it, too, Mom."

Ada straightened up, wrapped her arm around his waist. "One thing, Jack: I won't be so easily pleased again. I can't feel pride in your accomplishments unless you're doing what you want to do."

Jack rested his cheek on the top of her head. "That makes two of us," he said, knowing it was true. For too many years he'd felt like a victim of his own lies.

A loud snore ripped through the silence.

"Joe's at it again," Ada said. "I'd better go turn him over." She eased away from Jack's hold, walked toward the hallway, and paused under the threshold. "Tell me, Jack: *Do* you have a girl?"

Jack rolled his eyes. "Tell me, Mom: Did you and Dad get me drunk on purpose this afternoon?"

Ada shook her head and stepped into the hall. "It's a sad thing when children become smarter than their parents."

Not so smart, Jack thought as he swiped at the back of

his neck and walked toward his bedroom. Smart was Steve figuring out what had gone wrong all those years ago and why. Smart was his parents getting him drunk so that they could confirm Steve's analysis without Jack being able to field the truth, avoid the pain of knowing how right they were.

Smart would have been keeping his hands to himself instead of reaching out for the hot silk and wild magic Angie had so freely offered.

In his room, he took the leather case off the shelf and stretched out on his bed, his back supported by the maple headboard. The camera seemed heavy, intimidating, as he carefully pulled it out of its nest, the body smooth and finely fashioned and cold. Once he had held the Hasselblad like this, seeing in his imagination what the viewfinder would see—life, emotion, dreams shining brightly in the eyes of his subjects, images of the world as only he saw it, unique and infinitely diverse.

He'd been going in circles for years, and now he was back at the beginning. Full circle. Only this time he would be flying blind into a new direction.

His hand relaxed as the camera settled into his lap. His eyelids dropped between one thought and the next. The soft cotton of his shirt collar tickled his nose as his chin dropped. In a minute, he'd take the shower he'd been craving all day.

His mind drifted from the camera that seemed to warm in his hands to the lingering scent of Shalimar on the collar of his shirt.

Full circle—a dream he could hold and a woman he shouldn't have touched. A woman who had the power to hold him with a single memory.

24

Obstacles are those frightful things you see when you lose sight of your goals.

Angie stood at the portal to the Link International headquarters and read the sign above the door. She'd seen those words, deeply etched into a large bronze plaque, for years, yet now they seemed to take on a significance beyond the obvious. She'd been doing that a lot since Saturday morning—applying odd bits and pieces of thought to more personal concerns. Yet she felt detached, as if she were standing back, observing the creation of a separate being.

Thankfully, she hadn't had much time to think about it. After Jack left—walked out on her, she reminded herself—she'd come to Link.

Gena always scheduled important staff meetings for Saturday, when voice mail took over from the switchboard and no appointments were scheduled. Everyone showed up in grungies and were more relaxed and focused on a day when nothing else was going on to break concentration. It made for a less stressful meeting where important decisions had to be made and tricky problems needed to be addressed. Gena inevitably served food and drink and promoted an atmosphere of friends getting together to plan their next outing. It helped that everyone in management and planning were friends and close to one another in age.

Sunday, Angie had slept past noon, then spent the afternoon in her studio, singing to fill the silence and dancing to work off the restlessness she hadn't been able to shake since Jack had written her with the news that he might be coming home. She'd tried crying, but just couldn't get into the spirit of being broken-hearted. More than once she'd caught herself smiling for no reason, yet she felt detached, numb.

It made no sense at all.

Unless it was because she had a goal, and not enough time had passed for her to acknowledge obstacles. She stood back to read the plaque once more, to study the place that ironically had become as important to her as to Gena.

Link International was housed in a low sprawl of modern architecture combined with Old World charm. Built in a Roman villa style, a hollow square, the plastered adobe structure looked more like an oversize home than the traditional office building. Trees and walkways surrounded the outside of the building on three sides, and all the offices and workrooms opened out onto a central courtyard that was beautifully landscaped with trees, flower beds, and velvet lawns that invited staff to smell the roses during breaks and lunches. There was even a sign that said RELAX IN PEACE. Gena was big on signs and posters that carried a message.

In front of the building was a large evergreen bush trimmed and sculpted in a sphere, with darker patches to indicate land masses on the planet earth. Between Saturday and this morning, someone had cleared its branches of the snow and icicles that had made it look like the arctic landscape of an alien world.

Inside, Allie, the receptionist, was busy working the buttons on her telephone console like a ten-key calculator. Every line was lit up, and the fax machine beeped a signal for incoming transmission. It was, as usual, going to be a busy day.

Picking up her messages, Angie walked through the lobby and down the hall, her feet sinking into plush pale gold carpet as she passed offices and waved to the occupants on her way to Gena's office. Gordy, their computer expert, stood before the bank of coffeemakers in the employee lounge, filling each one with precise movements, studying the controls on each machine as if he'd never seen them before.

"How long before we have caffeinated?" Angie asked.

"Uh . . . approximately seven minutes and twenty-two seconds," Gordy said. "Where do you want it?"

"I'll be in Gena's office."

Gordy nodded absently as he moved on to the electric kettle used to heat water for tea.

When Gordy applied for a job at Link, he'd been so desperate for a job that he'd made the rash statement that he even made coffee. It had been part of his job ever since.

"Thanks, Gordy." Angie waggled her fingers at him and moved on. Gena had a policy of hiring according to desire to work in a team environment and a willingness to learn rather than for actual experience. Gordy had come to them as a college sophomore with a major in computers and a minor in psychology. The combination of knowledge in mechanical logic and the foibles of human behavior had appealed to Gena.

The door to Gena's office was cracked open. Angie paused, listening to see if Gena was on the phone before knocking. All was silent except for the muted sound of Enya playing on the CD player.

Angie rapped once.

"If it's anyone but Gordy with coffee or Angie with a report, go away."

"A case of the Monday morning cranks?" Angie asked as she strolled into the office.

Gena sat on the thickly padded sofa set in a cozy grouping by the French doors that led out into the courtyard, her feet propped on the heavily burled cocktail table that matched her desk. She glanced up at Angie and held out her hand.

Without a word, Angie opened her briefcase and pulled out a spiral-bound report.

Without a word, Gena took it and began leafing through the pages. "I can't believe that you have everything done for the benefit," she said. "Even the orchestra—I watched the video they supplied. They're good. Where'd you find them?"

Angie perched on the arm of a dark blue chair. "You specified locals."

Gena pinched her fingers over the bridge of her nose. "I can't believe you have everything under control."

"You already said that, though I distinctly remember you saying I was next to useless last week."

"I lied."

"Coffee!"

Gena checked her watch as Gordy walked in carrying a tray with a carafe, cups, cream, sugar, and croissants. "Right on time. How do you do that, Gordy?"

Grinning, Gordy set the tray on the cocktail table and walked out. He only answered questions he considered relevant.

"Right to the second. How *does* he do that?"

"He spent his lunch hour timing each coffeemaker right after you hired him," Angie said as she poured coffee into the cups and added cream and sugar to both. "What's the occasion?" She held up a croissant.

Gena sipped her coffee. "For the first time since we started Link, we're actually caught up."

"We can't be."

"We wouldn't be if it weren't for you. I'm beginning to wonder how we managed for so long without you."

Something expanded inside Angie, a warm, quiet feeling of pride. It had never felt like this before, never touched her as it did now. She *had* been doing a good job at Link. Her presence made a difference. She knew it and gloried in that knowledge. And then she realized that she had felt like this before—Friday night, when Jack had looked at her and told her she was beautiful. When they had made love and he had shattered in her arms.

"Thank you," she said.

"I don't believe it! No protests? No foot-shuffling and blushes?"

"Nope. I've changed."

"Uh uh," Gena said. "People don't change, remember? They improve."

"Okay, I've improved."

"You're not even bummed out because the major didn't call."

Heat climbed Angie's face as she bit into her pastry and averted her gaze.

"What's going on, chum?" Gena asked quietly, her expression somber as she reached for a croissant. "You were a million miles away during the meeting Saturday. Something happened."

"He showed up at the house Friday night."

Gena paused in mid-bite. "The major? He went to your house?"

"Uh huh."

"Oh, boy," Gena muttered in a voice of doom. "What happened?"

"We were overcome by instant and blinding passion."

"Sure, Angie."

Angie shrugged. "He spent the night, Gena," she said because she had to say it. The experience was too new, too overwhelming to keep it locked up. She hadn't been able to make sense out of her own actions or Jack's, and needed some kind of feedback to get her mind working again.

"Holy shit! You're serious!" Gena's feet hit the floor and she leaned forward. "He spent the night? Just like that?"

"Just like that."

"On the sofa, right? *Alone.*"

"No. On the floor. With me."

"Angie . . ." Words seemed to fail Gena. She shook her head and slumped back on the sofa.

"I know, Gena. I don't do things like that." She raised her head, stared out into the garden.

"No, you damn well don't. For cripes' sakes, Angie, how could you do that? You just met the man."

"I wanted to, Gena. He was everything I'd imagined— quiet and broody and so serious about life." She took a deep breath, met Gena's gaze. "He was the man I've known since New Year's Eve."

"In letters. Not the same thing, Angie, as knowing him in person."

"No. It's better. He came because of me, not my face or my boobs or—"

"I get the picture," Gena said impatiently. "A meeting of minds nine months before a meeting of hormones. So when do I get to meet him?"

"I don't know."

Gena glanced at her sharply. "When do you see him again?"

Angie shrugged.

"Uh-huh. The . . . uh . . . encounter was disappointing."

"No."

"He was disappointing."

"No."

"Dammit, Angie, don't you dare tell me half a story and then leave me hanging. What happened?"

Suddenly, the numbness was gone. The entire episode flashed through her memory: her excitement and awkwardness, his anger and kindness, the magic of their shadows echoing their movements and the shattering sound of silence as he slept. Angie swallowed, waited until she was sure her voice would be steady, light. "He didn't respect me in the morning."

"What do you expect, giving in to him like that?"

"He gave in to me, Gena," Angie said softly. It was so clear now—how she had thrown herself at him, almost begged him. Maybe she'd even played on his sympathies with her "true confessions."

"I don't believe it."

"It's true."

"What possessed you, Angie?"

"Jack," Angie said simply.

"Well, how does it feel to be used and discarded?"

The bitterness and sarcasm in Gena's voice ripped into Angie like a dull blade. She blinked at the tightness of Gena's mouth, the blaze of anger in her eyes. Even during that first year at Collingswood, Gena's criticisms had been more like good-natured prodding delivered with humor and a hint of caring. Caring was what Gena was all about, what made her a crusader.

"I don't regret a minute of it, Gena."

"No, I guess you wouldn't. You've been trying to devalue yourself all your life. A one-night stand with a stranger follows the pattern."

Angie's joints seemed to lock. Her muscles stiffened. Her nerve ends seemed to shiver once, then freeze into numbness again. She placed her coffee cup on the tray very precisely. "Sometimes, Gena, it's real hard to love you," Angie said. "Maybe you've had a bad weekend. I'll try to believe that." Leaning over the table, she gathered her briefcase and purse. "Since we're all caught up here and the newsletter layout is finished, I think I'll take the day off."

The numbness carried her out of the building and all the way home and remained through the better part of the afternoon. She made calls to the shops she'd supplied with greeting cards and heard the same story over and over again.

"I really like your cards, Ms. Winters, but designs like yours are pretty common—have been for longer than I've been around. Nowadays, it's off-the-wall humor and cartoon characters that sell. Photographic cards do well, too. Pretty and sweet is boring. Still, we like to give local talent a chance. I wish it had worked out."

Of course Angie had known all that for a while. She'd gone into her business feet first, developing her product before studying the markets. The consumers had given her cards a trial run and gone on to more exciting and imaginative products.

In a way Jack had done the same thing.

So how does it feel to be used and discarded?

Devalued.

The pain was a little sharper, a little deeper. Resentment began as a tiny spark that caught and flared. She had come so close to striking back at Gena, saved only by the unfamiliarity of the impulse. For once a comeback had been on the tip of her tongue. Thank God she'd counted to a thousand, waiting until it was ten minutes too late.

Thank God undisguised anger was still too new, too frightening for her to react spontaneously.

This past week had been a time of beginnings and endings. She'd never dreamed that they could come so close together that it was difficult to distinguish between the two.

The music of *Footloose* blared from the stereo system, the beat of the varied pieces trapped by the soundproof walls and ceiling of Angie's studio. Hardwood floors so smooth, the seams joining the strips of varnished wood could not be felt by the most sensitive fingers absorbed the impact of every movement in Angie's dance as she leaped and whirled and swayed. Moisture stained the back and underarms of her shiny fuschia leotard. Tendrils of hair escaped the confines of a banana clip to stick wetly to the sides of her face. Her teal tights were old and bagged at the knees. Purple leg warmers bunched around her ankles. A strap had broken on her soft leather ballet slippers.

There were no mirrors mounted behind the barres in the large square room. Mirrors meant that she would watch herself dance, see her mistakes and try to correct them. To Angie, mirrors symbolized performing for the sake of others rather than dancing for her own sake.

She ground her hips to the beat and tossed her head back as she executed a half turn and kicked high. Again she whirled around and around, perspiration streaming down her face until she couldn't see, couldn't "spot" to keep from losing her balance. She stumbled over her own feet and crumpled into a heap, breathing hard, feeling battered by the pace she'd set in an attempt to purge frustration and resentment and anger. She leaned over, her body doubled as she rested her forehead on the cool wood of the floor. The tape ended.

Slowly, she became aware of a slight breeze from the open doorway, the shifting of another body in the room. She'd closed the door when she came in. She'd been alone.

As alone as she'd been after every pageant, every performance.

Raising her head, she focused on the threshold, the familiar camouflage fatigue pants topped this time by a thick and heavily ribbed black turtleneck sweater, the vase holding dozens of dainty rosebuds in red, yellow, pink, and white.

Roses and baby's breath and delicate sprays of fern. An offering to take the place of words that could not be found. Angie raised her knees and wrapped her arms around them, curling into herself, holding herself against the memory of crushed petals and scattered hopes.

"Hi," Gena said.

"Hi."

"I let myself in when you didn't answer. I figured you'd be pounding the floorboards and trying to wake the dead."

"Yes." Dead emotions. Dead illusions.

"I—can we talk?"

"Not like this morning, Gena."

"No. Not like this morning." Gena's voice was thick and wary. "Now, Angie, before I lose my nerve."

Angie rose on trembling legs, trembling because she'd pushed too hard for too long. Because she knew that this would be a confrontation, a turning point, maybe a repeat of other times. Only this time she could not—would not—hide behind herself.

Silently, Gena grabbed the towel hanging over the barre and, one-handed, draped it over Angie's neck as they passed through the enclosed breezeway that connected her studio with the back of the house and walked into the kitchen.

Silently, Angie drank Gatorade straight from the bottle sitting on the counter and wiped her face with the towel.

"I know you're not crazy about roses, but I never understood why except that you always got a bouquet when you won a pageant." She touched a yellow bud. "These—they looked special somehow."

"I offered my bouquet to Sara, a friend in the same pageant, and she let them drop on the floor. She was so anxious to get away from me that she trampled them into pulp." Angie swiped a strand of hair away from her face. "Do you want something to drink?"

"Water." Gena laughed nervously. "I'm going to need it for all the talking I have to do. Would it help if I dumped these on the floor so you can walk all over them?"

Angie pulled a bottle of Evian water from the refrigerator and poured it into a glass. "No. And actually I love roses, but the only time I ever received any was when I earned them."

Gena smiled. "These are 'just because,' Angie. Because I'm a royal first-class bitch. Because my conscience is killing me. Because I love you and I don't know how to convince you of that after being so nasty this morning." She accepted the glass of water and followed Angie into the living room.

"Try telling me why." Angie sat down in the chair and raised her legs onto the ottoman.

"That's why I'm here. After you left this morning, it all came together. Dr. Landon and I have been piecing it together, but you were right. I needed to tell myself what was wrong. I've known for a while now, but it seems so damn stupid that I didn't want to tell you or the doc." She drank some water, stared down into the glass. "This afternoon I saw Dr. Landon. She didn't think it was stupid—why I'm the way I am. She didn't trivialize it, either. I couldn't have stood that. Never in a million years will it be trivial to me."

The bright, I'm-okay-even-if-you're-not smile was there as it always was when Gena came too close to her own problems. "Anyway, since I seem to be on a roll, I figured I ought to tell you why I'm so hard to love sometimes."

"I said 'hard,' Gena, not impossible."

"Yeah. I was counting on that." Gena perched on the edge of the sofa, her body angled forward, the glass sandwiched between her hands. "I'm so sorry, Angie. I don't know why I—"

"Yes, you do, and for once I deserve an explanation," Angie said with a calm that surprised her. "Jack didn't devalue me. I didn't cheapen myself. It was a good experience—wonderful. For the first time in my life I was glad of the way I look. I've never felt as if I had any power, in my life or over myself. Jack gave me power, and a choice. It made me feel like a million dollars."

"I know," Gena whispered. "I could see that. It pissed me off. Dammit, Angie, I was jealous. I felt betrayed."

"Excuse me? Jealousy I can understand, but betrayal? How?"

Gena swiped at her eyes, though Angie could see no tears. "You were a symbol. The last holdout—proving that not all of us are stupid enough to believe the only way to hold on to a man or even get one is to give him what he wants. I had this crazy rationale that sex isn't all that important. That a person could live very nicely and happily without it. What's an orgasm? Who needs it—really needs it? And why in the hell do we—I—feel so freakish because I can't have one of my own?"

"I don't have an answer for that, Gena."

"Did you . . . ? Oh, hell, forget I asked. It's none of my business."

Angie's breath shuddered at the memory of pure feeling soaring beyond the limit of endurance, of shutting down just for a second because otherwise the body might very well die of pleasure. It was melodramatic perhaps, but true. No wonder the books didn't adequately describe it. They couldn't. "Yes, I did, Gena. So have you."

"Right. My lover is a mechanical wonder. I love myself because I'm too afraid to completely love a man." She drained the glass and thunked it down on the cocktail table. "It happened once, you know—with a man. A boy, actually. I was fourteen years old and madly in love for the first time. He was twenty and gave me the old line, 'If you love me you will.' I did. At first it was great. He was in college and experienced. I had no business going with a college man, but Mom gave me advice and choices. What the hell did she expect? Besides, Dad was fooling around with a woman half his age. My family was falling apart, and I needed someone—anyone—to hold on to. I needed some kind of direction even if it was wrong."

Angie didn't know what to say so she listened and kept silent, barely moving for fear of startling Gena out of the trance she seemed to be in. Angie knew all about trances, about pulling back a part of herself while exposing another, pulling back away from the pain.

"It's an old, sad story. I lost control every time I was with him. I didn't think, didn't take precautions, didn't remember anything but the way he held me and touched me and made me forget the shit going on at home. I got pregnant, and he gave me a wad of money and orders to get an abortion." Gena's hands began to tremble, and tears slipped down her cheeks. "He gave me another classic about how everything would be okay if I did what he said. Dad was gone by then, and Mom was busy coping with the bad press over an advice columnist getting a divorce. She was so brittle, you know?"

"Yes, I know," Angie whispered, remembering how fragile her own mother was when Angie hadn't placed in a pageant for the third time in a row.

"My body was in control; I was so sick, and there was no one else to take over, make decisions, except for Trent. Do you believe it? I fell for a man named Trent. Naturally, he was a Big Stud On Campus. I found out later he was screwing half the cheerleading squad while—" Gena shook her head, swiped at her cheeks again, and stared at the moisture on her fingers.

"I had the abortion, Angie," she said, her voice broken. "And I've never been able to live with it. My life wasn't threatened by the pregnancy. I hadn't been raped. I wouldn't have been ostracized by my family."

"You were fourteen, Gena."

"I could have given the baby up for adoption!" Gena leaned back on the sofa, sprawling in an attitude of exhaustion. "As you know I fell apart, went bonkers, lost it. I can't speak for other women, and I wouldn't want to try. All I know is that it was wrong for me. I didn't make the choice for me but for *him,* and I knew better."

"Gena, none of us are too bright at fourteen."

"That doesn't help, chum. I'm still not too bright at

twenty-nine. I shot myself in the foot at fourteen and didn't have the sense to know something was wrong. I *was* bright enough to fool the psychiatrists in the fancy hospital Mom put me in. I assumed control and kept it. I control my life and my body. No way was I ever going to give a man power over me again. No way was I ever going to let my body take over from my brains."

Frowning, Angie thought back to Friday night, tried to see it in terms Gena had described.

"That's not the way it is, is it Angie?" Gena asked as if she'd read Angie's mind.

"At fourteen, maybe. Adolescents run on emotion and hormones."

"You didn't."

"Not obviously, but now that the subject has come up, I remember times when I'd wake up in the middle of the night and . . ." Embarrassment warmed Angie's skin, rushed into her face. "I don't think males are the only ones who have wet dreams. As far as emotion goes—no, I didn't operate on them consciously, but they came out in dreams —horrible, distorted dreams."

"Yeah, I remember. If emotions don't get out one way, they'll get out another." Gena sprang to her feet and began to pace. "So tell me what it's all about."

"Suddenly I'm supposed to be an expert?"

"You saw. You conquered. You *came.*" Dimples flashed in Gena's cheeks as she grinned. "And obviously you're okay with it. Tell me why."

Angie caught the corner of her lower lip between her teeth as she thought about her answer. "I trusted him, Gena. I trusted myself, too. Yes, making love can incinerate common sense and control, but not completely. I chose to lose control, and I was aware of what I was doing. I almost backed out because the vulnerability scared me. Jack didn't push, didn't issue ultimatums."

"But?"

"But he pointed out his own vulnerability—physical and emotional."

"Physical?"

"Think about it, Gena. A woman is vulnerable because she is opening herself to her lover, allowing him to . . . invade her. I didn't realize that the man is . . . um . . . entrusting his . . . um—"

"Pride and joy?"

"That's it! He's entrusting his 'pride and joy' to his lover. I think that maybe at that point, he's more vulnerable and less in control than the woman."

"Jack told you this."

"Not in so many words, and don't ask for more details. It really is none of your business."

"Why does it have to be so complicated?"

"So we'll appreciate it more?"

"Good guess."

"Gena?"

"Hmm?"

"I think the most important thing is to wait for the right person and to make sure you trust him, and work up to it gradually."

"Like you did?"

"It may have been through letters, Gena, but a relationship did grow. So did trust. Maybe it was better that way because I knew he didn't come here because of the way I look. He came here because of the way I am."

Gena snorted. "Yeah, until he saw you. You're gorgeous, Angie. It stood to reason he'd be turned on. Looks don't hurt."

Angie sighed. "No, they don't, and yes, Jack is tall, dark, and sexy. But we talked first. I acted like a total idiot, admitted to him that I'd been doing a lot of fantasizing. From something he said, I knew that he'd been doing the same thing—*before* we met face to face." Angie knew she was blushing again and wondered when it would stop. How much sophistication was required to banish the reaction? "It was funny, really. We both fumbled around. I fell on the floor, and he couldn't get his shirt off, and the whole thing was awkward until . . ." She shook her head. "Anyway, it didn't matter. It was natural—no pretenses and slick, well-practiced performances."

Crouching by the fireplace, Gena began arranging kindling and logs in the grate. "What now?"

"I don't know."

"Are you going to wait around for him?"

"For a while."

"Then?"

"If he doesn't show up or call, I guess I'll formulate Plan B. I'm not giving up without a fight, Gena."

"You're asking for trouble, chum."

"Probably, but he's worth it. So am I."

"Am I worth it, too?" Gena asked softly.

Tears fell without warning, burning Angie's eyes, blurring her vision. She'd never known Gena to show uncertainty, to ask for anything, to admit she needed anything from anyone. She was a giver, to her family, her friends, the whole world, not because she wanted something in return but because she wouldn't allow herself to feel obligated in any way to another person. To Gena, each obligation was like relinquishing a small measure of control.

"If we didn't have 'downs' occasionally, how on earth would we be able to appreciate the 'ups'?" Angie waited until Gena lifted her gaze to meet hers. "I love you, Gena, hard as it is sometimes. I believe you feel the same way—hard as it is sometimes."

Gena sat back on her heels. "Yeah." She flattened her palms on her thighs, stared down at them. "Today, I realized that you have a lot of control over me. I hadn't thought about friendship in those terms before." She looked up and smiled. "And it doesn't hurt a bit. I'm going to get really profound long enough to admit that it's given me more strength, not less."

Angie smiled back and eased herself up out of the chair. "Enough of this heavy shit. I'm going to call for a pizza and then I'm going to go smell my roses."

25

The snow and bitter cold had vanished like a figment of the imagination. The temperature had climbed to a balmy fifty-five, and the ground held only the surface moisture of early morning dew on the velvet lawn. Autumn splashed the landscape with fiery blazes of color on trees that shaded the headstones spaced over the cemetery grounds as precisely as soldiers in formation.

Heedless of the dew, Jack sat on the grass, his legs cocked up, his elbows resting on his knees. He'd been here only once before, a day when Bryan was forever denied the sight of any roof other than the satin-lined dome of his casket. His last memory of this place was of the casket, still above the ground and surrounded by flowers. It didn't matter that flowers, any flowers, had made Bryan sneeze. Later, strangers on a time clock had lowered what was left of his brother into a hole, filled it with dirt, and walked away.

He sensed a presence, heard the faint crush of grass and the shuffle of arms and legs. He glanced to his right, saw Steve sitting beside him, staring at the headstone.

"If it weren't for the pictures at home and that . . ." Steve nodded toward the grave. ". . . I wouldn't know that he had ever been real."

"So what are you doing here?" Jack asked.

"I followed you. Thought you might like some company."

Oddly enough, Jack was glad to have Steve there, relieved not to be alone with memories of two boys who no longer existed.

It's only pain. No big deal.

Steve's voice was quiet and smooth, blending with the light breeze ruffling through the trees, the distant whoosh of traffic on the highway beyond the gates. "I only have two clear memories of Bryan. One is of the day Dad took the pictures for the poster. Bryan was so tall that I just knew Dad would never get us all in the picture without cutting off Bryan's head or cutting me out altogether. And I remember being hyper because he'd promised to help me build a model B-52 bomber."

"You only asked him ten times a day, and you were always hyper."

Steve ran his hand around the back of his neck. "I hated being the baby of the family. I think I was trying to hog all the attention."

"I hated being in the middle. Bryan wasn't too happy at being the oldest."

"Damn," Steve said. "We were three pissed off individuals."

"Bryan said you weren't too bad when you were asleep."

Steve's chest rose and fell in a silent sigh. "Remember that last day? We were on our way out the door to go to your game, and I ran back to my room for my baseball cap. The doors between all our bedrooms were open, and I saw Bryan fold a sheet of paper and slide it under your pillow. He stood there, staring at me, as if he wanted to say something. I waited until he went back into his room. I was going to get the note and give it to you."

"Why didn't you?" Jack asked as he waited for anger or regret. By the time he found the note, it had been too late. If Steve had brought it to him . . .

. . . it seems to be the only thing I want to do now.

"I was pretty ticked because he didn't say anything, and because he never wrote notes to me. He called you 'bro' and me 'rugrat.' You two were always doing things together —building model airplanes, going to see the Broncos play, air shows on Armed Forces Day."

Out of the corner of his eye, Jack saw Steve turn his head to look at him. "You're never going to tell the parents what was in that note, are you?"

"Nothing to tell."

"No? Then why did you burn it?"

"I was pissed off, too."

Steve shook his head, lowered his gaze as he flexed his fingers between his knees. "I didn't think much about it at the time, but I never forgot it, either. After we got home that night and we were in bed, I saw you cry as you read that note and went into Bryan's room. You just stood there and watched him and then you stopped crying and went back to bed. It all makes sense now. He used to stare at that damn ceiling all the time. That night was more of the same."

"How do you know he was—"

"Because I went into his room after you went to sleep—"

"Why?"

"I had this sick feeling in my stomach. I didn't know what it was, but I wanted to cry, too."

Jack winced as Steve cracked his knuckles. " 'Kiss the rugrat for me.' "

"He said that?" Steve asked with a catch in his voice.

"It was in the note."

Steve swallowed. "It wasn't an accident, was it—the overdose?"

So I can get through what's left of my fucking life.

"No." Jack closed his eyes against the inscription on the headstone in front of him: BELOVED SON AND BROTHER. "I called him a chicken who sniveled like a girl."

"And I didn't give you the note before we left."

Don't mess with my head. . . .

All these years, Jack had carried that guilt, assumed sole responsibility for not saving Bryan. All these years Steve had blamed himself for not saving Bryan. Why hadn't they realized that only Bryan could have saved himself? "It's not your fault."

"I know. What about you?"

What about him? Jack wondered as he closed his eyes against the inscription. He tried to see Bryan, gluing pieces of plastic together, hammering nails into the treehouse, hiding Steve's favorite blanket just before bedtime. Instead, he saw Steve curled up on his side in bed, hugging that blanket and staring at him through the connecting door while sirens wailed and their parents cried. He'd forgotten how he and Steve had stared at each other for what seemed like hours, unblinking, silent . . . *connected*.

He felt the easing of a pressure that had been with him so long, he hadn't realized it was there. All he saw in front of him was a piece of stone. All he felt was the air around him, Steve's presence beside him, an incredible lightness in his soul. *What about him?* "I'm okay with it, Steve."

Hearing himself say the words, he knew it was true, knew that all that was left of Bryan were memories. His hand poked around in the grass and paused as a ladybug daintily made her way across his forefinger. "Don't tell the folks, Steve—about the note."

"No. I think they know that Bryan checked out on his own, and if they don't, there isn't much point in bringing it all back. They're finally okay with it, too." Pushing to his feet, Steve extended his hand.

Jack took it, accepted Steve's help to rise, stood beside him as they stared once more at the headstone with the airplane engraved in the granite.

"All he ever wanted to do was fly the bombers," Steve said thickly.

"Yeah, the one thing I didn't do. Beyond recreational flying, I just couldn't get into it."

"No, but I did," Steve said.

"For who?"

"Maybe for all three of us, bringing Bryan's ambitions full circle." Shrugging, Steve leaned his head back, stared at the sky. "Good flying weather today. I have a feeling Bryan is enjoying the hell out of it."

"Yeah. He's probably pushing the flap of that envelope all the way to—" Jack's voice broke, the rest of his sentence scattered on the breeze as moisture trickled down his face. He felt a hand clamp down on his shoulder, saw Steve's face through a salty haze.

"I'd like to think you're right—that Bryan isn't in there."

Steve jerked his head back toward the grave. "He's probably a hot stick in God's own Air Force."

They reached the parking lot in silence, and Jack paused before getting into the Volvo he'd borrowed from his parents, propping his arms on the roof as Steve straddled his Harley.

Steve looked up at the same time and grinned. "Wanna trade for the ride home?" He dismounted and tossed his helmet to Jack before he could answer. "It's like swimming. You never forget how."

Catching the helmet, Jack strapped it on just in time to catch Steve's leather jacket. "Why not? It's been a long time since I've caught bugs in my teeth," Jack quipped, feeling lighter and younger than he had since he was ten. He lobbed his car keys to Steve from the seat of the motorcycle and kicked on the starter.

"I have to go to the shop, so why don't you keep it all day? Visit a pen pal, maybe take her for a ride." He grinned slyly. "Oh, yeah—a letter came for you this morning. Lucky I got the mail instead of Mom. It's in my jacket pocket. Smells of Shalimar." Steve watched as Jack dug into the pocket and found the letter, shrugged as Jack frowned down at it. "Or shop for your own car—a big van maybe, to hold your photography equipment."

Jack ignored Steve's less-than-subtle hints that he needed a woman and wheels, ignored the way his blood began to race and burn, denied the sudden urge to sprawl beneath the nearest tree and read the letter, smell the fragrance, remember how it had smelled on Angie's skin.

He had to forget.

He jammed the letter back into the pocket, glanced up at Steve, and called, "Hey, bro."

Steve paused in the act of strapping himself in, his body still, his voice silent.

"Don't expect me to give you that kiss Bryan ordered."

Steve grinned and shifted into gear. "You just did—*bro*," he shouted back, and peeled out of the parking lot, flashing Jack a thumbs-up as he passed. "It was worth the wait."

Dear Jack,

For too many years I've forced myself to stand still while the rest of the world passed me by. But not now. The more I think about it, the more I know I have to write to you one last time. I'm betting that the J. Caldwell in the phone book is your father. If not, someone will have a good laugh on me. It won't be the first time.

Besides, a letter seems to be more fair to you than if I brazenly showed up on your doorstep. How on earth can one explain such a bizarre situation to one's family?

Words are often cheap, yet so many times I've been comforted by them. Your words in particular. I miss them more than I thought possible. Unfortunately, letters are no longer enough. I want to hear the words, watch you as you speak. For now, though, I need the illusion of being close to you. Ironic, isn't it, that I need to pretend now that you are nearby?

Did you feel safer, Jack, writing to me from half a world away? I know I did. The reality of your presence is frightening, yet distance no longer offers safety. It didn't keep me from falling in love with you before I saw you for the first time last night. Until then, I'd never seen love as a particularly positive experience, and certainly not one I wanted to pursue. How drastically you've changed my life, confusing me and altering my beliefs until I don't know top from bottom. All I know is that I cannot and will not fade into the woodwork and make life easy for either one of us. It's only fair.

Though I have no idea what I'm going to do, I'm sure I'll think of something. The women's magazines are full of advice for the lovelorn that consists of game playing and subtle deceptions. I probably should play it cool and wait for you to make the next move. But I'm not cool, and I can't play games with you.

It's been said that there is bad writing and good writing, and then there's communication. That goes for letters, too, Jack, as I discovered when you began communicating with me. And last night you communicated beautifully.

Bad mistake, Jack. You communicated so well that I

received a message maybe you didn't mean to send. You like me. You care. You want me.

Does that sound smug? Well, you're right. If you wanted to fool me into believing you don't care about me, you never should have looked me up, never should have stayed for dinner. You definitely shouldn't have come back after your sudden exit and shown me what kind of man you truly are.

You'll never know how difficult it was for me to watch you go that morning without asking when or if there would be another time for us, another chance. Now I understand why people get angry. I feel it, somewhere deep inside, yet I can't seem to do anything about it. As a child I learned my lessons too well, to avoid or deny the existence of anger, even my own. And now I know that I was angry because I felt as helpless and frustrated as I feel now.

I couldn't find the words to stop you from leaving. I don't understand why you stormed out of the house as if it had just been quarantined. All I have is the belief that your anger is unjustified, unreasonable.

I suppose that's where the anger comes from, and I almost wish that I knew how to express it. I felt the same way after receiving your first letter. Don't ask me why, but you put me in a mood to argue. I never argue. Do you know how you touched me with that letter, how important you've become to me? Gena told me that if you called or came over, it would be because I was important to you, too.

You haven't done or said anything to convince me otherwise. Something tells me that you're going to do your darnedest to change that, to fool us both.

I know that you wanted me as much as I wanted you. Selfishness stretched both ways between us last night. I gave you several opportunities to escape the situation. As far as I can tell, you didn't give a single one of them more than a second's worth of consideration.

I can only conclude that Gena was right.

At some point I'm probably going to be appalled at writing this letter and actually mailing it. I'm already feeling foolish because of its length.

But I don't feel guilt or regret, regardless of how the morning turned out. Actually, I feel pretty darn good. I lived the night on my terms, acted independently, paid no attention to the rules that have been drummed into me from birth. The world hasn't ended. Lightning didn't strike. The ground hasn't swallowed me up. I have no inclination to take back a single thing I've said or done. Except maybe for the sappy greeting-card sentiment that passed for the last word. Surely I could have said something more intelligent and gripping.

Unfortunately, it would have been ten minutes too late— as evidenced by this epic declaration of my intentions.

Angie

26

Nothing worked.

Jack turned off the highway and sped up one street, then another. A woman digging up bulbs from a flower bed frowned at him as he zoomed past. Automatically, he slowed down and raised his arm in a backhanded wave. He'd gotten the message. There was no hurry.

He'd taken Steve's advice and tried to pay attention to the features of various models of used vans, to make a rational decision on which one to buy, but he'd ambled past several models, barely glancing at each one before choosing one based on the comfort of the seats and the size of the interior. He couldn't believe what he'd paid for that two-year-old customized baby that looked like a studio apartment on wheels.

He'd tried equally hard to enjoy a ride up Monument Hill and back, then thought about cruising through the Black Forest, which bore no resemblance to the original in Germany, either in size or population. Instead, he'd headed back toward town, following a route he shouldn't be so familiar with after only one visit.

He tried not to feel the burn of Angie's letter in his jeans pocket, tried to convince himself that he should simply write back—a "Dear John"—except that he'd seen what letters like that did to men who were too far away to do anything about it. Too far away to do anything but accept rather than argue.

He tried not to read her letter a second time, not to think about how Angie argued with her own version of psychobabble and body language.

He wasn't ready for more of the same.

Coward.

The accusation acted like a cattle prod every time he

hesitated or thought about turning tail. He revved the engine of the Harley as if he were about to take off, but he knew better. Thinking that she'd be put off by a letter now any more than she had in the past was the same kind of self-delusion that had landed him in this mess to begin with.

He'd told himself to forget about Angie. He'd already said good-bye to her once. But he'd known that he had to make sure she was all right, appease his own guilt.

He had to see her again—just once more.

He studied the house, mellowed by age and faced with climbing vines that cast lacey shadows on the gold-tinted stone. It looked vaguely Victorian, vaguely gothic, with its round tower and stained glass that made up windows on both floors, the broad porch surrounding the first floor, and widow's walk encircling the roof, the dormer windows, and the chimneys that indicated more than one fireplace.

The house was an original, full of texture and contrast, shiny and dull color that ranged from neutral to vivid primaries, inviting whimsy, inviting the attention of a camera and enough film to capture every change in shadow as the sun moved from east to west. He squinted, diverted by the thought, seeing dawn wash the house in gold, seeing it at noon when shadows would be subtle smudges beneath indentations in the stone, in the afternoon when the leaves of ivy would have a dark gloss and the light slanted, burnishing the tower with deep gold.

It was the ideal setting for a woman like Angie. Only there weren't any other women like Angie. He doubted if there were any other houses like this one. He thought of the copperplate print he'd bought in Rothenburg and imagined a candle burning in the window of that upstairs tower, spilling color into a dark, lonely night, Angie's silhouette outlined in the vivid glass as she sat on a cushioned window seat.

Ten to one the second floor of the tower was part of her bedroom.

No way did he want to see that bedroom.

He had it all planned out—how he would repeat to her

all the common sense he'd been handing himself. Maybe the stars in her eyes had fallen and she'd save him the trouble. They could part friends and then drift into separate lives.

Maybe he wouldn't regret it fifty years from now.

Maybe she wasn't home.

The garage door was open, revealing a candy-apple-red classic Cadillac convertible with tail fins big enough to fit on a rocket to the moon. The engine was probably big enough, too.

Swiping his hand over the back of his neck, he glanced at the dark blue Bronco in the driveway. A crash came from the back yard, followed by a feminine voice. She was home. And from the creative combination of four-letter words she was spouting, she was not a happy camper. Curiosity overrode cowardice as he walked to the gate at the side of the house. It was hard to tell if she was angry. The last time he was here, it had been obvious that her nose was out of joint over his stubbornness, but she hadn't yelled or thrown a tantrum. She hadn't lost it to the point where she was incoherent. She'd merely insulted him in a calm, matter-of-fact voice.

"Dammit!" Angie had graduated to six-letter words. "Why wasn't I brilliant enough to label the tools?"

Jack stood at the cedar fence and watched her drop to her knees and sort through a pile of hammers, screwdrivers, and wrenches. A row of plastic bowls flanked her, filled with, as near as he could tell, washers, screws, nuts, bolts, and nails. Patches of grass fading from green to winter gold showed between the large metal rectangles that were laid out in neat rows. She looked ready to kick the circular saw, power drill, and electric sander into next week.

A first-aid kit sat on the edge of a wood platform. A large patch Band-Aid was wrapped halfway around her forearm. She paused in mid-cuss and looked up, her eyes widening as she saw his head above the fence. A wrench dropped from her hand, and her smile was brilliant. So much for falling stars, he thought with resignation. They were all there, shining in her eyes, and her smile made the sun look downright feeble.

Her jeans had a hole in one knee.

He opened the gate and strolled into the yard. "I was in the neighborhood . . ."

Talk about original.

She bit her lower lip, then smiled again. "Thank goodness. I have no idea of what to do with this," she said, waving her hand over the mess sprawling all over her yard.

"What is it?"

"Well, I paid for a storage shed, but I'm beginning to wonder if they delivered a do-it-yourself space station instead. I could swear the salesman told me that the material was lightweight." She held up the sheaf of papers in her hand. "I *know* he told me the instructions were idiot proof."

"A shed," he said, bemused by the size of the pieces.

"Uh-huh. A large shed—for potting and garden tools."

Jack studied the plastic bowls, and how she'd separated the hardware according to type and size, then read the labels taped onto each section of the shed. It looked like the same model he'd put up for his parents last time he'd been home on leave, only bigger. Much bigger.

Forget it, Jack. You turned in your hero badge, remember? You came here to prove what an S.O.B. you really are.

"I'm not staying, Angie." He watched her wrestle with a wall section and lose. Automatically, his hand shot out, stabilized it before it flattened her. He noticed more Band-Aids, on her thumbs, on the ankle that flashed as her jeans rode up when she bent her knee.

That knee was driving him crazy.

The power tools worried him. He stared at the lethally sharp corners on the sheets of metal. "Angie, did you hear me?"

"Yes, I heard you, and I don't blame you one bit, Jack. This is a disaster."

"Maybe we should lay this section down while we attach it to the next one," he suggested.

"Why didn't I think of that? What's a ratchet?"

He sorted through the tools, picked up a ratchet, and handed it to her. "I'm not coming back," he said through what felt like rocks in his throat.

"Mmm. What goes first—the nut or the bolt?" She studied him with a grave expression, then studied the hardware she'd plucked from the bowls with equal concentration. "Oh, I see what they mean by 'male' and 'female.'" She held up the nut and bolt and demonstrated. "See?" And then her smile smoothed out as she blushed fire-engine red.

Jack saw, and remembered what it felt like, how it had looked in shadows dancing on the wall. He frowned as he noticed that her sweatshirt was on wrong side out and remembered her yellow silk nightgown with the seams exposed and the way she'd exposed herself, a rare and unique woman. A fearless ladybug that could be crushed by one second of thoughtless handling.

Raking his hand through his hair, he forced himself to meet her gaze, to give every appearance of being honest as he recited the speech he'd been practicing all morning. "I'm burned out, Angie."

"I know."

"I'm no good at relationships."

"A little out of practice, maybe." She kneeled on the ground to fit two corner sections together and line up the predrilled holes.

If he didn't stop staring at her bare knee, he was going to be as hard as the damn bolt she was rolling between her fingertips. "I don't have a job."

"Is there a hurry? You have money to see you through for quite a while. You have talent—"

"How the hell do you know I have talent?" He snatched the hardware away from her, began doing the job himself.

"It's perfectly obvious from the images you sent me."

He let that slide. What was obvious was that she was irrational. "It might be years before I build up another career. I don't even know what I want to do."

"Could've fooled me."

He was getting desperate. "I'm thirty-five years old and living with my parents again."

"Good. I'll bet your mother hugs you. You badly need hugging, Jack."

He did need a hug—badly. But not from his mother.

A raw edge caught and ripped a hole in her jeans over her other knee. Fool that he was, he insisted on applying iodine and a Band-Aid over the scrape. The scent of Shalimar and woman on overheated skin filled his nostrils. She had to pick that moment to raise her arms to secure her hair in the clip holding it back from her face, her breasts clearly defined beneath the old sweatshirt.

As he bent over her leg, she touched his cheek, traced the line of his jaw. He was going to feel that touch all night long.

"Hold this steady," he said, jerking away from her and fitting another bolt. A cold sweat broke out on his face as he wondered who was going to hold him steady.

"Ouch!" Blood welled on her forefinger, and she reached for the first-aid kit, her grasp on the wall slipping and barely missing his head.

This wasn't going well, Jack thought as he caught it an inch above his scalp. "Angie, I have a foul temper, and I'm about to lose it. Listen carefully. I was married for almost thirteen years. By the time it was over, my wife hated me. I'm a stuffed shirt. I don't believe in affairs or one-night stands. You want a lover? Find a man who has the experience to at least take off his clothes, and yours, with enough finesse that you don't have to sew them back together in the middle of the night. Find a man who won't fall asleep on you."

"No, thanks."

"What the hell kind of answer is that?"

She smiled. "I'd tell you, but in the mood you're in, it wouldn't make you happy—you did that very well, Jack. What do we do next?"

Somehow, he'd managed to join the two walls. Belatedly, he remembered what a bitch his parents' shed had been to put together. "I don't want a woman in my life, Angie. I don't need the aggravation."

"No, neither do I." She glanced over at the metal strips leaning up against the fence. "What are those?"

Jack clenched his teeth. A silent *but* hung at the end of her sentence. He wasn't going to ask. Besides, he was getting a cramp from half sitting, half standing, with a fourth of a shed balanced against his body. "You didn't read the instructions before you had the cement poured?"

"Only enough to know what size foundation to have poured. I read the rest last night. The raised wooden floor was my idea," she announced proudly. "I built it myself."

"You'll have to tear it down," he said, feeling like an idiot for not noticing the important details of her little project. Some hero.

"Jack, I'm extremely proud of that floor," she pointed out.

"Isn't it supposed to be on the inside of the shed?" he asked, resigned to finding a way to release the assembled corner section without damaging it.

"Well, of course it is."

"Angie, the cement is supposed to extend *beyond* the walls."

Frowning, she looked from the floor to the illustration of the finished shed. "Uh oh."

"And I think those are the supports for the walls. They have to be bolted into the foundation."

"Oh. Can't we just stick them in the ground? Use cross-pieces to support the supports?"

"What do you know about cross-pieces?"

"Nothing," she mumbled as she pushed herself up and rose from the ground to walk over to her cache of tools.

"Well, neither do I," he said, fighting to keep calm as he unscrewed the nuts and removed the bolts. It was a little like trying to talk to Angie, having things fall apart five minutes after he thought he had it all together.

Angie brushed off the back of her jeans, then helped him slide the disassembled sheets back into the appropriate piles. "Why are you here, Jack? Why didn't you simply stay away?" she asked as she frowned at the dirt stains on her knees.

"Because, I don't know how to handle the situation." His knuckles turned white; his jaw was beginning to ache.

She shrugged. "Neither do I. Ignorance is supposedly bliss. If we don't know the rules, how can we break them?"

"The rule is: Shy little virgins don't get mixed up with sonofabitches like me."

"And I suppose another rule is that I should say 'Goodbye, and have a nice life, Jack,' " Angie said as she bustled around the yard, covering everything in sight with plastic tarps anchored at the corners with concrete blocks. Her lawn would never survive this.

"It would help."

She shook her head. "I don't think so—at least not at my end. I have this crazy idea that I should fight for you, or at least ask for a fighting chance. Earlier, I was contemplating asking you for a date. Gena is throwing a wonderful weekend bash at Cordillera in October—"

"Don't."

"I'd already came to the conclusion that you're too old-fashioned to appreciate the gesture." Her gaze remained fixed on the paraphernalia around her. Her voice lowered, becoming softer, smaller, like her handwriting. "No one seems to understand the concept anymore. After all, who ever heard of a twenty-seven-year-old virgin in this day and age?"

"Don't remind me," he said under his breath. He'd felt like a virgin, too, that night. Right now, he felt like a statue, standing as still as possible, as straight as if one of those steel supports were tied to his back. He was, he concluded, a barely living monument to hormones that just kept standing up for a head count. Whoever heard of getting turned on in the middle of a one-sided argument? What happened to male pride?

"Why aren't you listening to me?"

"I'm listening." She glanced up at him and planted her hands on her hips. "And if you'd been listening to yourself, you'd be ashamed for trying to con me into believing such nonsense."

"Oh, hell." His gaze swerved from her hands, the way they pushed in her sweatshirt, defining her waist, the flare of her hips. "Listen harder," he ordered, carefully enunciating each word. "I am a social misfit. A nerd in high school with no friends. A loner at the Academy with no friends. A married hardass in the service with no wife."

Angie lowered her gaze back to her knees, twisted her hands together as she took a deep breath. "A social misfit," she murmured as if it hurt to say the words and would hurt worse if she said them any louder. "That's a tough one to argue with." Staring down at the ground, then up at the top of the tower, she caught her bottom lip between her teeth as if she were searching for an elusive answer to the problem. "I take it you got my letter?"

"That's why I'm here," he said, controlling his need to shout.

"Didn't that tell you anything?"

"It told me that you don't listen and you like to argue."

She dug her tennis-shoe-clad toes into the grass. "No, I don't like to argue," she said, then sighed heavily. "Will you come inside with me for a few minutes? I want to show you something."

Without looking back at him, she walked toward the house.

He let her go, waiting until he heard the back door slam and knew she was no longer in sight. He could leave now, without having to say good-bye, without knowing that she was watching him.

He had to concentrate to ease the grip of his hands on the fence. His ears rang as he walked, one step at a time, toward the gate. He should have stayed away, should have given the memory a chance to fizzle out into just another day in his misspent life.

Only it never seemed to happen that way with him. He'd never been very good at trivializing . . . forgetting.

And while he'd been trying to convince Angie that a relationship between them wouldn't work, his convictions had become as stable as her goddam shed.

27

Angie waited in the kitchen, barely breathing, feeling each beat of her heart in every part of her body. She wrapped her hands around her middle, kneaded her stomach to ease the spasms, the panic.

Suddenly, he was there, standing by the rear staircase, watching her, his expression grim, brooding, his mouth tight, his eyes wary and angry at the same time.

Her mouth was dry with fear. The spasms in her stomach became more violent, more threatening. She had to do this. She would think of the distance, as she had a long time ago. Distance she had learned to create as protection against the nightmares of a fairy tale.

Without speaking, she brushed past him and began to climb the stairs, listening to the familiar squeak of boards echo behind her as he followed her up to the second floor, followed her through a small arched door, and up another flight of enclosed stairs.

Blindly, she groped for the switch inside the room, blinked at the sudden light, saw the life of a child who had never existed arranged in a carefully constructed shrine to dreams that had never been realized.

Behind her, she felt the heat of Jack's body, heard his harsh intake of breath at the ghostly shapes beneath dust covers. It had always affected her the same way: a room carpeted and arranged with furniture, brightly illuminated with track and recessed lighting. A room designed for lingering with illusions and regrets.

Jack stood in the small hallway that divided the attic into two rooms, winced as the light flared, watched as Angie yanked off dust covers and crossed the attic room to stand in front of the fireplace on the outside wall.

She explained nothing, said nothing, and kept her gaze fixed on a distant place he couldn't see.

He stepped inside, onto the thick Aubusson carpet, richly patterned in pastels that seemed pale compared to the vivid colors in the rest of the house. The ceiling sloped from a center beam into dormer windows—three to a side —set with the diamond panes of glass he'd noticed earlier. A large Boston rocker sat at an angle to the fireplace, with plump blue cushions tied to its seat and back. Glass-enclosed shelves were fitted against the walls with curio cabinets in the corners. Everywhere he looked were trophies and plaques and portraits, some candid, some posed. The only books he saw were photo albums and scrapbooks. The only sound he heard was Angie's slow, measured breathing as she stood as stiff and still as the trophies, her back to him and her arms pressed tightly over her stomach. Her silence seemed sacrosanct, unbreachable.

He glanced at the portrait to his right and saw a small child, more baby than toddler, with strawberry curls framing a porcelain doll face with big brown eyes that were calm and serious, even though the mouth curved in a smile that looked more practiced than natural. The dress enveloped her with ruffles, its skirt a wide, carefully arranged circle that was barely disturbed by the pudgy hands clasped so ladylike in her lap. The ankles were crossed just so, the patent leather shoes shiny as a black mirror.

Frowning, he moved on to the next picture. A beautiful child, with high cheekbones, perfectly arched brows, and a patrician nose stared back at him, still serious, shrouded in a velvet cape that looked too heavy for such small shoulders. A tiara sat on her head, a delicate piece set with glittering clear stones that were too cold and hard for her youth and coloring.

As silent as the girl in the portraits, Angie didn't move, didn't speak.

Another large picture incorporated oval vignettes surrounding a full-body view of the same girl, a little older, a little taller, with legs that started at her armpits, captured in a high kick. The costume was spangled with black and white sequins, an abbreviated tuxedo complete with top hat and cane. Her hair had darkened, become richer, and each vignette showed it set in a different style. The smile was the same, only more controlled and not quite as wide. The eyes were serious, yet different from the first two photos, their color dull and flat.

"Beauty contests," he stated.

His head jerked up as Angie moved, her hand groping behind her for the arm of the chair, finding it, wrapping around the wood with a white-knuckled grip, supporting her body, until she sat down and stared straight ahead.

The rockers creaked as she set the chair in motion. Her skin was nearly translucent in its paleness. The cords in her neck stood out with tension. Her expression was blank, as if a vacuum had smothered her emotions, as if something inside her were dying and all her energy concentrated on staying alive.

He'd seen that look before. On his mother's face after Bryan's link to life had been severed. On Angie's face a week ago when she'd told him that she knew she was beautiful. And he recognized the void that couldn't be filled with the dreams of others. A hollow grave where his own dreams had turned to dust.

He made a fast prowl around the rest of the room, seeing beauty without vitality, captured movement without animation, seeing a face and body that had hidden its soul where it couldn't be touched or hurt. And he saw smooth wood and cold metal engraved with words meant to honor beauty and talent but somehow made them seem vulgar instead.

Suddenly what had been an attractive, airy, and comfortable room became obscene, stifling, oppressive. Bile rose in his throat, and he felt the slow burn of anger. The child had existed in the first picture. She'd faded in the second. Nothing was left of her after that.

Pausing at what appeared to be the most recent portrait, he alternately studied the picture and its subject as the rocker creaked in time to a slow heartbeat, to the flare of Angie's nostrils with every slow, controlled breath.

I have a great body . . . since the age of eleven.

The body, encased in a lace gown, was an eloquent promise for the future of developing breasts and lean hips tapering outward into a feminine flare. The auburn hair glistened with gold and copper highlights and was swept away from her face to fall down her back in a tumble of artfully arranged curls. In the portrait she couldn't have been more than ten, yet the face was older than ten, wiser, every feature sharp and clear, as beautiful as it was now.

As vacant as it was now.

He felt as if he were on the last leg of a long race—tight chest, hard breathing, an adrenaline rush that made everything around him seem distant and hazy as he stopped at the last portrait on the wall beside the rocking chair, a large frame holding two separate photos, as if neither one merited the honor or expense of individual casings.

He homed in on her immediately, in the center of a group of other girls. Girls who looked like children next to her. She hugged a large trophy to her chest, the fierceness of her hold almost tangible. As she gazed down at it, her expression was soft and wistful. The second shot might have been a continuation of the first, snapped only a moment or two later. Her head was high, as if someone had said, "Smile," and she had obeyed automatically, without time to arrange her mouth, control her response. Her eyes sparkled, yet in that brightness, he saw something beyond the excitement of the moment, stronger than the pleasure.

A void expanding outward. A girl shrinking inward.

Jack swallowed hard, cleared his throat, startled by the abrupt sound competing with the groan of old, dry wood. He took the final step toward Angie, stood in front of the chair, stared down at her.

Her head turned; her gaze focused on the fireplace. "You're a photographer. What do you think?" she asked without inflection.

"They're masterpieces."

"Nothing but the best. You like them, then."

"Technically, yes. Emotionally, no."

"No," she repeated in that same hollow voice. "Why?"

Abruptly, he bent over, covered her hands with his on the arms of the chair, stopped the movement. "Because I watched a baby grow into a woman between the first picture and the last," he said harshly. "About twenty portraits in half as many years."

"Less than half."

"You really hated it."

"I really hated it."

Catching her chin with his hand, he forced her to look at him. "What else? I see it in the second shot where you're dancing, and in the last two, but what is it?"

"Fear," Angie said, her voice a strained whisper. "When you're performing, you don't hear anything—you can't because it will distract you—and so everything seems quiet except the music. And then, when you're waiting for the winner to be announced, it's quiet . . . so deathly quiet." She closed her eyes, and he heard the silence in the room, felt it like a cold wind.

Her voice softened even more as she went on, keeping her eyes closed. "Suddenly there's so much noise—shouting and cheering and applause. Can you imagine what that sounds like to a small child—so loud, it . . . crushes?" Her breath and her body shuddered at the same time, and her hands clutched the arms of the chair more tightly. "It's like an explosion. So much noise, and the lights are so bright, and the applause doesn't stop, and it's all so frightening. I'd walk down that runway wearing a crown that pulled at my hair and a cape that smelled bad, and all those faces were smiling up at me—all those hands clapping. I still hear it sometimes in my sleep, and I wake up and go to my studio to dance so that all I'll hear is music."

Her eyes snapped open, wide and unblinking as if she'd awakened from a nightmare. "The other—I won Miss Congeniality. That trophy was the least important of all, as you can see by where my mother placed it on the bottom shelf." A whimper escaped her—a dangling thread of emotion she couldn't contain. "Being liked didn't matter. And no one liked me after I won the crown. Even that wasn't real."

"Being liked mattered to you."

"I wanted a friend. I tried everything to make friends."

"Like the letters, the pen pals?"

She shrugged. "It worked. I have friends all over the world who like me for something besides my face and figure—my *talent*."

"Didn't anyone see it?" The tremble of her chin vibrated through his hand, through his body, shaking him. He released her chin with a lingering caress of his finger as he lowered himself to the floor at her feet and unconsciously rested his arm on her knee.

"The general saw it. That's when he and mother started fighting—discussions at first, then arguments, then shouting matches. Then they stopped talking except to their lawyers."

"The divorce," he said, hating himself for even thinking it, hating the implication that a child actually could be responsible for a divorce, that the responsibility would produce a crushing guilt that could never be lifted.

"Mother was horribly depressed when I began losing and finally dropped out altogether. I agreed to go to an exclusive girls' school that was near an equally exclusive school of dance." Angie spoke quickly in that fast-forward way she had when she was nervous. "It worked better than any pills the doctors gave her. She decided that we should move back here permanently rather than follow my father to his next assignment. He set up a trust for me with old family money and left. When mother remarried, he deeded the house to me. I've seen the general's lawyer once a year, and I've seen the general himself once since then."

Clearly, she believed her father blamed her for the divorce. Clearly, judging by the man's absence in his daughter's life, she was right. There was nothing he could say to that. Nothing that would help. The flesh of her knee was chilled and clammy. That bothered him. Everything bothered him.

Like remembering all the clues in her letters, the vague unease he'd felt when he tried to read between the lines. It had been easy to forget those blank spaces, attach normal explanations to what he saw in black and white.

"You don't hear from him at all?"

"He sends me money on birthdays and Christmas, tells me to pick out something nice." Again she shrugged, and he was beginning to see it as another defense, an affirmation that all was well. She was a survivor. She'd learned to live with the pain. "I donate it to Link."

Absently, he rubbed her knee above the Band-Aid, stared at the goosebumps on that tiny patch of exposed skin. "Why didn't you tell your mother to lay off?"

"Because mother wasn't—isn't—a monster, Jack. She loves me and I love her. But I couldn't stop her from dreaming, and I couldn't stop myself from trying to fulfill her dreams. Because it was so important to her, and she was so proud. What child doesn't want its parents to be proud?"

"It's a trap we fall into," Jack said bitterly.

"Yes," she said, without surprise at his agreement. "Besides, Mother Nature took care of the problem. When I developed earlier than the other girls, I began losing. With all the dancing, I shouldn't have developed so early nor so well. I didn't fit the mold, and I saw my chance before the other girls caught up to my bra size, and we would all move into a different competitive classification."

She smiled in a perfect imitation of the portraits. "Maybe I would have told Mother eventually. But I couldn't do it then."

"Not overtly. You learned to be shy—the only choice you had," he said, remembering pieces of conversation, seeing them suddenly make sense and fall into place.

"No, not overtly," she agreed. "I'm not an aggressive person, Jack. I've never been good at confrontations and anger."

Personally Jack thought Angie was damn good at confrontations, slipping under his skin so smoothly that he didn't realize it until it was too late. Today, for instance. He was still here, though he'd meant to say his piece and run like hell. He still wanted her, more than ever, though all week he'd been convincing himself otherwise. He should be disgusted with himself, but he couldn't pull it off, couldn't keep from touching her.

The chill had left her knee, and the life was back in her eyes. He slipped his hand under her sweatshirt, wanting to make sure she was warming up, needing to warm her if she wasn't. It was a protective gesture, an instinctive act of possession. It made him feel significant to have her share her nightmares with him, to know that she trusted him. To know that it was *him,* Jack Caldwell, burned-out, antisocial sonofabitch, that she trusted rather than Jack Caldwell, a hardass major who lived strictly by the book.

Somewhere in the last week, he'd obviously forgotten what the book said. His body was making up rules as it went along.

Her midriff was warm, so his fingers dipped beneath the waistband of her jeans. He could spend his life touching her, keeping her warm.

Angie sighed, and her fingers began drawing invisible images on his forearm where his shirtsleeve was rolled up. "You do know what I'm talking about, don't you, Jack? You've been there—in a different way maybe, but still you know."

He knew. He had performed for the sake of others—a misguided and stupid goal rather than a noble one. "I've been there," he said, and heard the choke in his voice. Angie's life had been as extreme as his—her actions, her motivations, her pain. She'd dropped out, and so had he.

Right out of their own lives.

"You don't talk about this." For a moment, he thought about how odd it was to be talking with her about old nightmares while his hand indulged in a conversation with her body.

"Only with my therapist. I told Gena, and she understands that I hated it, but she doesn't understand why. How could she? Beauty contests, modeling, all that attention and glamour—it's every girl's dream."

"Why tell me?"

She met his gaze then, her eyes focused and bright. "Because you said you were a social misfit, and it takes one to know one. Because no one wants to be alone in their misery. Sharing is a natural instinct." Hesitantly, her hand lifted to his face, her fingertips tracing his cheekbones and nose, eyebrows, and mouth. "Because when you stayed the night, I was, in a sense, performing again—with you—and I hadn't had any lessons or experience and didn't know what to do or how to act. I acted like a fool and probably embarrassed you, yet you stayed anyway."

"I shouldn't have." He became aware of the rough texture of a Band-Aid as her fingers soothed the tension between his brows. She had so many scratches, so many hurts.

"Do you really believe that, Jack?"

"I don't know," he said quietly, and felt it inside—the lack of certainty, the desire to be wrong about himself, about the rightness of being with Angie. "I don't want to hurt you, Angie."

Her hands framed his face, as she leaned over to meet his gaze. "I'm willing to risk it."

"Well, I'm not!" he said, his voice raised and angry. Her hands fell away as she jerked back away from him. "That's what I've been trying to tell you." He snatched his hands away from her, pushed himself to his feet, and made tracks for the other side of the room. "I said it before, Angie. Affairs are not my style. I'm lousy at commitments. I don't just lose my temper—I destroy. *You don't want a man like me.*"

"No, I don't. I want *you.* I think the feeling is mutual." The chair groaned as she rose, walked slowly toward him. "It's so frightening, Jack. I don't blame you for being wary. I have my share of hangups, and I'm so good at putting you on the spot, embarrassing you. That's why I brought you up here, so you might understand why I'm so inept. So you'd know that I understand about being a misfit." Heat burned through his shirt as she laid her palm against his chest, wrapped her other hand around his neck.

Just that fast, he grew hard, felt the pressure of tight jeans increase, constrict. His arms raised, he began to circle around her, answering the need to hold her. He knew he

was on dangerous ground, thinking that self-preservation
lay here with Angie rather than in his own solitude.

"Jack, haven't you ever heard of going with the flow?"

Just that fast, he grasped her wrists, pulled her hands
away, and stepped back before *he* began to flow. Inside his
jeans, he felt as if he were permanently embossed with the
pattern of his zipper. Teenage boys had more control than
he did when Angie was around. He was too old for this.
Supposedly, he was too smart for this.

Striding to the opposite wall nearest the door, he stared
out the window. "I did that last week, remember?"

"Yes, I remember."

The husky note in her voice made him nervous. And
desperate. Nothing in his life had prepared him for the
spontaneity that caught him unawares when Angie was
near. He'd never imagined that he could have so much
feeling that control would be impossible. It scared the shit
out of him to need so much that it was almost violent. He
needed to make love to her. He wanted to shake her until
her teeth rattled for being so trusting, for offering so much
of herself.

"Well, remember this, Angie. Until last week, I'd been
with one woman, period." It was suddenly hard to talk. He
had to swallow against the dryness in his mouth. "That
woman left me over a year ago. That's a long time for a
man who's used to regular sex. You were there ready and
willing to"—he stopped himself from using a crude term,
searched for one more acceptable in mixed company, and
failed—"willing to put out. I was feeling pretty raw for a lot
of reasons. *You were there, and dammit, I used you.*"

Her face blanched, and she sagged back against the wall
as if she could crawl behind the sheetrock.

He was on a roll. He should be relieved, but he wasn't.
Sickness churned in his stomach, and his head was pounding. He couldn't look at her. If he did, he'd take it all back,
take her word for it that he was a hell of a nice guy who
had it all together. A calm rational man who deserved her.
A man who could and would take care of her and never
step on all those fragile emotions of hers. Rubbing the

back of his neck, he halted abruptly at the door. "What did you expect? I've been doing a lot of irresponsible things lately. Coming here in the first place was the kicker."

She shook her head, ran her tongue over her lips. "You came here because—"

"Because I was curious about a woman who can't take no for answer. My mistake. The word doesn't exist in your vocabulary. *Not with your mother and not with me.*" He winced at the sound of his anger that seemed to echo in the room, at the way she stared at him, her expression exactly like the one in the portrait hanging on the wall beside her. That should have done it, but he'd forgotten that she always had to have the last word.

"I wish I could believe you, Jack. It would make both our lives so much simpler if I did."

"What in the hell is wrong with you?" he asked, hearing his voice as if it belonged to someone else.

"I'm in love with you, Jack."

She'd said it before, but not like this, not with pain, not with silent tears. He was a coward when it came to a woman's tears. Heaving a sigh, he glanced at her one more time and said, "I'm sorry, Angie." Turning on his heel, he walked through the door and took the stairs two at a time. He'd had the last word after all.

And if he hadn't convinced her that he was no good, he'd sure as hell convinced himself.

28

They said she had the brass balls of a fool and the wings of an angel. Somewhere along the way, her halo had slipped down around her ankles, so she'd kicked it away and kept going.

Gena Collier had never claimed to be an angel. Only a fool would presume to meddle in the affairs of man on a worldwide scale. That instinct coupled with the guts to jump in with both feet had made Link into the success it was today. Sometimes she glided to the bottom and touched down with soft landing. Other times, she fell according to all the laws of physics, her plans shattered into a million fragments. Her greatest talent was to climb back out, carrying those pieces and finding a new way to make them work as a whole.

Once she started meddling, she didn't stop until things worked out—her way.

Angie was a mess, though no one would know it to look at her. It was driving Gena nuts, watching Angie take each day with serenity and smiles, floating around in limbo, waiting for a dream to happen. It just wasn't natural for a woman to be so normal and efficient after handing her heart over to a man who didn't know what to do with it.

Angie honestly believed that he wanted to find out, that all he needed was time.

Who would have thought Angie would take Jack up to the mausoleum in the attic and reveal her childhood or lack thereof?

As sure as Gena had misplaced her halo, something had to be done. Given her druthers, Gena would like to boil a pot of tar, pluck a few million feathers, and run the man out of town on a rail.

But from what Angie told her, Jack Caldwell wasn't a

villain. From what Angie told her, he was worse. He was one of those misguided males who thought women were too flighty to know what they really wanted, too weak to hold up under a problem or two. Someone had to show him the error of his thinking—as soon as she found him, which was turning out to be harder than she'd expected. From what Angie told her, he didn't even know where he was.

Gena parked in front of the four-bay garage and stepped out of her car. The sign above the bays read CALDWELL & DAD. Cute. Real cute. Evidently changes had been made. The ad in the Yellow Pages had said J. CALDWELL'S.

She sauntered into the first bay and stopped dead at the sight of the lower half of a man sticking out of the jaws of a black Lincoln stretch limo. Assuming his top half was rooting around in the innards of the monster, she took a moment to admire the tight male buns and long, muscular legs, encased in shrink-to-fit jeans that had certainly lived up to the promise. A clean shop rag fluttered out from his hip pocket like a warning flag.

"Nice model," she murmured.

"Is someone there?" The voice coming from under the hood was like imported chocolate, deep and smooth, with a smoky hint of hazelnut. The voice was irritated.

"I'm looking for the owner," Gena said.

"You got him."

"J. Caldwell?"

"S. Caldwell," came the muffled response.

"Oh."

"No—S, as in Steve." The body emerged slowly: a lean waist, belted with old, cracked leather, a flat midriff that wedged outward to a broad chest and even broader shoulders wrapped very nicely in a gray shirt that might have been clean yesterday. From what she could see, all the appropriate muscles were there, appropriately developed for efficiency and strength, as tight and ropy as the buns and legs. She was a sucker for streamlined men.

Wiping his hands on the shop rag, he turned to face her, his clear blue gaze cutting straight to her face, then gliding down her body and back up again. His face was carved out of rock, all sharp planes and angles. Grooves cut into tight flesh from his nose to the corners of his mouth. Smile lines were etched by the sun at the corners of his eyes. Furrows of concentration marked his forehead, softened by a forelock of chocolate brown hair.

Meddling had its rewards.

"I'm looking for J. Caldwell, as in Major Jack, formerly of the U.S. Air Force," she said, holding his bold stare. "Any relation?"

"Why?" He leaned back against the fender of the limo and crossed his ankles.

"I've been trying to find him for two days."

"He's not here."

Gena scanned the spotlessly clean shop. All the dirt and grease she associated with auto repairs seemed to be on his clothes. Tools were lined up in the neatly labeled compartments of several huge red metal cabinets. An emissions tester and diagnostic computer occupied the last two bays. "Where can I find him?"

Steve watched her with hooded eyes. "You can't be the pen pal."

"Nope." She stepped forward, held out her hand. "Gena Collier. The pen pal's friend and employer."

"Gena Collier," he repeated slowly. "As in Link International?"

"As in desperate for a photographer."

"You lost me."

Rifling in the carryall that passed for her purse, Gena produced a brown envelope. "I received this from an A. Caldwell—do all of you go by your initials?—last week in answer to my ad in the classifieds, but I'd already hired a man. He didn't work out."

"So you want my brother," Steve said.

"*I* don't want him, but *Link* needs a good photographer, preferably last week. The letter inside"—she waved the envelope at him—"was signed A. Caldwell, and she said—" Gena jumped at the sound of casters rolling on cement, the sight of feet and legs appearing from under a car in the next bay. A torso slid into view, with a thickening waist and stevedore's chest that barely cleared the undercarriage of the car. The face had to be the model for the younger one that kept drawing her attention over and over again.

The older man got to his feet and ambled over to her, his brow lowered in a frown. "Joe Caldwell, Ms. Collier." The frown didn't ease. "You say Ada sent you that package?"

Suddenly, Gena was nervous, tongue-tied. A thundercloud had nothing on Joe Caldwell's expression. She'd been amused when the letter had come. Obviously Ada was a meddler—a woman after Gena's own heart. It hadn't occurred to her that the poor woman would have to answer to six-foot-three of angry man—presumably her husband. "I'm glad she did," Gena said quickly as she hurried after him, trying to head him off at what was plainly the office door. "These shots are really good."

Joe glanced at her over his shoulder. "Glad to hear it." He shook his head and stepped into the office.

"Listen—"

He shut the door firmly in her face and pulled down a shade over the window that made up the top half. Gena glared at the door, then swiveled around to glare at Steve. "You could have warned me."

"Would it have made a difference?"

"Of course it would. I don't want to get anyone in trouble."

Blue eyes leisurely strolled over her breasts and down her legs. "I'm open for a little trouble."

Gena lowered her eyelids to half-mast and gave him a vampy smile. "Swords at dawn? Karate? Russian roulette? Name your seconds."

"How about pillows at sunset?"

"How about telling me how to get in touch with your brother?"

Steve's expression switched from leering to annoyed. "If Jack wanted a job at Link, he would have applied in person."

Rubbing the bridge of her nose with thumb and forefin-

ger, Gena wandered back into the shop proper. "I must be
losing my touch."

"Which one?" he asked, his mouth twitching.

"Obviously, I'm here to meddle. I understand he's at
loose ends."

"You could take lessons from my mother." He shifted
and buried his fingers up to the first knuckles into his front
pockets, his thumbs hooked over the edges. "So you're
here on behalf of the pen pal."

Gena opened her mouth and shut it again. There was
something about this man that invited confidence, honesty.
It wouldn't do to be *completely* honest. "No, I'm here because I've seen your brother's shots before. He sent a few
to Angie—the pen pal—from Germany. Then I get this."
She held up the envelope. "He's good, just what I want for
Link."

"Angie, huh? I wondered what her name was," he said
musingly. "And of course she works at Link. You trying to
matchmake?"

"Hardly," Gena replied with her fingers crossed behind
the shield of her bag. "Link's photographer would be out
on assignment most of the time. We're going into publishing. He wouldn't have much contact with office staff."

"Is this the usual way you hire people?" He was distinctly amused now.

"Actually, this is one of my more conventional meth-
ods," she said wryly.

"Jack doesn't have professional experience, except for
what he did in the service. Those shots were strictly hobby
stuff."

"Well, he has a good eye—and don't tell me he hasn't
had any technical training. I don't want a discount-store
photographer. I want someone like your brother who isn't
afraid to be creative."

"And the pen pal has nothing to with it."

By shoving the envelope into her bag, Gena bought two
seconds to compose her features. She wished she had another six hours to compose the rest of herself. "If you knew

me better, you'd know that Link comes first, last, and always."

"Now, there's a challenge," Steve said as his gaze wandered over her. The interest was unmistakable and scary. She wondered if it was possible to overdose on hormones.

"You always dress like this on a work day? You look like a terrorist."

"I am a terrorist. Ask my contributors." She glanced down at her camouflage pants, black cotton shirt and high-top black tennis shoes, and wished she'd worn something else. Something like silk and jewelry and perfume and makeup. Makeup would definitely be nice. "So," she said as she developed a fast interest in the garage, "are you any good?"

"Lady, I'm the best."

Smart-ass, she thought, ignoring the rush of excitement in her blood, the heat gathering in unmentionable places. No man had ever done this to her this fast, with an innuendo here, a double entendre there. Mike had never flirted with her, never indulged in sexual teasing. With her, he'd taken sex very seriously and very personally. She'd loved Mike, but he'd never made her feel like a hundred pounds of unstable dynamite.

Definitely scary.

"Do you work on T-Birds?"

He strolled to the bay door with a hip rocking gait. "That two-seater yours?"

"Yep."

"Nice," he said as he sauntered around the car, his eyes never leaving hers. "The front quarter panels could use some attention," he mentioned as his gaze skimmed her breasts like calloused fingers. "The rear bumper is original. Great body style." Angling his head, he stared at her bottom, then straightened to study her eyes. "Headlights are nice and round." He grinned then as he passed her on the way back inside. "It would be interesting to see if I'd fit in the passenger seat."

Finding a sudden interest in the walls, Gena tried to remember the last time she'd honest-to-God blushed. That was Angie's department. So was shyness. And contrary to what she'd told Steve, she *was* here because of Angie, the one person who came before Link. That meddling in Angie's life would also solve Link's problem was pure gravy.

The photographer's brother had a remarkable resemblance to dessert.

"What, no pin-ups?" she said, noticing that the walls were bare.

"I like my women warm and moving."

"You're so full of yourself, Caldwell, I doubt you'd notice if she wasn't," she shot back.

"Jack is on his way over," Joe announced as he stalked through the office door. "I'm going home for lunch." He disappeared out the bay, and a moment later, Gena heard tires squeal.

"Look, I didn't mean to cause trouble—"

Steve crossed his arms. "No sweat. Mom apologized, and all is forgiven."

"How do you know?"

"Because Dad is going home for lunch." Before she could absorb the implications of that, his fingers plowed through his hair as if he were suddenly impatient, suddenly tired of playing games. "What do you know about my brother?"

Relieved that the game had no winners or losers, Gena was only too happy to answer. "Not much. He's divorced, fresh out of the service, takes pictures as if the camera were his third eye on the world, and he likes Easter candy."

"I told you he doesn't have much in the way of experience."

"I can't remember the last time I hired anyone with experience," Gena said as she paced in front of the door, hauling in fresh air. "Experience means habits developed according to someone else's standards. It makes my life easier if I don't have to deprogram everyone I hire."

"Makes sense."

"You sound surprised."

"I am." He tinkered with what looked like a twisted piece of machinery. "I had you figured for a rich girl who doesn't give diddly squat about causes except as a way to seem useful without exerting too much energy."

Gena snapped her fingers. "Well, that explains why I only work twelve hours a day, seven days a week. I do it to avoid getting a real job."

The grin was back, a lopsided slash this time. "You're good at what you do," he stated.

Propping one hand on the corresponding hip, she tossed her head. "Mister, I'm the best," she said, lobbing his own words back at him.

"Here's your chance to prove it. Jack just drove up."

"Well, it's about time. Another day of trying to find him, and I'd have to work three days past my own funeral to catch up on my backlog." She glanced up at the door to see an electric blue van park smack across the bay, completely blocking it.

With a knowing look, Steve flashed her a thumbs up. "Break a leg."

"Thanks," Gena said under her breath, not the least surprised that Steve seemed to know more than she'd told him.

With impatient strides, a man walked into the shop. A tall man who was obviously poured from the same mold as the other Caldwell males. No wonder Angie had gone off the deep end.

And Angie had to be a lot braver than Gena gave her credit for. Where Steve was laid back and full of the devil, his brother was angry and tense and loaded for bear. His eyes were narrowed, his mouth a flat, tight seam, and his cheeks were flagged with color.

Good. He knew who she was in relation to Angie. The suspicion in his eyes told her he expected her to slip Angie into the conversation so he'd have an excuse to throw the job in her face.

"Ms. Collier? I'm Jack Caldwell." He held out his hand, gripped hers as if he'd like to tear it off.

"I never would have guessed," she said dryly.

"Look, Ms. Collier—"

"Gena."

His nod was short, abrupt. "I saw your ad—"

"Good. Then you know what I need."

"I'm not qualified." He bit out each reply as if he were in a hurry to say something else.

"So your brother said. I disagree. You have equipment?" Predictably, Steve choked on a laugh.

"A medium format Hasselblad, a thirty-five millimeter Nikon, a used large format Horseman I picked up at auction—I haven't tried it out yet."

"How about training?" Gena bit back a grin. She had a feeling that he'd just keep rattling out a list of equipment. It was so much babble to her. She wanted to keep him going, not give him a chance to think or to argue.

"High school courses, university extension every chance I had, the Air Force Academy."

"Field work?"

"Hobby stuff, if you don't count recon shots from the belly of an airplane."

"I'll count them if they were as emotional as the snaps you took in Germany."

From the corner of her eye, she saw that Steve had gone headfirst under the hood of the limo again. From the sounds of metal on metal, bangs and clinks and scrapes, she knew he was really working. She'd bet her last million that he was also listening. Neither Caldwell was dumb. They could both talk and chew gum at the same time.

"What do you want, Ms. Collier?" Jack asked.

"Someone who knows the difference between posing children for twelve ninety-five package deals and using film to x-ray a soul. Preferably someone single who's willing to travel wherever I send him. Someone . . ."—she was careful to emphasize each word—"someone who won't mind if he only checks in at the office once in a blue moon."

"What do you want," he repeated.

"Can we leave Angie out of this?" she asked mildly, cutting straight to the chase.

He didn't blink. Funny, but she hadn't expected him to be cool under fire. "You tell me."

Giving a good imitation of Distressed Female, Gena flut-

tered her hands and did her best to look the part. "I know
how this looks, Jack. I knew when I came here, but I'm
desperate. The last photographer I hired didn't know a
viewfinder from a light meter. The next one insisted on
posing candid shots." She moved in for the kill. "Link has a
benefit coming up in December and several book projects
in the planning stage. I need posters and shots for greeting
cards—decorative stuff to please the masses—for fundrais-
ers—"

"Greeting cards?" he asked in a dangerously soft voice.

Gena nodded briskly. "Angie's already done the copy,
and she'll be in charge of production. Once you've provided the images, you're out of it."

"How does she feel about that?"

"Better than you. Angie isn't petty or jealous. And she's
on to other things. Believe me, the last thing she's worried
about is what you're doing."

Imperceptibly, his head reared back, and his nostrils
flared as if somebody had clobbered him.

Flaring nostrils were good.

"The job pays very well." She named a sum. "We offer
all the usual benefits—hospitalization, expense account
within reason, and so forth. Pick your own hours, as long as
each job meets deadline." Pausing for effect, she studied
his reaction. There wasn't one. He stood perfectly still, his
eyes fixed on the far wall as if there really were a pin-up
there, as if he were seeing visions come to life.

That look touched Gena, changed her perception of
Jack Caldwell from the-man-who-broke-Angie's-heart to
simply a man with a dream. A man who needed that dream
to feel alive.

In that moment, Gena knew she had found another
cause.

"I do need to see your portfolio, Jack," she said softly.
"To satisfy the board of directors."

"I don't have one." His hand raked through his hair,
rubbed the back of his neck. "I told you, I'm not a professional."

"Okay." Again, she snapped her fingers. "Tell you what.

The fall colors are spectacular up in the mountains. I can get you a room at Cordillera, and you can do a job for me personally—" Her voice faltered at the sudden flare of his eyes, the hard clench of his jaw, the way his mouth opened as if he had been about to say something.

She rushed ahead before he did. "I need landscape shots for my own Christmas cards. Mix in candids and architecture in Vail—whatever turns your crank. I can also hire you as a consultant to set up darkroom facilities at Link. You can use them—"

"No."

So the man was afraid to see Angie. Better and better. She felt like smirking. Instead, she went on as if he hadn't spoken. "You can use them after hours when everyone has gone home. *Everyone,* Jack."

Steve emerged from under the hood of the limousine, his gaze suspicious as he watched Gena, his brows raised as if he were telling her that he'd figured out exactly what she was up to. She flashed him a challenging smirk. *You don't fool me, Caldwell. You're your mother's son.* She'd suspected it before, when he'd gone back to work as if he had no interest in the proceedings. She knew better. By keeping his mouth shut, he was aiding and abetting. It amused her how men denied involvement by being passive accomplices.

"What's Cordillera?" Jack asked, glancing at Steve.

"Damned if I know," Steve said with a shrug. "I've been away from home as long as you have."

"It's fairly new," Gena said offhandedly. "An inn west of Vail." She said a silent prayer, asking forgiveness for the gross understatement. "I already have reservations for this weekend, but I can't make it, so the room will be ready for you."

"Uh-huh," Jack muttered.

"Sounds good, Jack," Steve said. "What have you got to lose?"

Making a great show of frantically searching through her carryall, Gena hauled out a handful of papers. "I knew they were in here somewhere. Here's a map of how to get there. Take a sport coat and slacks. Most of the restaurants in the area are upscale. Oh—sweats and a bathing suit, too, if you're so inclined. Cordillera has a pool and exercise room."

"At an inn?"

"The whole area is a playground for the rich and famous. The smaller inns have to compete." Hoisting her bag over her shoulder, she headed for the open bay and squeezed past Jack's van. "I'll expect to see you when you get back—with lots of images. And thanks for giving Link a chance." An imp with her voice called out to Steve, "The room has two beds. You're welcome to go with him."

Hopping in her car, she heaved a sigh of relief. Jack hadn't said no, and he didn't strike her as a man who would go back on an agreement, even if it was an unspoken one. He was a rigid man, with rigid principles.

She merged onto the freeway and stepped on the gas, putting as much distance as she could between herself and Jack.

Between herself and his devil of a brother.

29

Gena had done it again.

But then, Angie wasn't surprised. Once a year, the director of Link International put every other employer in the country to shame by throwing a weekend office party at one posh resort or another. Gena claimed that the staff at Link deserved it, and paid for the extravagant show of gratitude to employees and tolerant spouses with a personal check.

Posh was one thing. The Lodge at Cordillera was quite another. An exclusive mountaintop retreat, the Lodge provided its guests with the finest European traditions in architecture, decor, and amenities. Tall, ornate gates flanked the entrance to the retreat, promoting the atmosphere of a place separate from the outside world, inviolate.

Angie appreciated the serenity of thirty-something-thousand acres of mountain forests surrounding the stucco and stone lodge. The slate roof complemented the sky and picked up the shadowed hues of the mountains themselves. It was easy to imagine that, rather than being less than a half-day's drive from home, she was far away, experiencing the magic of the Spanish Pyrenees.

She found solace in the furniture that invited relaxation and continuity with the colors of nature brought inside, as if walls and glass were an illusion to be indulged. She relaxed knowing that the Lodge offered relative solitude with a total of only twenty-eight rooms and suites.

Gena had taken the whole lodge for three days. No crowd of strangers. No roommates. The facilities were exclusively theirs. Already, Gena's guests had spent the afternoon hiking on the nature trails and through the folds of the mountains and drooling over the golf course that was being thoughtfully created to blend with several high meadows. She and Gena had indulged themselves in the spa, enjoying massages, hydrotherapy, facials—the works.

Angie had never felt so pampered in her life, and if she didn't feel the inner glow all women in love were supposed to have, she knew that her exterior more than made up for it.

Perhaps here, away from a normal and familiar world, she'd be able to think, find a way to approach Jack in a dignified, nonthreatening manner. But dignity, she'd discovered, was often a sacrifice one had to make in the name of love. Still, she wasn't going to give up on him, on herself, on *them*.

She was about to give up on getting through dinner.

Gena had insisted on five courses, with a pause between each for conversation and appreciation of the original art on the walls and the view outside the arched glass doors that lined the restaurant.

Gordy had stared at his appetizer and commented that it lived up to the restaurant's name, Picasso, after the artist whose signed originals adorned the walls. The girls who worked in the mail routing room couldn't keep their heads still, turning this way and that as servers made frequent rounds with large baskets of fresh rolls and kept the wine and water glasses filled. The second course had been whisked away and palettes were again being cleansed with conversation between friends.

Friends. Angie had worked with these people, spent more than one weekend on troubleshooting marathons with them, argued with them in meetings, but until now she hadn't realized that they all had a common bond. Away from the office, they were connected by respect and genuine liking for one another.

Even her mother and Ben were here, serving as host and hostess and occupying the appropriate chairs at the head and foot of the table, with Angie on Ben's right and Gena at the opposite end on Charlotte's right. Angie appreciated Gena's gesture of respect, and she knew her mother was in her element.

They were thirty-two in all, dressed in satin and velvet

and silk and worsted tuxedos. Gena had insisted on that, too.

"Bring the LBD Ben sent you from Paris," she'd instructed Angie. "We spend our lives in casual or business clothes. Dressing up is fun. Even the guys are going black tie."

"Even Gordy?"

"Yep. Men may grumble and groan about wearing 'monkey suits,' but they preen like peacocks when the women start noticing how civilized they look."

Angie had obediently worn the black dress because arguing with Gena would have upset the careful balance of emotions Angie had struggled to create and maintain since Jack had left her in the attic room three weeks ago. For hours after that, she'd acted mechanically, carefully packing her mother's treasures in boxes, labeling each one, exorcising the ghost of a child who no longer had power over the woman.

It hurt, being a woman.

A gentle touch on her arm interrupted her thoughts. She smiled up at Ben as he leaned over her to pull out her chair.

"I want you to see something," he said, guiding her to the wall of glass doors. The whole group stood at the floor-to-ceiling glass doors framed in natural wood, watching in reverence as a full moon rose over the Gore Range in the heart of the Rockies. Without the illumination of city lights, the stars sparkled like glittering chips being scattered over a black velvet sky as a heavenly hand carved and polished the frosted crystal moon.

Ben's arm circled her shoulders, and she noticed that her mother had taken her place within the family embrace as the moon climbed in a graceful arc and brushed the mountain peaks with ethereal platinum light.

Below, an amphitheater rose from the meadow, catching the light, casting a man in shadow. Curiously, Angie watched the man and realized he held a camera as he captured the ascent of the moon on film. He was completely engrossed, tireless, his body conveying excitement and care and absolute concentration. Another figure sat on the ground beside him, digging in a large bag, handing his companion one object and then another.

She imagined that those two people were herself and Jack, silently sharing the excitement that the man's movements conveyed, sharing the wonder of a magic night.

Shaking her head, she slipped from beneath Ben's arm and took her seat at the table. Others followed, and the third course arrived.

"You look beautiful," a man said from her right.

"Thank you, Gordy. You look beautiful, too."

He grinned sheepishly. "Gena told me she'd send me packing if I showed up in a pastel tux with lapels broader than my shoulders." With the distracted expression he was famous for, he mumbled, "How did she know I own one like that?"

Angie chuckled, feeling on an even keel again. "A lucky guess?"

"I knew that dress was for you," Ben said smugly, then glared at Gordy for staring so pointedly at Angie's breasts.

Angie poked Gordy in the ribs before Ben became inclined to defend her honor.

Self-consciously clearing his throat, Gordy raised stricken eyes to Angie. "I was just trying to figure out how they managed to put the dark stuff exactly in the right places," he explained.

"It's handmade lace, Gordy, and fully lined," she said, knowing that if he wasn't given an explanation, he'd be staring at her chest all night trying to find the answer.

"But the laws of gravity—" He shook his head. "I'm afraid it will never stay up."

Ben choked on a sip of wine.

"I promise it will," Angie assured him solemnly. Poor Gordy was as dippy as they came. She had a real fondness for dips. "There are stays in the bodice that hold it in place, Gordy."

"Oh," Gordy said, apparently satisfied and relieved that he wasn't lying unconscious—at Ben's hand—under the table during dessert.

The inner room of Picasso had gathered more diners as she'd explained the laws of fashion to Gordy—a party of six, a couple near the door, two men hunched over, engrossed by conversation in a shadowed corner.

All of a sudden, Gena seemed in a hurry to move her chicks into the lounge for coffee and liqueur. Angie looked up as her mother appeared at her side. "It's such a lovely evening. Come outside with me, Angie?"

Ben nodded at his wife as he again pulled out Angie's chair, and a waiter opened the door to the terrace and bowed them outside.

Angie had been dreading the confrontation she knew would come after she'd sent the boxes of trophies and portraits and even the Aubusson carpet to her mother. Charlotte didn't make her wait any longer.

"Angie, why did you send me those boxes? Those are your memories."

"No, Mother. They're yours."

"Ben said the same thing, but I didn't want to believe him." Charlotte's sigh echoed in the stillness. Inside, a classical pianist began to play "Claire de Lune" on the Steinway. "Was it so terrible, darling? Was I so terrible?"

Angie hugged her arms. "Yes, Mother. I'm sorry, but it was terrible. I'm sorry that you had to find out."

"Why? So we could go on misunderstanding one another for the rest of our lives?" Charlotte turned her back on the view and leaned against the low stucco wall surrounding the terrace. "*I'm* sorry, Angie. Your father tried to tell me, and I didn't listen. I think you tried to tell me, too, in your own way, but I didn't see. I was too selfish to see." Her voice hushed to a whisper.

Lowering her head, Angie clasped her mother's hand, held it between both of hers. "I didn't see, either. You wanted to give me what most girls would have died to have, what you never had. I didn't see that above all else, you loved me."

"You were too young to know those things, Angie. I don't have that justification for my blind selfishness."

"Would you have listened, Mother, if I'd told you?" Angie asked, her voice thick. She had to ask. She had to know. Somehow, she thought it would be easier to lay the nightmares to rest if she knew, if for once she and her mother could address the past with honesty.

"Oh, God." Charlotte's voice trembled and shattered as she covered her mouth with her hand. "Angie, I was so shallow, always so proud of your beauty and your accomplishments, your talent and your victories." Tears gathered in Charlotte's eyes, trailed down her cheeks, reflecting moonlight. "I didn't realize how much happier we both would have been if I had simply been proud of *you.*"

Tenderly, as if her mother were a small child, Angie reached over to wipe away the tears with her fingertips. "I think you were, Mother. All those things—the talent and beauty—they were a part of me, a part of my life."

"A life you were forced into. A life that deprived you of your father." More tears flowed. "I have so much trouble living with that."

Angie lifted the hem of the lace overskirt, dabbed at Charlotte's face with the fabric. "I was a bright child, Mother. At a young age, I chose to do what you wanted. I wanted you to be happy."

"And I pushed you because I thought it would make you happy," Charlotte said on a choked laugh. "All that happiness caused a lot of damage."

"Nothing that can't be fixed," Angie said softly. "As for the general—I used to think it was all my fault, because I disappointed him, because I didn't do what he wanted. But not anymore. You didn't deprive me of him. If he wanted to be my father, he would be my father regardless of what we did or didn't do."

"It hurts you, though."

"Yes, it hurts very badly, but that isn't your guilt to bear, Mother. Parents screw up and so do children," she said bluntly. "We have to forgive ourselves. We have to remember that we love each other and go on from there."

A sob escaped Charlotte, and Angie breathed deeply as she crushed the fabric of her skirt in her hand. She kept silent, giving her mother time, giving herself time to contain the tears that never seemed far from the surface lately.

I don't just lose my temper. I destroy. The memory slipped like a shadow into Angie's thoughts, and she wondered what Jack had to forgive himself for, wondered if he could.

But Jack was miles away in Colorado Springs, and her mother was here, and Gena and Ben kept peeking out at them.

"Angie—your dress. You'll have water stains, and you're crushing it."

Smiling at Charlotte's return to normalcy, Angie opened her fingers and her skirt drifted back into place over the satin lining. "It's all right, Mother. A few tears never hurt anything."

"The last time I saw you cry, Angie, was when you lost that last competition. You sat in the back seat of the car and didn't make a sound as you cried." Charlotte smoothed back her hair. "They were happy tears, weren't they? Relieved tears."

"Yes, Mother, they were. It was finally over—"

"Angie," Gena hissed as she poked her head out the door. "I refuse to nurse you through a cold this weekend. Get in here before you freeze."

Ben squeezed past Gena, wearing his topcoat and holding his wife's mink. "It's not as if you two live thousands of miles apart," he said gruffly as he draped the fur over Charlotte's shoulders and held on to her. "I've already said our good-byes to Gena."

"You're not staying?" Angie asked. "Mother will enjoy the pianist."

"This is a party for young people, Angela." He winked. "Your mother has duly looked your friends over, so there's no reason to stay."

"Yes," Charlotte said, "and they're perfectly wonderful, darling. I'm quite satisfied that you're a social success."

Again, Ben winked. *It's all right. Don't worry. Have a hell of a good time.* Ben's winks were so eloquent, so reassuring.

Angie didn't argue. Her mother's eyes were puffy, and her makeup was streaked. She wouldn't want anyone to see her this way. "I'm glad you like my friends, Mother. I'm glad you came."

"Angie?" Charlotte said. "We added a solarium to the back of the house—a lovely place to sit and talk. Will you come?"

"Soon," Angie promised, and hugged her mother, holding tight.

"Yes," Charlotte said, her hold just as tight.

"Charlotte, Angela is cold."

"Yes, all right, Ben. I'm coming," she said as she pushed Angie toward the door to the lounge. "Angie, I've made arrangements for a moving company to pick up all that furniture and take it to the battered women's shelter Gena sponsors—Wednesday morning at eight."

Bemused, Angie slipped inside and lingered to watch Ben snuggle her mother under his arm. A battered women's shelter?

Would wonders never cease?

"Either we've been had, or Gena Collier classifies anything less than a palace as an inn," Steve said.

"We've been had," Jack confirmed.

"You finally tipped to that, huh?"

"The only thing subtle about Gena is her height," Jack grumbled as he finished off his drink.

"Yeah, five-foot nothing of ballistic blonde," Steve said with a lopsided grin. "You knew all along."

"Angie mentioned an office party at Cordillera. It wasn't hard to figure out what Gena was up to."

Steve shrugged. "As you said, Gena is not subtle. So why did you bite? The pen pal or the job offer?"

"Curiosity."

"Bullshit. I was with you today, remember? You were on a high I thought only jet jockeys experienced."

"Maybe."

"Maybe, hell. I know it when I see it."

"See what?" Jack stared down into his fresh drink. He knew what he'd felt; he just couldn't put a name to it, a description. All he remembered was long stretches where his mind had become a part of the camera, burning with visions of the images he wanted to reproduce on film. It had never been so strong and consuming that he felt as if he'd blacked out.

"It's emotional orgasm," Steve said succinctly. "It's being juiced up and straining on high revs. It's that split second when the forward gear of a bird are an inch off the ground, and the rear wheels are pulling against gravity, then all of a sudden the plane lifts under you. You're weightless for that second, suspended, and then you fly."

"Yeah," Jack said, his scalp prickling at Steve's description, at the emotion, and he realized that he had felt like that today with his cameras. He'd felt like that a month ago, with Angie.

"I used to feel sorry for you, Jack, that you didn't care that much about flying. I thought you must be as dead as Bryan not to be able to feel it."

"Different strokes."

"I guess it's true about pilots. We're arrogant as hell, thinking we're the only people in the world who touch heaven every time we go to work."

"Then why did you take the discharge? Why aren't you still flying?"

"Because I wasn't just touching heaven. I was delivering hell, and it didn't balance out. This time, the bombs were clean—all smoke and noise and fire. But I kept wondering: What if next time my payload is the dirty stuff? What if I dump a thousand years worth of hell on a city?" Steve tossed back his whole drink in one swallow. "Politics and duty and high patriotic ideals weren't enough justification anymore. I got soft, Jack. It was time to call it quits, settle down."

"And you found out that there are other ways to touch heaven," Jack said, thinking of Angie, remembering moments when he'd jumped free of control and touched heaven. Moments filled with more than her body. Like reading a letter, listening to her talk, knowing she trusted him.

Discovering that he trusted her.

"Now what?" Steve asked. "You're the victim. How much are you willing to be manipulated by the blonde?"

"I'm taking the job, Steve."

"And the pen pal? That's what this is really all about, isn't it? If those images are good, you'll get the job anyway. Smart lady, the blonde."

Smart lady, Jack agreed silently. And she was formidable. Any woman who defied the pessimism of society at large to help and protect the less fortunate elements of that society wouldn't hesitate in pulling out the stops to help and protect a friend. The way he figured it, she'd looked him up primarily to look him over. If he failed the test—with God only knew what bizarre rules—she would have turned bully in the blink of an eye. Evidently he'd passed, or he wouldn't be here now.

He couldn't have stayed away. He hadn't even tried. Angie's friend was shrewd and had hit him where he lived. First the job, then the unmistakable maneuvering to get him to Cordillera. He'd known that Angie would be here.

It was damn hard to believe he was lost when people like Angie and Gena and Steve kept finding pieces of his dreams, fitting them together. It was up to him to finish the job.

He'd come to that particular conclusion after hearing Angie's story, seeing how far she'd come and how determined she was to go farther. No matter how hard he'd tried, he couldn't make himself stop wanting to go with her.

"We going to sit here all night or join the party?" Steve asked as he waved his hand in front of Jack's face.

"What party?"

Steve rolled his eyes. "Remember the nerdy guy that came by the table while we were eating? He made it a point to tell us about the party going on in the lounge. Said his boss had taken over the *whole* lodge for the weekend and invited us to join in."

Vaguely, Jack remembered. But when they'd come late into the restaurant, he'd been too tired to pay attention to any friendly nerds. He and Steve had spent the day prowling the countryside and at eight thousand feet or better, that was enough to waste a man when he was used to breathing at five thousand feet. They'd asked for a picnic lunch and found champagne in the basket. He'd guzzled water all day and through dinner, then common sense appeased, he'd ordered a Scotch.

"His boss took the whole lodge, huh?" Jack said tongue in cheek.

"Yep. *Exclusively.* A company party, according to the nerd. No one here but people who work—"

"At Link," Jack finished for Steve, and matched his brother's grin. "Does that mean I already have the job?"

"You had the job the minute the boss lady saw those images you shot in Germany."

"Somebody needs to upgrade the boss lady's opinion of a man's intelligence," Jack muttered as he signed the check.

As they walked out of the restaurant, Steve caught Jack's arm, stopping him just inside the door. "This is for real, Jack. You really want to see the pen pal? I got the impression you'd declared her off limits."

Jamming his hands in his trouser pockets, Jack propped his shoulder against the wood frame of the door and stared at the crowd gathered in the lounge, searching for a familiar face. No, he didn't *want* to see Angie. But she'd been the one to teach him that want and need were entirely different. And lately, he hadn't been paying much attention to limits.

The nerd hoisted a five-foot-nothing blonde onto his shoulder, and she began issuing orders in a loud whisper. The crowd instantly hushed and listened with rapt attention, as if she were reciting the Ten Commandments.

Jack didn't listen. He'd found a familiar face, but not the right one. Smiling wryly, he glanced at his brother. "She's not here, Steve."

"You sure? Maybe she's in the powder room."

"Maybe." Jack kept searching the crowd for a woman with hair the color of autumn.

"We couldn't have been wrong," Steve said, his own gaze

scanning the crowd, though he didn't know what he was looking for.

Jack jammed his hands deeper into his pockets and settled more comfortably against the wood molding. Already he was feeling uncomfortable, restless, stifled, as he always did at parties. This was worse because he didn't know a soul there except for Steve and the midget blonde who had flashed him a cheeky grin, then made it a point to keep at least twenty bodies between herself and the two men she'd tried to con.

Rocking back on his heels, Steve kept his gaze focused on Gena, as if a tunnel connected them and everyone else were out of sight. "Well, since we were invited to crash this bash, I think we ought to do just that. There's still the little matter of the blonde. She has to be up to something."

Jack agreed. But if Angie wasn't here, then why was he? Giving up on trying to second guess Gena Collier, he turned his back on the room and walked over the small cubicle where drinks were being mixed and dispensed. Dutch courage seemed to be in order.

Under the circumstances, crashing a party seemed to be an appropriately desperate act.

30

There should have been some kind of warning, like a sudden lull in conversation, a cessation of movement, an arc of awareness—*something*. But the pianist didn't miss a note on the Steinway, the fabric of expensive clothing still rustled in the background, the noise of thirty or so voices still buzzed in his ears and scraped on his nerves. The only change in atmosphere was the waft of night air as one of the outside doors was quickly opened and closed.

The pianist made the transition from "Moonlight Sonata" to "Happy Birthday" as if it were part of Beethoven's original composition. The buzz crescendoed into a sudden chorus of, "Surprise!" without a single hesitation or pause.

Jack felt the quick chill and the return to warmth, heard the change in the music, the voices, yet didn't react. Maybe because the transition had been so smooth and the party atmosphere had already existed. Maybe because he had been too preoccupied with his plan to wait until he finished his drink, then gather his own intelligence as to Angie's whereabouts—a simple inquiry to the night manager, a climb up the stairs, a knock on Angie's door.

She had to be here.

Jack accepted his drink, thanked the bartender, and faced the room as if nothing had changed and all thirty bodies hadn't converged into a circle, as if a server from the restaurant wasn't wheeling in a giant, elaborately decorated cake.

Spaces opened up in the circle. Voices died down to a low roar. He saw the guest of honor in the center, her hair pulled high on her crown and cascading down her back as radiant as flame.

It still didn't register, the way being handed a cashier's check for a million dollars didn't immediately register.

Angie looked better than a million dollars.

His body caught on before his brain. Her hair caught the light and blazed with color around her head as she whirled in a circle, laughing, her hands pressed to her cheeks. His gaze was fixed on that motion. His forehead beaded with moisture. Adrenaline pumped through his veins, gathered in his groin as he watched her.

He couldn't stop watching her.

She was here. Surrounded by people. Being touched and hugged and even kissed. His jaw locked in frustration.

A hand nudged his arm—Steve's, holding a camera case. "The blonde wants to know if you'll snap a few," he said dryly.

"The blonde can shove her pictures where—" But Jack bit off the rest of his sentence as Angie's face lit up with laughter and her eyes glowed with pleasure. He checked the film in the Nikon while Steve handled the light meter. He wanted pictures, too: of Angie's face, flushed with surprise, of her suspiciously bright eyes, of the way her dress floated around her as she turned to smile and speak with each person.

He hadn't known it was her birthday.

He should have known.

"Wow!" Steve said in awe. "That is one beautiful woman. And that is some dress she's almost wearing."

Jack had been too busy staring at Angie, absorbing her presence to notice what she was wearing, until he heard Steve, until he focused on Angie through the viewfinder.

The fabric was lace, fine and light as cobwebs, black as a midnight shadow, plumping her breasts above the strapless top, nipping in at her waist, flaring out into a circle from her hips and ending at her knees.

Her knees were perfect. No Band-Aids, no scrapes and scratches.

The fabric must have been rare, too rare to waste on completely covering her back. Instead of the usual zipper, there were laces criscrossing the wide wedge of skin where the edges of the gown didn't meet. Her arms, sheathed in black gloves, were the only part of her that could possibly be warm.

She was wearing lace, but not little-girl lace. There wasn't a ruffle in sight. All he could see was the woman wearing the dress. All he could do was snap the shutter, over and over again.

"Damn. I wish she'd sneeze," Steve said wistfully.

"Shut up, Steve," Jack growled, barely able to strain the words through his clenched teeth.

"Cool your jets, Jack. The lady's gorgeous. There's not a man here who isn't—"

"The *lady* is the pen pal," Jack said, and deliberately stepped in front of his brother to obscure his view.

"Holy shit. The pen pal? *Her?* You?"

Ignoring Steve, Jack kept snapping pictures, alternately focusing on Angie and every man there. Fourteen men, not counting lodge employees. He could take out two or three, maybe. . . .

"Back off, Jack," Steve said as he gripped Jack's arm, exerted pressure.

"Oh, Christ," Jack muttered, and lowered the Nikon, backed away until he and Steve were in a secluded corner of the lounge. Jealousy had damn near swallowed him up, blinding him to reason, making him immune to restraint. The emotion was new to him, and it alarmed him with its power.

"You need all the help you can get," Steve agreed. "I was just kidding, Jack—about the men. Look at them." He nodded toward a group of three men. "They're lusting, but they won't touch. They like her too much."

"Yeah."

"She's so damn beautiful, she doesn't seem real." Steve handed him a fresh Scotch. "Most men are intimidated by a woman like that. They'd rather dream about her than find out if she has cellulite on her thighs or that she wears control-top pantyhose to hold in a spongy stomach." Angling his head, he gave Jack a sharp look. "But you don't give a shit whether she has ripples on her thighs, do you?"

"No." Hauling in air, Jack felt it scratch his dry throat,

strain his lungs. His gaze shot from one man to another, and he saw that Steve was right. Judging from their loosened ties and unbuttoned jackets—two were down to vests and rolled-up shirtsleeves—the whole group had been dressed to the nines for hours. They'd seen Angie for hours. No one had mauled her, and knowing her, she'd have crawled up the chimney if anyone had so much as hinted at a postparty grope.

Another cart, loaded with elaborately wrapped gifts, was rolled out from the office with Gena navigating. Angie's eyes widened, and her lips parted. She didn't so much as twitch as she stared at the packages.

"Jack, aren't you going to let her know you're here?"

"Later." Suddenly, Jack felt out of place, out of sync. Besides Steve, he was the only one not wearing a tux. Besides Gena, Angie's was the only familiar face.

She hadn't noticed he was here.

"You'd think she'd never had a birthday party before," Steve mused.

Shoving his glass at Steve, Jack raised the camera again, captured the stillness of Angie's expression as she stared at the gifts, the cake, the party hats being passed around. Someone had tied a fancy mylar balloon to her wrist. Through the lens of his camera, he saw, with every shot he took, the emergence of a child, a child who had been absent from the twenty portraits he'd seen in an attic shrine.

She squeezed her eyes shut and scrunched up her nose as she made a wish over the birthday cake. A long wish, as if she were covering all the angles of a particular dream. She clasped her hands together in front of herself, maybe strengthening the wish with a prayer. And she leaned over and blew out twenty-eight candles, then opened her eyes slowly as if she were afraid that one might still be burning. Everyone cheered.

Angie started to cry and wiped her eyes with her gloved fingers.

In that moment, Jack remembered the little girl in the attic, imagined her celebrating her birthday at home with her parents or at some fancy restaurant that served up a fancy cupcake with a single candle stuck in the top. He saw her clothed in ruffles that stood out like angel's wings from her shoulders, saw her sitting at an elaborately draped table, surrounded by other tables occupied by strangers. Her ankles were crossed, her hands folded in her lap just so when she wasn't eating with tiny ladylike bites and drinking her milk from a goblet, careful not to get any on her upper lip and even more careful not to spill any on the table.

I wanted a friend. I tried everything to make friends.

No, she'd never had a real birthday party before. How could she, when she hadn't had anyone to invite?

"What do you see, Jack?" Steve asked, as Jack took one shot after another.

He saw the child Angie should have been. He saw Angie the woman. "Is there any more film in my bag?"

Wordlessly, Steve handed him a fresh roll, then stuffed more into the pockets of Jack's Harris Tweed sport coat for easy access.

Jack didn't notice when Steve disappeared from his side.

Gena had again been hoisted onto a broad male shoulder, this time to deliver a speech.

"Heads up, everyone! For heaven's sake, will one of you gentlemen give the poor girl a handkerchief?"

The nerd complied.

"Thanks, Gordy," Gena said. "Angie, this party is brought to you compliments of your parents. The dinner was your mother's idea."

It figures, Jack thought, and remembered the large group in the other room of the restaurant. She'd been so close even then.

"Ben took it the rest of the way with this." Gena waved her arms expansively. "The general sends his regrets."

And a check. Jack would bet his Hasselblad on it. Clenching his fists, Jack wished he could take back the salutes he'd given General Winters when they'd met.

"Anyway, Charlotte and Ben didn't tell you because it would have spoiled the surprise. I tried to get them to stay for the duration, but Charlotte said that we were all 'quite acceptable' and much too old to need chaperones."

Fresh tears trickled from Angie's eyes.

"Will someone please give Angie another glass of champagne?" Gena said with her hands on her hips.

Steve reappeared with a large bouquet of roses in his hand. "The blonde is really something," he said, his gaze frankly appreciating Gena's curves outlined in a red velvet dress that sheathed her arms to the wrists and framed her neck, collarbone, and the top of her chest with a dramatic square neckline. "With a friend like her, no one would have the guts to be your enemy."

Jack frowned at the flowers. "You planning a party with her after the party?"

"With the blonde? Hell, no. Not yet, anyway. Credit me with a little class, will you?" He leaned forward a little and confided in a whisper, "I thought you might want to give the pen pal something, so I swiped these from the spa downstairs and conned the night manager into opening the gift shop for some tissue paper."

"You can't go around swiping someone else's flowers, Steve."

"I can when the owner of the flowers gave me permission."

Blinking, Jack averted his gaze from Steve, swallowed the lump that suddenly climbed into his throat.

"I'll hang on to them until you're finished."

"Thanks," Jack said, and raised the camera to take a picture of Gena perched on a man's shoulders as if she were on a throne.

"Angie," Gena said, "open the big white one first. It's from your folks. And remember to take your ruffles in the spirit with which they are given."

Grinning, Angie untied the yards of lavender ribbon and carefully began to pry open the tape holding the wrapping paper in place.

"Rip it off!" several voices ordered.

With a mischievous twinkle in her eyes, she slowly peeled a glove down her arm. The pianist took the cue and played a suitably suggestive melody. Her hips rotating in a modified bump and grind, Angie twirled the glove above her head and tossed it into the crowd. A waiter grinned as it landed on his head. Then Angie blushed and pulled off the other glove without any flare at all.

He knew she was unprepared for the occasion. Behaving spontaneously—like chattering at fast-forward or throwing snowballs—was a typically Angie thing to do under the circumstances. This, he realized, was the real Angie, full of life and sparkle and impulse.

Cursing, Jack buttoned his jacket over his zipper and downed his Scotch.

Paper ripped and cardboard tore when the lid of the box didn't immediately come off. A second later, Angie jammed the lid back on again.

"Sweetcakes, if you don't show us what it is, I'll have Gordy do it."

Glaring at Gena, Angie hissed, "It's lingerie, Gena."

"I wanna see," everyone chorused.

Defeated, Angie reached into the box and pulled out a handful of silk, holding it up for everyone to "see."

"I'll be damned," Gena whooped. "It's rose instead of pink—and no ruffles!"

"My mother always gives me flannel granny gowns," a woman grumbled.

As if she were surprised, Angie studied the low bodice of the gown, the seed pearls and lace that made up the cups, and the classically simple robe. "Heavens," she said, and quickly went on to the next gift.

Jack couldn't stop taking pictures. It was as close as man would ever come to bottling happiness.

That gown and robe stayed in Jack's mind while he alternately snapped the shutter and watched Angie tear through package after package. Ribbons wound up draped around her neck and wrapping paper landed on the floor, only to be whisked away by members of the Cordillera staff. The gifts fell into two categories, producing either laughter or blushes and whistles.

"Gena, I refuse to open this one in mixed company—it's from your mother."

"It's safe. No survival kit, this time, I promise."

Dubiously, Angie opened the box, then grinned and held up an oversize T-shirt, the neon lettering turned toward the crowd.

Jack adjusted the settings on his camera and snapped, the letters on the shirt perfectly focused: IF YOU LOVE SOME- ONE, LET HIM GO. IF HE DOESN'T COME BACK, HUNT HIM DOWN AND SHOOT HIM.

At the hoots and shouts of agreement from her friends, she turned it around to read the message. Her expression was thoughtful, musing, and a tiny, secret smile tipped up the corners of her mouth.

Jack had the crazy idea that she was thinking of him, and the idea gave him pleasure.

"Did my mother by any chance tuck a shotgun into the box?" Gena asked, then stared directly at Jack as she clapped her hands. "Okay, kiddies, that's all the loot. Now, before we get down to some serious celebrating, I have an announcement to make." Her gaze swept the room, then settled on Angie. "I could swear that this room isn't all that huge, but I could be wrong. We've had a man here for hours and not one of you has noticed him." The gaze turned into a glare directed at Angie. "Link finally has a photographer worthy of the name." She pointed toward the corner, toward Jack and Steve. "The big, serious guy is Jack Caldwell, our new wunderkind, and the other hulk is Steve, his brother. If you'll all be polite and trot over to that corner, you might even persuade them to take a break and join the fun."

Heads turned in Jack's direction, but he didn't see any- one but Angie, raising her head to meet his gaze. Her lips parted, and her smile disappeared.

Everything seemed to disappear, the people, the furni- ture, the music, as Jack stared back at her. Still, he was painfully aware that they were not alone.

It shouldn't have happened this way. What could he say in front of an audience? An audience, he realized, that seemed to sense Angie's tension, his tension, and backed away, opening the circle they'd formed around her.

It was all wrong. He couldn't make small talk, shake

hands, and make nice with strangers. Not now. He couldn't just stand here and watch Angie when there was so much to say to her. Private things. Painful things.

The pianist began playing the Warsaw Concerto.

The nerd put his hand on her shoulder, and her head whipped around. He spoke to her; she backed away, shaking her head. Gordy moved with her, then around her, and gathered her in his arms, arranging her body for a dance. She didn't shake her head again, but followed his lead as the others encouraged a performance.

A performance with the fanciest footwork Jack had ever seen. He'd expect it from Angie—but the nerd?

He could have sworn she'd been saying no to Gordy at first. But not now. She was Ginger and her partner was Fred, not just enjoying a sociable turn around the room but dominating it, as the others watched in appreciation.

It might have been because Angie had changed her mind so fast, or maybe it was his own irritation, but he felt a growing uneasiness, a need to do something. Yet like the others, he kept watching, spellbound by the way she moved, her feet never seeming to touch the ground, the way she became the dance itself.

He caught sight of Gena, circling the floor, her expression worried, her hands fluttering up and down as if she were trying to catch someone's attention. The uneasiness grew, and Jack stepped forward.

Steve's hand caught him, stopped him. "They're dancing, Jack. Leave it."

Jack strained against Steve's hold.

"She's enjoying herself, Jack. Look at her. She's smiling."

Jack saw the smile, perfect on the surface, conveying pleasure, but her eyes were wide, and focused inward. The smile didn't change. Her eyes didn't change.

The pianist switched to a tune with a Latin beat, and the dancers followed suit, hips swaying and feet moving in intricate patterns and the flashy heart-shaped balloon bobbed above Angie's head like the famous bouncing ball on TV singalongs.

Gena's circuit of the room ended at his side. "I couldn't stop it," she said hoarsely. "He's drunk, and I couldn't stop it."

Jack shook off Steve's arm.

"Don't, Jack," Gena said. "I told the pianist to wind it up without being obvious. Angie would hate a scene." She looked up at him. "You know that, don't you?"

He knew, and so he remained where he was, fighting himself for control. Fighting not to see to it personally that Gordy the nerd passed out prematurely.

Angie twirled away from her partner, and her skirt floated around her, baring her legs to the thighs, to the black garters holding up her stockings and the enticement of those few inches of flesh peeking out between scraps of sheer smoky silk. She moved like water, her hair blazed like fire, and Jack had never seen anything as erotic in his life as Angie dancing.

Her body creating movement, while her mind huddled someplace far away.

The women watched with envy.

The men would step on their tongues if they took a step.

Gordy reeled her back in and lowered her in a dip so low her hair brushed the floor. She held the pose and stared at the ceiling of carved wood, her mouth frozen in a doll's smile.

Jack shifted on the balls of his feet, clenched his hands into fists. Gena stepped in front of him. He'd have to go through her to get to Angie.

The goddam nerd kissed her.

Angie's arms suspended in midair, then clutched Gordy's shoulders. In the position she was in, all she had to do was raise her knee to make sure no little nerds would ever be born.

She didn't. Gordy raised his head and glanced around at the applauding crowd. His eyes were glassy, his pupils dilated. The bastard *was* wasted. And Angie stumbled away from him as he straightened up and released her.

Gena frowned. "He doesn't know what he's doing, Jack. Please trust me on this. He'd shoot himself if he did." She raced over to the center of the cleared floor, took Gordy's arm, and led him to one of the other women in the group, who helped him up the stairs.

Jack heard the applause and cries for an encore, saw Angie cringe, then straighten her spine and lift her head as she walked toward the stairs with slow, precise steps.

With a muttered curse, Jack shoved the Nikon at Steve at the same time that Steve shoved the flowers at him. "Maybe these will help," Steve said, looking confused.

Automatically, Jack's fingers closed around the bouquet as he took long strides in Angie's wake. He wasn't thinking about roses or birthday gifts. He'd seen the portraits and thought he understood. But he hadn't. Not until he'd seen the emptiness in three dimensions, the firelight reflecting back from her eyes, as if she rejected anything that brought the world too close.

He caught up with her on the first landing of the stairs, reached out for her arm, and pulled her around to face him. Her shoulders and chest rose and fell, her lips parted slightly as if she were regulating each breath. She stood, unmoving, her eyes fixed on him, yet not really seeing him, not seeing anything. Then she inhaled deeply and calmly stared up at him, so damn calmly that he wanted to shake some emotion out of her.

It was as if he were invisible, insignificant, just another friend who had drifted out of her life, all but forgotten. It made him feel helpless, inadequate, an idiot who had done too good a job of convincing her that he didn't belong in her life.

An idiot who had begun to think he might have been wrong.

A man who searched for a sign that she needed to be held, by him. That his warmth would bring her back.

Idiotically, he held out the flowers, because he didn't know what else to do. "These are for you," he said as he traced the path of a long dried tear on her cheek with his forefinger.

Something flared in her eyes, dark and raw, like an old

nightmare, and she shuddered and stared at the flowers. "Yes, thank you. I was very good tonight, wasn't I?"

"Angie—"

She jerked her head away. "Not now, Jack," she said, her words spaced between breaths. "Just leave me alone, please."

It was like the kick in the balls she hadn't delivered to the nerd, the slap in the face that the nerd deserved. Like a crippling blow from behind. Only there was no power in her voice. She was calm, always calm, and he took it as an insult to the emotions he didn't understand and couldn't control.

Control, Jack. Fast, before it's too late.

He dropped the bouquet at her feet and walked away.

He looked back once as she rounded a corner and saw her run up the stairs toward the guest rooms, her hand over her mouth, leaving the flowers scattered on the floor.

A cool hand pressed against Angie's forehead; an arm encased in red velvet wrapped around her waist, supporting her as she bent over the toilet and heaved until she felt turned inside out.

"Oh, God, I'm so sorry, Angie." Gena held a washcloth under the faucet.

"You should be." Angie wiped her face and secured her hair back in a jet-beaded banana clip.

"Angie, I didn't tell Gordy to do that. I wouldn't. He just can't hold his liquor—"

"And you can't mind your own business." Angie squeezed toothpaste onto her toothbrush, feeling pushed and squeezed, feeling pressure build inside with nowhere to go.

"You're not talking about Gordy."

Rinsing her mouth, Angie capped the tube and shook out her toothbrush. "You should have left it alone, Gena. You don't know Jack. Manipulating him like that, promising him a job just because—"

Gena held up her hand. "Hold it, chum. First of all, you know better than to think I'd give anyone a job unless it was the best thing for Link. *You* showed me the photographs he took in Germany. His mother sent me others. I happen to believe he's capable of giving Link exactly the kind of images we need. In the second place, Jack Caldwell knew he was being manipulated from word one. He went along with it."

Angie washed her face, fussed with her dress, caught Gena's gaze in the mirror. "No. Not Jack. He wouldn't do that."

"He wasn't fooled for a minute," Gena said, as if Angie hadn't spoken. "He knew exactly what was going down. His being here would've meant zilch otherwise."

"Why don't you tell me what it does mean," Angie said softly.

Gena sighed dramatically. "Angie, would you have wanted him to come here only because he was set up? Would you want *him* if he was gullible enough to buy into whatever he was told?"

"No." Angie thought about all the years she had done just that, and her hands clenched at her sides.

"Trust me, Angie, I was about as subtle as a jackhammer —and that man may be stubborn, but he sure as hell isn't stupid. He knew he was being conned; so did his brother. He came anyway. What does that tell you?"

"I don't know." Angie opened the bathroom door and stepped into the main room of the suite. But she did know. The truth was bitter as betrayal. There were no more implications, just certainties.

Only she had been manipulated. She could accept it from Gena, had accepted Gena's meddling nature long ago. It was a part of Gena. Take it or leave it. The decision to take it had been Angie's. Jack, on the other hand, had given her precious few choices about anything.

Blindly, she crossed the room, opened the balcony door, and breathed deeply, needing air, needing to ease the ache in her chest. "So you're playing matchmaker."

"Try fairy godmother," Gena quipped. "Heaven knows you need one."

The fresh air was making her light-headed, and she was

too antsy to stand still. She snapped the door shut and began to prowl the room, then stopped dead at the table and chairs arranged in a corner. "What is this?" she asked, staring down at the table, then the room service cart against the wall. She hadn't noticed it before, but then she hadn't been looking. More implications.

"Canapes, fresh coffee, champagne and brandy, leftover birthday cake. It was supposed to be waiting for you when you came up after the party," Gena said. "I guess they saw you leave and brought it in while we were in the bathroom."

"Very efficient," Angie said as she glanced over the champagne chilling in a bucket on the table, the gourmet snacks, the large carafe keeping the coffee hot. Plates, champagne flutes, brandy snifters, cups and saucers were in obvious twos. "Very nice. Thank you, Gena. Obviously I need you to plan when and where I'm to be seduced."

Rubbing her temples with her fingertips, Angie lowered her head, closed her eyes against the light that felt like a knife slicing through her head. "The Honeymoon Suite, the fire, all this—such a lovely *setup*," she said, shocked at the harsh note in her voice. But she couldn't seem to stop herself from speaking her mind, couldn't stop feeling as if a fingernail were scraping a blackboard in her head.

"What's wrong with you, Angie? It was a spur-of-the-moment gift."

"A gift," Angie muttered under breath. "You know, Gena, when Gracie sent me the vibrator and condoms, I was flattered. It meant that Gracie saw me as an adult, perfectly capable of making my own choices. With all this, you've made me feel like a high-class hooker being set up by her pimp."

From the corner of her eye, she saw Gena sag into a chair, her head lowered, her face bleached of color. "I can't believe you said that."

"Neither can I," Angie said. "But I'm not going to take it back."

In spite of her obvious distress, Gena managed a note of sarcasm in an otherwise shaky voice. "If that were my intention, I'd have sent Gordy up here. He's been in lust with you for a long time."

"And of course you thought I was too naive and helpless to know that," Angie said. "I've been aware of Gordy's feelings for several months now, Gena. Why do you think I danced with him?"

"You got me. I figured that you went on automatic. You looked like there was no one in the pilot's seat."

"There wasn't. And it was automatic, but I chose not to make him feel like a fool in public." A chill prickled Angie's skin, and she wrapped her arms around herself. "What's one performance more or less?"

"All for nothing," Gena said. "He made a fool out of himself without your help. Poor Gordy."

Rubbing her arms, Angie rounded on Gena, spoke in a low, fierce voice. "Help the lonely, the homeless, and the culturally impoverished, Gena, but don't even consider trying to help Gordy through this. It's my problem and his, and believe it or not, we're capable of dealing with it on our own."

"No problem." Gena pulled her diminutive frame forward in the large chair and rose to her feet. "We'd better get back downstairs. The party—"

"Is over. I'm sure you'll find a way to explain my absence."

"But—"

Impatience emphasized Angie's movements as she resumed her pacing. "Tell them I'm too drunk to stand up. Tell them the altitude got to me. Tell them you have to take care of me. *That* they'll understand."

"Right." Gena walked to the door, paused with her hand on the knob. "I didn't mean to hurt you, Angie."

"I'm humiliated, Gena, not hurt. And yes, I know you meant well. That's why I love you. That's why I'll forgive you—tomorrow."

"I sure as hell hope good intentions count for something."

"That's why I'm not hurt, Gena." It was getting harder to talk, harder to think straight, harder to be civil. "I appreciate the intentions, Gena, but what I need is respect—the same respect I showed for your privacy when I didn't ask about what happened to you before we met."

"Okay, I get the message, Angie. I feel like shit." Staring down at her hand curled around the doorknob, she took a deep breath, then met Angie's gaze. "I feel like you've grown up and left me behind."

Pressure built inside Angie, pushing harder, looking for weak spots. She didn't know what it was or why she felt it. All she knew was that it frightened her, the intensity that just kept growing. Her chest hurt and blood pounded in her head. "I can't talk about this anymore, Gena."

"Sure, chum. We'll make up in the morning."

"Yes. In the morning."

Gena pulled the door open, hesitated. "You'd better take some Tylenol for that headache, and put something in your stomach. You don't want that ulcer coming back to haunt you." She scooted out of the room, closing the door fast, as if she were afraid Angie might throw something at her.

Angie wanted to throw something badly. Something like a good old-fashioned childish temper tantrum.

But she didn't know how.

31

Dammit! She didn't want to feel better.

Angie tossed the unopened bottle of aspirin back into her purse and stalked across the room, snatching a canape as she passed the cart.

She was conditioned well enough to know that an empty stomach was not good, even for an ulcer that had healed over. The nausea had disappeared along with the remains of one of the best meals she'd had in years. It always happened this way, as if there had to be a purge to make things right again.

She didn't feel purged.

Everywhere, she felt tense and achy, as if all her muscles were contracting, closing around something inside her, hemming it in. She couldn't stop her rapid pacing, across the room one way and then another, snaring a tidbit or two from the cart with every circuit. Her stomach closed around every drop of nourishment as if it, too, were guarding itself. Even her skin felt tight, like shrink wrap holding her together.

Holding emotions in as she'd been conditioned to do. Conditioned to be perfect. Perfectly calm and rational and controlled. Perfectly willing to measure up to everyone else's expectations. Willing to let everyone—anyone—else decide what was best for her.

"Aargh!" She heard the sound of frustration, yet didn't immediately identify it as her own.

Temper tantrums didn't belong in the life of a professional symbol of beauty. Anger always seemed to result in endings to marriage, to friendship. And anger was easily transformed into fear, a silent, private emotion that grew without encouragement and smothered healthy growth.

Fear could be quite comforting, an excellent excuse not to take chances, to let others call the shots.

Like Gena. Like Jack.

Why hadn't she sensed his presence downstairs, felt it somehow? More than once she'd been distracted by the flash of the camera, the whir of the motor drive, but each time she'd glanced up, she'd seen more spots than detail— a man's form, a camera body obscuring his face, another man behind him in the shadows.

She should have known it was Jack. But how could she, when he'd convinced her that he wouldn't be back? She'd believed that their next meeting would be up to her. The idea had terrified her. How did a woman fearlessly chase a man without chasing him away?

It was a tricky business, especially when that man had a past that sat like a giant chip on his shoulder.

There had been so many clues, between the lines of his letters, beneath the surface of his words: his mistrust of her in the beginning when she'd simply been a pen pal, then his acceptance of her friendship when he'd revealed to her the man who cared about a young lieutenant and worried about irreconcilable differences because in his book everything in life should be reconciled, balanced, and closed out nice and neat.

Something in his life hadn't ended so neatly. Something in his mind didn't balance. And she was beginning to feel the scapegoat in the piece.

Neither did she feel particularly balanced. Vaguely, she recognized the anger, and shoved it away again, stuffing it back into a locked mental drawer.

She was, she realized, as much a control freak as Gena and Jack. But Gena's need for control was blatant, spilling out, knocking down obstacles in its path. Jack's was rigid, self-contained, keeping people out, holding him back. And hers? It was focused and personal, directed solely toward herself, an amazingly effective ability bred from need. Her need to overcome. The need of others for her to comply.

Who was she to cast stones at Gena?

How could she justify her frustration with Jack?

That settled, she made another circuit of the room, her pace fast, her muscles beginning to relax. Thinking always helped. She smiled wryly as she popped another snack into her mouth. Control always helped.

Jack's control was slipping. He wouldn't be here otherwise.

So cocky, Angie.

It felt good to be cocky. Hope always felt good.

She jumped, startled by the sharp rap on the door, and mechanically veered her course to answer it. While the doorknob was still out of reach, she hesitated, glanced at her watch, checked the room. It was past midnight. The down comforter on the bed had already been turned down.

It had to be Jack.

With panic clawing up her throat, she took another step toward the door, then abruptly angled her way to the bed to pull up the comforter, smooth the pillows.

She jumped at the second rap, louder than the first. Panic strangled her, knotted up her muscles again. Every rational thought she'd had in the last half-hour disintegrated under the force of an emotion she didn't dare acknowledge. Her palms were damp as she quickly smoothed her hair and rushed to the door.

He stood in the hallway, his tweed sport jacket unbuttoned and pushed back on one side by the hand he'd stuffed into the pocket of his navy slacks. In his other hand he held a vase of roses that dripped water all over the carpet. His hair was tousled, as if his hands had combed through it more than once, and his eyes were grave and hooded by half-lowered lids as he stared at her.

Silently she stepped aside, and silently he walked in. She went to the table, poured coffee into two cups, and all the while she felt his gaze burning on the exposed skin of her back between the criss-cross of laces that literally held her dress together. "Would you like a snack or some cake?" she asked, delaying whatever moments were in store for her.

"I'd like you to turn around and look at me."

Very carefully, she set the creamer down and flattened

her palms on the table as something jumped inside her, like a prisoner trying to jump over a wall. Slapping it back into place, she sighed and turned slowly to face him.

"These," he said in a measured tone as he held out the vase, "are for your birthday."

The scene on the landing shot through her memory: the flowers, his hand holding her back when all she could think of was getting to her room, his other hand holding out the flowers, as so many others had done after a performance.

He'd picked them up from the floor, gone to the trouble to find a vase and fill it with water. "Thank you," she said with all the graciousness of her upbringing. She took the vase from him and placed it in the center of the table.

Again silence, stillness.

Angie returned to the comfort of a simple task.

"Nice room," Jack said.

The strain in his voice made Angie aware of details as she hadn't been before: the drift of air from the partially open door to the private balcony, the intimate grouping of two sofas and a table in front of the hearth, the king-size bed skirted with an exotic print that matched the draperies, the armoire that was an antique reproduction imported from Spain. A freshly lit fire blazed and crackled in the fireplace angled across a corner.

"It's the Honeymoon Suite," she said as she balanced cups and saucers in her hands. "A very nice setup and about as subtle as a jackhammer."

"What?"

Glancing at him over her shoulder, she placed the coffee on the cocktail table between the sofas. "Gena told me that you've known all along what she was up to. She said she was very careful to be obvious."

"She was," he said.

She watched him as he averted his gaze, and his jaw clenched and unclenched in agitation, and she felt her stomach do the same thing. It was one thing to know the truth, quite another to hear it admitted without apology.

She was entitled to an apology.

She took a sip of coffee and sat down, willing her muscles to relax, willing herself to think before she spoke. "I'm sure I should be grateful for her interference. I imagine my heart is supposed to be all aflutter that you went along with it."

"You're pissed off."

"I'll let you know," she said pleasantly. "It's not very flattering to be considered incompetent to manage my own life. I'm surprised that it doesn't bother you."

"I don't give a rat's ass about Gena's plans. I was going to see you anyway."

"That's good to know." She looked around the room, then met his gaze as she arranged her mouth in a perfect little smile. "Why don't you sit down, Jack? Tell me how long you would have waited to see me if Gena hadn't interfered."

Jack sat on the opposite sofa facing her, his expression guarded as he watched her. "What the hell is wrong with you?"

"Gee, what could be wrong?" she asked, her eyes wide, ingenuous. "I've been treated to a surprise birthday party where I received oodles of neat presents like lingerie and perfume and the man of my dreams to test it all out. I really think Gena should have tied a bow around your head." Her voice rose at the last, and she felt it again, that leap of emotion inside her, anger scaling the wall of fear. The strength and persistence of it frightened her, and she reminded herself that it was inside, contained, that only she could let it out. "Why didn't you tell me you were here?" There. That was a reasonable question.

Evidently Jack didn't agree. He loosened his conservatively striped tie, popped the top button of his shirt, and lunged for his cup of coffee as if it held the elixir of life. "I was walking on a thin edge," he finally admitted, and his voice was as calm as hers, as civilized.

"Why?"

Leaning forward, he set his empty cup back in its saucer. His fingers raked through his hair. His mouth quirked in a mocking smile. "Your dress. Every man in the place staring at you . . ." His voice trailed off, and he looked away from her, the cords in his neck standing out with tension. "I was jealous. And you intimidate the hell out of me."

"Heavens," she said, unexpected pleasure rushing through her. A purely feminine pleasure for his jealousy that for the moment canceled out other feelings. She knew her face was coloring, heating up. "Intimidating?" the thought of it was as foreign to her as a display of temper. It was embarrassing.

Tantalizing.

"My brother said you're the kind of woman men feel safer dreaming about," Jack said, still averting his gaze. "But all I saw was you—not a dream. I was more comfortable with you when you *were* a dream, Angie."

The coffee had cooled and she finished the cup, then rose to fetch the pot and the bottle of brandy and poured for both of them, splashing a measure of spirits in both cups. Just then, she needed some spirit. Jack was talking to her rather than warning her off. From the raw glitter in his eyes, she knew he didn't like it one bit.

She didn't like his hunted expression, the appearance he gave of being herded into a trap—and she was the bait, already trapped.

She was fed up with being trapped.

Pleasure disappeared, crowded out by memories that had been too close lately, too confining. "Why? Because dreams are what you want them to be? You can't be jealous because no one else can touch a dream. Because a dream gives and expects nothing back?"

"Yes, dammit!"

She felt herself crack inside, felt the shake of composure, the leap of anger through the breach. "Keep your dream, Jack, but leave me out of it."

"I wish to hell I could," he growled looking savage enough to eat raw meat.

"Who's stopping you?"

"You are. First with the goddam letters—"

"You mean the *goddam* letters you answered? The ones that inspire lewd fantasies and wet dreams?" Ignoring the warning flags waving in her mind, she lurched from the sofa with fast, jerky movements and snatched the half-full cup of coffee from Jack's hand. "But you weren't a lonely, impressionable boy far from home for the first time. What was in your dream?" Carrying both cups back to the table, she set them down with a clatter.

"I was a hero to you," he blurted, then snapped his mouth shut. Embarrassed color flared in his cheekbones. He shifted on the sofa, rubbed his hand over his face as if he could erase what he'd just said.

"Well . . . good . . . for . . . you."

She spat the words out like sixteen-penny nails, sharp and cold and shocking coming from Angie. Jack snapped his gaze to hers, spoke without thinking, seeing red as his anger went from simmer to boil. "Isn't that what you were looking for?" he shot back. "A lot of women plug into the fantasy of a hero in uniform."

"Right, Jack. That's just what I needed—someone else in my life who thinks all I'm good for are fairy tales and illusions. It's so *damn* perfect," she said bitterly. "Gena is my fairy godmother, and you're my hero, come to save me from my tower just so you can put me on a *damn* pedestal and cover me with glass."

"That's not what I meant—and stop cussing, dammit!"

"Why? Because it destroys the image, makes the dream too real? Because heroes always fall in love with ladies as perfect as they are?" She stalked across the room, lace flying around her as she spun on her heels for the return trip. With her hands on her hips, she stopped and glared down at him. "Not to worry, Jack. You're not a hero, remember? That's why you're here, isn't it? To tell me just what a sonofabitch you are? To tell me how you destroy?"

"That's why I'm here," he bit out.

"So tell me, Jack. Pour it on thick. Convince me what a menace you are to sweet little things like me. Make me hate you—*make my day.*"

Jack shot off the sofa and reached for her, his hand closing around the satin cords tying her gown together. She just kept walking, and the bow pulled free, one of the ties ripping off in his hand. As she spun around, the strapless front of the dress gave way to gravity, falling away from her breasts, revealing a bustier that was all but sheer.

That stopped her. With one hand, she grabbed at the top, holding it up while the other hand groped behind her for the ties.

He held up his hand, a satin cord dangling from his fingers.

With a distinctly unladylike snort of disgust, she grabbed the T-shirt off the pile of gifts stacked in a chair and yanked it on. "Okay, Jack. Nice try, but not good enough," she said, her voice muffled by the shirt that had snagged on her nose.

"What do you want?" he shouted.

"For you to either convince me that you're a rotten son-ofabitch or leave me to my own conclusions," she shouted back as the shirt finally fell into place. "And stop shouting. I have a neighbor."

"*I'm* your neighbor."

"Naturally. Silly of me to think you and Gena would have missed the obvious."

"What the hell do you mean by that?"

She rolled her eyes as she stood there, her fists clenched at her sides wearing white cotton over black lace. "Well, you said you planned to see me. Gena's plan was better than yours, so you went along with it."

"So what?"

"So what did you plan to do once you got here?"

"Talk to you."

"So talk! Tell me what a bully you are, Jack. What did you do—break someone's toy when you were six?"

"No, I tore down a tree house when I was ten—after I called my brother a chicken while he was committing suicide, then I trashed every single thing he'd ever given me."

Her mouth dropped open, then clamped shut.

"I knew what he'd done. He left me a note. I didn't tell—"

"You were ten!"

"Yep."

"You were angry."

"Really pissed," he agreed.

"If you're still feeling guilty over that . . ." Her gaze narrowed. "But you don't feel guilty, do you? Not anymore. You're too smart for that."

"That's all you have to say?"

"I'll want to hear the details later. I'll sympathize later when I can cry and tell you how badly I feel for what happened. But right now, we're on a roll and I want to hear something really gory."

"Cold-blooded—" He swallowed the rest of it, knowing it wasn't true. Angie had fought hard to live beyond the past. She'd said nothing that Steve and the parents hadn't already said, only she'd reduced it to simple, basic truth, putting it in perspective. He'd been a kid incapable of making adult decisions. He'd reacted like a kid.

And now he was a man, arguing with a woman—like a kid.

"Pretty lame, huh?" he asked, feeling a weight lift from his conscience, feeling charged by Angie's continued challenges.

"Pathetic," she agreed. "So what else, Jack? Did you steal candy from a baby? Beat your wife?"

"Close enough," he said, feeling the shock of hearing the words, relieved that she'd said them first.

"Close?" Angie blinked and shook her head. "Isn't that like being a little bit pregnant?"

"Maybe." Taking advantage of her confusion, he grasped her arms and steered her to the sofa. "Sit," he ordered, and she flopped down onto the cushions, angled herself in the corner, pushed against the arm as if she were bracing herself.

Jack did the same, mentally, emotionally, as he dredged up memories he was afraid to talk about. Afraid that they'd sound as bad as they'd seemed at first, afraid that the doubts he'd had lately were nothing more than feeble justifications for his actions. Afraid that Angie would judge him guilty.

"You're serious," she said, dazed.

"I'm serious," he said grimly as he jammed his hands into his pockets and stalked over to the balcony door.

"Oh, boy," she said. "I've got to hear this."

The way she said it—in disbelief, as if she were humoring him—helped him pull up the memories, helped him look at them without feeling as if he'd been gutshot. "Then listen," he said more harshly than he intended. "I'll tell you once, start to finish—no interruptions or smart-ass remarks."

Her gaze never left his face as she nodded.

He missed her anger, the way she'd zipped haphazardly around the room like a deflating balloon. It had helped to be goaded, to be pushed into a corner. He closed his eyes, saw the memory in stark detail. With Angie so silent, it was easy to pretend he was alone, yet he forced himself to stand back as he talked, to try to see it all through Angie's eyes as he shared the past with her. . . .

32

"**K**ay and I started dating while I was at the Air Force Academy," he said, and described how well she'd fit in with his carefully planned life, how it had all happened exactly the way it was supposed to. They'd been married in the Academy Chapel, Kay in a wedding gown straight out of *Vogue*, himself in his dress uniform, both of them stepping into a picture perfect life.

It had been perfect for a while, following patterns they'd both agreed upon. But things had deteriorated with every transfer to another base, with every promotion Jack received and the increasing demands of his job. Kay had agreed on the glamour and excitement of military life, not on the pressures and politics.

His career became the nemesis of his marriage. Kay wanted children, yet with him eating, sleeping, and living his job, she didn't think those children would have had two parents. Jack hadn't wanted children at all, hadn't wanted to set himself up for the kind of heartbreak his parents had suffered.

Germany had been the last straw.

A year into his tour, he went TDY for two weeks for a round of briefings at the Pentagon. He'd expected her to be ticked that she couldn't go with him on the Temporary Duty assignment, but there was no scene, no argument that raged until he stepped onto the jetway. For once, she'd waved him off with equanimity, if not a smile.

He'd thought a lot about Kay, their marriage, while he was stateside, and he decided that as soon as he got home, they were going to talk, learn to do something besides argue. Kay had made the first move by not bitching about his trip. He'd make the second by offering her a compromise he thought they both could live with.

A new department was opening up in intelligence. While not his first choice, he'd already put in for the job of heading up the special team. It would mean stability, a long assignment in one place. Kay would like that. Back home, with the opportunity to pursue her career as a convention consultant, maybe she'd forget about having a baby.

When the briefings were over, he'd made a flying visit to the Springs. His mother had talked about children, dragging out all the clichés: she was grateful for having Bryan as long as she had; children were on loan; life doesn't come with guarantees.

"Eventually children go away, and they either leave you with memories, or if you're very lucky, they share portions of their lives with you," she'd said. "It's enough, Jack, if you have your own life to live."

Maybe it was that simple, he'd thought. If it was, maybe he could take it. He liked kids. Having one had never been his problem. Losing one was a different story.

So he'd decided that if Kay wanted a baby, then he did, too. Why should she suffer for his hangups?

A marriage was worth saving, wasn't it? It had been good once. He had loved her once. He wasn't sure if he still did. But he had to, didn't he? The vows were as binding as his oath of service. As far as he was concerned, they were engraved in stone.

Except he'd forgotten that stone can be broken as easily as crystal if you hit it just right.

As soon as he'd arrived back on base, he'd gone to the office and been informed of a "command performance" at a farewell party for a retiring colonel who Jack considered the biggest jackass Uncle Sam had ever commissioned into the Air Force, a man who was all brain and no action. By the time he analyzed a situation, it was over.

The party was one more delay and Jack resented the hell out of having his good intentions put on hold for another few hours. In another few hours, he'd probably be asleep on his feet.

At the retirement party, Jack had performed all right. He'd saluted the jackass with as little snap as possible. For once, Willis hadn't been inclined toward conversation, and Jack headed for the bar. He and another major indulged in the usual after-hours discussion on politics and the role of military intelligence in keeping the peace in a world that seemed to be crumbling faster than it could be shored up. Military cutbacks were more than a gleam in the congressional eye. There was a freeze on promotions. Though Jack had made major below the zone—before it was time according to the military's schedule—he knew future advancements were going to be a matter of being in the right place at the right time and sucking up to the right people.

Jack wasn't about to polish anybody's apple for a silver cluster to pin on his hat. With that attitude, he knew it was unlikely he'd make Bird Colonel before his twenty years were up.

When they stopped talking to stare grimly into their glasses, he decided he might as well head for home. He was in the perfect mood for more frustration, more catch-22's.

His feet feeling like hundred-pound weights, he climbed the concrete steps that led to the apartment he and Kay shared in a building with twenty-four other families, hoping that Kay was asleep. He was in a lousy mood. The three glasses of Scotch on an empty stomach seemed to be fermenting in his blood, adding to his exhaustion.

He unlocked the door and found Kay sitting at the dining room table, staring into a cup. "I defrosted the fridge for you, stocked up on groceries, and gave the place a good cleaning," she said without looking at him.

Jack took off his hat and hung it on the hall tree by the door, then loosened his tie, unbuttoned his uniform jacket, took another step into the living-dining area, and nearly tripped over a stack of suitcases. "You go to East Berlin on a shopping trip?" he asked.

"I'm leaving tonight." She glanced up at him. "For home."

A rush of panic-induced adrenaline propelled him closer. "What's wrong? Your folks or mine?" he asked as he tried to think of transportation and emergency leave.

"They're fine. I'm leaving you, Jack."

He rubbed the back of his neck as he looked down at her. God, he was tired. This wasn't the time, not when he couldn't think straight. "No more head games, Kay. We need to talk, but after we've had some sleep."

"No more head games," Kay agreed. "No more talk, Jack. It's too late."

"We've never talked," he pointed out, hearing the edge of impatience in his voice. Calm. Stay calm and reasonable, he coached himself. Hooking the chair across from Kay with his hand, he swung it around and straddled it, propping his arms on the back, propping himself up. "There's a new department opening up. It means a long stay in one place, close to home. I put in for it."

"Don't, Jack. Duty at the Pentagon is your best chance to make colonel."

He shook his head. "Too much stress. More hours. Less stability. We need the time—"

"We're out of time, Jack. I'm filing for divorce." She rose from her chair, picked up the cup, and went into the tiny kitchen to rinse it out. For once, Kay wasn't shouting. Her voice seemed to come from a long way off, like the sound in a bad movie.

"Just like that?" he asked, another bad line from a bad movie.

Turning from the sink, she braced herself against the counter as she faced him. "No. I've been working on it for a while."

"What kind of wife takes off without trying to work things out?"

"The kind of wife you wanted, Jack," she said without inflection. "I did my duty. I've wasted years playing a game I hate with people who bore me silly. I've tried to talk about our problems while you lived and breathed your job. The kind of wife who has been trying to work things out without you." She smiled then and touched her stomach. "I even got pregnant without you."

Pregnant. It was the only word that registered. He felt his stomach clench, heard the roar in his ears. Other men were happy to hear news like this. He'd promised himself—had intended to promise Kay—that it would be all right, that he would be happy *if* and *when* it happened.

It had happened, and all he could think of was his parents crying, then walking around like zombies, remembering, mourning, shrouded in guilt. "You can't be," he said hoarsely. "You used a diaphragm—"

Kay nodded as she pushed away from the counter and brushed past him. "And for good measure, you used a condom. Don't worry, Jack, we always had 'safe' sex. We never touched—inside. The baby isn't yours. A man and a woman have to touch to create life. You can't be touched, and if you could, you wouldn't feel it."

No? Then why did he feel as if she'd cut him to the bone? The baby wasn't his, and for some reason, he felt regret. His chair slid through the doorway and slammed against the kitchen counter as he stood and kicked it out of the way, advanced toward Kay, down the hall and into their bedroom. "Did you ever try, Kay?" he asked.

"You should know better than anyone how hard I've tried," she said in a bored tone. "You should know, but you don't, do you? Just as you never knew what I wanted."

Driven by a fury he hadn't seen coming and couldn't control—didn't want to control—he shoved her up against the wall. "You wanted the dress uniform and the rank. You wanted an officer and a gentleman. You wanted travel and excitement and security." His voice was low, rasping as he held her against the wall. "You got exactly what you wanted, Kay."

She met his gaze squarely, not flinching, not showing fear. If she had, he might have let her go, might have stopped holding her so tightly that his hands cramped. Her voice was steady, still calm, still bored. "I wanted a man, not a tin soldier."

It should have struck his ego, caused pain—something—but he felt no reaction to the insult. More than anything else that passed, that fact fed his anger, made him feel impotent, less than the man she claimed she'd wanted, not at all the man he thought he was.

"Who is he?"

"Ed Willis."

Jesus! Fury surged and peaked, swamping him, pulling him under. He felt his arm move back, then forward, heard the wall crack before he felt the shock of the blow spike from his fist up to his shoulder.

Kay turned her head to look at his hand still embedded in the hole in the wall next to her. Her mouth turned up in the barest hint of a smile. "You missed. Want to try again?"

He stared at his hand as he pulled it out of the sheetrock, stared at the blood on his knuckles. Had he missed? Swallowing down bile, he concentrated on releasing his hold on her, flexing his fingers, stepping back. He'd started to hit her.

For one disconnected moment, he'd *wanted* to hurt her.

He still did, just to get that nasty little smile off her face. He took another step back as he inhaled, let it out again. "If Willis is your idea of a man, then I'm damn glad I don't qualify," he said, struggling for some kind of normalcy.

"He's not perfect," Kay agreed. "He's a lousy officer, but—"

Jack walked out of the bedroom before he could hear the rest, before the rage took over completely, before he did more than bash in a wall, before he did more than leave bruises on Kay's arms.

Dimly, he heard her take her coat out of the closet, pick up the purse with the chain strap, open the door that led into the communal stairwell. "Will you carry my suitcases downstairs?"

An officer and a gentleman would have obliged. A decent man would have, in good grace, done the right thing and spared a pregnant woman from carrying heavy suitcases down a flight of stairs. But he was a tin soldier, according to Kay, not a man at all, and he sure as hell didn't feel decent.

He held up his bloody hand. "Sorry. You'll have to carry them yourself or wait for Willis to do it for you." Bending over, he slid the largest case across the floor, knowing it was childish, knowing it wouldn't accomplish anything.

He didn't want to go anywhere near her.

The other two cases followed. It was a wide hallway, and he aimed for the space well to the side of her. It would have been fine if she hadn't stepped over to catch her cosmetics case before it tumbled down the stairs. Nothing would have happened if she hadn't tripped over the long coat he held over one arm.

Reflexively, Jack started toward her as she stumbled down one step, landed hard on the next, and thumped down to a third before he caught her arm, held her steady, as he checked her for injury.

"I'm fine, Jack. Just let me go."

The main door opened at the bottom of the stairs. Jack saw Ed Willis and rose. "Here's your *man*, Kay. You'd better give him five minutes to figure out the best way to carry your luggage."

As usual, Willis stood still, taking in the scene, probably extrapolating the facts as he saw them. Probably scared shitless to get within striking distance of Jack.

Without a word or a backward glance, Jack walked into his apartment and shut the door.

The next day he'd gotten the call from the hospital. Kay had suffered a miscarriage, and a hysterectomy had been performed. She'd been spotting for days and had been warned not to lift, to avoid emotional extremes. Kay had always wanted kids, but it had never happened for them. Now it would never happen for her at all.

"Ed Willis caught his plane without her," Jack said, and forced himself to walk over to the sofa, meet Angie's gaze.

But Angie was up and running again, shadowing him, barreling into him as he turned. She looked downright disgusted as she poked a finger at his chest, her head thrown back as she glared up at him.

"You're not an S.O.B., Jack." Her finger poked again, once for every word. "You're a donkey's ass. A *pompous* donkey's ass, thinking you have to take responsibility for everyone else. You think the rest of us aren't capable. Your wife sneaks off to another man behind your back, insults you, and you take the blame. Shame on you for expecting her lover to carry her suitcases. Shame on you for taking the blame because she was more worried about saving a few bottles of perfume than she was about her baby." Breathless, she gasped as she poked him again. "Shame on you for dragging poor little helpless me kicking and screaming into your violent and depraved life."

He grabbed her hand, held it suspended between them before she broke her finger and left a permanent bruise on his chest. "Are you finished?"

Defiantly, she glowered up at him. "I'm hitting you, Jack. I called you names. Go ahead, hit me back." She pointed to the side of her jaw. "Right here. Beat the living daylights out of me. I deserve it, don't I? After all, I've made you do things you didn't want to do, writing those *goddam* letters, forcing you to come and see me, seducing you. Clobber me good, Jack."

"Don't tempt me," he muttered under his breath.

"You're tempted? Well, shame on you again. It's a sin, don't you know? Heaven forbid you should get mad when someone hits *you* below the belt. You'll fry in hell for wanting to hurt Kay. Whether you did or not isn't the point, is it? Who cares if you almost broke your hand to avoid it?" With a look of disgust, she shook her head. "I really can't believe you bought into this crock of nonsense."

"I wanted to hurt her, dammit!"

"So? Right now I want to paint a target on your behind and aim a cannon at it." Some of her anger died, but the defiance was still there, making her eyes glitter, her body shake. "I want to—"

He wanted her to shut up. Hauling her close, he wrapped his arms around her, trapping hers at her sides where they couldn't do any damage, and he clamped his mouth on hers before she could say another word.

Her mouth opened, her tongue assaulting his, continuing the battle while she glared up at him. He fought back, holding her tighter, thrusting his tongue into her mouth, only to have it pushed back by hers. Her hips ground into his. Her breasts pushed against his chest, her nipples firm, pressing into his flesh.

He didn't understand how they'd gone from angst to passion, and he didn't care. Apparently Angie didn't care either. She was the one in control, taking, provoking, demanding, still glaring up at him. It was her aggression that resurrected sanity, prompted him to tear himself away from her, release her arms, step back.

"What did you do that for?" she asked belligerently.

"This is a hell of a time to be horny," he answered bluntly. "We have to talk."

"Wrong, Jack. I've said my piece three times over. You've said yours in agonizing detail—"

"Angie—"

She shook her head, took a step back. "You know, Jack —*you know*—that you're not a violent man. You know you wouldn't have hurt your wife, and you know you'd never hurt me. You feel too much—inside, where it counts. The worst thing you can be convicted of is being a driven, misdirected donkey's ass."

He knew. Suspicions he'd had about his own self-appointed guilt turned to certainties with Angie's reaction. He'd needed that—the confirmation that he hadn't simply been rationalizing, glossing over actions that had been abhorrent to him. The reasons for that abhorrence were equally asinine.

He'd been obsessing on control and had hurt himself more than he'd ever hurt anyone else.

"Say it, Jack."

"I knew," he said quietly.

She held her ground. "Okay, we have to talk, but not now. Now we're going to make love."

"Why?" he asked, trying to keep his mouth from twitching in amusement. He had a feeling Angie wouldn't appreciate amusement right now.

"Because I'm a little drunk and feeling really brave, and tomorrow I'll probably turn back into a shy wimp who talks too much. Because I love you, and I'm horny, too, and having a great time acting like a spunky heroine. I expect you to make me feel like one."

"Not fair," he said softly as he shrugged out of his jacket, unbuttoned his shirt, and began to stalk her. "And you always talk too much."

She tugged off the T-shirt, let her dress fall to the floor and stepped out of the pool of black lace. The bustier was sheer, ending just above equally sheer black bikini panties, baring an inch of fair porcelain skin on her belly. "Okay, you can be a hero—tonight."

He advanced, his hands busy unbuttoning his shirt, unzipping his trousers. Without a break in stride, he shrugged out of his shirt and tossed it aside. Angie met him, slid her fingers beneath the bands of his pants and jockey shorts. "Let me," she said and knelt to slide them down his legs, her mouth a bare half-inch away from him. She glanced up at him, uncertainty showing for the first time in her face. "Um—can I . . ."

He would have been disappointed if she didn't blush, a blazing fire of a blush that washed out the rich color of her hair. "Spunky, remember?" he reminded her.

"Right," she muttered, and gave him a timid little peck.

"Careful, Angie, that's virgin territory."

Another little peck. "You're kidding," she said as she examined every growing inch, investigating textures, over, under, and around, driving him crazy with her teasing explorations. "Your wife never did this?"

"No." He barely got the word out. He didn't want to talk, didn't want to remember the uninspired sex he and Kay had shared.

"Good," Angie said happily, and closed her mouth over him, inspired.

God, was she inspired! He stood still as long as he could, as long as he dared, then croaked, "Angie . . . the bed."

She ignored him as she tasted and teased. Her mouth drew on him, gently, fiercely, gently again, her teeth raking provocatively over sensitive skin.

She rose then, launched herself into his arms, propelling them both back onto the bed, then rolling over to lie on her back, breathing heavily. Running her hand up her sides, over her breasts, she stared up at him, her eyes dark, intense. He'd seen scenes like this in movies—the heroine passionate, erotic, graceful, as she reached for the hero as if she'd die if he didn't move over her, take her with hot, urgent power.

"Jack," Angie whispered as her fingers worked the garters free, then the fastenings on the bustier. It fell open, framing her breasts.

"Hmm." He couldn't stop staring at those breasts, anticipating the first touch, the first taste.

She reached for him, opened for him, guided him, took him in. "It's time, Jack. I can't wait."

Neither could he. Like the good hero he was for the night, he ripped off the last scrap of fabric, found her hot and wet, the look in her eyes primitive and wild. He lowered his body, claimed her mouth, and plunged into her, fast and hard, as she arched up to meet him.

The night was still dark, a lingering moment to savor the memory of learning the taste and scent and texture of one another, a moment Jack wished would never end. The room was a shadow cast by the dying embers in the fireplace, yet even that small glow found Angie's hair, touched it with light.

She slept peacefully with her head on his shoulder, no longer the reckless heroine who had taken everything he had to give, every way he could. The angry woman who had called him a donkey's ass and told him she loved him five minutes later was gone. Only Angie remained. Angie, who had given him her trust by revealing herself—her weaknesses and fears—in painful detail, by revealing the secret part of herself that shouted and challenged and demanded. Angie, who had opened her body to him, encouraged him to find his own pleasure without fear that he would forget about hers.

It had been wild and spontaneous, without barriers, without shyness or modesty, an act of trust on both their parts.

She stirred and her hand brushed his groin, trailed up and down his diminished length. The hero was gone, too.

Gently, he took her hand in his, lifted it to his lips, kissed each finger one by one, and she sighed, stared up at him with drowsy inviting eyes. "No?"

"Can't," he said as he nibbled her fingers. "Maybe when I was sixteen and had a perpetual hard-on." A flush blazed up his neck and into his face. He was getting as bad as Angie.

A fingernail raked his palm as she snatched her hand away and rolled over to lie on her back, staring up at the lofty ceiling. "I missed it—not having a normal childhood, not being reckless and fearless like the other kids."

"Yeah," he said as he matched her pose and stretched out his legs. "I think we're making up for it." He glanced over at her, saw her bite her lip as her hands twisted and tortured the strands of hair lying on her shoulder.

Breath whooshed out of her, and it sounded like regret, grief, resignation, and when she spoke, it was tentative and wary. "I didn't mean to sound so cold-blooded about your brother. Will you tell me about him?"

His chest rose on a heavy sigh as he returned his gaze to the ceiling. Bryan was the last thing he wanted to talk about just then, but Angie needed distracting before she tied knots in her hair and her stomach worrying about how "cold-blooded" she was.

"There was seven years between us, but we were tight. Bryan was special somehow, more alive than anyone I knew. He had it all—personality, brains, the kind of looks that had the girls hanging all over him. Everyday things were interesting when he was around." Layering his hands beneath his head, he paused, waiting for the familiar sense of loss, the anger and guilt that always followed, but they didn't come. All he felt was peace, acceptance.

"Bryan left the suicide note under my pillow, but I wasn't sure what it meant." He condensed the details, recited them as he and Angie lay side by side without touching. He told her about Bryan's dreams, the accident that ended those dreams, the anger and betrayal he felt when Bryan left him to make impossible decisions. When Bryan forced him to take responsibilities he didn't understand.

"It scared me—the way my mother cried, the way my

parents held each other as if no one else existed. They shut down, like you do sometimes, only they didn't seem to be there at all. I'd try to hug Mom, but she didn't feel it. I'd talk to Dad, and he'd nod and say, 'Fine, son. I trust your judgment.' " Breath escaped his lungs in a fast whoosh, a last expulsion of the emotion that had ruled his life for so long. "Jesus—I was a kid; I didn't have any judgment. Then Steve started hanging on to me, expecting me to answer his questions, give him advice."

"You resented it," Angie whispered.

"Yeah, I resented it. So he separated himself from the family, did his own thing, and raised hell."

"What did you do, Jack?" She was smoothing her hair now, over and over on her shoulder.

"I was lost and scared. I wanted my parents back. So I reasoned, if losing Bryan had made them that way, then I'd damn well give him back to them. I made good, and except for washing out on jet fighters, I did everything Bryan wanted to do."

"Then you fell into the trap you'd set for yourself. Your parents came out of their grief, and at your age, with your overdeveloped sense of responsibility, you were convinced that you'd done the right thing. It was too late for you to do anything but carry on."

"That's about it," he said. "It worked, so it must be right. I was one screwed-up individual."

Now she was mangling the sheet. "No. You cared—too much, maybe. But you have your own life back—your decision. You're okay now. You're free."

It sounded flat, like a bad note in a good song, and he frowned. "Where do you get this shit?"

"I minored in psychology, fit in extra courses whenever I could after graduation."

"Well, that explains it." Jack rolled his eyes, then his body, and raised up over her.

"Explains what?" she asked, staring up at him.

"Why you always make sense." He nibbled at the corners of her lips. "How you get me to talk about things I've kept to myself for over twenty years. Who can argue with sense? You know too much for my own good." He frowned as she averted her face from his kiss.

"What now, Jack?"

"This is your party. You tell me," he teased. His grin slipped when she still wouldn't look at him, when she shifted onto her side, bunched her pillow under head, and hugged it tight.

"Maybe tomorrow." It might have been a quip if her voice didn't sound as if it had curled up into a ball, as she was trying to do.

Tomorrow sounded good. He was wiped out, and so was Angie. He had plans and ideas, but at three in the morning, they were blurred together. "You're right." He lay on his side and wrapped himself around her. "We need to sleep," he said gruffly, and tightened his arms as she tried to ease away. "Together, Angie." It tasted sweet, to hear it, to say it, to feel it.

"Yes," she whispered so low, he barely heard her. "Together is good."

Nothing was wrong, he told himself. She was just tired. So was he.

Their bodies conformed to one another as if they had been cast from corresponding molds, sharing warmth, giving comfort and reassurance as she relaxed and made a slow descent into sleep. Jack listened to Angie's deep, even breathing as he stroked her hair, inhaled the scent of her body mingling with his.

His eyes burned, yet his cheeks felt cool as the autumn air dried the moisture trickling down his face. He didn't fight the tears he'd never shed for Bryan, the sorrow he'd refused to feel. It was his last debt to Bryan, to the love he'd had for his older brother.

Images drifted like shadows through his memory—of transient moments, fleeting lives, lost hope. Of a boy who had learned that what was lost could never be regained. He wondered if the man that boy had become was strong enough to hold on to the dreams he had found, strong enough to accept their reality, as Angie had done.

He closed his eyes, gave himself up to sleep as Angie curled into him, giving him the true experience of belonging, togetherness.

In the morning, she was gone.

POSSIBILITY

Possibility hangs before me,
Like eternity.
Long thin haunted fingers reach into the space
That fills up my room.
With deaf ears I listen
To unspoken words,
Questioning feelings.
Do I miss the flowers I never had,
Or just the possibility of them?
It's purely and simply
A fairy tale
Brought to life by your magic.
                    —Jennie Cissel Thompson

33

She'd cut off her nose to spite her face. She should have stayed at Cordillera, played it out to the end, faced whatever problems the night had created. She should have fought for what she wanted. But no, she'd just had to think first.

She'd been gone for two weeks, visiting her mother, finalizing arrangements for the benefit in Denver, driving aimlessly through the mountains. Long enough for her mind to work its way from good excuses to the real reasons she'd cut and run.

She was a coward.

Her suspicion that love severed all connections between brain and heart were confirmed. No conclusions had come to her, only more questions. Decisions eluded her. Possibilities dangled from every thought, hanging over her head like dreams neglected, opportunities unexplored.

She'd left Jack without a word, without knowing what he felt, what possibilities existed for them—if any. She'd only questioned the "if any," only recognized the fear of learning that a life with Jack wasn't a possibility at all.

Angie opened Dracula up, let him suck up the miles between Denver and Colorado Springs. She checked the speedometer. Three reckless miles over the speed limit. Good enough to feel rebellious without being irresponsible.

Responsibility had been the motivation for her departure from Cordillera, from Jack. As usual, it came ten minutes too late. She'd almost asked him for promises and offered commitment. Again they'd made love without precautions. Being the honor bound, by-the-book man that he was, he'd have taken her up on it for all the wrong reasons.

It was the right time of the month. Jack would have

taken responsibility for that, too. He would have felt it his duty to wait it out, stand by her if nature took its natural course.

Really, life was such a cliché.

Really, she was such a liar.

Out of desperation, she'd asked herself if she could survive the worst that could happen. She could. Put that way, she didn't see where she had anything to lose except pride and a chunk of her heart. If she didn't explore the possibilities, she'd lose anyway.

The house was just as she had left it two weeks ago, the grass looking as trim and freshly mowed as it had when she'd left. That was odd. Shaking her head, she smiled. The lawn was fading to dull gold. Leaves were beginning to fall, spattering the ground with color, signaling an end to growth. It seemed as if she'd just raked, but that had been last year, before Jack had answered her first letter, before she'd fallen hopelessly, sappily in love with him.

Love was so irrational, linking the most inconsequential turn of mind into high drama.

Pulling the Cadillac into the garage, she switched off the ignition and left Dracula to rest in his coffin. The car deserved a rest. No one should subject a block-long classic to the narrow switchbacks and hairpin turns of Independence Pass on a whim. The car would probably need a brake job.

She needed an attitude adjustment.

An envelope stuck out of the mailbox—one-tenth of her usual daily mail. Evidently her neighbor had missed it when she'd collected the rest. She set her suitcase and tote down and frowned at the letter. There was no return address, no postmark canceling the "Love" stamp in the corner. An old twenty-cent "Love" stamp. Her name and address were neatly typed—no clues there.

Too curious to wait, Angie sank into the cushion of the rattan Papa San chair on the porch and tore open the envelope, pulled out the two sheets of plain paper with doodles all around the edges. *Her* paper. *Her* doodles—Jack's name written and printed and animated, an adolescent urge she'd indulged in more than once. . . .

Her head snapped up with the realization that he'd been in the house. He didn't have a key, but Gena did.

She was going to kill Gena—maybe—after she read the letter.

Her hands trembled as she smoothed out the last fold. A roar in her ears replaced birdsong and the chatter of chipmunks in the yard. The scent of Skin Bracer added tang to the rich odor of decaying leaves. She forgot to breathe as she read the bold angry scrawl that snagged the heavy vellum in places.

Dear Angie—

I don't know what I want to do most—shake you silly or love you senseless. You're not being reasonable, sweetheart. What are you trying to do—see if love can be treated with concealing cream? A wasted gesture, Angie. I don't want a cure for what ails me. You've been worrying about that, I'll bet. Maybe you're giving me an easy out because you think you've backed me into a corner. Maybe you like the fantasy too much. Who can keep it up? It's not real, right?

No problem. That's what dark nights and locked doors and sexy lingerie are for. Hell, we can even throw in a couple of dirty movies on alternate Saturdays. If you've developed a taste for rough and ready, we could have a good rip-roaring fight once in a while to set the mood. Your choice, Angie.

Choices open up a whole new world of problems. What do we do with the ones we don't understand? Is that the problem, Angie? Can't you decide between fact and fantasy, hero or ordinary man? Love me, or let me go? TV dinners for one, or cooking for two? Interfere in my life, or leave me to find myself on my own? By the way, I'm not lost anymore. You found me, showed me where I was. And if I forget, all I have to do is look at you, see myself in your eyes.

At the risk of sounding sappy, I'll tell you that you can find yourself in my heart.

If you're feeling embarrassed about losing your temper, then you ought to know that more than once, I've wished

*you'd cut loose, blow off steam—sort of equalize our tem-
peraments. Besides, you're sexy as hell when you're fighting
mad and looking for blood. Women aren't the only ones
who like to know they're being protected. You've probably
noticed that I've tried to pick fights with you, only to be
defeated by your own brand of sweet reason and sappy
sentiment.*

*If parts of this letter sound familiar, it's because I'm
throwing your own words back at you Angie. You've chased
me, hassled me, seduced me, and left me without asking if
I'm pregnant or not. I'm not, but hell, where's your sense of
responsibility and obligation?*

*For the record, I talked to Gena since she knows how
your mind works. We decided that you meddle and manipulate with the best of us. She gave me your spare house key.
By leaving, haven't you decided what's best for me? You
need to practice what you preach.*

I miss you, Angie. Being alone is beginning to pall.

Jack

Dazed, Angie read the letter again. Try as she might, she
couldn't find hidden meanings between the lines. He
pointed out the faults that she'd become painfully aware of
during endless hours of driving. He'd described some of
her fears exactly. He wrote in future tense but gave no
specifics.

That, too, produced anxiety—and hope. Always hope.
She needed the commitments and the trappings that went
with it, and she was very afraid that she'd cheat herself by
settling for less. Her not-so-great escape had produced one
certainty: no more cheating. She couldn't save another
dream for a rainy day. All the hiding places inside herself
were full.

Vaguely, she heard her neighbor's Doberman bark and
wondered what had disturbed him. A door slammed
loudly, and she imagined it was her back door. She followed the wraparound porch, saw the dog clawing to scale
her eight-foot fence and her screen door swinging on its
hinges.

She saw the shed, its door open, inviting.

On legs that had turned to pudding, she descended the porch steps, crossed the yard, peered into what should have been a dim interior. But the shed had been wired, and a small Casablanca fan complete with three lights hung from the ceiling.

The plank floor was sanded and varnished to a high gloss. Sheetrock lined the walls, covered by wainscoting and wallpaper. An elegant fairy-tale wallpaper with butterflies and flowers surrounding Beauty and the Beast—so obviously a message. Gardening tools hung above shelves lining one wall, and the shed was furnished with a worktable and a feminine rattan loveseat.

She blinked her eyes furiously, ignoring the persistent burn behind them, the pressure and sting of tears, the clog in her throat that throbbed, as if it were her heart. She backed out of the shed, ran into the house, leaving the screen still swinging on its hinges.

The house was exactly as she had left it two weeks before, cluttered from the rush of packing and the frenzy of being late to pick up Gena for the drive to Cordillera. No one sat in the window seat or stood at the kitchen counter. Everywhere she looked, she saw only memories and caught the scent of Skin Bracer lingering in the air. He had to be here. She could feel him, sense his presence.

She heard a "cuckoo," then the music box strains of "Edelweiss." Her head jerked up, and she glanced around the house, finding nothing. The sound seemed far away, above her. She listened to the music, remembering the words, hearing the promise of a flower thriving where nothing should grow. High up, close to heaven.

On shaky legs, she followed the music and blind instinct, up the stairs, one flight, then two, and hesitated outside the arched door leading into the attic room she'd so recently emptied of unhappy memories. Empty except for the music, the large cuckoo clock with dancing figures hanging on the wall by the door, the fire crackling in the hearth, the candles burning on the mantel, and the top of the shelves that had been filled with books collected from wherever she'd left them.

Pictures hung on the walls.

She followed one wall, her fingers trailing over the images preserved under glass. Images of a woman laughing, the black lace of her skirt floating around her as she whirled. A pensive woman whose eyes were squeezed shut as she said a prayer, made a wish, and blew out twenty-eight candles. A woman wearing a necklace of ribbons and bows with a heart-shaped mylar balloon tied to her wrist as she tore greedily into a gaily wrapped package. A bold woman with a naughty smile stripping off a black satin glove.

Angie saw herself, candid, natural, revealing. She was real, alive with motion, as candlelight flickered on the images. For the first time, she felt as if she belonged in this room.

More photographs were grouped on the wall by the door, some in color, some with the dramatic contrast of black and white—of mountains sprinkled with late wildflowers, a waterfall skipping over mottled rocks, a grove of aspens reflecting the gold of the sun, a frosted crystal moon brushing the mountaintops with ethereal light.

Jack belonged here, too.

Above the mantel, three pictures, identical in size, identically framed, hung side by side—on the left a tower of mellow stone with a lacework of ivy and shadows cast by an afternoon sun whose light played in the colors of stained-glass windows. To the right was the same tower, backlit by moon and stars and spilling color and warmth into darkness. And in the center hung a copperplate print of a medieval tower all in blue shades of night and shadow with the golden glow of a single candle reaching out into the gloom. Below them, on the mantel itself, she saw a folded sheet of notepaper propped up by a small crystal vase holding a single rose.

Hesitantly, she reached out, picked it up, flipped it open, and saw a drop of moisture spread over the rich finish and smear the ink. Swiping at her eyes and face with the sleeve of her copper silk blouse, she tried to focus through the sudden blur and sobbed impatiently when more tears fell.

A large hand appeared from behind her, slipped the paper from her fingers. A rich baritone, curiously flat, read the words.

"Dear Angie—

"God knows I've been blunt about my faults. I've forgotten how to be spontaneous. I know zip about individuality. I'm a stuffed shirt with outdated standards and the resulting guilt complexes when I don't live up to those standards. My temper is on a hair trigger. I've told you I don't want a relationship and you don't want a man like me. Stubborn woman that you are, you refuse to believe me. I'm not sure I believe me anymore. You've halfway convinced me that I'm a hell of a guy." He faltered, paused. The paper crackled and he went on, his voice no longer flat, but thick, strained.

"Didn't you tell me that you've left too many things unfinished in your life? We aren't finished, Angie. Not by a long shot." Again he paused, and she heard the shudder of his breath, felt its heat on the back of her neck. His voice changed again, becoming a rough whisper, low and gentle and clogged with emotion. "P.S. You show me yours; I show you mine. You love me; I love you back. I ask you to marry me; you say yes. That's the way it is. We've done two out of three. It's time to finish what we started."

She heard the snap of paper as he finished, listened to the silence as he waited. The tears wouldn't stop running down her face, into her mouth, onto her blouse, spotting the silk. Through the blur, she stared at the rose, the facets of delicate crystal.

The three bands of gold ringing the neck of the vase— two plain, and the other studded with a square-cut emerald surrounded by diamonds.

"I'm sweating bullets, Angie," he said thickly.

She found a tissue in the pocket of her jeans and blew her nose, wiped her face with her fingers, but she couldn't stop crying, couldn't stop feeling the pain flowing out of her. So much pain held in for so long, ragged and tearing at

her, unwilling to disappear without a fight, without leaving
a trail of fear.

She heard his feet moving on the polished wood floor, a
step back, a retreat, as if he, too, were struggling with pain
and fear. And she heard it in his voice, that sound of tattered emotions. She wanted to stop him, but couldn't speak
just yet. There was so much to say and the words had to be
right. She had to think.

"Okay, Angie, say it. Tell me exactly why you left. I need
to hear it before I give up."

She heard another step backward, increasing the distance. Urgency forced the words out, forced her to aban-
don thought for the simpler language of the heart. "*I* gave
up," she cried, and gulped down a sob. "I was embarrassed
by what I'd done, by how I acted when we—when—" Another sob to swallow before he heard, before he knew that
she was falling apart. "Darnit! All I know are the dirty
words."

"Rocked and rolled? Made love?" A hint of amusement
eased the strain in his voice, encouraged her.

She took a deep breath, wiped away more tears, pushed
all the words out, one after another. "I wanted you to know
what you'd be missing, but I felt as if I'd used you, tried to
use my body to keep you. I was ready to take you on any
terms you wanted. I've done that, Jack. It never works. I
had to leave."

"Shame on you."

She shook her head, and strands of hair stuck to the
moisture on her cheeks. "You're free for the first time in
your life, Jack. I know how important that is. We've been
acting like adolescents, exploring life and grabbing as much
of it as we could before we have to grow up. I'm glad you
like to . . ."

"Rock and roll."

". . . with me. But I want more, and we never seem to
think about what we're doing, and that can't be all there is.
I want marriage—"

His hands grabbed her from behind, held her arms as he
frogwalked her around the room and stopped in front of

the mantel. "Dammit! What does this look like to you? That's *me* on the walls—you and my photography, the two most important parts of my life, what I want it to be."

She stared at the bud vase, at the set of rings, one a promise, the others commitment. "I want children, Jack," she whispered, out of energy, out of words.

"Ah. So that's why you ran away."

More tears flowed, too many tears, as she thought of Jack and his brother and the way a child's loss had deprived other children of their parents when they needed them most.

"Is that a possibility?"

All she could do was nod.

Hair whipped around her face as he turned her to face him, shook her once, twice. "Damn you, Angie! I'm *not* an adolescent with a permanent hard-on. We've done damn near everything together in the last year. We were friends before we were lovers. You think I don't know what I'm asking for with you?" His voice was raw and hoarse. Bleakness dulled the color of his eyes. "I thought about having kids after that first night with you. I had to think about it. Everyone's scared of having kids, of losing them. Every parent screws up. I want children—*with you.*"

His anger obliterated her doubts. She couldn't contain it any longer, knowing that she'd hurt him. Relief, too, brought tears.

She sobbed once, then again and again, and laughter deepened the sound, forcing out the last of pain, the remains of fear.

All color washed out of Jack's face as he heard the tortured sound, brushed the tangle of hair away from her face, saw with horror the tears streaming from her eyes, the way they'd soaked the front of her blouse. "Oh God. I made you cry." Abruptly, he released her, strode to the other side of the room, stared at her with panic and desperation and helplessness.

Her laugh was strangled amidst the sobs, yet she managed a shaky smile. "It's okay, Jack. I've been waiting years to let go of everything."

Still he kept his distance, his hands jammed in his pockets, his legs braced apart, his face still pale, his expression tight.

The smile slipped from her face as she sniffed loudly, blew her nose even more loudly. "I made me cry, Jack. You didn't hurt me. You wouldn't, and you know it."

His mouth flattened, as if he were trying to hold something back, maybe words, maybe tears of his own.

"Say it, Jack. Tell me what you already know."

"I wouldn't hurt you, Angie," he said through a crack in his voice, then focused his gaze on hers, his eyes flaring to life. "I love you. I want to make those empty bedrooms into nurseries with connecting doors. I want to make the room next door into a darkroom."

She stared at him, at the truth in his face, the strength in his voice, the conviction, and she swallowed and swallowed because she didn't want to cry anymore. He'd fall apart if she did.

"Shit!" In the way that had become so familiar to her, he plowed his hand through his hair, shifted his stance, still staring at her. "I feel free with you, Angie. I need you."

"Jack?" she whispered. "I need a hug."

"Say it, Angie," he ordered softly. "Say it before I go out of my freaking mind."

She turned her back on him, removed the emerald and diamond ring off the neck of the vase, slipped it on her finger. Facing him again, she held up her hand so he could see the perfect fit, the way the stones sparkled in the sunlight streaming in through the windows. "Yes."

The next thing she knew she was being hugged and lifted and kissed as her body slid down his. Somehow his hands had freed her shirt from the waistband of her jeans and glided up her ribcage as he lowered her. It seemed only fair that her hands burrow beneath his sweater and count his ribs, too.

Retaliation was swift as he brushed her nipples with his thumbs, stroked her sides with his fingers. She raised her face, parted her lips. He accepted the invitation with nibbles, a quick, teasing dart of his tongue, then a groan as he sealed the kiss, invading her mouth, giving no quarter.

Dipping her hands beneath the waistband of his jeans, she explored the cleft at the base of his spine, kneaded the tight muscles below, and fitted her hips against his.

Her bra came loose in his hands, freeing her breasts to rub against cool, smooth silk, and he found her nipples puckered and hard.

As hard as he was against her belly.

She felt the hot rush of moisture between her legs, the urgency that flared whenever he touched her, the need that was always so desperate whenever she touched him. Again, she pressed closer, felt his erection imprinted on her stomach, exactly where it would be inside her.

Freeing the first two snaps on his jeans, her hands slipped inside as his tongue thrust deeply into her mouth, stealing her breath as surely as he had stolen her reason.

His arms tightened, a vise around her, holding her still as he tore his mouth away from hers, rested his chin on the top of her head, his breathing harsh and loud in the silence. And then he eased away from her, propped his arms on her shoulders, allowing air to come between them. "No," he said.

"No?"

"We're going to date, Angie. We're going to be engaged—"

"We already are," she reminded him.

"We're going to date," he said firmly, "and like the good adolescents we are, we're going to wait until we're married."

She couldn't believe what he was saying, couldn't believe he planned to leave her hanging. No way was she going to let him get away with it. "Jack, I ache." Her hand closed around him. "So do you. We have to make it better."

"No. I don't want you thinking—ah, Angie, stop . . . that all I want is your body, that . . . easy sweetheart— I'm using you."

She stroked him, up and down, applying pressure where she thought it might do the most good. "I don't want to be a good adolescent, Jack. I'm a woman with a great body that needs to know it's appreciated." She increased the pressure and unbuttoned her shirt with her other hand, slid it to either side of her breasts, and the touch of breeze wafting in through the windows was an erotic caress. "We can't wait, Jack," she said firmly as she unzipped her jeans, wiggled out of them and her bikini panties at the same time.

He inhaled sharply as he watched the bob of her breasts, the shake of her hips, the triangle of auburn hair revealed as she kicked her clothes away. "You were a lot easier to control when you were shy," he croaked.

The buttons on his fly cooperated with her, slipping free easily, and she lowered his Jockeys just enough to give her easy access. "You control me; I control you. That's the way it is, Jack."

Beads of sweat formed on his brow, his upper lip, and he threw his head back. "You're right. It's your turn."

It wasn't, but she wasn't about to say so. "My bedroom is—"

"Uh." His hands swooped around her, cupped her bottom, lifted her until she had to wrap her legs around his waist. "We're not going anywhere."

His mouth closed over a breast, drew on her nipple, and she sobbed at the exquisitely sharp sensation shooting through her. "Here, Jack? Like this?"

Raising her hips, he probed, found her on the first try, and lowered her, slowly filling her as he supported her between himself and the wall as he drove home.

She shuddered at the fullness inside her, the friction of his movements, the unbearable need to meet each thrust, match it, exceed it. Where and how didn't matter. Feeling Jack's urgency mattered. The quickening inside her mattered. The primal dance of shadows cast by fire and slanting sunlight on the wall mattered.

Knowing that even in this, she and Jack were so perfectly attuned, coming together and sliding apart in perfect rhythm, giving way to one another at precisely the same moment, breathing in sync, hearts beating faster and harder at the same tempo, and then the last thrust, the final bearing down, the moment's pause in life itself.

The coming together.

He shuddered once, twice, leaned into her. Moments passed before he lifted her, gently lowered her to stand on shaky legs and turn his head. She knew he saw the shadows and remembered. Shadows not of the past but of the present, a future memory to give pleasure rather than pain.

His gaze wandered over the pictures on the wall, the memories already created in new lives and new awareness. They were promises, too, of freedom to be themselves, to share what they were becoming with one another.

Jack's voice was low and smooth with certainty, with confidence. "It had to be like this, Angie—no inhibitions, nor holding back. It had to be here, where we both are—together."

Eyes of the future, eyeing the past.
I knew her. I know it.
I think it was me!
                              —Jennie Cissel Thompson

EPILOGUE

It was a landmark occasion, full of pomp and circumstance and the goodwill and magic of the Christmas season. Overhead, stars twinkled festively through the glass atrium in the heart of the large office building. The winter moon had just begun its ascent, a pure white light surrounded by an aura of angel-hair haze.

Beyond the lobby the atrium was fashionably set with tables and upholstered chairs and the accoutrements of the most elegant night club. A specially constructed dance floor fronted the raised bandstand where the orchestra played the best of Benny Goodman and a sultry siren tantalized the audience with torch songs. Soon, there would be a special performance reminiscent of Ginger and Fred.

They had come from all over the world: diplomats and dignitaries, royalty and movie stars, crusaders and corporate heads. No one was immune to Gena's special brand of meddling. Anyone with sense paid attention to jackhammers and steamrollers.

Pledges were generous and discreetly handled while men and women strolled from table to table showing off designer gowns and hand-tailored tuxedos and jewelry from stores whose names were spoken with reverence and longing.

Across the atrium Steve stood with Gena as he whispered in her ear, and Gena glared at him, shot some remark back at him. Then Steve grinned in that wicked way of his, and Gena actually blushed.

Charlotte and Ben sat at another table, placed there by Gena to save Angie from her mother's constant expressions of concern.

The general had sent his regrets along with a check.

Angie smoothed the folds of her gown of white silk chiffon, light enough to drift with every movement. Crystal beads and cracked ice were sewn into the draped halter top to catch the light, and the knee-length skirt cut from yards and yards of fabric was exactly measured to show her legs to the best advantage.

So far she'd managed to keep the excellent meal they'd just finished in her stomach.

She turned her head to admire her husband. No man there looked as important or wickedly devastating as Jack in the black tux he'd bought for their evening wedding, sentimentally insisting that he didn't want to start out their marriage wearing rented clothes that didn't fit right.

Angie smiled at Jack as she remembered the small but formal wedding. Jack had insisted on small. Charlotte stuck to her guns on the affair being formal. Each yielded gracefully to the will of the other. Surprisingly, Jack had taken to Charlotte and rather enjoyed joining forces with her in his efforts to "protect" Angie. Not so surprisingly, Charlotte had welcomed Jack as her new son-in-law with open arms. He was, after all, handsome, devoted to her daughter, and destined, she was sure, for fame and fortune as an artist of photography.

Some things never changed.

Ben approved wholeheartedly of anything that made Angie happy, and he admitted to feeling relief at having another man in the family. Ironically, when differences of opinion popped up on the care and feeding of Angie, as they often did, Ben and Angie inevitably squared off against Charlotte and Jack.

People never changed. They only improved.

From the side of the atrium, Gena summoned Angie with a wave, anxiety in every feature of her face. As she checked her watch, Angie's stomach rolled, then rocked, then shimmied. It was almost time. Chills rippled her skin as she rose from her chair.

Gena rushed to her side. "I've cleared the decks for you, chum. The little girls' room is empty. You sure you want to do this?"

The best Angie could do was nod, her hand over her mouth as she followed Gena to the ladies' room. Just in time, Gena threw a plastic cape around Angie's shoulders and jerked down over her gown. Just in time, Angie reached a stall, ber over the bowl, and tossed up her socks.

A strong hand braced her forehead. A black-encased ar wrapped around her waist, supporting her until the last heav Gena waited with wet washcloths, and Steve was squeezing o toothpaste on her brush. Charlotte charged in the door in rustle of burgundy velvet with Ben on her heels.

"I don't remember selling tickets," Angie said as she blotte her face, careful not to streak her eyeshadow.

"Angie, you do not have to do this," Charlotte said, her fac as pale as Angie's.

"She is not going to do this," Jack said firmly. "I'll stand c my head, pull faces at the audience—whatever—but Angie not going through this."

Steve grinned at Angie and handed her the toothbrush.

Ignoring her audience, she leaned over the sink to clean he teeth.

"You're not listening, Angie," Jack said.

Angie grinned at him around her toothbrush. "I'm fine, Jac and I have to do it. I'm looking forward to it." Actually, sh wasn't too sure about the wisdom of her idea to perform, t face the demons she knew once and for all. But she'd found th perfect partner, a man who had been ballroom dancing sinc his days at the Air Force Academy and had kept up his skil during countless affairs at Officers' Clubs all over the worl During their practice sessions in her studio, she'd learned a lc about "dirty dancing."

With Jack, she knew she could do anything.

"Bullshit. You are not fine. And you'd rather clean this batl room than go out there."

"Angie, please, if you're doing this for me, don't," Charlott wailed.

"Mother—out!"

Ben winked at Angie and steered his wife out of the re: room.

"Gena, tell her. It's not as if the crowd is counting on thi No one even knows who the hell we are."

"Leave me out of it," Gena said as she touched up Angie

makeup, secured Angie's hair high on her crown. "I gave up meddling, remember?"

Steve and Jack snorted in unison, "When donkeys fly."

"Um, Gena, do you have it?" Angie asked.

"Yeah, right here." Avoiding Jack's gaze, Gena pulled a shopping bag from under the counter.

Angie took the bag and handed it to Jack. "Happy One-Month Anniversary."

Jack trusted Angie, unless she was making a big show of avoiding him—like now. She never fussed with her appearance, always doing what had to be done and take it or leave it. Thirty seconds was long enough for her to look spectacular. But she was busy brushing color on cheeks that were already rosy and fussing with hair that couldn't look better. Warily, he looked in the bag.

Suddenly, Gena found a hundred things wrong with her own meticulous appearance. Steve watched with morbid fascination.

His hand connected with gray fur, latched on to long ears, and pulled out a two-foot-long stuffed donkey with a replica of Jack's uniform hat stuck jauntily on its head, a major's insignia pinned to its chest and a target painted on its ass. The miniature saddle blanket thrown over its back was embroidered with big red letters that spelled out MY HERO.

Angie glanced up, met his gaze in the mirror. Her smile was secret and a little mischievous. "Two minutes, Jack, and counting down. Are you ready?" They were normal words under the circumstances, but their gazes held, speaking a language that needed no words. He'd thank her later. She was looking forward to it.

"My big brother has to be the only man on the planet with his own collection of stuffed animals," Steve quipped.

Ignoring Steve, Jack frowned at Angie. "You can't soften me up, Angie."

"Jack, I've done this on a thousand stages and survived. This time is different; I want to. It's important." The secret smile that made promises, gave way to feigned nonchalance. "If you're getting nervous, Gordy can—"

He grabbed her hand as Gena whisked the protective cap away, and they headed for the dance floor.

"I'm doing this because it's important to you," he growled

"I know."

"Not because you're trying to manipulate me."

"No. Never that."

"And not because I don't want him touching you."

"Of course not. You haven't a jealous bone in your body" Angie patted his butt.

"Dammit! Are you sure you're all right?"

"Much better than I expected."

"What does that mean?"

Angie shushed him as the band leader began the introduction. Her hand flattened on her midriff. She focused on the stage, regulated her breathing.

Jack was beginning to feel queasy. "We're not doing this."

But the lights dimmed, a spotlight beamed on them, an Angie took his hand as she glided out onto the dance floor "Do you see anyone, Jack?" she hissed.

He shook his head.

"Right. There's nobody here but us."

He nodded and his eyes glazed. "You're sick. We're not—

"Get used to it," she whispered. The music began, an somehow, Angie was in his arms. His feet moved mechanically

He focused on the scent of Shalimar, the brush of her ha on his hand, the pressure of her thighs as they danced in pe fect time to one another. His moves weren't complicated. Ho many times had he grumbled that she'd do fine with a fenc post anchored to the floor?

The room was silent but for the music. The spotligh gleamed on her hair as she whirled away from him, struck pose, drifted back into his arms, her skirt billowing away fro her body, giving him a glimpse of her legs. She danced. Sh floated. She swayed with his body, then whirled away from hir again, her body turning and turning and turning as her ha turned to flame beneath the light.

He moved automatically, knowing what to do, knowing tha with Angie on the floor, no one would notice if his pants fe around his knees. She was the most beautiful, the brightest, the most talented woman he'd ever known.

His body quickened with awe, with pleasure as she became the dance itself.

And then she came back to him, picking up the change of beat from the orchestra. "Get used to what?" he whispered.

"Morning sickness," she whispered back.

He stared at her blankly and stepped on her foot.

"Remember Cordillera? The Honeymoon Suite? Rock and Roll?" she teased without flinching, without missing a beat.

He frowned, and she pinched his arm as he tried to absorb what she'd said. There was no time to react. The music was winding down, and he swooped over her, dipped her so low, her hair brushed the floor.

She felt light as a feather. She couldn't be pregnant. It was a joke, like the donkey.

As rehearsed, he stared into her eyes as she placed her hands on his shoulders. They held for the count of ten, long enough for him to see the truth. Long enough to see her close her eyes as applause erupted and grew in intensity.

Alarmed, he hissed at her, "Angie, look at me." Jack forgot about morning sickness and babies, forgot the lights illuminating the atrium. He tightened his arms protectively, ready to carry her away before the deafening sound sent her running in panic.

Her face wasn't pale or strained. Her smile was bright, genuine, her skin warm, soft. He shuddered as the applause continued, afraid of what it would do to Angie, dreading the moment when she'd retreat inside herself and look at him with that vacant stare.

She opened her eyes, met his gaze, and he saw triumph, happiness, life. . . .

He saw Angie, only Angie, and—dammit!—she was laughing at him.